The Tree of Ruin

Joshua Porter

KITSAP PUBLISHING

The Tree of Ruin
First edition, published 2017

By Joshua Porter

Copyright © 2012-2016, Joshua Porter

Cover Illustration: Joshua Porter
Cover Design: RubyRose Marie Neeland

ISBN-13: 978-1-942661-56-6

Published by Kitsap Publishing
P.O. Box 572
Poulsbo, WA 98370
www.KitsapPublishing.com

Printed in the United States of America

TD 20170328

50-10 9 8 7 6 5 4 3 2 1

When a child is born, she enters a world made of stories. Already she has learned to recognize them, for she has heard the stories in the varied beating of her mother's heart, in the sounds that fall like muffled magic through the caves of her tiny ears, and in the rising and falling rhythms that course through the whole of her private universe. By the time she takes her first breath she has known many stories, and she can sense that she has emerged not into a new world but into an old one, one whose story has seen countless chapters before her own. She cries, for she has come late to the telling and already missed so very much. She mourns, for she must struggle to understand the things the tale has taught her elders. She must fight for a lifetime to make sense of this middle without having known its start.

Today, the children cry harder still, for even before they have the words to shape their troubled thoughts, they can sense that the story is nearing its end. They have opened the book and in dismay found themselves consigned to its final chapter. They know stories well, well enough to dread the coming of the end, and so they cry out against it with what little force their infant lungs can wield. But no parent can stop its coming, no nurse soothe away its pain, and so they cry, and cry, and cry.

As they grow, this dark, lurking knowledge of the children remains an unnamed guest in their minds. It wears the clothes of anger, or sadness, or desire, but it is none of these. It mingles with their dreams, but even the touch of dawn cannot drive it from their heads. When they speak it is on their tongues, and when they labor it is in their sweat. It lies like a fog over fields and towns, over roads and crooked woodland paths. Moats cannot keep it at bay, nor towers rise above it. It is fear, crawling on its belly across the pages, turning them with rough, regular strokes.

The children know stories, and they know the end is coming.

Table of Contents

PROLOGUE

Firelight lapped against the tunnel walls as the troop crept single-file through the darkness, a centipede of men bristling with torches and long, slender lances. The ground was smooth and bare, worn down by centuries of miners burrowing ever deeper beneath the steep slopes and high peaks of the mountains above. Now, however, the tunnel was empty but for these men and the echoes that followed closely on their heels.

The soldiers moved ever downward, the white of their uniforms and their halting pace making them appear as pale, witless ghosts blindly seeking the gates of the underworld. Should the torches fail, they knew, they would feel the pure isolation of death, of warm bodies slowly yielding their heat and their life to the perpetual night that filled the Iron Mines.

Eventually they passed out of the narrow tunnels and into a vast open space known as the Miner's Moat: a great natural crevasse spanned wall to wall by a plank-and-rope bridge. Ancient and strong, the suspended pathway barely shuddered under their feet as they crossed. The reflections of their torches on slowly moving water danced silently for any who were brave enough to glance into the depths below.

Edwin Aloise looked down without fear, torch held out over the rail. Unlike the other men, he had plumbed deeper mines than this as a child, the guards who should have kept him out too afraid of his family name to stop him. Those days of wonder and exploration were far behind him now, but he still felt a yearning at the sight of that abyss. When he had journeyed alone through those caves of his youth, the shadows that stole his sight had not shied from him at the sound of his name, nor had the rocks that cut his hands muttered darkly behind his back about his house and lineage. If only things could have been as simple above ground.

"Hold!"

The command bounced between the sheer walls as if trying to beat its way out into the sunlight. Edwin stopped, just beyond the midpoint of the bridge, and looked up. One of the officers at the front of the line was uncoiling a rope and lowering it toward the water below. The rest waited in silence so complete that Edwin clearly heard the plunk when the weighted end hit the surface. The officer holding it beckoned for a torch to read the depth markings.

"Fifteen-reach," he said in a hushed voice, though the stone walls repeated the words back again, mocking the attempt at privacy.

"That's trouble," the commander beside him growled, and a map was hurriedly drawn from its tube and consulted. "At that height, it'll be flooded all the way up to the twin tunnels already. Incredible."

A pair of shadows slid from their places at the center of the line, hardly visible but for where they passed in front of pale uniforms. They reached the front quickly, but with their backs to him and the rest of the men, Edwin could not tell which one of them spoke.

"When was the last measure taken?" The voice was male, sharp and restless, like an awl on fresh leather.

The commander seemed to have as much trouble identifying the speaker as Edwin, for he glanced back and forth between the pair before answering. "Two days ago. It was eighteen-reach, then."

The voice spoke again. "How far to the next bridge?"

"That's at the Spider's Leg, here," the commander said, stabbing at the map. "But if the twin tunnels are under water, we won't be able to reach it."

There was a pause. The two dark shapes seemed to be conferring, but no echoes reached Edwin's straining ears.

"This will have to do," the now familiar voice said.

The two figures turned, revealing the masks that covered their faces. Edwin had seen them before, above ground, but they had been mostly unremarkable in the daylight. Cut from unpolished bark, the masks were flat across the brow and curved at the chin, devoid of features save for two narrow slits for eyes. In the torchlight, however, they were ghastly. Shadows oozed from fissures in the wood, black tears dribbling out in a silent, constant stream. The eyes grew and shrank with the guttering fire like pupils spinning open to hideous size, taking in sights beyond the apprehension of ordinary men. For the first time, Edwin shuddered at the sight of the Masked.

The two figures moved back down the line, making their way to the center of the bridge. They passed Edwin last, and he caught a strong whiff of sweat and dirt and musk, no doubt from the thick furs that draped their shoulders like forest moss. They stopped, not five paces beyond where Edwin stood, at the place where the bridge sagged lowest over the water. Again they conversed, but this time Edwin was close enough to overhear.

"It's a slow leak," said the one who had spoken earlier, tilting his head to peer over the rope rail. "Not the worst kind of breach to contain, but still dangerous. It will be worse for having gone so long unnoticed by the Listeners."

"How could they have missed another one?" the second Masked said worriedly. "If this keeps happening, what will happen to the world? The breaches will tear-"

"This isn't the time or place," the first cut him off. "Focus on what we can accomplish here, in the present." From the way he spoke, he seemed to be the senior of the two.

The Masked did not address each other by name, Edwin noticed, nor did any of his fellow soldiers know what they were called. It was whispered by some that the Masked did not even have names, and worse, that there were not even proper men hidden behind those wooden masks and hairy mantles. Such rumors were inevitable, given how rarely Masked visited the Iron Kingdoms. From what Edwin could see, however, they moved like men and spoke like men; surely they also had the names and bodies of men, even if they kept them well hidden.

"Of course, focus on the present," the junior Masked said hurriedly. He looked left and right. "Whatever energy has gathered here since the breach opened must still be dormant nearby."

"In the water," confirmed the senior grimly.

Edwin did not know exactly what they were talking about, but he could tell it was nothing good. He looked back toward the other soldiers, who had begun to chat unconcernedly amongst themselves and were paying little attention to the Masked. Most of them thought it was a fool's errand to be down there in the first place, Edwin recalled, and few bothered to hide it. What could two men do to fix a flooded mine, even if they were Masked? What could any man do? Their superiors had obviously thought differently, however. A flooded mine was an unproductive mine, and to preserve the wealth of the Iron Kingdoms, they were clearly willing to try almost anything.

"The water?" the junior Masked said. "How can you tell?"

"It's too warm." The senior Masked removed a glove and held his hand out over the side of the bridge, and the junior did likewise. Their hands looked perfectly ordinary, if a bit worn and scarred, and certainly weren't made of anything more exotic than Edwin's own.

The two Masked stood silently for a while, the senior shifting from side to side every few seconds. He walked with a slight limp, and Edwin wondered whether the leg was paining him.

"It's a bit warm," the junior acknowledged, "but only a little. That's good, right?"

The senior withdrew his hand. "Don't underestimate what we face. These underground waters can run for a hundred spans or more. Power great enough to heat them, even a little, could be immense."

The junior drew his hand back deliberately. "When we try to disperse it . . ."

"Then we'll find out."

"But what about them?" The junior nodded in Edwin's direction.

The senior crossed his arms. "We aren't responsible for them. We needed no escort, but they refused to let us come alone. The Aloise guard their mines jealously, and the consequence of that greed will be on their heads, not ours."

"We could at least send them back, now that we know the danger?" The junior's voice was strained. "Aren't we supposed to be protecting-"

"They would not go. If that pride proves to be their end, then so be it. Our duty is to all mankind, not a mere handful of men." The senior's word was final.

Edwin turned with growing unease to the soldier behind him, but it seemed the few paces separating them had dulled the Masked's words beyond recognition, for he saw no alarm on the other man's face.

"Let's begin," the senior Masked said. Edwin watched them warily, body tensed as he looked for signs of danger, but neither one moved. Time dragged on, and still the Masked just stood there, staring down at the water.

Edwin reached up absently to wipe his forehead and was surprised when his sleeve came away darkened with sweat. It had become notably warmer in the cavern in the space of just a few minutes. Nor was he the only one to take notice – the other soldiers had ceased their talk and were peering about with torches held high as if hoping to spot the source of the rising temperature.

A splashing from below drew the men as one to the rail, but it was as dark down there as when Edwin had looked before. Another splash echoed up, and then another. Edwin squinted down at the points of reflected torchlight. Unless he was mistaken, their dance was quickening.

Focused on the water, he barely heard the order from the front of the line. "Form up. Form up!" the commander repeated. Looking up, Edwin found his vision dimmed by a haze that had not been there moments before. The splashing from below grew louder and faster, swallowing up whatever else the captain had to say.

The soldier nearest Edwin turned back to look at him, his worried face softened by the mist filtered torchlight. "I don't like this. We should-"

His words were cut off as the bridge shuddered beneath them, throwing Edwin and the better part of the rest to their knees. A second bucking of the planks tossed Edwin onto his stomach and knocked the torch from his hand. He watched helplessly as it skittered to the edge of the bridge, teetered, and then fell like a comet through the darkness, briefly illuminating the churning, bubbling waters below before being extinguished in them.

The others must have seen the boiling waters too, for a mad scramble toward the end of the bridge had begun even before Edwin had the chance to find his feet. He used his lance to haul himself into a crouch and started to follow, but he made it no more than a few steps before hearing a sudden rushing sound and a crescendo of agonized screams from ahead in the mist. The bridge lurched sharply to the side, and several more torches went spinning into the chasm, some with men still attached and howling all the way down.

One of the dropped torches licked at the ancient rope railing, setting it ablaze and quickly creating a barrier of flame between Edwin and the end of the bridge. The fire was hampered by the dampness in the air, but it spread nonetheless, closing off Edwin's escape and dividing the body of panicking men in two.

The other way! I can still go back the other way! Edwin thought, whirling and preparing to make a sprint for the opposite wall. What he saw, however, froze him to the spot with fear.

It was as though gravity had been inverted. A monstrous, boiling waterfall was rising up on one side of the bridge, curling over it and cascading down on the other, with the two Masked standing squarely beneath it. Sizzling droplets splashed around them, but the two robed figures seemed to be dry and unharmed, at least for the moment.

Edwin stumbled as the soldier behind him pushed him aside and darted toward the unnatural waterfall, undeterred by the roiling abomination. Edwin did not even know the man's name, but still his chest tightened with dread as he watched him hurl himself into what could only be certain death.

The soldier flung himself past the two Masked, under the boiling archway, and finally came to a tumbling halt on the opposite side. Edwin could see him, little more than a clouded outline through the steam, rising slowly from his hands and knees as though he had not been expecting to make it that far.

Edwin's relief was short lived. A geyser erupted sideways from the waterfall, shooting toward the soldier like an arrow fired with uncanny precision. It was mere feet from striking him when the junior Masked, in the first motion Edwin had seen either make since the chaos began, reached out his arm, and the liquid jet froze in place. It did not disperse or splash to the ground. It simply hung in the air, undistorted, like a sculpture of glass suspended by invisible threads.

"Fool!" the senior Masked shouted.

The shape of the waterfall contorted, like a snake coiling more tightly around its prey. The area beneath it grew smaller.

"Run!" the junior Masked called to the soldier. He needed no further urging, and seconds later Edwin lost sight of him in the dense haze.

The Masked had been facing the railing throughout the ordeal, but behind them Edwin saw something new appear. A pillar of water that did not hiss or spit like the rest was slowly reaching upward, nearing the level of the bridge, its tip silently probing the air.

"Behind you!" Edwin shouted, but the roar of the waterfall drowned out his warning. As he watched, the silent pillar drew itself back in an unmistakable motion: that of a serpent preparing to strike.

With hardly a moment to think, Edwin dropped his lance and dashed forward as the liquid horror struck. The blast of water hit the junior Masked in the back, lifting him off his feet and smashing him into the rope rail with such force that his limbs bent around it like a doll's. There was a snapping sound as his body went limp, and Edwin reached him just in time to catch him before he could slip under the rail and off the edge. His head lolled back, revealing a deep crack between the eyes of his mask.

Out of the corner of his eye, Edwin saw the watery pillar rear back again, and he braced himself, unable to get out of the way. His fear, which had retreated during his mad lunge to rescue the wounded Masked, came screaming back, pounding against the inside of his head with helpless rage.

Then the senior Masked turned, and Edwin had the sudden sensation of being surrounded by a great flurry of movement, though his eyes saw nothing. The liquid pillar struck, but as it reached toward them its movement slowed, then came to a quivering halt. Narrow bands began to appear along its length, as if it were being bound and constricted by whatever force held it fast.

The same thing was happening to the waterfall over Edwin's head. In some places it had been strangled to nearly half its original size, and still the invisible cords drew tighter. The water wriggled in a way that Edwin had never seen water move, and he had the sudden impression of a rat with its neck pinched hopelessly in a trap.

As the water squirmed and struggled, the standing Masked turned his gaze downward. Edwin could not tell if the look was for him or for the man cradled to his chest, but he had the uncomfortable, inexplicable feeling that it was one of disdain.

There was a blast of air and a flash of heat so intense that Edwin felt his eyelashes singe, and the water above exploded, erupting into a shower of cool droplets that traced relief across his burned skin as they fell upon him, the two Masked, and the few soldiers that remained. The fires on the bridge hissed out, and darkness swallowed the sight of the first rainfall those depths had seen since the dawn of time itself.

Chapter 1

Where Dreams Touch the Earth

In the upper reaches of a tall Scarwood tree, under the bleary gaze of the sun's slowly opening eye, something miraculous was happening. On the underside of one of its many branches, nestled in the crook where arm meets trunk, a droplet of liquid was pushed out of a tiny hole in the bark. Its surface gleamed in the morning sunlight, and it wobbled with the caress of the wind like a newborn calf on untested legs. And, like the calf, it immediately discovered its inexorable attraction to the earth below.

Just like the others in the forest, the branches of this tree drooped rather forlornly, as though melting under the modest heat of the autumn sun, and the droplet found it had little choice but to surrender to its downward compulsion and slide swiftly along the underside of its branch. Unfortunately for the now rapidly moving globule, this tree was not a nurturing sort of mother. In fact, she was designed precisely to discharge her offspring with minimal fuss, and that was exactly what she did. The droplet, having achieved a remarkable velocity relative to its size, reached the tip of its branch and was flung unceremoniously into the open air.

It was here that the special fate of this droplet, out of all the countless others that had made similar journeys, became evident. As might be expected, the droplet fell. If it had possessed eyes, it might have remarked on the extraordinary vividness of the lapis sky that day, or on how the leaves of the forest beneath seemed to swell and deflate like scales of a lazy green crocodile belly-up in the sun. Unlike so many of its brethren, this droplet did not arrest its fall in the upper canopy, nor in the middle branches, nor even on the back of an unsuspecting songbird. It traversed all these obstacles with singular ease and instead landed upon . . . .

The young man jerked awake with a half-articulated cry, a fire burning through the flesh of his forearm. He grabbed a handful of loamy soil and rubbed it on the spot, and only when it felt like the fire had been banked to coals did he brush away the coating of cool, moist earth. Even in the dim light that forced its way through the forest's leafy curtains, he could make out the angry welt where the drop of acid sap had fallen on his bare skin.

Not for the first time, he wished his jerkin offered more protection than its sleeveless, hole-riddled cloth could provide.

The young man resumed his repose with a sigh, though he did not sleep, instead resting his head on a pile of leaves and waiting for the pulsing ache that always followed sap burns to subside. Something he had been dreaming stirred in him, something of vast open spaces of blue and green and a sensation like flying, but the feeling faded into the mists that hid the land of sleep from waking eyes before he could call it back.

After a while he rolled onto his side and watched a caterpillar delicately pick its way up the small incline of a nearby rock. When it reached the peak of its miniature mountain, it reared up, probing the air for a way to proceed. The young man held out his finger obligingly and felt its many legs take up their march onto the back of his hand.

"Where are you going, little one?" the young man murmured to himself, although for a moment the insect stopped, almost as if it had heard the question, before once again tickling him with its soft rain of light footfalls. As slowly as it moved, it journeyed with purpose, driven by something inside its tiny green head that would not let it worry over the vast distances before it or the likelihood that it would become breakfast for an enterprising avian before the day was through. It pressed on because that was what it was born to do, pulled by the twin threads of nature and fate from here to there, from one moment to the next, from the first second of life to the last. The young man felt a kinship with the tiny creature, for he too knew the tug of that same pair of reins. If life had given him any say in the matter, he would not have chosen to end up here.

A nearby huddled shape stirred, uncurling into the form of a yellow-haired girl. She yawned and brushed her bangs from her eyes, blinking inquisitively at the young man through the gloom of the forest understory.

"Who are you talking to?" she asked, peering about.

"It's nothing. Go back to sleep," the young man said.

Not to be deterred, the girl slid closer, dragging her ratty leggings through the dirt.

"I was having such a nice dream about the Listeners," she said sleepily. "You'd better show me what you woke me up for."

"How can you have a dream about people you've never met?" the young man said bemusedly.

"It's easy," the girl said. "They're all tall and handsome and smart. Now come on, show me!"

The young man sighed and held out his hand.

"It's just a caterpillar," the girl said, looking disappointed.

The young man laughed. "I told you it was nothing. Here, take him." He deposited the insect into her cupped hands. Though perhaps less than a year from her twelfth harvest, there was still enough child left in her to be appeased by this simple tribute. She leaned back and giggled as the caterpillar crawled up her arm.

"I see you've made a friend," a gruff voice said from behind them, so close that it would have startled any normal person, but the two of them had become accustomed to the fact that true solitude was rare under those trees.

The girl sat up, careful not to drop the caterpillar, her face suddenly serious. The young man composed himself a bit more slowly, resisting the urge to spring to attention as he had once been taught to do for his elders.

The owner of the voice appeared as he always did: a simple bark mask covered his entire face, leaving only an elusive glint in its eye slits to indicate there was a man behind it at all. He was draped in an assortment of furs and pelts – gray wolf and red fox, black bear and white rabbit – layered thickly enough to conceal the shape of the body beneath. Despite their obvious weight, he moved with a silent, distinctive grace.

The masked man put out a hand, and the caterpillar crawled from the girl's arm onto it, picking its way across the patchwork of old scars that covered the toughened palm and fingers. He held it up to a beam of light that pierced the forest canopy and examined it.

"You don't have as much in common with your tiny friend as you imagine," he said, his voice low and thick. "His journey is one of consumption and greed, about feeding on the gifts of this world in a quest to transform himself. Yours is a transformation that, when you are ready, will protect the world, not devour it. You will become a part of the legacy that has held at bay the darkness of the world's end for ages beyond counting."

So you say, the young man thought to himself, trying to ignore the uncomfortable feeling that the masked man who served as their mentor had somehow read his thoughts. Not everyone held such a flattering view of the Masked as they did of themselves, nor did many accept their dire prophecies at face value. They might call themselves preservers, but world knew them better as harbingers of destruction. Suffering and death followed them like long, evil shadows, and it was stories of woe, not salvation, on which the young man and generations of others like him had been weaned. Wherever the Masked appeared, catastrophe was never far behind.

The young man had witnessed it himself, once, when he was still but a child. He had been too young to understand much of what happened that day, but the thing that he had always remembered, beyond the fear, was the Masked themselves. Mostly, he remembered their power, a strength so incredible that it could accomplish in an instant what most men would not dare to imagine in a lifetime. It had been that memory that, when he was most desperate, drew him here, to the forest of burning sap where no hunter dared to tread.

The masked man lowered his hand and deposited the caterpillar in the remains of a fallen log. The girl's eyes followed the its progress as it walked among the cracks and splinters, but she made no move to collect it.

The masked man spoke again. "Give it no more thought. When you are ready, come to the camp and join us for breakfast. After that it will be lessons, as usual."

His message delivered, he did not tarry. His departure was nearly as silent as his arrival, for it seemed that even the dry leaves made themselves soft under his feet as he strode among the ferns and branches that littered the forest floor.

Seeming to have heard the invitation for itself, the young man's stomach growled loudly, and the girl rolled her eyes. The young man made a face at her, but it quickly turned from jest to pain as he tried to stand. His legs were suddenly unsteady beneath him, his stomach twisted painfully. For an instant he felt like he was falling, colors of blue and green rushing past him, toward something he could not quite see . . . .

. . . . *His body hung in the air, helpless, a masked figure standing before him. "Your depravity is truly astounding," the masked man said, "to inflict such desecration on the one who cared for you most deeply. . . ."*

"Is it happening again?" the girl asked, the smile dropping from her dirt-smudged face. Her words punched a hole in the hazy vision, letting the light of the present pour in and dissolve it like salt in a kettle.

The young man shook his head, leaning on a nearby tree to steady himself as the nausea abated.

The girl crossed her arms. "You're lying. You can't keep hiding it from them."

The young man shook his head again. "No, really," he lied, trying to keep his voice unconcerned.

"You're really thick, you know?" the girl said as she fixed him with an exasperated look. "Even I can tell it's getting worse, and you don't know they won't help until you ask. Just tell them, otherwise I will."

The young man grumbled noncommittally, hoping the girl would let it go. She had made that threat before, though so far she had not followed through; the temperament of the Masked did not exactly invite the sharing of confidences. Besides, there was no shortage of secrets the Masked kept from them, so in a way it only seemed fair that they should have one of their own. He only wished it were not such a grim one.

Just thinking about the subject made his chest itch, but the young man resisted scratching, not wanting to betray yet another symptom. He had no desire to feel the patch of decay hidden under his jerkin leave its foul remnants beneath his fingernails. Nor did he want to confirm that it had grown a little bigger.

"Come on," the girl said. "Promise me you'll tell, or I'll really do it this time." Her voice was pleading, and the young man stared at his feet, hating the fact that his sickness was making her suffer nearly as much as it was him. He had almost been able to accept how unfair his life had been to him, but now it was being unfair to her too.

"The Masked don't heal people," he said. "And they never make exceptions. If they knew, they'd probably send me away."

"So you'd rather just shrivel up to nothing?" the girl said. "Don't be such a coward."

"I didn't come here to be healed," the young man said without meeting her eyes. "I already know it's going to kill me. I came because I wanted to do something important with my life before it did, that's all. Join the Masked and save the world, you know?"

The girl looked over her shoulder at the still forest around them, then made a flicking motion with her small hand. The young man yelped as an invisible force whacked him upside the head. They were not supposed to use the power of the Masked for trivial things, but the girl tended to employ it when she wanted to remind him of her greater skill.

"You are such an idiot!" she said. "All that talk is just to hide the fact you're scared. You talk to the Masked every day, something most people would soil themselves even thinking about, but now you'd rather roll over and die than ask for help?"

It made the young man feel rather foolish, being chided by someone at least seven years his junior. It was even worse because she was right. There was little rational reason to keep his sickness a secret, but a fear he could not quite name still gripped him whenever he entertained the thought of revealing it to the Masked.

"It's a fatal condition," he said defensively.

"And who told you that, some lowlander hedge doctor who waves his hands over a pot and tells you you're possessed by spirits?" the girl said with a smirk. She never did tire of poking fun at his country heritage.

"Humph," the young man said. "You're just afraid that if I die, you'll be stuck out here with the Masked all alone, with no one left to listen to you prattle on day in and day out." He could not quite believe he was joking about his own death. Even worse, he couldn't believe that it actually felt good.

The girl gave him her best wide-eyed, sad-faced look. The young man sighed in defeat.

"Fine," he said, "I'll tell them."

"Today," the girl demanded.

"Today," the young man agreed reluctantly. But breakfast would not be the time, not with so many Masked looking on in their uncomfortable, staring fashion. He would wait until after their lessons, when he might be able to get some privacy with their mentor.

"Good," the girl said, visibly brighter for having secured the promise. "I'm hungry!"

The young man chuckled a little at how quickly her mood could change.

"Yeah," he said, "me too."

Chapter 2
The Listeners

The young man and the girl followed the narrow trail away from their campsite, skirting thick trunks and root mounds and fallen branches. Ferns and spindleweed brushed at their legs, leaning over the track as if trying to absorb it back into the unblemished forest that surrounded it. The path between their campsite and the gathering place of the Masked was entirely of their own creation, for the Masked did their best to avoid making trails in the woods. It was just one more of their many eccentricities, though it was far easier to accept than their strangest tenet: the abhorrence of names.

It was this absence of names that had proven most difficult for the young man to adjust to. Among the Masked, names, and particularly one's own name, were synonymous with evil. They were considered a gateway to the realm of selfish desire, where one could conceive himself better than other men. The Masked, who wielded immense power, believed that every temptation for personal gain must be mercilessly stamped out in order to guard against its misuse. They reasoned that once names were abandoned and individuality given up, there could be no greed, no jealousy, and no hate to distract them from the task that they alone could fulfill. Violations of this tenet were, to all appearances, unforgivable. No burden was too great to bear for those who believed that the fate of mankind hung on their shoulders.

A yelp of surprise drew the young man's mind back to the trail. The girl had fallen to her knees and was blocking the path ahead of him.

"What happened?" the young man said, kneeling beside her.

"My foot's stuck . . . . Ow!" the girl exclaimed as she gave it an experimental tug.

Indeed, her left foot had disappeared into the flattened dirt of the path, leaving one pale leg sticking out like the trunk of a very odd tree.

"You must've stepped on a groundrat burrow. Don't pull on it, I'll get you out," the young man said, using his hands to dig away the heavy, moist soil.

"It feels sharp," the girl whimpered.

It took the young man only a second to determine why. Not an inch below the surface he uncovered the edge of a large, blackish rock.

"It's all right," he said. "Your heel just scraped a rock as you stepped in."

He started digging on the other side of her foot, but stopped in confusion when he encountered a second, nearly identical rock surface. Her bare foot was wedged firmly between them.

"What's wrong?" the girl asked, pain adding a sharp pitch to her voice.

"Nothing," the young man said, frowning. "Though you sure picked a bad place to step."

Working as fast as he could, the young man scraped the layers of moss and dirt off of the rock that was pinning the girl's heel, revealing a rectangular block as long as his arm. It was heavy, but with the dirt cleared away he was able to shift it a few inches, allowing the girl to wiggle her foot free.

"Ouch . . ." she said, sitting on the path and holding her foot with both hands. It sported some nasty scrapes, but at least it did not seem broken.

"Do you think you can walk?" the young man asked, taking the girl's arm and helping her to her feet. She took a few hesitant, limping steps, and then she nodded, wiping the wetness from her eyes with a dirt-encrusted hand.

"I'll be fine," she said, controlling the quaver in her voice. "But what did I step in?"

"It's no groundrat burrow, that's for sure," the young man said. The hole, rather than filling with dirt, continued to gape.

The girl leaned over the opening and peered inside.

"It looks deep," she said, curiosity distracting her from her injury. She picked up a pebble and dropped it down the hole. A moment later there was a clack as it ricocheted off something hard.

"Not that deep," the young man said, "it sounds like there's something down there." He knelt and widened the gap some more, knocking the increasingly thin layer of dirt around its edges down into the space beneath. When the hole was big enough, the young man braced himself over it and poked his head inside.

"Sticking your face into animal dens isn't very smart," the girl observed dryly.

"I told you, it's not an animal den," the young man replied, his voice muffled by the dirt. All he could see was darkness. He turned his head, blinking several times to clear the spots from his vision as the blood rushed into his inverted skull. He thought he saw a tiny light, or maybe one that was just far away.

"Hello?" he called into the darkness.

Hello? his echo called back to him.

The young man pulled his head out of the hole, a smile on his face.

"It's a tunnel!" he exclaimed, his hands already diving into the dirt with renewed energy. "I can see a light farther in, maybe the other end. The whole thing must be made out of stone to carry an echo like that."

The girl gave him a skeptical look. "You can't be thinking about going in there?" she said. "We're already supposed to be at breakfast by now. And besides, do you think the Masked want us poking around in their tunnels without permission?"

The young man shrugged. "They're always telling us what to do. Don't you want to do something on our own for once? We don't even know if it's their tunnel or just some ruin."

"I still think it's a bad idea," the girl said. "You're going to get caught, and then they'll already be mad at you when you tell them about your . . . problem."

The young man groaned. He wished she would not bring that up.

"Aren't you curious?" he said. "We might even find where the Masked go every night. I told you it had to be a cave or something, didn't I?"

"It isn't worth getting into trouble," the girl said. "If they wanted us to know about it, they'd tell us. I'm sure we'll find out eventually. Why can't you just be patient?"

The mention of patience made the young man bristle. He might not have a choice about dying, but at least some things were still under his control, and he was getting tired of waiting. The way things were going, he might not have much time left.

"Nobody's making you come," the young man said. "I'll just stay here and find out all their secrets while you enjoy breakfast with our faceless friends."

The girl stamped her uninjured foot. "That's not fair! You can't make me eat alone with them! You know I hate how they stare!"

"Do what you want," the young man said, "but I'm going to see what's down there."

The girl pouted, but it did not take her long to acquiesce.

"Fine," she said dejectedly, "I'll come. You'd probably get lost on your own anyway."

The young man knew he had not really given her much of a choice. Without each other for company, they probably would have gone mad from loneliness months ago. They were still technically outsiders, and aside from their mentor, the Masked took great pains to avoid having too much contact with them. Conversation stuttered to a halt whenever they came too near, as if the Masked believed that merely speaking with them could infect them with some sort of disease. While the young man would have preferred someone closer to his own age to spend time with, the girl, and their arguments and their laughter, were the only things that made his life among the Masked bearable. It hardly seemed to matter that they did not know each other's names.

"Suit yourself," he said with feigned indifference. "Just don't jump down until I'm out of the way." He sat on the edge of the hole, dangling his legs into its mouth. Even now that he had made it wider, not enough light fell into it to reveal the bottom. Before his nerves could fail him, he took a breath, closed his eyes, and jumped.

The fall was farther than he expected, and he was just starting to panic when his feet hit the ground. He landed hard, bruising his backside on the stone floor when his legs gave out beneath him. He coughed as the trickle of dirt landed on his head in a dusty shower.

"Are you all right?" the girl's voice said from above. Her head appeared in the ring of light overhead.

The young man patted himself for injuries and wiggled his toes, but everything felt intact.

"I'm fine," he called up, "but you might not want to come down after all. It's all stone down here, and you might hurt your ankle more."

"You'll just have to catch me then," the girl said. Her head vanished.

"I'll have to . . . what?!" the young man said, barely having time to scramble to his feet before the girl came plummeting down on top of him. Thankfully she was much lighter than he was, and he was able to absorb the impact without falling again. She clung to his neck fiercely, but let go when it became evident that he was not going to drop her.

"It's so cold down here!" she exclaimed, rubbing her hands together as the young man set her feet on the floor.

She was right, he noticed. The morning air of the forest was chilly, but down here it was positively freezing. Goosebumps stood out on his bare arms, and he had already begun to shiver.

As his eyes adjusted to the dim light, the young man took stock of where they had landed. It was in fact a tunnel: he could almost touch both sides if he stretched out his arms. Just a few paces in one direction, the passage was blocked by a mound of dirt and large stone blocks that reached all the way to the ceiling. Several thick tree roots ran across the pile, having pushed in the walls that supported the ceiling as they grew. In the other direction, the tunnel disappeared into the darkness.

"Well, now that we're down here, I hope you have a way to get us out," the girl said.

The young man pointed down the corridor. "I can see the other end just down there," he said. Now that his eyes were better adjusted, the pinpoint of light he had spotted earlier was clearly visible.

"Then let's go already," the girl said. "I don't want to miss breakfast completely."

The young man put a finger to his lips.

"Sound carries down here," he said quietly. "If you're worried about getting caught, try not to make any noise."

The girl snorted and stomped away down the tunnel, though less noisily than she might have.

The two of them moved slowly toward the distant glimmer, feeling their way with hands and feet. The light ahead of them grew appreciably brighter as they walked, and within a few minutes it became evident that it was not the glow of the surface. Rather than having the greenish tinge of leaf-filtered sunlight, this radiance was almost blue.

"That doesn't look like a way out," the girl whispered. "We're not going to get stuck down here, are we?"

"Of course not," the young man replied. He did not sound frightened, but his concern was growing. He had not figured there would be any source of light down there other than an exit.

All thoughts of escape disappeared from the young man's mind, however, when they found the source of the light. The tunnel opened into a room of substantial size, its ceiling supported by rows of thick stone pillars. Despite being underground, it was surprisingly well lit.

The light was emitted by mushrooms, hundreds if not thousands of them. They sprouted in circular clusters scattered across the floor, their cumulative luminescence bathing the whole place in an unearthly blue glow. In the center of the open space, three waist-high pedestals stood in a triangular arrangement, obviously the focal point of the chamber. Otherwise, the room was empty.

"Yuck," the girl said, holding her nose against the smell of decay. "These mushrooms stink."

Undeterred by the smell, the young man tiptoed across the threshold and took a quick look around. Still satisfied that they were alone, he crossed to the center of the room where the pedestals stood. Unlike everything else they had seen underground, the pedestals were made of wood, not of stone, and looked like roughly hacked segments of tree trunk. It was exactly the sort of unrefined workmanship the young man had come to expect from the Masked and their reliance on only the most primitive of tools. What rested upon the pedestals, on the other hand, took his breath away.

Three strange devices, all apparently identical, lay atop the crudely worked wood. Disk-shaped and hardly thicker than a finger, they gleamed silver even in the dimness, betraying their rare composition. They were not large, but even so they contained more metal than the young man had ever before seen in one place. Their value was almost incalculable.

"What are you staring at?" the girl asked, approaching from behind. She too drew a sharp breath when she beheld the treasures before them.

Six concentric rings were inlaid into each disk's surface, each one a different color and composed of a different alloy. Tiny letters and symbols were etched into them, but whatever language it was, the young man could not decipher it. Even more remarkable than their metallic composition or runic inscriptions, the rings seemed to possess a life of their own.

It was beyond the young man to even guess at the principle that animated the rings, but they were most definitely moving. Their rotation was leisurely, and a few turned so slowly that it was hard to tell that they were moving at all.

"What do you suppose they are?" the girl whispered, her voice quieted more by awe than fear of detection. She moved to join the young man beside the pedestal, but as soon as she stepped closer, a whirring noise started up from the nearest metal disk. The innermost ring began to spin faster, and then it clicked into a locked position and stopped. The largest symbol it bore, an arrow, was pointed directly at where the girl stood. Clicking sounds from the other two devices indicated that they had followed suit. The young man and the girl waited, but nothing more happened.

"Why are they pointing at me?" the girl asked uneasily. She slid to the side, but the rings followed her. "Do something, make it stop."

The young man waved his arms, feeling a little silly as he tried to distract the devices from the girl, but they seemed wholly uninterested in him. Only when she moved far enough away did the rings resume their passive rotation. Even when the young man was the only one nearby, they continued to ignore his presence.

"I don't like these things," the girl said from behind a pillar, unwilling to approach the pedestals again. "Let's get out of here before we're caught."

"All right, just give me a minute," the young man said. Each of the rings had an arrow symbol just like the central one, he noticed, and the ones that were hardly moving were all pointed in the same direction. If he had just a little longer, he thought, he might be able to figure out what they were for.

Seemingly without provocation, the central rings once again began to speed up, and then they fixed themselves pointing directly away from the young man. When he looked up, he was shocked to find that they were no longer alone in the chamber.

The masked man stared at them from the across the room, the mushrooms' blue light too weak to penetrate the folds of the furs that cloaked him. Lit from beneath, peculiar shadows on his mask made it appear to be grinning.

"Are they what you imagined?"

The young man immediately recognized the voice as their mentor's. He was not sure whether he should be relieved or dismayed that they had been discovered, but at least now they did not have to worry about finding a way out. The voice did not sound angry, though that probably meant little. The Masked did not betray emotion easily.

"They?" the young man said.

The masked man gestured to the three pedestals. "The Listeners," he said.

The young man balked. The Listeners? These things could not be the Listeners, could they?

"Those can't be the Listeners," the girl said with conviction, coming out from behind her pillar and giving voice to his thoughts. "The Listeners are people."

"And who told you that?" their mentor asked.

The girl frowned. "No one, but the way you talk about them . . . ."

"Yes," their mentor said, approaching the pedestals. The Listeners' rings rotated to follow him. "We speak of them with reverence, for they are more important than any living person. They are our most valuable asset and our most effective ally."

The young man frowned. It was on the Listeners' orders that the Masked came and went, battling breaches across the world. He had always assumed that they were a secret enclave, an order within an order, too important for someone like him to know about.

"If the Listeners aren't people, how do they work?" the young man asked.

Their mentor crossed his arms. "You've already deduced much of it."

The young man was irked at having his thoughts apparently read again, but curiosity overcame his irritation.

"They point to where the breaches are," he guessed. "That's how you know where to go, isn't it?" He looked around. "And I bet there's enough room down here to fit all the Masked in the forest."

"Very observant," the masked man said. "But you've overlooked one thing. The Listeners don't just tell us where the breaches are. They tell us where they will be." He cupped one of the devices in his hands. "They sense subtle shifts in the distribution of energy throughout the environment and predict where it will coalesce."

"But how?" the girl interjected, not wanting to be left out. "You told us that you'd have to be very close to where a breach was going to happen to feel it."

"Ah, but the Listeners are very close," their mentor said. "They are close to all of our world of Altissara."

"Close?" the young man said. "How can they be close to everything, even things on the other side of the world?"

The masked man ran his finger across the device's concentric rings. "Remember your lessons. These rings were crafted long ago, made from countless pieces gathered from all corners of the world. Those pieces remain connected to the places from which they were taken."

This concept had indeed been part of a lesson, the young man recalled vaguely. "So each Listener can feel as if it were everywhere in the world at once," he ventured. "No matter how far away the breach, if the Listener has a piece from that place, it can sense it."

"Indeed," their mentor said, nodding approvingly. "Through the Listeners we can observe every breach in the natural order of the world, near or far."

"Then why did they point at me?" the girl asked. The young man had been so caught up in the details of the Listeners that he had almost forgotten. Now that he thought about it, the rings had reacted to both the girl and their mentor, but not to him.

Their mentor shook his head. "Enough questions for one day, especially from those who venture where they are not invited. Come, it is time we leave this place. You are not too late for breakfast, if you want it."

The young man protested. "But the rings-"

"Don't press your good fortune," the masked man warned. "You might have been punished instead of indulged if another had found you here."

"You aren't going to punish us?" the young man asked.

"Curiosity alone is not worthy of punishment. Do you plan to do this again?"

The girl and the young man stole a glance at one another. "No," they said vigorously and in unison.

"Then there's no reason to speak further of it."

The young man nodded in resignation. Being ignored by the rings bothered him, but there was little he could do about it now. The girl was right. Sometimes, it was better to be patient. The day was only just beginning, and he already had more than enough to worry about.

Chapter 3
The Masked

The journey out of the tunnels was surprisingly short. One hall and a narrow flight of stairs later, the young man found himself emerging into a small, low-roofed structure that he recognized as one of the many huts of the Masked encampment. Their mentor held aside the pelt that covered the entrance, and they stepped out into the comparative brightness of the mid-morning forest.

The camp of the Masked filled the area under the trees before them, though it looked little like what an outsider might imagine. Even now, the young man could feel a hint of disappointment tugging at him, an echo of what he had felt when first laying eyes upon the strangely mundane place where the saviors of the world dwelled.

Though the Masked occupied the camp year-round, the place had the look of a temporary settlement. There were no true buildings, only squat huts built from fallen branches covered with mounds of leaves that resembled piles of waste waiting to be burned. Not one was tall enough to stand up straight in, and they were rarely used for anything but sleep and shelter from the rain. For the most part the Masked lived, ate, and worked with only the trees around them for protection, and not a single one of the acid-dripping flora had been cut down to make room for their dwellings. There was no shared well that served the scattered huts, nor a common latrine. In fact, there was little to distinguish the lives of the Masked from those of wild beasts, and their garb of furs only served to reinforce that impression. Predictably, they avoided many of the conveniences they could easily have had. Comfort, after all, was just another invitation to corruption.

Most of the Masked in the camp were squatting around small fires, roasting pieces of the venison that served as a staple of their diet. The young man guessed that nearly a hundred lived in the forest in total, although an accurate count was impossible because it was so hard to tell them apart. Their voices were one of their few telling features, but most of them spoke to him so rarely that it seemed he was in the company of perfect strangers who time never made more familiar.

The young man, the girl, and their mentor joined three more of the Masked at the nearest fire. The fur-covered forms ate with their fingers, masks still in place, bits of food disappearing eerily behind the unmoving faces as if consumed by bodiless phantoms.

The young man, feeling their concealed eyes were upon him, picked up a skewer propped by the fire and quickly consumed the morsels of charred venison, diluting the musky taste with a few swigs from the shared water-skin. In the excitement of his underground discovery, he had forgotten how hungry he was. Two more skewers of meat disappeared the same way, and finally the young man's stomach gave an appeased sigh and was quiet. The girl also ate ravenously, too famished to be put off by the sensation of scrutiny that was inevitable among groups of the Masked. Then, their appetites sated, the young man and the girl sat by the fire, fighting the urge to fidget as their mentor finished his meal with no great haste.

Trying to look anywhere but at the silent figures who seemed to be watching him, the young man cast his gaze to the other fires. The low murmurs of conversation were everywhere, but the words were muffled by distance and the fire's soft crackle. They were probably sharing news of the world outside the forest, he speculated. The Masked traveled frequently, but there was no way of knowing when one had gone and another arrived to take his place. Responding to the breaches took them far and wide, yet they owned no beasts of burden to aid them, and he had yet to figure how they made do without. It was maddening, being so completely in the dark even when it came to such small things, but he held the feeling in check. The Masked displayed an uncanny ability to pick up on his emotions as well as his thoughts, and that tended to be even more intrusive and embarrassing.

Despite his efforts to hide it, their mentor must have sensed his restlessness. "If you're finished, you may go on ahead and prepare for your lessons. We're late today because of this morning's detour, so it would serve you to be ready and attentive."

The young man needed no further encouragement. He stood up, nodded respectfully to the other Masked at the fire, and set a brisk pace toward the edge of the camp with the girl at his side. They headed north, in the direction of the usual place where they took their lessons.

"I wish they wouldn't stare at us," the girl said. "It's creepy."

The young man nodded in sympathy. "Their conversation isn't exactly thrilling, either." This sort of commiseration had become a ritual between them.

The girl put her hands on her hips and looked at him pointedly, as if suddenly remembering something important.

"You had better not try to use what happened this morning as an excuse to get out of what you promised," she said.

The young man raised his hands and laughed at her seriousness. "I wouldn't dream of it. A promise is a promise."

"Good," she said. She meant it this time, he realized, and was not about to let him beg off like he had so many times before. He was not sure whether to feel irritated or comforted.

The air in the woods was gradually warming, though the exercise of walking did more to ward off chills than the slowly ascending sun, which peeked at the moving figures intermittently through the screen of branches overhead. Thin wisps of steam rose from the damp soil where golden rays fell, and clumps of knobby Scarwood saplings jostled one another for their father sun's attention as the pair passed by. A family of squirrels took it upon themselves to monitor their progress, poking their heads out briefly from behind tree trunks to ensure that they were behaving themselves. The smells of the forest were deep and strong, and filling in a way more fundamental than that of their hastily eaten breakfast. They brought a simple peace that allowed the young man to briefly forget his worries over what he had promised to do.

Soon the two of them arrived at a place where the ground was wiped clean and the exposed dirt still bore the markings of previous lessons. No sooner had the young man taken a seat than their mentor stepped into view, his furs bearing a few grease spots that he seemed not to notice. If he had truly been following them so closely through the forest, they had detected no sign of it as they walked. Such was the way of the Masked, and the young man had long since learned to take it in stride.

Instead of beginning the lesson by selecting a stick for writing, the masked man drew a short bit of string from inside his furs. When the young man saw it, he could barely disguise his groan. The pleasant feeling from the walk through the forest vanished far more quickly than it had arisen.

"Your enthusiasm is not required for this lesson," the masked man said bluntly.

The girl patted the young man's arm sympathetically, though for her this exercise was nothing to dread. For him, however, it might as well have been the punishment their mentor had promised to forgo.

Unwound, the pale strand of sinew dangled from the masked man's hand like one of his many scars risen from the flesh, weighted at the end by a small animal vertebrae that swung back and forth in short, unguided arcs.

"Watch closely," the masked man said. He began to swing the bone on the end of the string more purposefully. Then, using his other hand, he gave it a gentle flick whenever it reached the bottom of its arc, bouncing it back the way it came. He did this several times, and then he removed his hand.

The bone swung downward, and the young man saw something sparkle for a brief instant, like the invisible tip of a cracking whip, and the bone bounced back just like before. Again and again it bounced back, turned away by some unseen force. No matter how closely he watched, the critical moment passed before his eyes could take it in.

"Now you," the masked man said.

"I'll go first," the girl said, allowing the young man to breathe a momentary sigh of relief.

Their mentor said nothing, but merely began swinging the bone again. The girl furrowed her brow, and after a few seconds the bone was deflected just like before. It did not rise to the same height as at the hands of their mentor, but otherwise her mimicry was perfect. After just half a minute of this exercise, the masked man snatched the bone from the air and turned to the young man.

"Now you."

The girl backed away, giving him an apologetic look for not being able to delay any longer.

The young man's heart sank, for this was the part he dreaded. He wanted to shout about the unfairness of it, but instead he held his tongue, focused his mind, and tried his best. *Bounce back, bounce back*, he recited quietly to himself as the masked man once again swung the bone before him. *Bounce back!*

The young man's gut lurched as something reached out from his body and struck at the dangling bone, bouncing it sideways and setting it spinning violently. It was a terrible feeling, like when he had nearly lost a finger to an accident with a glass-edged scythe back home.

He tried again, not quite certain how he was making it happen, and again the bone leapt in a different direction. A wave of nausea pulsed outward from his chest, pushing up against the back of his throat like a boiling pot against its lid. He looked pleadingly at their mentor for encouragement or advice, but as usual found neither in his mask's impassive stare.

"You haven't been instructed to stop," their mentor said. "This is your most important lesson. It is the way of the world, and you will practice until you accept and master it."

This time the bone bounced so erratically that it pulled loose from the masked man's hand and landed in the dirt an arm's length away. The young man fell forward onto his hands, choking, feeling the bits of meat in his stomach making their bid for freedom. The patch of blackened skin hidden beneath his tunic burned in throbbing waves, keeping time with his fluttering heart, and he felt a shooting pain as if someone had tightened a fist around his insides and begun to pull . . . .

"*. . . . Your treachery is impressive,*" *the masked man said,* "*but no lie can last forever. Tonight, we right the wrongs you have committed. Then, you die. . . .*"

The young man clenched his teeth, sagging in the dirt when the nausea and hallucinations finally released him from their grip. Anger boiled up to take their place. He was useless, just like always, and it felt so terribly unfair. Unfair, just like everything else.

"Haven't you figured it out yet?" he asked the masked man bitterly, wiping spittle from the corner of his mouth. "You can see I'm not getting any better. Doing the same thing over and over again isn't helping. If anything, I'm getting worse!" His eyes fell on the bone, the object of his anger, still lying where it had fallen.

"And what good is this thing anyway?" he said, picking it up and dangling it distastefully in front of him. "It's pointless!" He tossed it at the other man and started to stand up.

A faint coughing sound issued from behind the mask, and it took the young man a moment to realize he was being laughed at.

"Correct," the gruff voice said. "That is your most important lesson. Now that you know it, you are ready to learn the rest."

Chapter 4
The Initiate's Path

The young man blinked several times, mouth slack.

"Do you mean . . . ?" He looked at the girl beside him, her face frozen in wide-eyed surprise. Neither of them was quite ready to believe what they thought they had heard, not after so many months of waiting.

"Yes. You are ready. Both of you." The fur-draped figure rose to his feet. "But there is still the matter of initiation. Now, show me your arm."

The young man's hand went to the spot where the Scarwood sap had burned him.

"What does my arm have to do with it?" he asked.

The masked man did not answer, reaching out and grabbing the young man's arm without waiting for it to be offered. "How recent is this mark?" he said.

"Just this morning," the young man replied, wondering what he was getting at. Living in the shadows of the Scarwoods meant that sap burns were inevitable, and he could not even count the number of times he had suffered them before.

After gazing at the raw spot for a moment and stretching the skin between his fingers, the masked man picked up a twig and scratched something unintelligible in the dirt. He looked eastward through the trees, then back at the young man. The mask hid his eyes in darkness, but the young man had the feeling that he was not looking at his face. If he had not known better, he would have said the masked man was staring at his chest, exactly where the hidden blemish marred his skin. It was all he could do to avoid revealing his sudden fear that, mere moments from acceptance, the truth of his condition would be discovered and he would be cast out.

"Dusk," the masked man said finally, standing without further explanation. "Come. The place we must go is far, and we have little time for travel."

"Don't you want to look at my arms too?" the girl asked. Their mentor made no reply, and she did not insist, though she did appear slightly crestfallen.

Rather than head back toward the camp or deeper into the forest, the masked man turned toward the morning sun and the forest's edge. The tree line was not far from where they took their lessons, and it would take only minutes of walking to reach it.

"As we walk, listen well. This is important, and there will not be time to repeat it. Do you understand?" their mentor said.

The young man nodded, still trying to grasp what was happening. Why today, after so long of the same routine, day in and day out? He had been burned by Scarwood sap a hundred times before, and he had failed to control the power of the Masked just as many. What about today made them ready, when yesterday they were not? The only difference had been their intrusion into the chamber of the Listeners, but that had gotten them scolded, not praised. Nothing had happened in there that could possibly have proven them ready.

"Once initiated, all Masked are equal," their mentor said. "There are no students among us, and no masters. However, each Masked must abide by our code, and it is the job of all to ensure the compliance of all. It is this code that has preserved us through the millennia, and at its foundation are three rules." The young man swallowed hard, trying to commit everything to memory.

"Regarding our power, you must never use it without true need. And when you do, use precisely what you need and no more. If you remember nothing else of what you hear today, remember this. That is our first rule."

Again the young man nodded. This rule was known to everyone, not just the Masked. Few bothered to question why - it was just a part of who they were, who they had always been. Yet to the young man, the why of it suddenly felt very, very important.

The masked man spoke as if to answer the silent question. "You know that we keep no possessions for ourselves. This extends even to our power, for it is a thing borrowed, not owned. Just as in all things, to borrow too heavily is to bless the present while cursing the future." It was not much of an explanation, but it was still more than the young man had been expecting.

Their pace was a brisk one, and the girl was struggling on her sore ankle to match it. Ahead, the young man could see the tree line and the meadow bathed in warm sunlight beyond. He shivered a little, suddenly reminded of the chill of the forest's shadows. Their mentor continued to speak.

"Once you receive your mask, you must wear it always in the presence of others. Your face, your name, and all else that marks you as unique must disappear forever from the world of men. That is our second rule."

Their mentor seemed to be addressing only the young man with his words, as if he had forgotten the girl was limping along behind them. The young man paused for a moment to let her catch up, and when she did he gave her hand a comforting squeeze. This was what they had been waiting for, and she deserved to be a part of it just as much as he did, if not more.

The trees gave way before them, and a gust of wind passing over the meadow beyond pulled at the young man's hair, reminding him of how shaggy it had become. The dry grass sloped down a shallow hillside, turning to rocks and mud where a small stream gurgled at the bottom, then rose again to blanket a series of hills that stretched out almost as far as the eye could see. Seeing the horizon unfold before him outlined in pure, dazzling blue made the young man almost giddy, and his heart seemed to swell without the confining bars of the forest's trunks to contain it. He had been in the forest for some time, but he had never realized until now just how much his body longed for the wind and light of open spaces, the sight of circling hawks and the tides of clouds rolling across the sky. An irresistible smile drew itself across his face, one in which the girl could not help but join him.

The masked man paused as they left the cover of the trees. Sunlight filled the crevices in the bark that covered his face, scouring them of shadows accumulated over years spent in half-light. The wind brushed through his furs, making them seem alive with the spirits of rabbits eager to run and foxes eager to chase. He had the look of a primal beast come to the edge of its domain to gaze out on a world that had long since moved on to a new age.

As he observed their mentor, the forest's chill briefly returned to the young man's body despite the sun's warmth. He recaptured, for an instant, his first impression of the Masked: mysterious, imposing, and powerful, but above all, feral.

"Our third rule . . . ."

The wind pulled at the softly-spoken words, dissolving them into breaths of air almost before they reached the young man's ears. He looked hard at the masked figure, but there was nothing to indicate that he had spoken at all, and he continued to stare eastward in silence. In the direction of his gaze, the sun's golden orb sat two fists above distant mountains, white-capped and majestic gates that guarded the border of man's kingdom from the endless wild beyond.

His patience dwindled, and the young man spoke up. "The third rule?"

If the masked man heard, he did not show it. Instead he set off through the tall grass, leaving the young man and the girl to catch up. They headed down the hill toward the remains of an abandoned structure, one that might once have been a hunter's cottage or farmer's outbuilding. Only a single wall was left standing, and of that only the frame remained intact. The interior floorboards were split and sagging, and as they approached, the young man thought he saw a slinking shadow slip into the darkened space beneath them.

The masked man came to a halt facing the empty door frame. The floor beyond did not look up to supporting any real weight, and the young man eyed it incredulously, trying to guess the purpose of their visit. While the young man and the girl stared, their mentor drew out a small black bag from his furs and loosened the drawstring. The slits in his mask gazed blankly down at its hidden contents for what seemed like a very long while before a hand went in and pulled out a fragment of stone no larger than a fingernail.

"What are we doing here?" the young man asked, but he received only a dismissive wave in response.

With the stone chip in hand, the masked man traced the outline of the door, starting from the ground on the left and finishing at the ground on the right, then pressed the chip against the lintel. The young man expected it to fall, but instead it remained fixed when the masked man withdrew his hand. Other than that, however, it seemed the odd ritual had accomplished nothing.

"Are you ready?" the masked man asked.

It was a pointless question. Before the young man had time to open his mouth, the masked man seized him by the arm, slapped a hand over his eyes, and shoved him bodily through the door.

The young man imagined he was about to crash through the unstable floor into a nest of rats or snakes or worse, but his feet remained on solid ground, and his mentor released him almost immediately. A moment later the girl stumbled up beside with a yelp of surprise, having been manhandled in the same manner.

Even before his vision returned, the young man could feel the presence of wind – not the gentle, pleasant wind that had brushed through the grass of the meadow, but a powerful, turbulent wind that changed direction like an animal pacing the confines of its cage. With the hand that had been covering his eyes gone, he took in an incredible sight: instead of the rotten, crumbling interior of the hut, the young man saw a bridge of glaringly white stone shooting out from beneath his feet over a great chasm between two mountains. He spun around, looking for the place they had left behind, but saw only a bare mountainside through the stone arch that marked the near end of the bridge.

The sky that yawned overhead was a brilliant blue, though the sun itself was nowhere in sight. Below, the sheer sides of the mountains reached down so far that they met in a thin black line. The painfully tight grip that seized his arm told the young man that the girl had also noticed the bottomless void below.

"Don't fall," the masked man said, and the young man jerked away from the edge. The girl followed, still securely attached to his arm.

"What is this place?" he said, trying with little success to control the anxiety in his voice.

The masked man shook his head. "It's not. Come, this is not our destination, and it's best not to linger."

The young man obligingly took a few steps across the smooth white stones, but stopped as the girl pulled him back, her eyes full of fear.

"This isn't right," she whispered, leaning backward to pull him toward the arch where they had entered.

The young man knew what she meant, though he did his best to be reassuring even under the unsettling barrage of the wild wind. The two of them had already endured so much to get this far: nights spent wet and cold on the ground without so much as a proper blanket, a diet meager enough to trim all the fat from their bones, and the maddeningly blank gazes of a hundred masks always staring, staring, staring . . . . They had to get through this too. Only if they finished what they started would all that suffering have any meaning.

"It's all right," he said. "There's nothing to be afraid of. It's just a bridge, that's all, and all we have to do is cross it."

The girl shook her head, the wind pulling tears from the corners of her eyes and dragging them across her face. "It's not a bridge," she said in denial. "It's . . . it's . . . ." Again she shook her head, unable to find the right words.

About ten paces ahead, their mentor stopped and turned back. "A disciplined mind has no fear for itself, so it cannot be surprised, or shocked, or intimidated. Abandon your fear and your body will not resist your will." The sound of his words rose and fell as the wind played with them, pushing them closer and then dragging them away.

The young man scowled. Couldn't he see that what the girl needed now was not some discourse on the theory of discipline?

"Don't mind him," the young man said. "Here, take my hands. That's it." He clasped the girl's hands in his.

"We'll walk together," he said. "We've gotten through worse, remember? You'll stay right next to me, and nothing bad will happen. You can even close your eyes, and I'll make sure you don't trip or fall. How does that sound?"

The girl blinked her wet eyes. "You won't let go?"

"Not for a second."

The girl took a deep breath, then nodded. "I trust you," she said. The wind rushed and roared between them, pulling tangles of hair across their eyes and mouths.

"Good," the young man said. "We'll be across before you know it. Let's start with the left foot . . . ."

The young man wished he had been right. The crossing was long, longer for their slow pace, and made tedious by the continued lashing of the unpredictable winds. The angry gusts carried a smell that was faint yet disturbing, like singed hair, that only grew worse with each breath. The path seemed interminable and unchanging, but at least its course was true and its construction mercifully strong.

At what must have been the midpoint of the bridge, the masked man slowed his steps and skirted a circle carved into the stone of the walkway. More interesting than the circle, though, was what it contained: a freestanding block of stone roughly twice as tall as it was wide. The standing stone was of a different kind than the rest of the bridge, but its purpose was unclear. The young man could detect no immediate danger from it, but nevertheless he followed his mentor's lead and gave the circle a wide berth. He did not even bother asking what it was for. Given everything else he still did not understand, it seemed hardly worth the effort.

When at last they reached the far end of the bridge, the young man's limbs were aching, not from the physical strain of the journey but from the tension his body refused to release. It must have been doubly hard for the girl, who to her credit had never closed her eyes against the sunless sky, bottomless chasm, and stinking wind. In fact, once they had gotten properly underway she had never once complained.

Where their journey ended looked much like where it began. A simple stone arch marked the end of the bridge, which terminated just a few paces beyond in the sheer side of the mountain.

"Close your eyes when you pass through," the masked man instructed, halting before the arch. At least this time it did not seem like he would throw them through by force.

Eager to leave that unnatural place, they closed their eyes and stepped under the arch together. The wind died immediately, though its stench lingered, hovering just on the edge of perception.

On the other side, they found that the scenery had changed once again. Great piles of stone rose up on all sides to form what had once been the walls of an expansive structure, though no roof remained to obstruct their view of the sky. Between the great gray blocks, scarred by weather and time, grew elaborate patterns of thick green moss, binding the stones where the mortar had long since turned to dust. The flagstones of the floor were uneven, perforated by cracks from which sprouted millions of tiny blue flowers, each with five delicate petals and a yellow dot at its heart. Four towers were visible over the ruined walls, and though they were crumbling at their peaks they still rose higher than any the young man had seen. Shielding his eyes and gazing up at the spires in awe, the young man took in the welcome sight of the sun hovering beside them. When he finally tore his gaze away, he saw that their mentor had already moved on to the far end of the dilapidated courtyard where a rectangular block lay in the shadow of two gnarled trees.

The girl released her grip on the young man's hand, though she remained close as they moved to join their mentor. As they drew closer, the young man could see that the stone block between the trees was in fact a box, open at the top and overflowing with a mass of the abundant blue flowers. Its dimensions, he realized, matched those of a human body.

The masked man drew leather gloves from his furs and pulled them over his scarred hands.

"The flowers are called Memory," he said. "An apt name, for they bloom year round, like a constant memory of spring." He paused. "And, if one were to touch your skin, a memory is all that would remain of you." He brushed one of the tiny flower heads and came away with a bead of clear liquid on the leather of his glove.

"There are few places where they grow any longer. Some day soon they may disappear from the world entirely." The masked man passed his hand over the top of the casket, and the flowers within closed up their petals in unison, hiding their yellow eyes from sight. Then he reached carefully into the tangled mass of blue and green, his arm buried nearly to the shoulder as he groped about in the depths of the coffin. After a bit of twisting and pulling, it emerged with a wide, heavy-looking book.

The young man had seen few enough books in his life, but even so he immediately knew that this one was special. It was bound with leather and thin strips of metal, the value of which alone was remarkable. So far as he knew, not even the iron lords wasted metal on books. There was a small shape of the same dully gleaming alloy set into the cover, but no words to mark what sorts of things might be found within.

"This is our heritage," the masked man said, holding up the book. "All of this." He gestured to the towers, the walls, and the casket. "This was home to those whose mistakes we exist to correct. Though they lived and died long ago, their selfishness touches our world with pain and destruction to this day, dragging it ever closer to the abyss." Surprisingly, there was no bitterness in his words. They were facts so ancient that the feeling had died out of them generations before.

"It is their power we have inherited," he continued, "though we share little else. It is from their excesses that we learn our modesty, from their indiscretions our secrecy, and from their greed our selflessness. To keep their tools of destruction from petty hands, we vowed to hold them securely in our own."

The masked man splayed a hand across the cover of the book.

"Reading this is your initiation," he said. "You have until dusk, most likely, to finish. There will be no problems if you are done by then." He looked over the young man's and girl's shoulders as he spoke, the words seemingly directed as much to the empty air as to them.

Then he held out the book. The young man accepted it, and after a moment of hesitation the masked man let it go. It was heavier than the young man expected, and the dry leather of the binding felt rough against his skin.

"Let her hold it for now, but do not open it yet," the masked man said, nodding to the girl, whose fear from the bridge seemed to have vanished in favor of awe. "There's something we must discuss. Just the two of us."

The young man looked to the girl, but she seemed too eager to hold the book to be concerned. After handing off the tome, he followed the masked man on a slow, deliberate walk across the courtyard.

For what seemed like a long time the masked man said nothing, looking only downward as he placed his steps around the flowers clinging to life among the broken stones.

"The life of a Masked is full of sacrifice," he said suddenly, his voice low. "That is no secret, and we all know it before putting on the mask, but . . . ." He kept looking at ground. "It demands different things from each one of us, and some must give more than others. Some of us grow cold because it's easier than dealing with the full weight of the choices the mask forces on us. Some may even wish to give up choosing altogether, or think that our work would be easier without cares or memories to haunt us. But that is wrong." He drew a full breath.

"The truth is, what we suffer as a result of our choices is just as important as the results they achieve. Living with that pain is a constant affirmation of the choice that created it. To turn away, to wish in your heart of hearts to escape it, is to turn your back on your beliefs. If you choose what's right, then no matter the consequences, you can endure them."

The masked man lifted his head. "Now," he said, "there is only one question you must answer. Knowing this, do you choose the mask?"

The question caught the young man off guard. It was not a demand that he justify why he wanted to join the Masked, why he wanted to give up his name and all chance at a normal life. It was not even a demand for a pledge of loyalty. All it required was a simple yes or no.

Wondering why the question was only for him, the young man glanced over his shoulder at the girl. He noticed, strangley, that despite all they had just been through, she looked relaxed, and her dirt-smudged face was untroubled by worry. Even surrounded by the fatal blue blossoms, a single misstep from death, she was serene, lost in her own world as if she had not a care in this one. How could she be so at ease? The reason, suddenly, was obvious. It was because she felt safe. It was because she was not alone.

"Yes," the young man answered. "I do."

The masked man gave a slow, understanding nod. "Good. Always remember that. And do not judge me too harshly for the secrets I have kept, once you learn the truth. I always did what I thought was best." There was unmistakable pride in his voice, and also a touch of sadness. Then he turned, walked through the arch at the end of the courtyard, and was gone.

The young man stared at the empty archway for a minute before returning to where the girl sat on a cracked stone block, running her hands over the book she held.

"What did he want to talk about?" she asked, glancing up.

"He told me to look after you, that's all," the young man lied, still a little shaken by the unexpected emotion from their mentor.

"Oh," she said. Then, after a long pause, "What do you suppose the third rule was?"

"The third rule?" the young man said, distracted.

"In the field, before we crossed the . . . the bridge," the girl reminded him. "He never finished telling us the third rule."

The young man shrugged. Of all the unanswered questions that skittered about the edges of his mind, that was least among them. "You can ask him yourself when we get back to camp. Anyhow, let's have a look at this book."

The young man seated himself beside the girl and examined the volume over her shoulder. It was very old: the metal bands had tarnished nearly black, and the binding was worn and discolored. He ran his hand over its face in the same manner as the girl, stopping to finger the raised metal emblem on the cover. It was a tree, branches and roots fanning out in stylized symmetry to form an almost circular whole. The workmanship was exquisite, and even though it was no taller than his thumb, it was covered with textured bark and minute, delicately crafted leaves.

"Shall we open it?" the young man said, reaching for the lip of the cover.

"Wait," the girl said, suddenly sounding unsure.

"What is it?" the young man asked.

The girl looked down at her hands. "We're . . . going to be Masked after this," she said.

"I suppose so," the young man replied.

"I know we won't need each other any more, but . . . can we still be friends?" she said.

The young man laughed and put an arm around her shoulder. It was an absurd question, from someone he had come to think of like a sister. "Of course we can. Just because we'll be Masked doesn't mean we'll be different people. We can stay friends, no matter what."

"Promise?" the girl said.

"I promise," the young man answered.

"All right," she said, putting her hand next to his on the ancient book. "Let's open it."

Taking a collective breath, they lifted the heavy cover and looked inside.

Chapter 5

Heroes Born, Villains Made

The young man blinked. He was standing in the middle of a dirt road – the courtyard, the girl, and the book in his hands had all vanished the instant they cracked its covers. The air was thick and heavy with unseasonable summertime heat, and the sun shone down on fields that stretched across the flat countryside in every direction. In the southern distance, a bank of dark thunderheads fringed the horizon.

"At last, he has brought you to me," a voice said from behind him.

He turned to see a woman standing in the grass by the side of the road, dressed in a strangely cut and oddly colored gown. The bodice was intensely green, close fitting to the waist and then loose to the ground. Rather than sleeves, from her shoulders hung strips of red cloth that dangled nearly to her ankles. When she stepped forward, they rippled smoothly after like twin tails of flame.

The young man took a step away.

"Who are you?" he asked, bewildered. "Where am I? What happened to . . . ?" He hesitated, hampered for the first time by not knowing the girl's name.

"You may call me Lith," the woman said. She had long, jet black hair and a pale, thin-featured face seemingly untouched by sun or wind. The ghost of a smile danced between her eyes and lips in an almost imperceptible expression of anticipation. "I am the one who will complete your transformation."

A faint breath of southerly wind stirred the grass, cooling the beads of sweat on the young man's face.

"You're going to make me a Masked?" he said.

The woman called Lith laughed, the lightness of her voice echoed by a faint roll of thunder from the distant clouds. The sound sent a chill down the young man's spine in spite of the heat.

"Not exactly," she said slowly, as if savoring the moment. "I'm afraid that my friend, your mentor, had to deceive you in that regard, or I fear you would not have come to me willingly. Perhaps you have sensed it already, but I will let you in on a secret: the days of the Masked, like those of this world, will soon be at an end. You will not be joining them, at least not in the way you imagined. I have something very different planned for you."

•••••

"What have you done to him?!" the girl cried, cradling the young man's head in her lap and frantically trying to wake him from the stupor that had come over him the instant they had opened the book. He was still breathing, but his skin had grown pale and sweaty, and a quivering spasm ran through his body.

The strangely dressed woman who had appeared in the courtyard the very moment he lost consciousness stood over both of them, arms crossed.

"I have done nothing," she said. "At least, not yet. Your friend has a darkness within him, an injury he has carried all his life, and it is very near to claiming him completely. He thinks that he cannot be saved, but he can, with my help. And yours."

The girl looked up into the strange woman's angular face, tears welling up in her eyes as the young man lay unresponsive in her arms.

"What do you mean?" she asked.

•••••

"What do you mean?" the young man said warily, keeping his distance from Lith.

"I mean that the Masked have outlived the purpose for which I made them," she answered. "They have guarded this world well, but they were never meant to be a permanent answer to the forces that threaten it. They know only how to treat the symptom, not the disease. Soon, even they will not be able to protect it any longer. That is why I need you."

"You made the Masked?" the young man said in disbelief. This woman hardly looked much older than he was.

Lith's black hair cast a shadow over her face. "I am older than I look."

"Even if I did believe you," the young man said carefully, "what do I have to do with it?"

"That part, at least, is simple," Lith replied. "The Masked have reached the end of their usefulness, but I made them resilient, even . . . fanatical. It has helped them endure through the ages, but it also means they will never accept that their ways are now doing more to hurt the world than to help it. Before a better solution can be effected, the Masked must be dealt with. Permanently." She focused her gaze sharply upon the young man, a dark gleam in her eyes. "For that, I need someone who will help me stop the Masked from hastening the world's end with their ineffective attempts to prevent it. You will be my champion, and for me you will kill the Masked, each and every one."

•••••

"That's . . . that's . . ." the girl struggled for words.

"He will die if you refuse," Lith said simply. "It is your choice, of course, but there is no other way to heal him."

The girl looked down at the young man's face. It was twisted now, as if he were dreaming something terrible. She could feel his heartbeat getting faster.

"What kind of person are you," she said angrily, "to ask something like that?"

Lith reached down to touch the young man's grimacing face, but the girl pulled him closer protectively, and she stopped.

"I am someone who cares very much what happens to him," Lith said quietly. "I am someone who wants to see him attain his full potential. But before he can do that, he needs your help."

•••••

"That's crazy," the young man said, starting to back away again. "I'm not going to kill anyone!"

"You will." Lith said.

"Why would I?" the young man demanded.

"Because," Lith said, "that much, at least, is already written. There, upon your chest."

A flash of distant lightning lit the horizon, and the blackened skin of the young man's chest pulsed with burning like a second heartbeat.

"Once the Masked are no more," Lith said, "it will fall to you to be this world's true savior, and do what they cannot."

"No!" the young man said, fighting through the pain that was clawing at him from the inside. "If you want to hurt them, find someone else!" Surely this had to be a trick, a test that the Masked had set for him to measure his loyalty.

Lith raised a dark eyebrow.

40

"There is no one else, and soon you will understand why. Haven't you realized where we are?"

The smell of manure baking in the sun reached the young man's nostrils, and the angry reply he had been preparing died in his throat. He felt the parched dirt under his feet and heard the resonating tones of grasshoppers singing in staggered rhythm. It couldn't be . . . . He looked around again, and this time saw a small house on the edge of the dirt track, hardly a stone's throw from where he stood. The fact that it had not been there a moment before hardly crossed his mind, for recognition swept aside all other emotions. This was home.

A familiar voice cried out from inside, and he rushed to the door and threw it open. The interior was a single room, smaller than he remembered and more sparsely furnished. A woman lay on a straw pallet, attended by two others and a man in a sun bleached shirt and dirty trousers. The woman cried out again, and this time was answered by the shrill cries of a new life announcing itself to the world.

"Oh sis, he's beautiful!" one of the women exclaimed, wrapping the child in a blanket and holding him out for the new mother to see. "Look how strong his little legs are!"

The mother took the bundle in her arms, tears streaming down her face.

"Go on," the sister said, prodding the father as the midwife prepared a knife to cut the cord. "Give your son his name."

The father reached out and stroked the yowling infant's cheek with a calloused finger.

"He should be called Donvin," he said, clasping the mother's hand. "For your grandfather. It will be a name he can be proud of."

A shadow fell across the young man, and he turned to see Lith in the doorway. He tried to speak, but could not. Tears came unbidden to his eyes and fled down his cheeks in droves. It was a shock to hear his name spoken aloud for the first time after so many months, and the emotions it triggered threatened to overwhelm him.

"It was the first time you ever heard your name," Lith said. "But that is not what I wish to show you."

There was a cough from the corner of the room, and everyone turned their heads. There, camouflaged against the mud-colored walls, stood a man in a bark mask.

"The child must be tested," his familiar voice said.

"How could he have been there?" the young man said in confusion.

"He has watched over you for a long, long time," Lith said, "far longer than you know, and at great risk to himself. He has devoted a lifetime to preparing you for this day."

More shocking still than his mentor's presence was the disk that he withdrew from his robes and held out toward the mother and child. It glittered in the light of the small windows, and the young man recognized it instantly as a Listener. Why would his mentor have taken one of the Masked's most prized treasures from its hiding place?

His mother hesitated, then slowly laid the newborn Donvin on the metal disk. The young man shivered, as if he could feel the sharp chill upon his own back.

The masked man looked down at the baby he held, and the child's face contorted at the icy touch of the Listener having replaced his mother's warm arms. For a while the masked man waited, but nothing happened. The rings of the Listener were still.

"This child is special," he said finally.

"Very special," Lith whispered in the young man's ear.

Donvin's mother sat up sharply in alarm.

"No," she said, "it was not to be this generation! You told my grandmother it would be the third after hers!"

"Then the gods have smiled on us," the masked man said, his voice empty of emotion, "for delivering our hope a generation early."

"What would you have us do, then?" the father said sternly, putting a hand on his wife's shoulder.

The eyes of the mask stared at him. "Reveal this to no one, particularly no other Masked. Care for him according to my instructions. Protect him and make him strong, for one day he will need all the strength you can give him. Look: already his destiny is taking hold."

A tiny black speck appeared on the infant Donvin's belly, winking into existence seemingly from nowhere. The baby screamed, and the dark, corrupted flesh of the young man's chest burned in awful recognition.

"And a great destiny it shall be," whispered Lith, "for it is the one I have written."

The light in the room dimmed as dark clouds advanced across the sun. Thunder rattled the poorly fitted panes of the windows.

"But to attain that destiny," Lith whispered, "you must be healed. You must be infused with new life to replace that which was taken."

A light patter of rain began fall upon the thatched roof, tapping like a many-taloned hand scratching to get in.

"What are you talking about? What was taken? By who?" the young man said, but a loud peal of thunder drowned him out. A brilliant flash of lightning outside the windows temporarily blinded him, and when his vision returned, the ghosts reenacting the scene of his birth were gone, leaving the room empty and barren.

Lith stepped out of the cottage and into the rain that was turning the dirt track to mud. The young man watched her from the shelter of the doorway, unwilling to follow her into the downpour. She raised her hands to the sky and lightning flashed down again, obliterating one of the scrubby trees that marked the edges of the fields in a shower of smoldering splinters.

"Your body is not the only thing unfit for the task ahead of you," she said, pointing a finger at the young man. "You might be the one I have waited for, but you are still far from what I need. Your mind is weak. Your compassion for others, your gratefulness to the Masked, your experiences of joy and friendship – these things make you unable to do what must be done. It is my job to change that." She spread her arms, gesturing to the rain ravaged landscape. "The person you are will die here, and a new Donvin will rise in your place, one who is capable of being what I need him to be. What the world needs him to be."

A great wind blasted in the young man's face, and he slammed the door against the raging elements and the now terrifying visage of the woman called Lith. The walls protected him for mere moments before a roaring gust ripped a corner of the thatch roof clean off, allowing the deluge of rain to flood into the house. Mud began to rise through the floorboards, and before he knew it the young man was up to his ankles in a soupy mix of water and soil. One of the walls began to lean dangerously inward, and he threw himself out into the storm before the whole structure could collapse on top of him.

His senses were assailed from every side – wind and rain lashed his body, lightning assaulted his eyes, and thunder crashed upon his ears. The water was rising at an unbelievable rate, so fast that he could feel it climbing past his knees and up his thighs. Much of the landscape was already hidden under the churning, brackish liquid, and the house behind him was quickly sinking into the muck.

Standing on the surface of the stormy water as if it were solid ground, Lith raised her voice to the heavens as the land about them was swallowed up by the rising flood.

"Come forth, child of man!" she cried out to the storm. "Answer the call of your creator! Cast off the manacles of your past and embrace your future! Alasht ulat Dolmon! Alasht ulat Dolmon!"

The earth shuddered in response to her call, and the young man grabbed his chest in agony as something pressed outward from within. The water reached his shoulders now, and the roof of his childhood home disappeared beneath the surface as its walls dissolved into clumps of sand and straw. Water sloshed against his nose and mouth, and he spat out a mouthful of the gritty, foul liquid. Above the howling storm, Lith continued to shout her unintelligible summons.

"Through sacrifice of willing flesh, arise! Alasht ulat Dolmon! Alasht ulat Dolmon!"

•••••

The girl hesitated.

"And we'll be together?" she asked again. "Even after . . . ?"

"Yes," Lith said soothingly. "I can promise you that much. I cannot tell you what it will be like, because I do not know. But I do know that this is not the end. You will be together, and you will help him in more ways than you can imagine."

The girl nodded, wiping her eyes on her sleeve. "Then it's not so hard a choice after all," she said, taking the unconscious young man's hands in hers. "That was all I needed to know."

•••••

The ground quaked violently, creating waves that crashed over the young man's head. His face was tilted toward the sky, the only way to keep it above water. The thudding inside his chest made him feel as if he were about to split open, hammered by the angry fists of something terrible yearning to be free.

"It is time!" Lith cried. "From these waters, be born and reborn! Alasht ulat Dolmon!"

There was a roar as the earth split open with awful violence, though the young man could no longer tell if it was the earth breaking apart or his own body. Just before the waters closed over his head, he saw something massive and dark rising up from below, something nurtured in the bowels of the earth and the depths of his own heart. It broke the surface as he sank beneath it, but he still managed to catch one final, brief glimpse of its frightful shape and the ravenous, insatiable hunger in its eyes.

•••••

Donvin jerked up from the ground, eyes wide and heart pounding, his breath coming in desperate, greedy gasps. Overhead the sun was bleeding red into the clouds above the ancient courtyard, a sunset that had some significance he could not quite place. His hand went instinctively to his chest, feeling for something that should have been there, but was not. He looked down, unsure of what it was he was searching for, but the skin there appeared wholly unremarkable.

Something else was missing too, though not from his body. He looked about the confines of the courtyard, trying to remember what it was. The place was empty now; the growing shadows of evening hid nothing but moss and flowers under their darkening cloaks. There had been something else here, he was sure of it, something important, or someone, but now . . . .

"Do you feel better?" a woman's voice said from behind him.

Donvin craned his neck to see Lith watching from her seat on an overturned paving stone, her hands folded in her lap.

"I feel . . . empty," he said slowly, feeling the vibrations of his voice in his throat as if for the first time. He shook his head, trying to dispel the sensation of absence that continued to harry him, weak yet unmistakable, like the glow of the sun's waning light.

"That is to be expected after being cleansed," Lith said calmly.

"Cleansed?" Donvin said.

"Purified," Lith said. "Improved. Free of troublesome emotions and liberated from a controlling morality. What you are feeling is not emptiness, but freedom."

What Donvin felt was discomfort. His whole body was cold and full of aches, and the palms of his hands were smeared with some sort of black ash. His movements were clumsy, his legs shaky as though he had had too much to drink. He tried to remember why he had come to this place, but the more desperately he tried, the more the faint, familiar understanding hovering just beyond the edge of his thoughts seemed to slip away.

Then memories, like the mistakenly interred, began to claw their way up from the muck of his ravaged mind. They were conspicuously few, a handful of survivors from a sinking ship, one dragging himself ashore for every ten that perished, but all the more precious for their scarcity. Fragments of his time among the Masked and his journey to the ruins returned to him, glimpses that revealed just enough to contrast the absence of everything that came before. Just enough for him to realize the magnitude of what had once been there, and now was gone.

Donvin growled, turning on Lith with his nails digging into clenched fists. "What have you done to me?"

Lith gave him a tight-lipped smile. "I assure you that this is for the best. Soon you will thank me for what I've done. Removing your memories was necessary to make you into something greater than you could ever have been while they held you back. You will be my perfect hero."

"Hero?" Donvin spat. "Why would I help you after what you've done?"

"Because of what I can offer in return," Lith replied. She reached down, picked up a stone, and hurled it at Donvin's head.

Donvin raised his hands to shield his face, but more than just his hands obeyed. His eyes widened as visible lines of force rose from his flesh, glittering filaments that radiated from his body like thousands of fine hairs. The silvery, glowing strands of his will sliced through the flying stone two paces away, dicing it into little more than a cloud of dust to be caught and scattered by the breeze.

"Isn't power worth some small sacrifice?" Lith asked. "You can see it now, can't you? The power of the Masked that was always so elusive? It is no small gift, though it pales in comparison to what they once had at their command." She looked at Donvin out of the corner of her eye. "But I can promise you this: obey me, and one day you will taste of that forbidden might, that terrible force whose scars the world has struggled so hard to forget. On that day you will inherit a power that even the Masked have reason to fear."

So this was the truth of the Masked's power, Donvin marveled. This was what he had only glimpsed in hints and flashes. The luminescent fibers obeyed his every thought, moving as easily as if they were an arm or leg, pulsing with light in time with his excited heartbeat. A greedy thrill filled him, sharp and intoxicating for being untempered by reservation or doubt, emotions he could no longer feel. Lith might claim that there was something in existence greater than this, but in that moment, Donvin could not believe it.

The strands were not the only new things he could see, Donvin realized. His vision seemed more precise, and he noticed details that would have been all but invisible to him before. He could see the patterns in the growth of the moss and flowers that revealed their common roots, as well as the way the broken stones had once fit together to make the high courtyard walls even higher. His other senses were also awakened to new life, heightened in a way that made what few memories he still had appear dull and flat.

"I see you like my gifts," Lith said. "Do as I ask, and there will be more."

"What do you want?" Donvin said, suddenly suspicious.

"The same as before," Lith said. "Infiltrate the Masked, and kill them. You will be doing the world a favor."

"Suppose I still refuse?"

"Then you will die."

Donvin bristled. "Resorting to threats already?" he said, his aura of power pulsating around him with unspoken menace.

"I am not the threat," Lith said, looking into his eyes. "If you took even a moment to think, you would realize that the true threat to you now is from the Masked."

Donvin frowned. "How?"

"You came here to become one of them," Lith said, "but you are mine now, not theirs. I doubt they will be pleased to learn that their power has fallen into the hands of an impostor. They have not endured the ages by being tolerant or forgiving." Lith smiled sweetly as realization dawned on Donvin's face. "Yes, I think you understand now. If they find out what happened to you here, they will surely kill you. If they find out."

Donvin scowled at her. "Clever."

"I like to think so," Lith said lightly. "So, the choice is yours: destroy the Masked before they discover what you are, or do not. Live, or die. Those are your options."

"And if I choose to live?" Donvin said.

"I will assist you, of course," Lith said with an impish smile. "I am not completely heartless. Call it a partnership. You may not have chosen it, but it can still be profitable for you."

Donvin crossed his arms, but he knew she had trapped him. He had no particular desire to kill the Masked, but if it came down to a choice between their lives and his, there was no contest. With an empty mind, the choice was easy.

"I'll play your game, for now," he said to Lith, "but only because my choices are hardly choices at all."

"That's only natural," Lith said. "After all, that's precisely how I designed them. Now, you will be needing a plan, and I might be able to make a few suggestions. . . ."

Chapter 6

Fire from Ice

The forest of the Masked was still and quiet upon Donvin's return that night, its web of branches transfixed by the moon's hypnotic gaze. The hour was late, and no one was waiting to welcome him back. So much the better, he thought as he slunk through the trees to his old campsite. Better to be well rested when facing the others for the first time. Yet once he had found his leafy bed, he quickly discovered that all was not as peaceful as it appeared under that darkened canopy.

Donvin sat up sharply in the gloom, senses whirling. Something had yanked him from the jaws of sleep, something like a presence hovering so close that he had felt it even through the fog of coalescing dreams.

It would have been too dark for normal eyes, but Donvin's newly sharpened vision picked out the shapes of the familiar trunks with ease. Nothing was moving. He was alone.

He lay back and closed his eyes, but as his vision narrowed to a sliver, he saw a flicker of movement dance between two distant trunks, and his eyelids flew open again of their own accord. For a brief, terrifying moment he was convinced that it was the Masked, somehow alerted to his deal with Lith, coming to kill him for defiling their sacred order. But time dragged on, and he saw nothing further. His eyes began to drift shut.

Flicker.

Startled to alertness again, Donvin reached out with his palms and probed the air, trying to feel the faint breath of wind left behind by the motion, but none reached him. Whatever was out there, it was no Masked. He sat achingly still, holding his breath to avoid disturbing the perfect silence that froze the night in place like a sheet of black ice.

Flicker.

It happened when he blinked, far from where he had first seen it.

Flicker.

Donvin leapt up with a snarl and stalked toward the motion. The silvery lines of his will streaked outward from his skin, bathing the scene in a dim, shimmering light. Their radiance revealed only more stillness, more emptiness. He paced a wide circle around his bed, searching.

A movement to his right startled him, and he lashed out violently, experiencing a brief, pure satisfaction at having finally found the source of his irritation. A second look in the silvery light, however, dampened his relief. Beneath the deep gouge his threads had cut in a nearby trunk lay the remains of a red squirrel, its body severed cleanly in two and its twitching already growing quiet. There was no way such a small creature could have been responsible for what he had seen.

Markings on the tree around the gouge caught his eye, and Donvin stepped closer. The bark had been carved roughly into the shape of two figures, one tall and one short. Their faces were rounded, featureless, and they had nothing but simple lines for arms that came together where their hands would have been. The wound Donvin had inflicted on the trunk cut between them, dividing them in two as surely as it had the now-dead squirrel.

Donvin bent down and sniffed at the carvings. There was a human scent there, but faint. It was ticklingly familiar, as if remembered from a dream, but the telltale hints of recognition skittered away like startled spiders from the unexpected light of his attention.

Donvin continued to pace between the trees, trailing his own ghostly light with him, unwilling to return to his bed while whatever had been skulking in the darkness remained at large. Hours slipped past, and before long he found that he was able to see clearly without the light from his strands. He called them back, suddenly aware of the magnitude of his crime should this use of their power be seen by the Masked. That had been thoughtless of him. He would have to be more careful.

His bed of leaves, hardly comfortable at the best of times, looked unusually inviting to his weary eyes, and he collapsed onto it without another thought. Yet almost immediately his rest was disturbed by the sound approaching footsteps. Their rhythm, purposeful but not hurried, told him the identity of his visitor.

"Ah, this is a relief," the masked man said upon seeing Donvin's reclining form, halting his approach. "Not everyone makes it back."

His hands were full of something hairy, like a large dead animal with too many legs: the traditional Masked furs. Resting atop them was a mask of fresh, clean bark.

"A gift of welcome," he said.

Donvin was tired from his restless night, but he could not afford to show it. For all the Masked knew, his initiation had gone flawlessly, and if he wanted to stay alive, he could not let them think differently.

"Thank you," he said, rising to face his mentor. "I appreciate everything you've done for me."

It was not a lie, exactly. If not for the Masked, he would never have acquired their magnificent power. What he did not appreciate, however, was being dragged into whatever secret conflict they had with the woman Lith. Still, it would be dangerous to let that part of his sentiment show.

Donvin took the robes from his mentor and draped them over his lean form. They had clearly been tailored to his shape, for they fit snugly despite their bulk. In the morning's chill air, they were a welcome comfort.

The mask came next. It was freshly carved, and the edges still smelled strongly of sap. The narrow eye slits stared blankly ahead, as unexpressive as those of any other Masked, but Donvin wagered that few had ever concealed secrets as deadly as his.

His mentor tipped his head in acknowledgment as Donvin donned his new visage, and that was all the ceremony the occasion was offered. Donvin supposed he should not be surprised. Ceremonies and honors were the fuel of pride, and pride was just one of the many human traits that the Masked claimed to revile.

While Donvin was straightening his mask, his mentor turned his gaze to a spot on the ground, not far from Donvin's own bed, where the leaves were piled thicker than elsewhere. It was the spot where . . . .

Donvin's brain struggled, as if trying to scale an ice-covered hill and sliding back with each approach. No, he decided, there was nothing special about that spot.

"Things will be very different now," Donvin's mentor said, turning his head back after a few seconds. "There are few restrictions on the initiated, but with freedom comes duty. Wearing the mask does not make a man wise; to put it on is merely to begin that journey. Aiding our work is the only way to gain true understanding of the power that protects this world."

Donvin listened with only half an ear as he adjusted the weight of the furs across his shoulders. Things *would* be different now, he thought. Very different indeed.

Some of those differences made themselves known as soon as Donvin set foot in the camp of the Masked that morning. The Masked, who just a day earlier seemed like stories written in coded script, hardly seemed so mysterious now. Each had a distinct scent, posture, and stride so clear to his sharpened senses that he wondered how he could have thought them so interchangeable before.

Vastly different too was their attitude. They no longer shied away, and some even offered friendly greetings as he passed. A few also looked about expectantly, as if searching for something that should have been there, but was not. The looks confused Donvin, but he said nothing about them, and neither did the others. Better to feign understanding than reveal ignorance about something a true Masked would know.

Donvin felt his mentor's hand come to rest on his shoulder.

"There will be a group departing shortly to contain an impending breach," he said, pointing to a cluster of five figures standing together beside one of the huts. "It would be prudent to accompany them."

He drew away without waiting for Donvin's response. Perhaps to a careless eye he would have faded among the others who bore the same rough, plain face, but to Donvin he stood out as clearly as a wolf among sheep, slipping carefully and silently between them. It might have been Donvin's familiarity with his mannerisms, but his mentor seemed even more distinguishable from the group than the rest. Donvin followed him with his eyes until he reached the edge of the encampment, stepped under a low-hanging branch, and vanished.

Though Donvin did not care for the tone of the suggestion, he would follow his mentor's advice. Lith had warned him, in their brief time together, to accept any invitation that was made. A newly initiated Masked should be eager to contribute, and for his own protection, that was exactly what he was determined to appear to be.

Yet he would have to do more than just blend in if he wanted to stay alive in the longer term, Donvin knew. He might be able to fool them for a while, but the Masked were not stupid, and sooner or later they were bound to discover the truth. That was where Lith's plan came in. To have any chance at carrying it out, however, he would first need to earn their trust, and this invitation would be his first opportunity.

The five Masked acknowledged him with nods as Donvin approached and joined their circle.

"Now we have six, far more than we need. Two or three would be enough." The clipped words came from the man on Donvin's far left. He shifted side to side as he spoke, keeping his weight from settling on either leg.

The second from Donvin's right spoke in response, this one a woman. "It is no matter, far as it seems. What the Listeners say is that probably, if they are right, this will be the only breach we must attend to today, so there's no need to worry over how many we take. At least, that's how it's likely to be." She ended with a slight shrug. Donvin rolled his eyes behind his mask and suppressed a snort. She certainly had a way of getting to the point.

"Sounds fair 'nuff," intoned the heavyset man in the middle, visibly bulky even under the layers of fur. "The more the merrier." His words rumbled like a boulder picking up speed down a mountainside.

The other two Masked did not speak, but Donvin took the opportunity to size them up anyway. The shorter was rather unusual looking: a deep crack ran between the eyes of his mask like a furrow plowed in a field. For such a unique mark to be left unrepaired, the damage could only have been caused by a breach. Judging by its size, the man behind it was lucky to have survived at all.

The final Masked in the group, while unremarkable save for his above-average height, was behaving somewhat oddly. He did not seem to be listening to the conversation, and was instead looking upward at the trees with his head cocked to the side, as though merely enjoying the sound of the birds.

The Masked with the limp tensed when the others disagreed with him. "All right, all right, it doesn't matter anyhow. Shall we depart?" he said, biting off the words stiffly. Donvin caught a whiff of a distinctly unpleasant odor, musty and tinged with something that made his nostrils tingle.

"Yes, I do think we should get moving now. We would not want to be late, no indeed, that would be quite a problem," the woman said, once again wasting no few words to make her point.

She led the group a short distance out of the camp to a place where a tall root sprouted from the trunk of a tree, forming a sort of half-arch large enough for a person to pass through. She drew from her furs a black bag, no bigger than one of her small fists, and murmured to herself while poking about inside. The bag looked familiar, but Donvin could not place it, his memories still reluctant to come when called.

The woman eventually drew out a brownish pebble, pressed it to the base of the root, and began to trace its shape. Where the stone touched the wood, Donvin could now see that it left behind a glowing silver strand. When she had finished her tracing, she placed the stone at the top of the root and a fine curtain of silvery threads blossomed slowly downward from it, filling the arch and obscuring what lay beyond.

One by one the Masked ducked through the luminescent curtain, with Donvin bringing up the rear of the line. The last before him, the bird-watching Masked, halted just before the portal to look up once more at the trees.

"The squirrels are anxious today," he said in a thoughtful voice, the observation directed to no one in particular, and then stepped under the root and vanished.

Donvin looked up at the trees, but he saw no squirrels at all. Shaking his head, he followed the rest through the glowing portal.

On the other side, Donvin had been expecting to see the long white bridge again, the same construction on which he had traveled to and from Lith's courtyard, but what he found was something quite different. The cloudless, sunless sky was the same, as were the twin mountain peaks, but the bridge connecting them was gone, replaced by a massive fallen tree drawn straight out of a nightmare. The trunk, thick as it was, was twisted into strangely contorted shapes, with branches shooting out at odd angles and entangling messily with one another. Leaves grew not only from the branches but from the trunk itself, great waxy ovals that flapped this way and that in the familiar, rancid wind. At the far end, barely visible in the distance, was the same archway that had stood on the white bridge. The other Masked were nowhere in sight.

Donvin took a step forward onto the trunk. It sloped downward immediately, forcing him to descend with it and replacing his view of its great length with a storm of rattling leaves and creaking branches. He took another step, and one of the leaves slipped beneath his foot. When he tried to reach out with his threads to steady himself, however, the threads did not come.

A fierce gust of wind chose that moment to blast him from the side, and Donvin toppled over the edge of the trunk, branches pummeling his body as he crashed down, arms flailing for anything within reach. A sturdy branch clipped him hard under the chin, but his arms wrapped around it instinctively, bringing him to a jarring halt. He hung there pitifully, mask askew and head spinning as the wind buffeting his dangling legs over the bottomless drop below.

His face burned with humiliation. It would have been a fine thing if the others had been there to witness *that*, he thought as he waited for his dizziness to subside. He willed for the silver threads again, but again there was no response.

Cursing silently, Donvin hooked one leg over the branch he was holding and reached up for the next one. In this manner he climbed up, one branch at a time, until with a grunt he hoisted himself back onto the trunk and lay on his side, panting. The wind moaned through the leaves, disappointed that it had been unable to finish him off.

Using a pair of upright limbs for leverage, Donvin pulled himself to his feet. Determined not to make the same mistake twice, he kept his feet close to the center of the trunk and his hands firmly gripping whatever branch was nearest as he moved forward, pulling himself along with his arms as much as pushing with his legs. He quickly discovered that the only way to make any progress was to forget about his destination and focus instead on each step and each switching of his grip as its own little journey.

Somewhere near the center of the trunk, Donvin passed an odd-looking formation that called back memories of his previous bridge crossing. It was a large knot of petrified wood, almost rectangular in shape but for its rounded corners. Unlike the stone monolith on the white bridge, however, this one was imperfect: bumps and whirls covered its surface, and a thin, almost invisible crack sloped downward from its peak. Donvin made a note of its presence, but after taking a short breather to examine it, he found himself with nothing to do other than press on.

Ducking, weaving and squirming through the tangle, Donvin eventually crawled up a short incline and found himself face to face with the archway at the far end of the tree-bridge. It, at least, had not changed, nor had the sheer cliff face beyond it. The stench of the wind was even stronger here, and it made Donvin glad he had skipped breakfast. Eager to be away from it, he hurriedly walked the last few feet through the arch.

Intense light forced Donvin to shield his eyes as he emerged from the mouth of a shallow cave. Every surface he could see was white and glowing, burning with cold fire ignited by the pale sun above. An icy wind probed at his furs like an arctic snake searching for the warmth of life hidden beneath. Here and there, loose rock outcroppings broke the crystalline surface of the snow, which lay deep over the solidly frozen and sloped ground. Fresh tracks pointed to where the other Masked were seated, clustered around a feeble fire at the edge of a wood of scrawny, snow-laden trees.

"Any slower and it might have been all over," the furrow-masked one said to Donvin as he fed branches to the fire. "Good thing the breach is late."

Donvin bristled at being called a laggard, but caught himself before responding out of hand. He had only been delayed because his power had deserted him, but it was best not reveal that he had tried to call upon it at all. As much as he wanted to know why it had happened, the risk that he would give something away was too great.

"Quite right about the breach," the point-challenged woman said. "It appears that the Listeners were wrong about the timing." She had her hands stretched out toward the flames, but shivered a little anyway. Tiny ice crystals sparkled in her brown hair when she moved. "There's not much we can do now but wait. Some might find it inconvenient, but this country isn't so unpleasant, really." The wind moaned between the frozen dwarf trees behind her, and she inched closer to the fire.

Turning his back on the paltry comfort of the flames, Donvin surveyed the area around them. The terrain was made up of many short hills, each smoothed into the next by the heavy coating of snow. The trees, pathetic as they were, were numerous enough to screen his vision to the west, but to the east he could clearly see where familiar mountains began to crook westward, marking out the northeast corner of the civilized world. From this proximity they appeared colossal and wild, snow streaming from their jagged ridges like froth from fangs of earth and stone.

Donvin followed the line of gargantuan teeth with his eyes until it disappeared behind a hill to the north. He guessed that where he stood was probably only a few days from the foot of the mountains proper, which, based upon his limited exposure to maps, put them somewhere within the Springwild highlands, a region where nothing lived that had not made a bitter bargain with the frozen gods whose breath held the land itself on its knees. Even the trees cowered in fear, hunching low to escape their gelid masters' ire.

A rumbling boom, distant but clear, reached Donvin's ears from somewhere to the west.

"What was that?" he said as he turned.

"Battle," grunted the boulder-voiced Masked, looking into the trees. "Been going on since near two hours ago."

Donvin started. Two hours? Even with his fall, the whole of his crossing had taken less time than that, and he had begun the journey only a few seconds after the others. How could the timing of their arrival have been so different?

Setting the question aside, Donvin followed the large man's cue and looked into the densest part of the twisted wood, but saw nothing. "Who's fighting?"

"Coastmen, by the sound of them, though they're far from home. They're the only ones who'd go to the trouble of hauling a ship's cannon onto the battlefield," Boulder said. He crossed his arms and reclined thoughtfully. "Probably the Allied Forces of Falls Gate attacking the Prince of Springhold's men. If that's so, it's surprising the fight has lasted even this long, what with Springhold decimated by twenty years of infighting."

To Donvin, the names meant little. "They've come a long way just to pick a fight."

Boulder chuckled. "Land. Money. Pride. Women. Will these things not make a man travel any distance?" He chuckled again and shook his head. "War is generous to the victors, if those things are what they seek. Most likely it's land they want, land for their southern king and a new empire that will stretch from sandy beaches to snowy mountaintops. Or perhaps they think only of the coin that they will pluck from their fallen enemies." He shrugged. "Only the future can reveal the truth, because their motivations-"

"Are none of our concern," the limping Masked cut in, stamping his feet on the ground and rubbing his hands together vigorously. Donvin had not been the only one listening to Boulder's musings.

"What good is it to talk about them? They do what they will, and we go about our work just the same, loved as little by one nation as the next. The tides of armies are as predictable and trivial as the tides of the sea. Forget about them. They are a waste of effort." A thin mist trailed from behind his mask as he spoke, as though the heat of his words had set the bark aflame.

Boulder returned to looking through trees in silence, and Donvin closed his eyes and listened as closely as he could, trying to pick out the sounds of the distant battle. They were there, faint in the background, but there was something much closer . . . . He opened his eyes and squinted eastward once more. There, cresting a hill perhaps a mile distant was a dark, swelling mass that squirmed against the white snow as it moved.

Donvin abandoned the fire and walked a short ways up the hill to get a better look. Unless he was mistaken, this was the opportunity Lith had predicted, though he wondered how she could have known.

"Have somewhere more important to be?" Limp's voice creaked like a tether tied to his ankle.

"Something's coming," Donvin said, pointing toward it, and Limp, Boulder, and the reticent Masked who had been listening to the birds left their positions around the fire and came to stand beside him.

"So there is. Coastmen. See their black armor?" Boulder crossed his arms, and Donvin could smell the warm scent of self-assurance wafting from him.

Limp rubbed his hands together, warding off either the cold or nerves.

"What difference does it make? We have nothing to do with them. They will ignore us, and we should do likewise." He sounded less than confident. Even a fool knew that it was still possible to drown in predictable tides.

"Perhaps," Boulder rumbled. "But perhaps not. We are, after all, near a battlefield. They might think–"

A pair of shouts and a sound like a stone being cleaved in half halted Boulder in mid sentence, and the four Masked whirlded around in unison.

Point lay writhing in the snow, trails of black smoke and a sickening smell rising from her furs. Furrow was on the ground several paces in the opposite direction, wincing in pain as he tried to stand. Between them, the sickly fire they had been tending had become an inferno.

"It's the breach!" Furrow shouted.

His words were nearly swallowed by a roar from the flame itself, a guttural, unearthly sound. In the few moments they had been distracted by the approaching coastmen, the thing had become a hellish pillar twice the height of a man and was growing visibly by the second. A loud crack pierced the air, and a shard of splintered wood erupted like an arrow from the base of the fire, forcing Donvin to dive to avoid being struck through the chest.

He fell heavily, and the breath left him in a rush. Lying stunned and dizzy, mask half buried in the snow, he was able to watch but not to move as the chaotic scene unfolded around him. Limp was shouting ineffectually at the others; a mass of silver threads was pouring from Boulder's hands, forcing back a gout of flame from Point's prone body; Furrow had enveloped himself with some kind of glowing shell, but was pinned down by a barrage of flaming splinters.

Donvin coughed, and life spread back into his limbs with his first intake of breath. He staggered to his feet and shook off his vertigo, but already the situation had changed. The pillar of fire had sprouted several arms, moving separately from the body in a way impossible for a normal flame. Boulder and Limp's threads grappled with the infernal appendages, but they lashed furiously, resisting confinement. The pillar was still growing, though their efforts had forced it to relent in its assault upon Furrow, who was finally able to pick himself up off the ground. Bird had dragged Point to a safe distance, but Donvin could already see that she was sitting up on her own, clearly still alive.

"Don't just stand there, help us!" Limp snapped at him.

Donvin stepped forward to join the struggle, but before he could, the fire let out a roar and leaped. It stretched upward, its base becoming more and more attenuated until it broke away from the ground and became airborne, no longer connected to any visible source of fuel. Now a free-floating ball of heat and light, it soared through the air to land in the dry, withered branches of the nearby trees.

The resulting combustion was so powerful that Donvin and the others staggered back as it shook the ground beneath them. In a flash it seemed the entire wood had gone up in tongues of flame so tall they hemorrhaged red and orange into the formerly pristine blue sky. It was as if a great fissure had opened and the deep, fiery heart of the world had ascended in all its naked glory to the surface.

Spurts of flame coursed out in grasping tendrils, liquefying the snow as they shot toward the comparatively tiny masked figures. The silver ribbons of Donvin's will extended almost before he knew what he was doing, forming a wedge that channeled the oncoming blaze to either side. To his right he saw a wall of snow rise to shield Bird and Point, while to his left Limp, Boulder and Furrow took cover within an even larger version of Furrow's protective shell. The onslaught slackened, but the flames continued to reach ever higher.

"It's too big!" Furrow gasped between breaths, barely audible over the splitting tree trunks and boiling sap as the stunted forest burned. Donvin saw spots of blood on the snow by the other man's feet.

"What should we do then, give up? Let it burn the forest to the ground?" Limp said, his voice shaking, though with anger or fear it was impossible to tell. "Where will it go after that? We have to stop it. We don't have a choice!" The flames roared and crackled triumphantly behind his words, a kind of mocking laugh that was chilling even in the face of their overwhelming heat.

Bird and Point came up from the rear, Point moving stiffly but without support. The left side of her mask was heavily charred, and the furs covering her left arm were completely blackened.

"Are you all right?" Furrow said as he moved toward her, his own wounds forgotten, but Bird's low, clear voice commanded their attention to him.

"We still have a chance to stop this before it gets out of control," he said. "The breach-fueled part of the fire can't grow at such speed – most of what's burning out there is just ordinary flame. If we can find the core, we can disperse it before it does any more damage."

"Ridiculous," Limp scoffed. "Find the core, in all of that? There's no time! We need to put the whole thing out at once."

The stare of Bird's mask was directly at Limp. "An audacious plan. Some of us might not have the strength to carry it out." Donvin detected no insult in those words, but Limp nevertheless stiffened as if struck.

"Maybe not all of us are equally gifted," Limp said with barely disguised anger, "but that doesn't mean we can't do our jobs."

"That's all well and good, but we have another problem," Boulder interrupted. He turned and pointed to the armored men cresting the next hill over.

The coastmen must have been sprinting the whole way to have covered the snowy terrain so quickly. Crossbows were already visible in their hands. It wasn't an army that approached, but they were certainly too many to ignore.

Donvin recognized his opening at once. "Let me deal with them. I don't have the experience to be much help against the fire anyhow."

Bird turned to Donvin. He stood tall, apparently undisturbed by the sheet of flame raging behind him, showing none of the anxiety that had infected Limp's voice. "Those men must be persuaded not to come near, or we will not be able to protect them," he said. "Worse, they could distract us and put us all at risk."

Donvin looked to Limp, expecting him to try to give his own, contrary instructions, but he just snorted.

"Whatever happens to them is their own fault," he said. "They never learn. No matter where we go, it's always the same. Just keep them from getting in our way."

Donvin nodded. "Whatever it takes, so long as we stop *that*." He smirked to himself as he pointed toward the wall of flames. His inflection had been perfect, even to his own ears.

Whether or not Bird was convinced by his posings of dedication, Donvin couldn't say, but his mask gave a curt nod. "Good luck."

Bird led the others toward the burning trees, Limp stalking a few paces behind, while Donvin walked down the hill to meet the soldiers. A cursory count told him there were about fifty in the group, each armed with a crossbow and a short spear strapped to his back. They were clad in dark armor that gleamed a strange mix of colors in the sun, though it covered only their chests and heads. It was probably a scouting party, Donvin concluded, not an assault force. As they finished closing the gap, he took a few seconds to mentally rehearse how the encounter was to play out.

When they had come close enough for Donvin to smell their sweat and feel the faint currents of their labored breath, the soldiers stopped in two ragged lines. Their crossbows were out but unloaded, and they certainly did not seem prepared to fight. In fact, most of them appeared more interested in the conflagration that was consuming the scrubby forest than in Donvin.

Their leader stepped forward with a wave. "Hail! Thank the gods we made it in time. The other Masked said you were in need of urgent aid, and I feared we would not be fast enough. I take it that is the breach?" He nodded toward the flames.

Donvin hesitated. Another Masked had sent them? He had expected these men to be angry and dangerous, convinced that the Masked had come to bring ruin upon them, yet it seemed that violence was the furthest thing from their minds.

That, he thought, was a problem. His plan for earning the Masked's respect required these men to be hostile. How was he supposed to display his bravery and devotion by defending the other Masked without an opponent to fight against? It was a problem for which Lith had left him unprepared.

Confusion quickly turned to anger. What right did they have to spoil his plans and endanger his life? Outsiders were supposed to be fearful of the Masked, and seeing one near a battlefield should have given them more than enough reason to attack. But volunteering to help? Ridiculous!

That gave him pause. If the other Masked assumed the same, why not give them what they expected? Bird and the others were hidden behind the ridge of the hill and preoccupied with their task; they would not witness what happened here.

A cunning smile broke out across Donvin's face. It would certainly be more convenient for him if these soldiers proved dangerous, and the Masked would hardly question the truth of something they already believed. There was no reason he should let these soldiers' failure to cooperate ruin the part they were to play in his plan.

Silvery threads uncoiled silently from Donvin's hands, invisible to the soldiers who did not share his power, and slithered stealthily past the leader toward the rest of the men.

No!

The threads froze. Donvin put a hand to his head, feeling a pounding like a fist on a door, desperate to get out. There was some reason he shouldn't be doing this, he thought. If only he could remember what it was . . . . But then the pounding faded, and his head cleared. There was nothing wrong with what he was doing. He was doing it to preserve his own life. What did these people matter next to that?

"Sir?" the leader of the soldiers said, confused by Donvin's silence.

Donvin did not bother to answer. His threads resumed their movement, coiling about the hands and arms of several unsuspecting soldiers, who looked on in disbelief as they found themselves snapping bolts into their crossbows, cocking the bowstrings, aiming, and firing.

Three bolts shot forward with a twang, one striking their leader in the back and the other two narrowly whizzing past Donvin to kick up small plumes of snow behind him. Feeling as though he had done enough in the way of establishing provocation, Donvin raised his hands, and the light of his will shot out, piercing the bodies of the first line of men and lifting them into the air. The horror on the faces of those who remained standing was almost comical.

Donvin paused, and the bodies hung suspended like a flock of limp, meaty birds against the sky, where the deep blue of the alpine atmosphere merged with the fire's flickering red. For the briefest of moments, the sensation of wrongness returned. His hands quivered, and his heart beat with the fast, flailing rhythm of footsteps fleeing through the dark of night. But then his hands stilled and his heart calmed, and the sight of the bodies dangling in the air once again seemed unremarkable. Killing these men was good, Donvin's mind assured his hesitating body. Death was what they deserved for putting his plans, and his life, at risk.

The snap of crossbows releasing their bolts, purposefully this time, reminded him that he had more immediate concerns. He cut the flying shafts from the air with a thought, their glass tips scattering like broken icicles in the snow. His return salvo consisted of the bodies of his attackers' fallen comrades, which landed among the remaining men like crushing rounds of human artillery.

The confrontation hardly lasted long enough to be called a fight. The few who survived the initial exchange were quickly dispatched by Donvin's glowing strands, and that was the end of it. All told, it had taken no more than a few seconds.

Once the moans of the injured were silenced, however, Donvin noticed that the scene of the skirmish did not look nearly as hard-fought as he had hoped. It had all been over so quickly that the snow had barely been disturbed. Even worse, the placement of the bodies was all wrong, and there was hardly any blood to speak of. Donvin shook his head. That would not do at all.

It took but a short time for him to arrange things more to his liking. He dragged the bodies about in the snow, trying several configurations before finding one that satisfied him. Blood was slightly more of a problem. Once dead, the frigid conditions quickly sapped the bodies of their warmth, congealing their vital fluids to the point that cuts simply refused to bleed. As reluctant as he was to disturb his precise placement of the lifeless men, in the end he was forced to dismember one of them entirely to procure a suitable amount of gore to garnish the scene.

Once he had made the spectacle look a bit more convincing, there was just one more deception needed to add credibility to the story that it was meant to tell. It was not one he relished, but it was critically important, for if all went well, it would place him beyond reproach in the eyes of the Masked.

Donvin crouched and retrieved a short spear from where it lay beside its former owner. He checked the obsidian blade carefully, noting with satisfaction that it was clean and smooth, before placing its tip lightly against his left side, just below the ribs. He took a deep breath, grasped the haft of the spear with both hands, and pulled.

Designed for thrusting, the spearhead cut through Donvin's robes more easily than he expected and bit deeply into his flesh. The pain was incredible, and only grew worse as he jerked the weapon from his body and fell weakly to his knees, clutching the self-inflicted wound. Hot wetness ran between his fingers, matting and staining his furs and choking him with sudden nausea as it drained from the gash. At least, he thought with a grimace, he would not have to fake the agony it caused him.

Getting to his feet was nearly unbearable, and every step he took was like stabbing himself all over again, but only part of his plan was complete. For the rest, he had to get back to the others before they contained the blaze. Slowly he limped his way up the hill toward where the fire still burned in the trees, leaving a crimson trail behind him on the snow.

Half-formed curses whirled through his head with each torturous shift of his weight. If he had known how hard it would be to walk, he might have made do with more superficial wounds. The amount of blood he was losing was also worrisome. It would have been a simple matter to bind his flesh back together with his power, but that was hardly the sort of thing that would occur to a well-intentioned but inexperienced young Masked racing to the aid of his companions. For the lie to be convincing, he had to endure as he was.

He paused to catch his breath as he neared the conflagration, able to inhale only in quick, shallow gasps. He could see five figures standing just at the edge of the blaze, and above them the occasional glimmer of silver among the orange tongues that poured smoke into the sky. He need not have worried about his timing, he realized. Despite their efforts, the blaze had hardly shrunk at all. Its assaults against them had been halted, but the competing forces of the fire and the Masked seemed to have grappled one another to a standstill. Donvin could not have asked for anything better. He took another grueling step forward.

The first Masked to notice his presence was Furrow, who yelled something that was consumed by the roaring of the fire. Donvin kept up his agonizing pace, dragging his left leg behind him through the snow when the pain of using it became too great. *Almost there*, he thought to himself, *just a little farther.* It was no longer possible to tell which was larger: the fire raging before him, or the one that coursed through his gut, threatening to burn away all other sensation and all other thought.

Point risked a glance away from the fire to look at him. "Hurt," she said, her voice a startling rasp that surely must have pained her throat.

"I'm fine," Donvin said, squeezing his wound a little so that he let out an involuntary gasp and immediately wishing he had not. "I can help."

"Don't be a fool," Bird said, "there is no need for heroics."

Of course there was, Donvin thought. That was the whole reason he had come. He had prepared more to say, but a sudden wave of lightheadedness gripped him, and he swayed on his feet. He had lost too much blood already; there was no more time to talk. If he did not act now, unconsciousness would take him, and his chance would be lost.

Donvin spread his arms, gritting his teeth against the pain. The gesture wasn't strictly necessary, but it was dramatic. At first, nothing seemed to happen aside from a light dusting of snow swirling through the air. Anyone watching closely, however, might have noticed that the powdery, whirling flakes were in fact falling *up.* Snowflakes continued to rise in a thick mist all around the gathered Masked, soon dragging whole clumps from the snowpack with them. The other Masked began to take notice when the ground beneath their feet shifted uneasily, as if they stood upon the back of a slowly awakening giant.

Donvin, eyes closed, imagined what it must have looked like from outside his body. There he was, arms open, palms up, quivering as though carrying an immense, secret weight. The fire blazed before him, turning the shape of his body into a black shadow of defiance in the face of its hellish destruction. The daylight grew dim as more and more snow filled the air, covering the sun with layer upon darkening layer. Gigantic walls began to form, growing higher and thicker with each passing moment as more snow was drawn into them, squeezing the sky into a rapidly shrinking circle overhead. An unnatural night fell as the massive walls met and closed, sealing out the daylight and deepening until Donvin's shadow merged completely with the blackness. The flames guttered, gasped a suffocating breath, and died.

Donvin thought he had opened his eyes, but there was no change in the nothingness he saw. Something was wrong. He tried to take a breath, but there was no air left to breathe. The void he had created was not content with smothering just the fire, an unwelcome voice whispered in his mind. It wanted him as well.

A sudden flash of silver sheared through the darkness, and the killing night shattered, its black fragments reverting to white as the pieces of the gargantuan dome of snow crumbled to the ground. As the clouds of crystalline powder settled, the returning light illuminated four fur-covered shapes lying still on the ground. Donvin's eyes, however, were drawn to the fifth, and the only one still standing: a Masked surrounded by so many glowing threads that it seemed his body itself was the source of a pure, steady radiance. Bird.

Brightness filled the slits of the other's mask, and for a moment Donvin could see two vibrant blue eyes behind them lock with his own. They stared at one another, blue eyes into black, black into blue, until Donvin fell forward, taken fully by unconsciousness even before his bedraggled body struck the ground.

Chapter 7
The Plan Begins

Donvin woke to the sound of rain pattering on leaves, an irregular drumbeat that mustered his bleary senses to attention. The whiteness into which he had fallen was gone, replaced by dappled greens and hints of gray in the shifting cracks between the branches overhead. He was back in the forest of the Masked.

The dirt was spongy beneath him, and it clung to his hair in wet lumps as he sat up. A tightness in his side drew his attention, and he reached under his furs to feel the tender but restored flesh where his self-inflicted wound had been. As he did, the back of his hand brushed against a cold, hard shape in an inner pocket of his garment.

"You did very well," a woman's voice said. "Very well indeed."

Donvin jerked his head around to see Lith leaning against a tree behind him, dressed in the same strange outfit she had worn in the ruins. Here among the ancient trunks, Donvin could see clearly that its green was not any sort of forest green, nor was its red the color of sunset in the woodland air. It was the savage green of a child's forest memory, the bleeding red of a sunset as in a dream.

"How did you get here?" Donvin asked. His hand closed around the hard object in his pocket and drew it out. It was the metal tree sculpture, the same one that had adorned the cover of the book he had read with . . . .

Donvin struggled to remember. Had there been someone else, or had he read that book alone? And how had a piece of it made its way into his pocket?

"I go where my book goes. Or any part of it," Lith said. "But it is you I came to discuss. Your improvisation was brilliant, so I think we can consider this test a success."

"'Test'?" Donvin said, brow rising. He pointed to the place where his injury had been. "Are you telling me I stabbed myself for nothing more than a test?"

"You needn't say it like that," Lith said patiently. "This was as much for your benefit as for mine. I learned that you are clever and ruthless enough to do what you must to ensure success in our joint endeavor, while you learned that my instructions can be trusted. If they could not, you would not be alive."

"So that's all this was?" Donvin said with a sneer. "Something you cooked up so we could be better friends?"

Lith shrugged and gestured to the trees.

"Why not ask your comrades?" she said. "They certainly seem to think otherwise, judging by how they rushed off together."

Sure enough, there were no other Masked to be seen. Between the raindrops, however, Donvin's ears picked up the murmur of distant voices.

"How long have I been here?" he asked.

"Only a few hours," Lith replied, wiping her forehead to keep the water out of her eyes. Donvin noticed that her feet were bare, yet she trod on stones and roots without a hint of discomfort. "The rest of them are having a meeting, off that way."

"About me?" Donvin had trouble believing it could be about anything else.

Lith shrugged once more, causing the red fabric that hung from her shoulders to ripple and swing. For a brief moment, Donvin saw two long tongues of flame licking at the emerald trunk of her body.

"Shall we find out?" she asked.

She offered Donvin her hand, but he got to his feet without it, mindful of the tenderness that lingered in his freshly knit flesh. He followed the voices through the woods with Lith trailing silently behind him, the sound of their steps hidden by the persistent rain.

The voices led him to a place where a lightning-struck tree had fallen, leaving an open space on the forest floor exposed to the sky. Through the hole in the canopy the clouds poured torrents of water, turning the uncovered patch of ground into a deepening mire of sludge. In that waterlogged clearing sat more Masked than Donvin had ever seen together in one place, and though he did not take the time to count them all, there must have been at least a hundred. Their rain-drenched forms crowded in a circle around the edges of the clearing where the ground was most solid, focused intently on the two in the center who paced around the stump of the fallen tree, exchanging words in alternating volleys. A rut had been worn in the muddy ground at their feet.

Donvin halted at the edge of the gathering, taking stock of the scene before him. A few of the nearest Masked turned to glance at him, but they paid him little heed.

". . . inexcusable. The timing is not important. What matters is the intent that the timing was meant to serve." Bird's cool, clear voice was unmistakable. Several voices from among the onlookers expressed subdued agreement.

The Masked opposite Bird answered him, the long arms of his gangly figure gesturing to the crowd as he spoke. "Tradition has its own purposes. How much of that intent will be sacrificed by reminding them again so soon? We must not dilute the gravity of our message."

Bird shook his head, casting droplets of water from his mask. "We would dilute it far more by allowing this transgression to pass."

The rain fell unhindered on both men, who were already soaked through to the skin. Tiny rivers poured off their furs and cut channels in the mud, liquid snakes that crept their way out toward the attentive audience.

"The Dedication ceremony has a sacred history," the other speaker said. "Since our beginning it has been our only formal communication with those in our charge. Never before has it been used as a reprimand. It would be an unthinkable motive, even if the time were at hand."

Bird shook his head again. "The purpose of the Dedication is to renew the people's faith and remind them of the price we pay for their lives. Is there any doubt that their faith has failed? Is there any doubt the price has been forgotten?"

"The misstep of a few is not the failing of many," the gangly Masked said.

"Misstep?" Bird stopped moving. The few voices that had been agreeing with the other man died away. "A misstep?" He turned and addressed the onlookers directly. "Forty-seven. Forty-seven living, breathing people. That's how many one of our own was forced to kill with the very power that is dedicated to preserving them!" He whirled about, spraying water like a shaking wolf. No one else dared to move. Even the other speaker had stopped his pacing.

"They attacked us, knowing full well who we were. How could they possibly have been mistaken?!" Bird rapped his knuckles hard on his mask. His composure was fading, and it was causing more than a little unease among the rest. The earth underfoot squished and sucked as weight was shifted throughout the audience.

Bird was moving again, but erratically. The water that had been pooling in the rut around the stump poured forth as he broke the miniature wall of mud that contained it. He walked right up to the edge of the crowd, then abruptly turned and walked back to the stump.

"What foulness has touched their hearts that makes them turn against the guardians of their lives?" Bird gripped the front of his furs and shook them. "Can the evil that holds them do anything but grow, becoming a sickness that plagues not one man but all men? That evil must be stopped, the sickness healed, before it spreads and threatens our very purpose! How much more blood must be shed before we open our eyes?"

"Resilient," Lith whispered in Donvin's ear, "even . . . fanatic."

Bird paused for breath, and the other speaker took advantage of the opportunity. "Our tradition should not be lightly–"

"We do not serve tradition, tradition must serve us!" Bird stopped, daring the other man to interject. Perhaps wisely, he did not. When he spoke again, Bird's voice had calmed, a bark lessened to a growl. "We exist for one reason only: to protect this world. We do not exist to contain the breaches, or to keep our power out of undisciplined hands, or to administer the Dedication. These things have become our traditions because they serve our ends. If we must change to survive, to accomplish what we were made to do, then we must change, and no tradition must be allowed to stand in our way."

Bird took a moment to survey the crowd, assuring that he still held their attention. "We have suffered an unforgivable slight, but we have also been blessed. The festering betrayal that lies in the hearts of those we serve has been revealed. Should we fail to act, we truly are unworthy of their trust. It is a shame there is only the Dedication to call upon, for even it may not be enough to right this wrong." He ended his speech by sitting firmly on the ground with a splash.

The other speaker looked back and forth between Bird and the silent crowd. It seemed for a moment as though he might continue to argue, but decided against it.

"All that can be said, has been said." He sat as well, avoiding the spreading puddle that Bird had created. Those among the audience who were standing joined him on the ground.

The ensuing silence was, in fact, hardly silent at all. The rain splashed noisily in the puddles, among the leaves, and on upturned masks. The voice of the storm spoke with more ferocity than the men who had argued beneath it, and a roll of thunder pressed aggressively against Donvin's ears. For some reason he could not explain, the sound made his heart flutter, and an involuntary quiver ran through his body. The feel of the rain on his skin was suddenly uncomfortable, making his breathing labored, and he reached out to a tree to steady himself.

Bird rose slowly to his feet again. Mud dripped from his hands like clotted blood, and rain beat down heavily on his shoulders. With him rose others, Limp and Furrow the quickest among them. When the movement had stopped, two out of every three of the Masked were standing. Bird looked to the other speaker, who after a moment joined the standing majority, and the remainder followed suit.

Bird addressed the standing crowd. "The Dedication will be held in two months time. Pray that no more is necessary."

"This is the first step," Lith's voice whispered. *"This is the how our plan begins. This is how their doom shall be sealed."* Donvin turned, but she was gone.

The Masked dispersed, but Donvin lingered, having suddenly caught sight of his mentor. The man approached Bird and exchanged a few private words with him, their masks bobbing in silent conversation. Then he reached out and clasped Bird on the shoulder. In the instant before the persistent rain washed them away, Donvin glimpsed a few white specks clinging to the furs under his mentor's arm. They looked a great deal like flecks of snow.

Chapter 8
Elymia

Elymia's eyes preferred to follow the contours of the blown glass vase, which resembled a green flower turned inside out, rather than look at the women around her as they talked. It was not that she disliked them; on the contrary, she would not hesitate to call them friends. It was just that the glass gave her a place to rest her eyes where they would not betray her thoughts. It sat in the center of the marble tabletop, one of many in the rooftop café, and caught the sunlight like emerald fire. It was a beautiful day, with the scents of sea salt and fresh fruit mingling in the air and the sounds of happy conversation filling the street below. A joyous day for most, but not for Ely.

"That's preposterous! A winter wedding means no children, everyone knows that!" Tamalina Resposé clapped a hand to her breast in exaggerated distress. A pair of rubies glittered on her finger against the dusky blue of her blouse. "How could you have condoned such a thing?"

Remiana Aloise gave her an intense frown from across the table, her saffron dress clinging to her body in the unseasonable warmth, but the twinkle in her green eyes revealed the playfulness of the exchange. It was not her wedding at issue, but one of her many cousins', yet she answered the challenge.

"If we believed every one of your superstitions, Tamalina, I dare say we would all have turned into sea-snakes by now," she quipped, bringing forth a light round of laughs from the circle of women. All except Ely, that is, who was hardly paying enough attention to be amused. Even Matrice Pourin, who was often the solemn one of the group, added her titter to the mix, face aglow. A pervasive good mood had settled over the whole city – today was the day before the Dedication, after all, the first time in years that many families would find themselves all under the same roof.

From where the women sat on the rooftop, they had an excellent view of the long avenue leading to the city's north gate, which had been choked with arriving travelers since the break of dawn. The gate itself was a huge edifice of decorated stone rising to nearly twice the height of the surrounding wall, its opening the shape of a spread-winged sea eagle. Ely imagined it as the city's mouth, swallowing more and more people until the encircling walls would bulge outward like Wharfmaster Abrohl's belly after a feast.

The Dedication was not celebrated every autumn, nor even regularly. In fact, it had been five years since the ritual had last been announced. Perhaps that was why everyone was so exhaustingly eager, Ely reflected. It was the only holiday that required families to gather up all their branches in one place, and so the cities throughout the land swarmed with people drawn from all across the countryside for nearly three full days. The only problem was that Ely's was a family of ghosts.

Oh, she had her father, she reminded herself, swirling her cup of cool brown tea absently, but he was somewhere off in the north fighting a war that had been over for months. The other commanders had long since returned to lavish parades and rewards of titles and lordships and lands, passing through Falls Gate in garish exhibitions of flying colors and polished arms, but not him. He was still fighting for a distant throne and a people who had abandoned their family long ago. It made the prospect of enduring the three days of revelry alone feel like an icicle slipped inside her bodice.

"Oh, look at that one there!" Tamalina's sister, Eomila, gasped, pointing over the edge of the roof to a man in a brilliant red tunic and pointed hat.. "He looks like he's about to catch fire!" If Matrice was one to keep her feelings to herself, Eomila wore hers on her sleeve. The crowd in the street had come from all corners of the Deodar Basin, from the edges of the known world as far as many were concerned, prompting Eomila to remark on nearly every unusual sight. Though only a year shy of her sister, the younger Resposé had received more than her share of the pair's youthfulness and exuberance.

"Don't point, Eomila, it's rude," Tamalina scolded. "That's a priest from the high desert, show some respect."

Ely almost choked on her tea, disguising her laugh with a cough.

"Are you well, Elymia?" Remiana said with genuine concern, patting her lightly on the back. "Do not be drinking too quickly now, it is not good for you." Her accent was like the waterfalls cascading down the mountains of her native lands in the east, enchanting yet harsh around the edges.

A quick nod and a smile were enough to assure the others that Ely was not drowning in her own cup, allowing her to escape the collective eye. Wry mirth still bubbled inside her, although she did her best to smile only a little. The man Tamalina had called a priest was nothing more than a common hunter from the Deepwood; they wore red to avoid accidentally shooting one of their own in the forest. For one who prided herself on knowing all about the peoples of the Deodar, Tamalina was woefully ignorant. She aspired one day to take over the city census from her mother, but Ely imagined there was as much chance of that happening as a snowfall in midsummer.

For what was perhaps the hundredth time, Ely regretted being the only one of her friends who had received much in the way of real learning. Eomila could paint majestic landscapes and lifelike portraits, while Tamalina wrote beautiful poetry that belied her rather cynical nature, but neither knew history, or figures, or sailing, or war. Matrice was the daughter of the city's high recorder and intelligent in a distant sort of way, but her interests tended toward the abstract and fantastic, leaving her with little practical knowledge despite the many books she read. Some even suggested snidely that her simple, almost common name had been given to compensate for her sometimes glaring lack of common sense. Remiana was easily the most worldly of the group, an heiress of a great iron family who had had land and labor bought and sold in her name even before she had learned to crawl. She had even brokered a few deals of her own, though her success likely had as much to do with her blonde curls and winning smile as her ability as a negotiator.

As the women chatted and laughed, the streets clamored with vitality below. The people really were like food for the city, Ely thought. They gave it a kind of life she had rarely seen, coursing through it like new blood in old stone veins. Even the green towers of Cliffhome Keep at the center of the city looked like living, growing things that day.

The sun climbed toward its peak and the heat grew uncomfortable, even in a light silk dress. Ely had hardly noticed, so lost was she in her own thoughts, until Remiana spoke up.

"I do not know about the rest of you, but I am finding this heat dreadful. What do you say we move to the cliff gardens for the afternoon? The breeze off the ocean will do us all good."

"Last time I was at the gardens I caught a deathly chill," Eomila began, but the other women had already begun to rise from their seats, and after a moment she reluctantly followed. Ely, for one, was looking forward to the change of scenery. At least in the gardens she could wander away from the group for a little while and stretch her legs.

Remiana produced a slender glass disk and placed it on the table next to their cups. The sight of the blue flower petal suspended within the glass, flattened and preserved as perfectly as the day it was cut, stirred fond memories within Ely. In her youth, she remembered asking her father many times how they put the flowers inside the coins, only to be met with a sly grin and a wink. "It's a secret, Ely," he had told her, "but some day I'll take you to the mints and you can see for yourself." The mints themselves had proven unimpressive, but the sight of the flowers' trapped, unfading beauty had never ceased to conjure the image of her father's conspiratory look in her mind.

A whole petal was a great deal to leave for their five cups of tea, but Remiana was notorious for her loose purse. Having been born among the greatest stores of wealth in the world, she did not quite seem to fathom how much less others were accustomed to receiving. Even other women of high birth, daughters of lords and city functionaries, were taken aback by her free hand. Ely liked to think of it as a charming eccentricity of a far off land, though in actuality she knew it had little to do with geography.

Descending two long flights of steps, the women emerged indoors on the first floor of the café. While the upper level was reserved for those of the higher classes, the lower was open to all with coin enough to pay. It was packed to the seams with reveling travelers and had the rowdy atmosphere of a bar, despite the city council's mandate that no alcohol be served before the sun touched the walls. The smell of sweat was nauseating, and Eomila and Tamalina reached for their handkerchiefs in unison.

None of the women were especially eager to wade through the raucous sea of customers, but there was so much money to be had from the thirsty masses that the hostess and her two hired guards had turned to helping the servers carry drinks and were deaf to their shouts for an escort. At last Matrice threw up her hands and dove into the crowd without a word to the others, leaving them to exchange surprised looks before quickly following before the gap she created could close.

Being a lady of a high house offered little protection there. For every step they took, it seemed they were subject to a hundred pokes, grabs, and gropes, some accidental, some anything but. Men were ever so bold when you couldn't tell where the hand had come from, Ely thought, wincing as a slap landed firmly on her behind. By the time they emerged gasping onto the only slightly less crowded street, her face was twisted in a scowl and her body felt bruised in countless places. Eomila looked on the verge of tears, while Matrice seemed ready to use her bare hands to tear the head off the next man who touched her. Remiana came close to doing just that – upon reaching the door, she turned and struck the nearest man across the face hard enough to draw blood. Whether or not he had actually been one of the offenders mattered little to her, and she was the only one of the group who bore a look of satisfaction as they departed.

Their carriage was still parked outside, its Aloise insignia of a gold iron-smith's hammer on a white field granting it immunity from the jostling of the human tide. It was said that an iron lord's justice was the only kind all men feared, and that made their insignias better than a writ of passage from the king himself. Unlike some of her friends, Ely knew the history behind such sayings, and it was as cold as the ore that the Aloise brought up from the depths of their mountain mines. In the last five generations, more men had died in the name of iron than in the name of the gods, and house Aloise sat atop that bloody pile like an avaricious raven king.

Looking at Remiana, however, Ely could not fully accept the truth of those stories. She was kind and pretty, generous and thoughtful, even if she was a bit blunt at times. Her mother had brought her to Falls Gate only six months ago to find a husband, yet in that time she had made more friends than Ely had in a whole lifetime there. As it would happen, Remiana had ended up meeting far more women of the high houses than men. Many prospective suitors were still off with the northern campaign, and of those that remained, few were willing to endure the hardships, and even danger, that marrying an Aloise entailed, even if it also meant wealth beyond compare.

The carriage driver and the lone *beras* harnessed in front of him both appeared to be sleeping, the man with his chin on his chest and the beast with its belly to the warm stones, relieving its weight from its six slender legs. On the back of its brown shell was branded the same device as on the carriage, and the people in the crowd gave it a wide berth, though they could easily have torn the coach and driver to pieces before putting so much as a scratch on the great beast. Even at rest it stood as tall as Ely and must have weighed more than twenty men.

The five women clambered into the carriage, not bothering to wait for the coachman to rouse himself and open the door for them. A sachet of dried herbs filled the interior with a pleasant aroma, providing welcome relief from the human stench of the café and the street. While Remiana prodded the driver through the open window to wake him, Ely and the others arranged themselves comfortably on the upholstered seats. The ride from the northern gate to the cliff gardens wasn't terribly far on a normal day, since the city stretched out to hug the southern cliffs much farther than it extended inland, but with the streets so full, they settled in for a long trip.

The driver, once roused, reached out with his herding pole and rapped the *beras* sharply on the head, just behind the great horn that was longer than Ely's arm. The carriage shivered as the creature rose up on its legs, gaining at least three feet in height. A second tap set it moving slowly forward, though no faster than those walking around it. The driver shouted for them to clear a path, but most just laughed and kept walking, the beras plodding patiently behind them. They knew they were in no danger of being trampled – beras were tame as could be, unlike their male counterparts, the boras, which would sooner smash a cart than tolerate being hitched to one.

While the pedestrians might have been terrified of so much as scratching the carriage's paint, they had fewer qualms about slowing it to a near standstill. The driver menaced them with his herding pole, but it was far too long to be wielded accurately, and he nearly lost it to a boy who thought it might be fun to grab on and give it a tug. The women listened with amusement as he verbally dueled with anyone in the crowd who would respond, laughing when one of the strangers shouted back a particularly clever insult. Even Ely forgot her earlier gloom for a while when a plainly dressed man loudly complimented the driver on his "practiced handling" of his exceptional pole. At this the driver looked like he was ready to leap from his seat and chase down the offender before Remiana firmly commanded him to stay put.

The sun was past its peak when the carriage finally came to a rest beside one of the many entrances to the cliff gardens, nestled between two grand brick houses that looked south over the gardens and the ocean beyond. There was no need for city walls here: the five-hundred-foot drop to the water provided better protection than the thick stone barrier that ringed the rest of city. The cliff gardens sprawled to the very edge of the precipice, studded with dazzling star-flare trees and trellises of godsbreath vine. While the gardens stretched along the city's entire border with the sea, this section was gated to keep the common elements at bay, something to be particularly thankful for on a day like this one.

Ely squinted as she stepped from the carriage into the sun, relishing the cool, salty breeze as it touched her skin. The ornamental gates of blackened wood were already being opened for them by a watchman when Remiana dismissed their driver, and moments later they stood within the fragrant confines of the garden. Inside, the sounds of the city faded under the muted crashing of the surf below. Narrow gravel footpaths punctuated by ornate benches wound their way about clumps of trees and expanses of open grass, making it feel for all the world as if they were at a fanciful country estate. Best of all, there was not another soul around.

"I do love a stiff breeze," Remiana said as they strolled toward the cliff, pulling a ribbon out of her hair to let the wind catch it. "Back home the winds could pick up a grown man, in the right season," she added wistfully, as if this were something to be missed.

Tamalina rolled her eyes. Remiana often talked of home, but Ely found her descriptions enchanting rather than boorish. To hear her tell it, the Iron Mountains were the talons of the Gods cleaving the sky, ice coated and proud. Life there was vigorous and raw, filled with heights of passion and danger that lowlanders would never understand. To her, it was impossible to have truly lived until you had swum in a river not fifty feet from where it spouted off a mountainside into oblivion, or probed the depths of the Iron Mines for days on end with only a flickering candle as a guide. It was little wonder the men of the city were intimidated by her and all her clan.

The women settled on a grassy patch not far from the edge of the cliff, Tamalina and Eomila sharing one bench, Matrice and Remiana sharing another, and Ely sitting on the grass. Tamalina gave her a chastening look, but Ely ignored her. It felt good to relax, and the grass warmed her from below as the wind cooled her from above. She too let her hair down, and it hung heavy and straight down to her elbows, an auburn somewhat darker than the shell of a beras.

The talk turned to the coming day's activities, but Ely instead let her ears fill with the sounds of the ocean. She lay back in the grass, mentally daring anyone to warn her about stains. The others let her be without comment, and she closed her eyes against the sunlight on her upturned face. Perhaps she could avoid the ceremony tomorrow by making a visit to the graves of her mother and all her uncles and aunts and cousins. They were, after all, the closest thing she had to family left in the city. After that, she would spend the evening reading in her father's great plush chair, she decided. But that was the full extent of her plans, for she could think of nothing else to do. Normally she did not mind being alone, yet it was entirely different when she knew that everyone else would be sharing the comfort of their loved ones.

"Are you and your mother not returning to the Craghorn for the Dedication?" Eomila's question caught Ely's attention.

"Our business here is not complete," Remiana said simply, hands folded in her lap. "An Aloise never leaves a job half finished. Not even for the gods."

The answer brought a moment of uncertain silence, filled only with the rustling of leaves and the rumble of the tide.

Ely chimed in from where she lay, propping her head up with her hands. "You mean they haven't been able to marry you off yet."

Remiana gave a single, sharp laugh. "That is the right of it, and I do not believe they will, either. Your men are like spring river turtles. They look fine enough, but their shells are soft and weak. Still, my mother will find one who will not squash under her foot, and then she will bind his family to ours with the iron lash no matter the time it takes. Perhaps when your father returns he will bring sturdier stock home with him."

Ely could not help but smile at the thought of Remiana's mother testing men for marriage by stepping on them. She had met Oridine Aloise, the matriarch of the Aloise clan, only a few times, and the woman gave the impression of being one of the rocky spires of her homeland, tall and rigid, with a face of stone and eyes like jewel-lined caves. To think such a woman had birthed Remiana, or even lain with a man, was nigh impossible, yet it could not be otherwise – the Aloise family had no tolerance for bastard children, and those few who did manage to make it into the world were quietly helped out of it again with a knife in the darkness.

"My father is growing old and slow. I wouldn't expect him home before this time next year," Ely said, trying to keep the sadness she felt at speaking those words from her face. "And besides, war isn't for highborn men anymore. Why die when you can pay another to do it instead?"

Tamalina and Eomila seemed to find this quite amusing, but Remiana's eyebrows came together in a frown. "You dishonor your father, Elymia, and those who fight with him. I do not believe mine is the only house that still demands respect for its elders."

"Yours is the only one that enforces it with a blade."

Ely knew at once she had let her bitterness get the better of her, but words were not hounds to be called back once the hunt was on. Tamalina's mouth hung open, and even Matrice looked as though she were recovering from being slapped. To their great surprise, however, Remiana tilted back her head and laughed so loudly that she startled a blue-capped winglet from the branches above. When at last she quieted, she was confronted by four very confused looks.

"Mother told me the houses here had fallen far, but I did not believe. What a land this is, where one can slander her King's house and her father in the same breath!"

Yet to slight the gods is permissible? Ely thought, but she kept a reign on her tongue and lowered her eyes. Her own faith was hardly that of a priest, and she had few enough friends as it was without pressing her luck any further. Otherwise, she might have reminded Remiana that no Aloise sat the throne at present, nor would he for another few months until the end of the interregnum. Even then, he would not hold any direct sway in Falls Gate, which still had its independence until the unification campaigns were complete and the treaties signed and sealed. The treaties also contained provisions insulating the city from royal power, the reward for having joined voluntarily with the unification effort. Though Falls Gate would indeed become a part of one kingdom under the nominal rule of the Iron King, in practice its autonomy would remain intact.

The sun wandered toward its afternoon holdings in the sky, and Ely felt a weariness sinking into her, resting itself on her bones like a heavy black cloak. She could not keep her mind off her father and the day that was lurking beyond the sunset, and at last she excused herself as gracefully as she could manage and walked eastward along the garden paths, grateful to be alone with her thoughts as she made her way home.

Her father's house was one of the great manors that lined the private gardens, many of which were as tall as five stories and had chimneys as numerous as points on a crown. Although she had lived there for all of her life, Ely considered it her father's house rather than hers for good reason. Residences on the green line, as it was called, were granted only to those who held important office. When her father retired from his command, as was sure to happen soon, it would be given to another. *If he ever comes back,* she thought grimly.

It was agreed in all corners, particularly in Falls Gate and the other independent cities, that the war was a good thing, both for the conquerors and those being conquered. Unifying the divided lands of the Deodar would finally put an end to territorial squabbles, lift trade embargos, and bring security to those who had lived without it for as long as pens had been put to paper. The north was particularly fraught with strife, with two self-proclaimed lords each trying to claim Springuard Hold for his own, and each willing to build ramps of the dead up to its walls if need be. Word had come by pigeon several weeks ago that the cries of battle had at last been quieted in that place, but that was the last Ely had heard of her father's campaign.

Soon Ely reached the garden-side door to her father's house, made from a solid piece of washed oak and set into a recess in the brick. She let herself in and eased the creaking door closed behind her, letting the darkness of the back hall work its relaxing fingers through her body before moving toward the better-lit parts of the house. Her room was on the third floor, and she took the servants' stairs, pausing to peek into Barty's room to see if he was there. As a soldier, her father believed that being waited on made a man unable to care for himself, and thus Barty made up the entirety of their household staff. About of an age with her father, he gardened and cooked, tidied and washed, and had done so for as long as Ely could remember. At the moment he was out, and she expected he would not be returning for some time. Even a simple trip to the market would take hours with the streets as clogged as they were.

She took the remainder of the stairs two at a time and threw herself onto her bed, burying her face in the pillows. She could tell that Barty had changed the sheets, because she caught a faint whiff of the lotion he used on his scarred palm to keep it from stiffening. Barty had been a soldier too, once upon a time, and Ely imagined that was why her father had chosen him as their one and only concession to the expectation that people like them should employ servants. She tended to think of him more as one of her father's war comrades than as the man who was responsible for keeping the privy clean.

A breeze pushed its way through the delicate curtains and into the room, and Ely rolled over to look out the window. The descending sun highlighted the contours of the clouds, raising them out of the sky like the folding cutouts in her old children's books. Nostalgia and loneliness were like sisters in her heart, and she pushed the gilded memories of girlhood away so as not to deepen her already gloomy mood. Perhaps the gods would not notice if she slept away the next few days. She sighed and buried her face again. As much as she wanted to hide from the unfairness of her solitude, she would not. Obligations always outweighed desires. Her father had taught her well.

Chapter 9
Preparations

The sidelong rays of the afternoon sun cut sharply into the slits in Donvin's mask, forcing him to walk with his head tilted toward the ground. The scent of the sea on the stiff breeze was so heavy that it overpowered even the pungent smell of his mentor's hairy mantle, though the other man walked just a few steps ahead on the road that meandered across the windswept headlands. Furrow plodded close behind, bringing up the rear of their small party.

That they were there, on their way to administer Dedication ceremonies in some town called Falls Gate, meant that Donvin's ploy in the north had served its purpose well. There was now not a single Masked who could not recognize him as the one who battled the coastmen to protect Bird and the others. It was remarkable, in fact, how quickly he had gained celebrity among those who supposedly cared nothing for individuality or pride. Yet if Lith's plan was to work, he would need every bit of it.

Strangely enough, Donvin mused as he walked, his growing reputation was largely due to Point, who seemed to credit Donvin with her very survival. Though she had been lucky in many respects, she had not escaped the devilish flames of that day unscathed. Her throat had been badly burned, and her voice crippled. Still, what few words she could muster following the ordeal were about him. As Donvin remembered it, it had been Bird who had aided her, not him, but apparently his theatrics had overshadowed all else in her mind. So much the better. In any case, her words were potent. The Masked listened solemnly, and they remembered - Furrow especially so. It had come as no surprise, then, when Furrow appeared that morning to join Donvin and his mentor as they prepared to depart the Masked camp.

Donvin felt a sudden chill as a shadow fell across the roadway. He paused to look up, his eyes no longer assaulted by the sun's piercing light. His mentor's voice broke the long silence.

"Look to the west. We are nearly there."

Donvin's eyes followed the road as it snaked around isolated rock outcroppings toward the sun, which was now partially obscured by something tall and imposing rising out of the headlands.

"That tower is part of Cliffhome Keep," his mentor said. "It was here long before anything that could be called a city, and longer still before the name Falls Gate."

Donvin squinted at the tower. Cliffhome Keep. He had inquired about the place with Boulder, whom he had discovered was far more pliable than the other Masked when it came to information. His descriptions were impressive - the tower was built with rock excavated from an even bigger project, the port tunnels that spiraled down the cliff beneath it, wide enough for five wagons and tall enough for a ship's mast. Long ago they had been used to move ships between the Seadiver River at the top of the cliffs and the ocean at the bottom, an otherwise unthinkable task given the height that separated them. The Keep served as both a lighthouse and a seat of power for the lords who would use the tunnels to control commerce in the entire region for several centuries.

But, over time, the city had expanded westward to the mouth of Seadiver Falls, and the Cliffhome lords had been unable to prevent the merchant guilds from constructing their own transport system: a series of pulleys and winches that could lift cargo from seafaring vessels below to faster, shallow-bottomed riverboats waiting above. Not only was this faster than the tunnels, but it took only a few short years to build, and only a few years more to cripple the influence of the Cliffhome lords. The tunnels fell out of regular use, and Cliffhome Keep surrendered its place as the political, if not the physical, heart of Falls Gate. According to Boulder, all this had happened many generations ago.

Now the Keep was nothing more than an ancient place, a ruin still inhabited by people who had ceased to care that it was a ruin of something that had once been much greater. Its people had preserved it, after a fashion, though it no longer held much significance for them. Yet to Donvin's sharp eyes, even at this distance, the structure boiled with meaning. It burst upward from the landscape like an embossed letter from an earthen page, the start of a story that told of all the things human hands had once achieved and might, some day, achieve again. How could they have forgotten the story that such a bold letter began? Now having seen the tower for himself, Donvin found it difficult to imagine anything at all that people such as these could not forget.

Their neglect, puzzling as it was, would prove a boon to the tasks Lith had set for him. If Boulder was to be trusted, the lowest levels of the Keep were still used by the city governors for entertaining, but the rest of its many floors and countless rooms were largely abandoned. That would make what Lith had sent him for that much easier to obtain. And, of course, there was the matter of what he was to leave behind. The letter was folded safely inside his robes, an innocent-looking envelope that, according to Lith, held even more potential to shape the world than the power of the Masked.

Still, it would be no small feat to remain undetected while he carried out these tasks. The Masked were recognized everywhere, and he had yet to devise a plan to escape his two companions long enough to do what he must.

"This is no time to be lost in thought," Donvin's mentor said. "We are in the realm of men now, and they will watch us closely. We are to be their teachers, if only for the span of the ritual, and we teach as much with our bodies as with our words. Though we are not so different from them, we must hide our likeness if we wish them to listen, respect, and obey."

Donvin fell in again behind his mentor, keeping his eyes upon the spire ahead as they walked. Not so different? He kept the disdain confined to his thoughts, for the scent of his body could not betray an emotion that was merely thought but not felt. Not so different? The people who lived in that place were ants crawling across the remains of a history they neither knew nor cared to know. Lith had told him much about them that was beyond even Boulder's substantial knowledge, and little of it was flattering. They would leave nothing behind when they died, and the world would carry no memory of their passing. No, they were nothing like him.

Timing their arrival in Falls Gate for dusk, when their presence would be least conspicuous, the three Masked had seen few other travelers on their way. As close as they were to a major city, most people still made an effort to be off the road long before dark. The few they did encounter had given them a wide berth, shooting them furtive looks that alternated between curiosity and apprehension. One or two of the bravest had tipped a hat or made a stumbling curtsey, but by and large the Masked were rather aggressively ignored. It was for this reason that Donvin was surprised to hear a voice call out to them as they passed three wagons that had stopped in the windswept grass by the side of the road.

"Oy, you there! Lend us a hand, will ya? Three strong lads like you could . . . ." The portly man who emerged from behind the wagons faltered, wiping his brow with a cloth and squinting at them in the amber light. Donvin watched in amusement as he took in their furs and masks with quickly widening eyes.

"My apologies, sirs . . . or ma'ams . . . I meant no disrespect," the man said, running a hand through the sweat-darkened hair that fell to his shoulders. His eyes flicked among them, but he did not beat the hasty retreat that Donvin expected.

"None taken," Donvin's mentor said. "Do you need assistance?"

The man shifted uneasily, clearly conflicted. Looking past him, Donvin noticed that the first of the wagons was resting at a sharply uneven angle, the front axle on the far side touching the ground. The harnesses of all three lay empty.

"Had a bit of an accident," the man said slowly. "Wheel snapped clean in half, but the load is so heavy that my men and I can't lift the blasted thing to fit a new one. There are only three of us, and the whole wagon could collapse if we climb up there to unload the barrels first." The man glanced uneasily at the sun's position on the horizon. "I'd send one of my boys to the city for help, but even if they found someone willing to come out here at night, repairs in the dark are slow, and I doubt we'd make the delivery before noon tomorrow. By then, the markets will be closed for the ceremony, and I might as well drink the wine myself."

The wind calmed a bit, and Donvin caught a faint whiff of sweetness, fermented fruit, and roses coming from the large casks in the wagons. An idea began to crystallize in a dark corner of his mind.

Donvin touched his mentor's arm. "We should help," he said in a low tone, too low for the portly man to overhear.

"Oh?" his mentor replied softly. "With that many barrels, three more sets of arms will hardly make any difference." Furrow nodded slightly in agreement.

"That wasn't the sort of help I meant."

Donvin could hear the disapproval in his mentor's voice. "Our reputation has suffered enough among these people. We need not weaken it more by reducing ourselves to common laborers. And even if that were not so, such frivolous use of our power is unquestionably forbidden."

"Of course," Donvin said, doing his best to sound reasonable. "But think of it as an opportunity to begin to restore the trust we've lost. The first thing this man will do when he reaches the city is tell how we helped him bring wine to the Dedication. It's a kindness no one would expect from us."

His mentor crossed his arms. "As it should be. We are not in the business of curing mundane troubles. We already shoulder an unbearable weight for the sake of this world. To add to it for a few meager casks of wine would be criminal. We will do no such thing."

Donvin gritted his teeth. "If only-"

"No. Enough." His mentor turned to the wine merchant, who was tugging on his hair in a painfully obvious expression of anxiety.

"We regret that we cannot help you," he said, "but our business will tolerate no delay. We pray that you find the assistance you seek soon."

The merchant stooped in a bow. "Thank you for your wishes, good sirs. May your way be clear, good sirs." Relief was the dominant tone in his voice, and he remained staring at the ground until after the three Masked departed.

Donvin smoldered as they walked. He glanced back at the cask-laden wagons behind them, calming himself with steady breaths. He could wait. There would be other chances to create the distraction he needed to slip away.

The sun sank lower, and the road rolled slowly beneath their feet. The highest tower of Cliffhome Keep thickened from a distant needle into a black pillar as they drew nearer, surrounded now by its inferior siblings clawing up around it toward the purpling clouds. The wind grew colder, carrying with it the sound of a phantom surf crashing somewhere far below, down the cliffs and out of sight.

The sky was rapidly losing its memory of the sun's light when the road brought them at last before the city walls. The thick, moss-colored blocks reached so high that it hurt Donvin's neck to scan the battlements above. He saw no men atop the wall, only the irregular stone formations of what had once been crenellations. History had been kind to Falls Gate, for it had been long since these stones had felt the sting of arrows or the desperate steps of feet at war. Donvin wondered whether it was truly possible for a letter as small and unassuming as the one he carried to change all of that.

The city's eastern gate straddled the road easily, but at the moment the massive wooden slabs of doors, so large that they could only be moved on wheels, were shut fast. The same would be true of the western gate, so that all foot traffic was funneled through the northern one. The chaos caused by the crowds converging for the Dedication made for a smuggler's field day, and the city's governors were not about to give up the chance to collect trade taxes by allowing the city to leak people and goods like a thrice-pierced waterskin.

Tents covered the open areas on both sides of the road leading up to the gate, shelter for those who could not afford to stay in the city or who had arrived too late to claim to a bed. Large and small stood side by side, pristine linen beside patched rags hung over sticks, all jostling for a flat piece of soil right up to the base of the walls. Despite their great numbers, there were few people to be seen among them. This was the eve of the Dedication, and for now, at least, there was merriment to be had inside those looming, ancient walls.

The three Masked saw little hint of the true crowds until they followed the wall northward and turned to approach the northern gate. A great mass of people clogged the gateway, spilling out around it in roiling disarray like vomit trying to force its way back into an unwilling mouth. Everywhere there was pushing and shouting and cursing, and no few of the mob were waving bottles and tankards, evidently having found some source of liquor besides the taverns within the city. The deepening shadows of the evening hid most of their faces, though they did nothing to obscure their appalling stench. The intensity and variety of malodor was overwhelming, but Donvin's two companions seemed to take no notice as they made their way toward the ragged edge of the human sea.

Drunk and rowdy as the crowd was, no intoxicant was strong enough to withstand the sobering effect of the Masked. Every face that beheld them fell silent and tried to melt away into the crowd, an act which usually resulted in a shoving match with another who had not yet noticed the reason for flight. The mere presence of the Masked was enough to cut a narrow path through the masses, though that did not make their passage without incident. The noise was such that none could warn the others of their coming, leading to the occasional unpleasant surprise. One oblivious man had the misfortune of failing to notice he was in their way until they had drawn within three paces of him, and by the time he had collected his wits enough to throw himself to the side, Donvin was forced to step over a small puddle of steaming urine that had been left behind on the heavily trampled ground.

When they came to the mouth of the gate itself, the Masked encountered the source of the congestion. A line of uniformed men armed with clubs stretched out across the threshold, stopping and checking everyone who carried so much as a rucksack for goods to be declared and taxed. Each had accumulated a bulging pouch of collections on his belt and from time to time had to take a swing at some ragamuffin youth who, emboldened by the crowd, would make a grab for it and then dance out of reach. Normally the guards might have given chase, but the would-be thieves were well aware that they could not abandon their posts.

Donvin and the other Masked approached the nearest guard, who did not see them immediately, being too preoccupied with rifling the contents of a large travel pack under the watchful eye of its owner, a short, stocky man who had the build of a quarrier. The owner of the pack was the first of the two to realize who was standing beside them, and he began backing away slowly, past the guard and through the gate.

The guard reached out and grabbed him roughly. "Hey, we're not done here, don't think you can just be walking on th-" He stopped mid-sentence as he looked up from the bag to see the three Masked standing in front of him. Frozen as he was, he did not even react when an enterprising urchin darted up from behind and got both hands around his collections purse before being clubbed soundly by the next guard in line.

"Where's your head, Will? That one nearly made off with your -" The second guard, too, was arrested by the sight of the Masked, and Donvin was surprised to see that this one was a woman. While she wore the same white tunic emblazoned with a blue eagle as the other guards, she carried a writing board under her arm and an inkpot on a long cord around her neck in addition to the club in her hand. She, however, was much quicker to recover.

"Thank the deep you're finally here," she said, making a quick bow and pushing back her leather cap with her club as it threatened to fall over her eyes. Her not-quite-youthful face was hard-lined and freckled, with skin slightly browner than most of the others Donvin had seen that day and a single braid of light brown hair that dangled past her right eye. "Hope the crowd didn't give you too much trouble, they've been awfully-" She paused to point her club menacingly at a group of scruffy men who had been trying to tiptoe past unnoticed.

"Don't you lot take another step! Will! Get over there!" She gave the first guard a shove in their direction, then turned back to Donvin and the others.

"Follow me, if you'd be so kind. I'll take you to your escort."

The crowd thinned substantially once they were past the line of tax collectors. It was dim enough as they passed under the the wall that those about them did not immediately move away in fear, being unable to tell them apart from the normal travelers who were moving about in the gloom. The hard-packed dirt of the road turned to stone beneath their feet, which clattered noisily with the sound of hundreds of walking staves and boots.

Emerging inside the wall, Donvin discovered that the thickening dusk was in the process of being beaten back by a new sort of light. Two men were running up the side of the street, each carrying a curious set of long poles. As he watched, they stopped beside a tall post atop which sat an empty glass bowl. The first man used his rods to lift a bucket up to the lofty bowl and deftly tip in some of its contents, while the second man, almost before the first had finished, struck the tips of his rods together over it to make a spark. By the time the light from this odd sort of lamp had flared up and then stabilized, the pair had already moved on to the next post some twenty paces farther on.

The lamps illuminated the street and the facades of the buildings that lined it, all of them short compared to the towering wall under which they sheltered. The first two stories of each were cut from the same sort of stone as the wall, though many had a third or even fourth floor atop them constructed from wooden planks and painted a variety of colors that Donvin had no doubt would look dazzling in the daytime. The height of the buildings seemed unusual to him, though he could not say why. He had seen plenty of buildings with multiple stories in the towns he had visited with the Masked, but they were not the ones with which his mind was struggling to draw a comparison. He tried, and failed, to conjure a memory of where else he might have seen standing structures other than the tiny huts of the Masked.

Donvin's momentary concern over this failing was set aside when the guard they followed brought them to a halt beneath the third street lamp from the gate, which was casting its circular glow on a cluster of well-dressed and clearly disgruntled gentlemen huddled around its base. The guard waded in amongst them, utilizing her club somewhat more gently than she had done before, but still with enough force to produce a number of indignant yelps.

When at last she had managed to pry them apart, she revealed at their center a middle-aged, harried looking woman talking very quickly and making notes in a small book while each of the men around her tried to get her attention by shouting at ever increasing volumes.

". . . and I tell you they were already recorded and paid for last week!" One man practically screamed in her ear. "No, I don't have the receipt with me, but if you'll just come to my office I can show you the – oof! Hey!" He exclaimed as the guard prodded him in the stomach, forcing him to back up a step.

"Our guests are here," the female guard said, gesturing toward the Masked who stood outside the buzzing knot of men. The woman she spoke to was the first person Donvin had ever seen look genuinely elated at the sight of them. The frenzy of activity around her evaporated almost instantly, the flurry of hasty excuses fading quickly as their owners scurried like roaches from the presence of the Masked. The woman watched them go with lips curled in satisfaction.

"Thank you, Mae," she said, turning back to the guard. "You could have sent someone for me, you know."

"Oh, I know," the guard called Mae replied, "but when else would I have gotten to use this on that bunch of vultures?" She hefted her club and shared a quick smirk with the other woman.

To the Masked, Mae said, "My good masters, I leave you in the capable hands of the Lady Evana Resposé, Vice Chairwoman of the Census and Mistress of Accounts. Now I must return to my duties, if you'll excuse me." She turned on her heel and trotted back toward the gate, humming a tune with a quick beat that Donvin did not recognize.

"I apologize for her abruptness," the Lady Evana said, brushing a wisp of light brown hair behind her ear and leaving a faint smudge of ink on her forehead in the process. "I was forced to assign some of our accounts officers to double duty as inspectors, and she seems to have taken to it a bit . . . overzealously."

"It was no trouble to us," Donvin's mentor replied. "You and your staff have always taken good care of us, Lady Resposé, despite the many demands on your time."

A look of confusion crossed the woman's face briefly, followed shortly thereafter by one of recognition. This was obviously not his mentor's first Dedication here, Donvin realized, nor the Lady's.

"Please, you must call me Evana," she said. "I am flattered that one such as yourself remembers me. I was merely second adjunct to the chairwoman during the last dedication."

It felt odd to Donvin to hear a woman of her years speak so deferentially, though again the feeling had arisen without apparent source. But perhaps more remarkable was that she was talking to them without difficulty, he realized. Come to think of it, so had Mae. Clearly they were no strangers to the Masked, or at least to overcoming the feelings of intimidation that so often struck others dumb.

"We have long memories, and we do not forget those who have shown us kindness," Donvin's mentor said.

At this Evana blushed and looked away, squinting so that the wrinkles at the corners of her eyes became more pronounced. She was certainly not young, though her hair showed no signs of graying as yet. She made an awkward bow to acknowledge the compliment, and in doing so jostled the bottle of ink that swung from her neck, spilling several drops on her shoe. Donvin saw her wince almost imperceptibly, but she came up with a smile.

"Please, let me show you about the city. There have been a number of changes since you were last here." She hesitated, glancing at Donvin and Furrow, but decided to continue addressing Donvin's mentor. Irked at being so quickly dismissed, Donvin decided this was as good a time as any to interject.

"You might be interested to know that we passed a disabled caravan carrying wine about two hours east of here," he said. "The driver was distressed about making it to the city in time for the ceremonies tomorrow."

Evana's eyes came back to him. Given how close he and Furrow were standing, he was impressed that she could tell which one of them had spoken.

"They had lost a wheel," he added. "They need strong backs to help replace it."

"Wine . . . ." Evana said, putting the butt of the pen she held to the corner of her mouth. "Oh gods, I'd wager petals against leaves that it's the casks half the innkeeps have been asking after all day." She squinted in the flickering lamplight and pawed through the pages of her book, which Donvin now noticed had a fancy letter "E" stitched into the leather cover with gold thread. After finding a blank page, Evana scribbled something, then tore it out with a deft motion, put two fingers between her lips, and let out a piercing whistle.

Almost immediately, a gray-bearded man with a slight paunch and the now-familiar inkpot trotted up from the direction of the gate, wheezing. "Yes m'lady?"

Evana handed him the note. "See that it gets taken care of now, or we may have a hundred angry innkeepers breaking down the door tomorrow morning. Tell Bristole to take some men from . . . well, take them from anywhere he can find them, and tell him that if he hasn't set out by the time I get back, he'll be the one who gets fed to the innkeepers when they come calling."

The messenger left with a bit more spring in his step, and Evana smiled at Donvin. "You may have just saved us all a great deal of trouble. People around here are seldom more serious than when it comes to their wine. I thank you."

Donvin wished he could smirk at his mentor, but knowing how it would go unseen, there was little point. Patience, he reminded himself. His idea for a distraction might have a hint of life in it yet.

"Now, as I was saying," Evana capped her pen, snapped her book shut, and corked her ink bottle, "allow me to take you on your viewing of the city."

"If you do not mind," Donvin's mentor responded, "we would like to conduct our inspection of the stables immediately, and then retire to our accommodations. It has been a long journey. We mean no offense."

"The stables, certainly, they are ready for you of course," Evana said. "But please, if you desire a tour later, it would be my pleasure to be your guide."

Donvin knew little of these stables other than their inspection was the traditional first task of the Dedication, and that it related somehow to the ancient pact between the Masked and their charges. Boulder had spoken of it as if it were common knowledge, and Donvin had not pressed for what seemed like unnecessary details. He had to be judicious with his questions, for there was a limit to what he could pry out of the normally closemouthed Masked without raising suspicions. In fact, it was this very reticence that had put Donvin on the path to Falls Gate in the first place. According to Lith, there was knowledge here that the Masked were unwilling, or unable, to share, knowledge that he would need if he was to succeed in their extermination. It was an interesting coincidence that this was the place that his mentor, too, chose to come for the Dedication. Even more so that he had been here before.

Evana led the three robed figures through streets, which were now aglow with yellow light from lamps and windows. The burning oil gave off a thick smell, raw and slightly sweet and not at all unpleasant. Whale oil, if Boulder had been correct. At least, that was what the people here called it. So close to the ocean, it might well be the truth.

Though many of the people within the city were packed into alehouses and inns and gathering halls and homes, there were far too many to be contained indoors. Throngs clustered in the light that spilled from open doorways to tilt an ear for the music that emanated from within. Men and women met beneath the rippling glow of the lampposts, exchanging words and laughs and smiles, and then moved on, sometimes together, sometimes apart. Children

darted among the legs of their elders, caught up in the excitement that wafted about like the smoke from every burning candle and lamp. Pickpockets
and thieves lurked at the fringes, rejoicing in the haul that they would collect
this night. Through his mask, Donvin saw them all.

The group had not gone far before they rounded a corner onto a side street
that was bordered by a long, windowless wall standing about ten feet high.
Donvin let his hand trail along it as they walked and discovered that unlike
the smooth, cleanly cut stone of most of the city's buildings, this wall was
a rough mixture of mortar and crushed rock, with gradual bulges and dips
in the surface. Clearly it was not of an age with the rest of the construction
– such a material could not stand the test of time as well as solid blocks of
stone.

A ways down the street, the group came across a door in the wall possess-
ing no window or other ornament, not even a handle. Matching sconces of
clay on either side cast a flickering light, and between them a thin man in
uniform leaned casually against the door, tapping the toe of one booted foot
against the ground. When he saw the party approaching, he righted himself
and straightened his leather vest, which bore on one breast the now familiar
eagle in blue and on the other a green crescent cut by three red lines.

"Good evening, Mister Keth," Evana said after taking a brief moment to
conjure the name to her tongue. "We've come for the inspection."

"Aye, a good evening it is, Lady," said the man called Keth, rubbing the
drowsiness out of his eyes with the back of his hand. He looked to be about
of an age and height with Donvin, his face entirely smooth, with a head of
close-cropped hair oiled so that it gleamed in the dim light. "But we were
told not to expect you until later this-"

"Quite true," Evana cut in forcefully, "but we will be conducting the inspection now. If you would announce us?"

Keth scratched the side of his face for a moment, then turned and hammered on the planks of the door with a closed fist.

"Oy! The Lady of Accounts and the . . ." Keth's eyes flicked behind him to
take in the masked faces. ". . . guests are here for the inspection, open up!"

There was a short, muffled reply from the other side of the door, but it did
not budge.

"Is there a problem?" Evana crossed her arms and stared expectantly at
Keth.

"Er, no . . . ." Keth said, turning back to her after several seconds. "But the Master did say that he wanted to greet you personally. They're probably fetching him now."

"Oh, that's just wonderful," Evana said wryly, flipping open her book and preparing to make a note. "I'm sure the council will be pleased to hear that our honored guests were kept waiting in the street while . . . ."

The door in the wall slid sideways with an awkward screech, retreating into a slot in the mortar, and a short, bald man in burgundy robes bustled out as soon as the opening was wide enough to accommodate him.

"Now, now, my dear Evana, no need to be writing that, hmm?" he said, placing his index finger on the open page of her book and tipping it toward him so he could peer at what was written inside. Evana closed it with a snap, and the man withdrew his finger in a hurry and gave her a wide smile.

"This," Evana said coolly, "is Master Gill, Executive Handler and special representative to the city council. So pleased you could join us, Master Gill."

The bald man chortled. "Gillibardo Groundwise, actually, though Master Gill will do just fine. A pleasure to have you all here, a pleasure."

"And a pleasure to see you again as well, Master Gill," Donvin's mentor said, nodding his head politely. Furrow remained silent, unreadable, and Donvin followed his example.

"Too kind, really," the bald man said without missing a beat. "Now, might I show you inside?"

The door slid shut on their heels after they passed through, issuing another painful screech of wood on wood. Now that they were inside, Donvin could see that it was controlled by two men working a large crank on the wall beside it, one that seemed to require the full strength of both to turn.

"Security mechanism," Master Gill said when he noticed Donvin watching the process, as if that explained everything.

The paving of the street reverted back to dirt beneath their feet on this side of the wall, and Donvin looked about curiously. They were in some sort of yard full of waist high fences that divided it into many smaller sections, all of which appeared to be empty. What little illumination there was fell into the area from high windows of the surrounding buildings, making the gloom lie thick along the bare ground. The door they had come through stood at one end of a long path that ran down the middle of the fenced pens toward a long barn within which Donvin could see a hint of lights flickering. Beyond that, he could just barely make out the clustered outlines of three tall silos, each perhaps five stories in height.

Master Gill accepted a torch from another man who was dressed much like Keth, then motioned for them to follow him.

"I would tell you to watch your step," he said lightly, "but that seems to put a jinx on people around here. We do our best to clean up the dung, but there's only so much that can be done."

The warning prompted Donvin and Evana to check the area about their feet, while the other two Masked, if concerned, made no show of it. Master Gill led the group forward at a leisurely pace, holding the torch over his head and talking as they went.

"We have sixteen pens on the north field – that's where we are now, of course – eight on each side." He gestured to his left and right with his free hand. "A shame you didn't come tomorrow when it was light, you would have been able to see so much more. Some very clever new hinges on the gates, I assure you, very impressive." The loss of the opportunity to show his hinges seemed to genuinely disappoint him.

"Now, it may seem like we have a great deal of space here, but being inside the city is actually quite confining. Demand for eggs and chit-iron has never been higher, but production has been at the same levels since, well . . . ." Master Gill scratched his head and gave a weak, wheezing sort of laugh. "You'd have to check the histories for that one. Might as well be forever. A real shame, too."

Donvin sneered a little at the man's back. Humoring blowhards had no part in the Dedication as far as he was concerned, but his mentor allowed the bald man to ramble on unchecked.

Master Gill looked over his shoulder at the Masked. "As it happens, I've been trying to convince the Council to let us establish a second farm outside the walls. The traditionalists are against it, naturally, but I think a word or two from the right people could bring them around, if you know what I mean. It's an excellent plan, if I do say so myself, and well within the bounds of the compact. Another farm would provide room to grow, and the potential for revenue is just-"

"Why don't you tell our friends about the facilities here," Evana interrupted. "That is, after all, why they've come, and you wouldn't want to bore them with Council politics."

"Yes, of course. We wouldn't want that." Master Gill looked ahead stiffly, and Donvin could smell the irritation on him even over the heavy aroma of dung and soil that thickened the air.

"Where was I . . . . Ah yes, sixteen pens, and sixteen more on the south field, on the other side of the stables. As for the stables themselves, allow me to show you."

The group had drawn close to the long building. Instead of opening the large set of square, heavy-looking double doors, Master Gill led them to a vertical slit that had been cut in the wall beside them. It was quite narrow, but wide enough to squeeze through if one turned to the side.

"Just added this last year," the bald man said proudly. "Stroke of genius, really. Wide enough for people to pass through, but that's all. It lets us keep the doors shut most of the day to limit the risk of escapes. Not that we were having difficulties with that, mind you," he added hurriedly.

Donvin snorted. A hole in the wall didn't seem particularly ingenious to him.

Evana squeezed through first, followed by the Masked and then by Master Gill bringing up the rear. Before following them through, he snuffed the torch in the dirt outside and left it by the door, for they had no further need of it. Small, glass-enclosed lamps hung from the rafters inside, each burning brightly for its size. They illuminated an open space running down the barn's length and stalls with solid doors, all closed, lining the walls to either side. Despite the chill in the night air outside, inside it was warm, almost stuffy.

"I can personally vouch for the fact that everything is well maintained and of the highest quality," Master Gill said proudly. "You'll notice that for the flooring here we use fresh cedar shavings, changed weekly, to absorb excess moisture. Each stall has a separate trough to reduce competition for food, which we keep a full two weeks' supply of right here on the premises. As for the food itself, we purchase . . . ."

Quickly bored by the litany that was holding his mentor's interest, Donvin turned his attention to his surroundings. Having come in to the right of the large double doors, they were quite close to the nearest of the stalls. The door of each, which was wider than Donvin's outstretched arms, was painted with a large colored symbol. Nearly all of them bore a green crescent, but a few were marked with three red, horizontal lines, one atop another.

Donvin looked back at his companions. Master Gill was still talking and gesturing, while Evana watched with a look of mild impatience on her face and the Masked stood as still as if they were rooted, all silence and inscrutability. Since it seemed that his attention was not required, Donvin moved away from them a few steps to stand in front of one of the stalls marked with red lines.

There was a small flap of dark cloth hanging on the door near eye level, and when Donvin lifted it he discovered a narrow viewing slot into the stall. He peered inside, but the interior was hidden in perfect, inky blackness.

Suddenly the door shuddered as something massive slammed into it from the other side and a long, black horn stabbed out through the slot, missing Donvin's head by inches. He took a quick step back, body tensed, as the wood creaked and groaned and the protruding horn lashed back and forth, making an awful scraping sound as it strained against the wood. Then, slowly, it receded into the stall. The cloth fell back over the viewing slot, and whatever was inside fell quiet again.

Turning back to the others, Donvin found that the conversation had come to an abrupt halt. Evana was staring with her mouth half open, while Master Gill's eyes looked like they might never close properly again.

"If you're looking for an extra eye hole in that mask," Master Gill said, his voice loud in the stunned silence, "I can recommend a good carpenter. Getting one from a boras won't be near so gentle. Cheaper, though, I will admit," he added with a light chuckle.

Evana struggled for a moment before letting out a short, exhaling laugh, and then the tension was broken. Donvin could see the shoulders of the two other Masked shaking slightly, but they made no sound. Still, he could almost hear their laughter. It made his lips curl into a sneer and the blood hammer on the backsides of his eyes.

"Now, as I was saying, I can bring out a beras for your inspection," said Master Gill, addressing the other two Masked instead of Donvin, "or a boras, if a good thrashing is what you two are seeking as well?" Evana was avoiding looking at Donvin too, and making an unsuccessful attempt to hide her smile with a hand over her mouth, but her eyes were still squinting with restrained mirth.

"A beras will be fine," Donvin's mentor said, pointing to the crescent-marked door just to the left of the one Donvin had approached.

"An excellent choice," Master Gill replied, shuffling over to the door and lifting the timber latch that held it shut. Donvin tensed, but the bald man acted with a casualness that belied any danger. The door swung open, and Master Gill leaned into the shadows, reached out, and knocked on something dense-sounding with his knuckles.

The legs were the first things to emerge from the stall, two of them, probing side to side and clicking at their joints before planting themselves firmly on the ground. Then came the beast's colossal head, so large that Donvin could not have wrapped his arms around it had he tried. Bulging eyes as big as fists protruded from its sides, solid black and unblinking. More legs followed, six in total, propping up a body as massive as a small cart and covered in pockmarked brown armor. What drew Donvin's focus, however, was the giant, curved horn that pointed upward from the creature's head where its nose might have been. Overall it gave the impression of a beetle, albeit a massive one, but no beetle he had ever seen bore a weapon like this one. It was obvious to him that there was no way such an outlandish creature could possibly be natural.

"Please, have a look," Master Gill said, beaming as if this thing were an object of pride.

Unfazed by the appearance of the bizarre beast, Donvin's mentor knelt down beside it and grasped one of its many feet with both hands. Each foot had several wicked-looking barbs that jutted out at right angles, but they were so large that his hands fit easily between them. He articulated what Donvin could only describe as the ankle joint forward and backward, then, apparently satisfied, moved his hands up the leg, squeezing and probing at its roughly armored surface as he went.

Once finished with the leg, the masked man brought his face close to one of the great bulbous eyes and inspected it from different angles. He cupped his hands around it, shielding it from the light, then removed them quickly, all while the creature remained perfectly placid. Then, to Donvin's surprise, he lay down on his back and worked his way underneath its belly, tapping on the shell as he went. It was a remarkably undignified act for one of the Masked, and just watching it filled Donvin with contempt. What right did this man have to laugh at him when he himself was willing to crawl on his back in the dirt in front of these city dwellers? What had happened to remaining aloof and separate, dignified and unchallengeable?

After several minutes obscured beneath the beras's bulk, Donvin's mentor emerged and brushed himself off, sending a small rain of dust and wood chips falling from his firs.

"She is quite healthy," he said. "You are to be commended for your stewardship, Master Gill, and for your fulfillment of your people's part of the compact."

"You are too kind," the bald man said, flushing all the way up to the top of his head. "You may of course see others, if you wish. The one painted for the ceremony is down at the far end, and quite a beauty if you care to have an early look. This year's artist is young, but very talented. She's related to you, if I am not mistaken, isn't she, Evana?"

"My niece," Evana confirmed, lowering her voice a bit. "She's a wonderful girl, but it has been hard on her, keeping the secret for all these weeks. She has been looking forward to tomorrow's unveiling at the ceremony more than anyone."

"No doubt your niece's work is splendid," Donvin's mentor said, "but if we may, we shall wait until tomorrow to see it. We have had a long journey, and the hour is growing late."

"In that case," Evana said, the tired look that had been growing around her eyes vanishing instantly, "I would be pleased to show you to your accommodations."

Donvin's mentor nodded. "If you would. And thank you for your gracious assistance, Master Gill. This city is fortunate to have you."

It was just for an instant, but Donvin caught a glimpse of Evana rolling her eyes while Master Gill preened at the compliment.

The party departed the stable complex the same way they had entered, with Evana in the lead and Master Gill trailing behind, wishing them well all the while until they had crossed the yard of pens and passed through the wall back into the alleyway. Keth jumped up from where he had been nodding off beside the gate, giving each of them a stiff bow and getting a sympathetic smile from Evana in return.

"Now that that's taken care of," Evana said, talking over her shoulder as they walked, "I've arranged several rooms for you that I think will be to your liking. They are on the third floor of one of our finest inns, right on the green line overlooking the bluff, with south facing windows for an excellent ocean view. It's a bit of a walk to get there, but you'll find it a good deal more peaceful than much of the city tonight."

That seemed true enough; though the alley was as empty as when they had left it, the rumbling of thousands of not-so-distant voices was in the air. Donvin could feel the stones humming, their vibrations tuned to the hammering of a million moving feet. The city's blood was roaring. Yet a seaside room, however peaceful it might be, was not what Donvin required this night. He needed a room with a different sort of view.

"No," Donvin said from the rear of the procession. "It is not to my liking."

The rest came up short, and one startled face and two unreadable masks turned back to look at him. Good, he had their attention. Now he needed a plausible reason.

"We did not come here for your city luxuries," Donvin said, remembering the way Bird's righteous anger had captured the crowd of Masked at the Dedication debate. "Do not think we are children to be placated with petty gifts. If you were hoping to gain our favor, you had best remember why we are here, and pray that the gods accept your pleas for forgiveness rather than choosing to dedicate *you* to our cause tomorrow. We have bled and suffered for your mistakes, and your bribes only insult us. We will find our own accommodations."

"I did not mean . . ." Evana said, looking with bewilderment to the other two Masked. No doubt she was thinking about his incident with the boras, questioning whether his words carried any real weight. In his mind, Donvin could hear her laughing again. Laughing at him.

Donvin stepped toward her, drawing close and looking down into her widened eyes. "Make your excuses to the gods. We have no interest in them." He stepped around her frozen form and continued down the alleyway. Furrow's footsteps followed with hardly a moment's hesitation.

Perhaps it was Donvin's imagination, but he thought he could hear something more than just the sound of foot striking ground in those following steps. He could hear a hint of shame in them, shame at needing to be reminded of the sins of these coast dwellers, and of that disastrous day of pain and death in the north. He could hear echoes of long nights spent in Point's hut, changing the cool compresses on her throat throughout the hours while she slept. He could hear the blood that dripped from her mouth when she coughed, and the hoarse sobs that followed. He could hear the cold, steady march of revenge.

After a long pause, two more sets of feet followed them, Evana and Donvin's mentor walking together a ways behind. Satisfied that he was now leading the way, Donvin retraced the path they had followed on their way to the stables, heading for one of the inns he had seen along the road not far from where they had entered the city.

Though full darkness had fallen some time ago, the streets were even livelier than they had been at dusk. To Donvin's heightened senses, the smell of alcohol was thick in the air, wafting from nearly every door. Perhaps because of this, the three masked drew little attention as they slid in and out of the pools of light cast beneath the lamp posts. Between those illuminated islands, they were just three more shadows in a city already full of them.

With the night had come a cold, stiff wind from the sea that buffeted Donvin's furs about him and made him glad for their weight. The people that they passed on the street clumped more closely now, as much for warmth as to make themselves heard over the ale houses' din, which had grown just as much as their smell. The children were absent, tucked indoors away from the chill, and predators of purses prowled the narrow alleys and shadowed lanes in their place.

It was not a long walk, but Donvin's ears were stinging with cold by the time they reached one of the inns he had remembered seeing. Though the city's northern gate was mostly obscured by darkness, its location was marked clearly by the sudden end of the rows of streetlamps where they encountered the massive stone wall. Donvin counted ten lamps between here and there. Close enough for his purposes, he thought. He looked up and noted that there were several small wooden balconies hanging off the face of the inn above its entrance. Yes, this would do nicely. Without waiting for Evana and his mentor to catch up, he mounted the three shallow steps to the door, sending a few surprised loiterers scattering out of his way.

The door to the inn stood open to the night air, radiating light and noise into the street until Donvin's fur-cloaked form loomed up to choke them off. He paused on the threshold, turning his masked gaze slowly across the room. It was a large, open space with round tables arranged throughout and a wall of casks at the far end. Every chair was filled, and the interstices clotted up with even more patrons who made do with whatever standing room they could find. It was warm inside, and the air sticky with human breath.

The sound of earthenware shattering on the floor told Donvin that his presence had finally been noticed. It was easy to spot the culprit – the man stood frozen beside one of the nearer tables, his hand still lifted to his lips even though his ale and the pieces of his mug now covered his feet. A slowly expanding wave of silence washed across the room as more of the patrons became aware of the Masked who was blocking their only means of escape. Donvin was content to let them squirm in their seats, drinking in the panic on their faces, but Evana slipped past him through the door. Though she tried to avoid touching him, her elbow clipped him none too gently as she passed. The audacity of the contact made Donvin want to reach out and strike her.

"These gentlemen need a room," she announced breathlessly and to no one in particular, apparently determined to reclaim the control she had lost in the alley. Donvin's face was hot, and he opened his mouth even before he knew what was going to come out of it. Before he could speak, however, an unusually tall, slender woman emerged from a half-height swinging door in the back, bringing with her a strong smell of roasting fat and potent garlic. Her black, frizzy hair hovered like a dense thundercloud over a face full of freckles, which was pressed in a frown.

"I thought I recognized that voice," she said over the heads of the patrons. "But it's not bringing good news, I'll wager. Come to collect the tax yourself this time?" She wiped her hands on the rag she was carrying and tossed it over her shoulder back into the kitchen.

"I don't mean to bother you, Losha," Evana said, "but our guests will be needing a room."

"Well, you are bothering me," the woman called Losha said, not bothering to hide the disdainful look she gave the Masked. "And we're full, can't you tell?"

Evana looked rather uncomfortable, but that did not slow her down. "Now that I think about it," she said, looking at the casks piled up in the back, "I do believe we forgot to collect the duty on all of those. I'll just go ahead and mark that down, shall I?"

Losha's eyes narrowed. "You wouldn't."

Evana uncorked the bottle of ink about her neck.

"Fine, fine," Losha said, throwing up her hands in defeat and weaving her way across the room between the tables. "But you had better remember this the next time my husband asks for leave from work. We could be making twice as much from this lot if he was helping in the kitchen tonight." She gestured to the crowd, who had started to resume their conversations, albeit in whispers.

"You know I couldn't spare even one tonight," Evana said tiredly. "We're just as busy as everyone else."

"Yes, lots of honest people to bleed of their coin, I'm sure," Losha said bitterly, beckoning them to follow her through a narrow hallway off the entrance that led to a flight of stairs. "Still, you probably solved my problems just by walking in the door. It won't take the whole lot of them five minutes to clear out and find somewhere else to fill their stomachs. I won't need help in the kitchens then, will I?"

She took them up to the third floor, lighting their way with a lamp taken from a hook at the foot of the stairs, and followed the hall past a number of battered-looking doors all the way to the end.

"Our best room," she said, hanging the lamp up beside the last door. The door itself resisted her attempts to open it until she gave it a solid shove with her shoulder, and even then it groaned loudly before relenting. She went inside, and a moment later came back out dragging a heavy trunk with both hands.

"Like I said, we're full," Losha said with a grunt, "but surely these good people wouldn't mind giving up their room. Don't you think so, Evana?" She didn't wait for an answer. "I'll be back up with some food when I get around to it." She backed down the hall toward the stairs, bumping the trunk across the uneven floorboards behind her as she went.

Evana watched her go, and then she turned to the Masked. "I hope everything is adequate?" She made it sound as if it had all been her idea.

A glance inside the room told Donvin that it was. It was not so large, and the ceiling bowed and it smelled of must, but a balcony was visible through a tall, street-facing window.

"This will do," he said coolly.

"I'm glad," she said, but she didn't look anything other than tired. "There is more I must do tonight, so with your permission, I will take my leave. I will return in the morning to guide you to the cathedral square for the ceremony."

"By all means," Donvin's mentor said. "You have been very good to us."

Donvin said nothing, as did Furrow.

Evana smiled graciously at Donvin's mentor, bowed, and turned to leave. Her little book was already open in her hands before she was halfway down the hall.

•••••

Donvin lay still in the bed, but his eyes remained open. He waited. The breathing of his two companions slowed into the rhythms of sleep, and the sounds of the city outside grew gradually fainter as minutes passed, then hours. The creaking of wooden floors and chairs from below subsided, and the faint light trickling in under the door from the lamp in the hall was extinguished. Still, Donvin waited.

The growing silence was loud in his ears as they sucked in every irregular footfall, every click of a pebble upon the paving stones outside, every scraping of bristly rodent hair against the insides of the inn's walls. In the gaps between those tiny noises, the silence seemed to roar like a hailstorm pounding on the roof, so loud that it began to swallow the real sounds entirely. The harder Donvin listened, the more difficult it became to distinguish noise from silence. At times he thought he could hear Evana laughing at him once more, and he stifled a curse. At other times he thought he heard voices that he could barely make out.

A girl's voice sounded sorrowful. "I know we won't need each other any more, but . . . can we still be friends?"

"We can stay friends," a boy's voice said, "no matter what."

Donvin's head snapped up. The roar was gone, as were the voices. Had he slept? Something about the voices had seemed familiar, but now, sitting upright in the darkness, he could not pin down what it had been. Donvin's lingering confusion fled, however, when he heard the distinctive sound of wooden wheels upon uneven stone outside the window. Finally, they had come.

Donvin slid out of bed, ignoring his nakedness, and crept to the door that opened onto the small balcony. He lifted the short wooden bar holding it shut, eased it open just a sliver, and squeezed himself through. More than one splinter lodged itself in his back as he scraped across the old doorframe, but the pain was dulled by the numbing cold that seized his unprotected flesh once he was outside.

The street lamps that lined the roadway had burned themselves out, and the windows that Donvin could see from where he crouched on the balcony were all dark. Nevertheless, the moon and the stars, when they peeked out from behind a haze of low clouds, provided more than enough light for him to see his prey. They had come through the north gate, as he knew they would, and were trundling down the street at an unhurried pace: three wagons, each pulled by a beras and weighted by numerous stout casks of wine.

The beasts were a bit of a surprise; they had not been with the caravan earlier that day, though Donvin now remembered the empty harnesses clearly. Their presence made him slightly uneasy, but there was no reason that they should make any difference to his plan. He shook his head. The caravan was passing beneath him. Now was not the time to be pondering bugs, no matter how large they might be.

After a quick glance over his shoulder to check that the room behind him remained as still and quiet as he had left it, Donvin set to work. Silver tendrils drooped from his extended hand, casting a phantom glow that would have been obvious to the caravan's drivers had they possessed the ability to see it. Fine threads touched each barrel in the carts as they drove beneath, easily passing through the wood to caress the liquid within. Where they touched, Donvin could feel the wine change in response – he felt small things shifting, rearranging, like grains of sand trickling across an open palm. With this, the distraction he needed tomorrow would be ensured. Now it was just a matter of finding a suitable disguise so that when it happened, he could move about undetected.

The cart at the front stopped abruptly. On the balcony above, shielded from view only by the narrow slats of the railing and the cover of darkness, Donvin froze.

"What are you stopping for, you dumb lug?" A man's voice called from the back cart. "Let's get these delivered so we can get some bloody sleep!"

"It's not my fault!" came the hoarse reply. "The damn beras is trying to turn around!"

"Then give it a good whack!"

"Don't you think I'm trying?"

Donvin winced at the voices, hoping they would not wake the other Masked. For a moment he thought of killing the men below before they could make any more noise, but that might stop the wine from being delivered at all. Better to get back inside and pretend to be asleep before they got even louder. He pulled back his glowing fibers from the barrels.

"That's better. Git, you big lump, git!" The driver berated the beras, and the sound of wheels on the paving stones resumed. Donvin paused, holding his breath while the wagons receded down the street. After a while he stood and leaned over the rail to watch until the last one vanished from sight.

"Not bad for a night's work," a woman's voice said unexpectedly from behind him.

Donvin spun and put a finger to his lips, urging silence.

"Don't be silly," Lith said, refusing to lower her voice and leaning casually against the railing on the now-cramped balcony. "They won't wake."

"What are you doing here?" Donvin hissed, keeping his voice low. "I didn't call you."

She looked off toward where the carts had disappeared. "Simply making sure you have things in hand. But it seems there was no need. You do impressive work."

Donvin just smirked. This was nothing more than preparation. Impressive was still to come.

Chapter 10
Dedication

Ely woke to the sound of bells, the deep boom of the cathedral's Father Bell followed by the high chimes of the smaller Sisters.

Dedication morning, intoned the Father Bell.

We know, we know! replied his clamoring daughters.

The morning air was cold, and Ely shivered as she got up to shut her bedroom window. Thick, puffy clouds covered the sky, though cracks in the skyborne fleece were already revealing a clear blue latticework beyond as the waking land prepared to cast off her cozy nighttime blanket.

Despite the early hour, there were already people in the street below. One couple, leading a small herd of children in heavily patched clothes, stopped just beneath Ely's window to stare at the mansions on every side. The man, whose clothes looked even more well-worn than his children's, bent to say something in his wife's ear, and she laughed, tugging him forward by the arm while the children shouted and dashed after like disorderly ducklings.

After pulling the curtains shut a bit harder than she needed to, Ely lit two wall-mounted lamps to dispel the dimness in the room and sat before her dressing table to examine herself in the mirror. Lamplight was hardly the best for that purpose, and it did nothing to make the frown she wore look any more appealing.

The Father Bell boomed again. *Don't frown,* he commanded.

We smile! We smile! chimed the Sisters.

Ely poked at the corners of her mouth with her fingers until they turned up, and held them there. *Happy now, father? she thought,* but the silent room yielded no reply.

She sighed and pulled open the dressing table's wide drawer. Inside were her comb and brush, a few plain hairpins, several folded ribbons of varying colors, and a thin, discolored envelope. She removed the items one at a time, laying them out in a line across the empty surface of the table. The envelope came last, and she propped it up against the mirror so that she could see her name penned on the front of it in solid, no-nonsense script.

The white bone comb gleamed in the lamplight as Ely applied it to her hair. She could feel the delicately carved animal shapes of the handle making their familiar indentations in her hand with each long stroke. When the tangles yielded, she removed the stray hairs from about the comb's teeth, which had been spaced so as to look like the animals' many legs. There was a whole menagerie clustered on that short length of bone, but age and use had worn the details smooth until all the heads, legs, and tails looked the same.

Only halfway through the morning ritual, the comb came to a halt as the smell of eggs drifted up from the kitchen two floors below. Ely's stomach rumbled, and she set the comb gently beside the envelope on the table. There would be time enough for that later. Not bothering to change out of her shift, she rose, snuffed the lamps, and went in search of breakfast.

As expected, she found Barty in the kitchen, his tall form bending down to peer into one of the three brick ovens, the streaks of white hair at his temples glistening with sweat. He straightened when she came in, brushing flour from his hands onto the front of his yellow apron.

"Morning," Ely said, plopping down on a stool and putting her elbows on the slate countertop that divided the long room in half. It was pleasantly warm here compared to her room, though the stone of the countertop was still cold on her arms.

"Morning, Miss," Barty said, eying her elbows and her glum look, but making no comment. "An egg will be ready for you in a moment. I took the liberty of making them the traditional way. It is the Dedication, after all."

"That's fine." Ely slouched down and rested her chin on her crossed arms on the counter. "Do we at least have some redcorn powder for them?"

Barty made a little flourish with his hands, producing a small glass jar and planting it on the counter next to her elbow. "Just for you."

That coaxed a little smile from Ely, and she uncorked the jar to sniff the contents, which burned the insides of her nostrils satisfyingly. Barty always remembered what she liked.

"Are you going to be attending the ceremony at the cathedral?" Barty asked, turning back to the oven.

Ely shrugged noncommittally. "I was planning to visit the family instead. Besides, there will be far too many people in the square, and I don't much feel up for crowds today."

"Oh? With your father gone, you're the head of the house, so you should be the one to present the house offering to the Masked at the ceremony. I'll do it myself if you prefer, but you have more right to it, and I'm sure your father would be pleased to know that it was you who fulfilled the family duties while he was away."

"I'll think about it," Ely said, rolling the jar of redcorn impatiently between her palms. She did not need any more reminders about the things she should do. "Is that egg done yet?"

"Yes, just a moment," Barty said, moving around the end of the counter to get to one of the washbasins. He turned the handle, and a paltry trickle of water sputtered onto his hands. He shook his head.

"Every Dedication it gets worse. This poor city can't handle so many people," he said. He scrubbed his hands together vainly under the piddling stream, then turned the water off. "I'm afraid I won't be able to run a bath for you this morning, Miss."

"I'll just have to go to the ceremony, then," Ely said wryly. "Out there, no one would know if I hadn't bathed in a week."

"I expect that's true," Barty said with an amused smile, returning to the oven and reaching inside with a folded cloth to remove a glass dish holding a pair of delicious-looking baked eggs. He rolled them expertly onto two white porcelain plates, still steaming, and set one down squarely in front of Ely.

•••••

Donvin balked at the plate before him. "What's this?"

The dining room of the inn was virtually empty save for the three Masked sitting together at one table, but the waiter who had served them scooted back to the kitchen in such a feigned hurry that the door was swinging behind him before the question was fully out of Donvin's mouth.

Donvin's mentor looked up from his own plate. "An egg," he said simply. "Dedication tradition."

It did not look like an egg to Donvin. Roughly spherical and as big as his two fists put together, it was thickly covered with crusted breading and was still too hot to touch comfortably. He tipped the plate a little, and the egg rolled toward him slowly, leaving a smear of grease on the dark earthenware platter behind it. The thing smelled like salt and dirt, and plenty of each.

Furrow set his own egg back on his plate, a large bite in the top revealing a cloudy, gelatinous interior. "How long should we wait for Lady Evana?"

108

he said, lifting a cloth napkin to clean some hidden crumb from behind his mask.

"She will be busy this morning, certainly," Donvin's mentor said, chewing thoughtfully after taking a bite of his own egg. "Most likely she is occupied elsewhere, though it is not like her to be late. If she has not arrived by the next bell, we should depart for the ceremony on our own."

The swinging door to the kitchens opened again, and the innkeeper called Losha emerged carrying a large brown pitcher in one hand and three hefty clay mugs in the other. She plunked them down on the table unceremoniously.

"Drink up," she said. "Evana's paying for it, else I'll have her hide, so have as much as you like." She scowled around at all the empty tables, then disappeared back into the kitchen.

Whatever was in the pitcher smelled a good deal more appetizing than the egg, so Donvin poured himself a full cup. It was warm and tasted mostly of honey, and he took several long sips before speaking.

"I doubt she has anything more important to deal with than us," he said, leaning back in his chair and cradling his mug with both hands. "We're the main event, aren't we?"

Donvin's mentor shrugged. "Managing a city takes a great deal of work, and is not something easily done even at the best of times. One should not be too hasty to judge."

"No doubt," Donvin said between sips, "but I think her priorities need correcting if she thinks to make us wait while-"

Flicker.

Donvin sat up straight. Something had moved in the corner of his vision, by the stairs that led to the upper floors. The movement seemed . . . familiar, just like what he had seen among the trees the night he had earned his mask. He turned his head. Morning light was coming in through the large windows that fronted on the street, clearly illuminating the room and leaving hardly a shadow to play tricks on his eyes.

"Is something amiss?" Donvin's mentor looked up from the mug he had been filling.

"No," Donvin said, setting his own mug on the table with a thud. "Excuse me." He stood and walked toward the stairs. The other Masked merely continued their breakfast, but Donvin could feel at least one set of eyes upon his back. Furrow's, most likely. Though he could hardly be called talkative, Donvin was convinced that he lacked nothing in perceptiveness. No matter.

He could come up with an excuse for leaving the table if necessary, but silence frequently served just as well among the Masked.

He stepped into the hall that led to the stairs and paused. The floor was dirty from the many boots that passed through each day, and the layer of soil held tracks well. The freshest appeared to be those of the Masked on their way to the dining hall for breakfast, and no lingering scent suggested any other recent visitors. Donvin frowned. He was sure he had seen something.

Donvin climbed the stairs two at a time, poking his head out into the hall when he reached the second floor. All was stillness, the guests either having cleared out early to avoid the Masked or stayed abed late for the same reason. Seeing no evidence of movement, Donvin moved up to the third floor.

Flicker.

It was there: a movement at the far end, at the door to the room where they had slept. Donvin crossed his arms and smiled to himself. There was no way off of this floor other than the stairs at his back. Approaching, he found the door slightly ajar. A shove from his hand threw it open the rest of the way with a bang.

Light from the open curtains fell upon the scuffed floorboards, the bare chairs, and the fraying blanket that had been pulled up over the bed. All were perfectly undisturbed. Donvin growled, kicked the door shut behind him, and walked a slow circuit of the room. The door to the balcony was closed and latched from the inside, just as he had left it, and the window panes were all intact. There was no closet for anyone to hide in, and the frame of the bed was a mere two inches off the floor, leaving hardly enough room beneath for a rat, let alone a person. The only thing moving in the whole room was a lone caterpillar inching slowly along the wood of the window sill.

Donvin turned, disgusted, then stopped. On the back of the closed door hung a set of clothes: a white tunic with a blue eagle on the breast, and a thin leather vest with marks of red and green. That was strange, Donvin thought. The clothes had definitely not been there that morning. They looked to be about his size too, just like those worn by the man Keth at the stables.

Curiosity aroused, Donvin reached up and pulled them down, noticing for the first time the long tear that slashed the fabric of the tunic cleanly down the side from shoulder to hip, opening it up as one might peel back the skin of an animal felled in the hunt. Something else was odd as well. Into the wood of the door behind where the clothes had hung was carved a word, sliced in deep, angular cuts that failed to meet at the corners, as if made by a hand that found shaping just a few letters difficult. *Dolmon*, the tortured script read.

Donvin could not recall having heard or seen the word before, though something about it made his chest tighten and his lungs hunger greedily for air. Whatever it meant, he would have to puzzle it out later. He already had more than enough to do today, though these clothes, wherever they had come from, would make his work much easier.

As Donvin turned the clothes in his hands, remarking on how perfectly they would serve as a disguise, something small and dense fell from a pocket of the vest and landed on the floorboards with a dull thud. It was a little book. A golden "E" stood prominently on its cover.

A bell tolled across the city, heavy, hollow, and low. The time for the Dedication was coming.

•••••

Ely covered her ears until the deep reverberations of the Father Bell had subsided. Heard from Hallow Street, which ran along the back wall of the cathedral, the ceremonial bell was nearly deafening, making her glad that it was reserved for special occasions. Only wealthy cities could lay claim to a bell of any size, and Falls Gate had five, but in truth Ely did not much care for their thundering clangs and tooth-jarring echoes.

The children in the street unclasped their hands from their ears and pointed, open mouthed, up at the cathedral's tower where the bells were housed. The bell tower, though grand, looked like little more than a delicate silver pin when viewed against the imposing, if somewhat run-down, towers of the Keep behind it. Its proportion probably mattered little to the children, however. No doubt many of them who had come to the city for the Dedication had never heard a bell at all before today. But, being children, their attention did not hold for long after the bell fell silent, and they quickly returned to their games.

Ely stepped lightly around the squares and circles of reddish chalk that they had drawn on the uneven paving stones, careful to stay out of the way as the children bounded between them. The small satchel that dangled from her waistcord bounced against her leg as she walked, reminding her with every step of the ceremonial offering it contained.

The streets on that side of the cathedral were relatively clear, at least when compared with the swelling crowd that was growing on the other. The breaking clouds of dawn had indeed proven prescient, and the sun now beat down warmly from a clear sky, drawing the people out of doors in droves even though the Dedication itself was not due to start for at least another hour or two.

Though the ritual had great religious and historical meaning, it was the spectacle that most of them were gathering to see. It was rare to get a chance to observe the Masked from a place of safety, and people were drawn to it as they might be to see a caged bear, to feel its hot breath and hear its roar from beyond the reach of its claws. Breaches were uncommon around Falls Gate, but that did not mean its people did not know and fear them. In the last year alone, three ships had been lost to the sudden whirlpools that were the symptom of underwater breaches, and that unusual surge had done plenty to remind people what seeing the Masked ordinarily entailed. But for Ely, a deep sense of solitude denied her any pleasure that being part of that audience might have brought.

A short way past where the children played, she turned left through a narrow opening in the brick wall that fronted on the street and stopped, gazing south across the rows of tightly-spaced graves that sprouted from a field of closely-cut grass. The cemetery was not large, at least not relative to the size of the city, though it still took up at least twice as much ground as the cathedral across the street. Given the limited space, not many people were buried here any longer. Only those of noble blood who were willing to pay for the privilege could now secure a spot in those grassy rows.

The lines of erect gravemasts gleamed dimly in the sun, looking perpetually wet on account of the oil that warded off rot and insects from the timber. The grease tended to discolor the wood over time, marring it with yellowing splotches and streaks, but it was effective – even the oldest of the grave markers rarely needed replacing. Perfectly spaced, the masts resembled a miniature wood of branchless, leafless trees all standing at attention. A few pieces of ragged cloth rippled from their tops in the salty breeze, the remains of flags bearing family coats and colors.

Ely made her way between the rows, toward the back of the cemetery where the newer masts stood with unstained sides. The sun flickered as she walked through the shadows of the many posts, and a crow startled at her approach, taking wing with flustered flapping from where it had been unearthing worms from the soft soil. Only a few other people were about, placing shells at the foot of a grave or tying new flags where the wind had shredded old ones into rags.

The grave where Ely stopped looked much like all the rest, though it bore no flag, nor did any that shared the row. That had been part of the agreement Ely's father had begrudgingly signed all those years ago. No shells. No flags. That was the price of laying traitors to rest in a place of honor. When Ely was old enough to understand, she had asked him why he had done it, why he had not instead found a place where they would be allowed to mourn properly. The answer he had given had never satisfied her, nor did it now.

Ely sighed, touching the carving on the front of the gravemast before her lightly. The name written there was etched in rigid, blocky script, cut by a chisel that clearly held no love for it: Almestra Celundine. Ely's mother. Her fingers came away sticky with grease, and she knelt, wiping them on the warm grass beside the grave.

Instead of rising when she was done, Ely sat, pulling her knees up to her chest. The small satchel she carried ceased its tugging at her hip, but it would take far more than that to make her forget its presence.

Relenting, she opened it and took out the delicate bone comb, running her fingers across its carvings for the second time that day. They had been painted, once, though only the tiniest flecks of color remained after the wear of many years and the touch of many hands. In the absence of paint, the sunlight revealed all too clearly what the keepsake had always been: a piece of the crude stuff around which lives are spun, left useless and bare once those lives had come undone. It was a fitting token for a graveyard, and for her family, a fitting heirloom.

Resting her chin on her knees, Ely closed her eyes and tried to imagine herself in the presence of those who were buried beneath where she sat, the people whose deaths had brought ownership of the beautifully grim memento down to her. She did not need to look at the names on the other graves, so many times had she come here in her youth. The nearest was that of Gaalben Monsel, her mother's only brother and the one who might well deserve the blame for bringing the family to this end. Ely had tried many times to hate him, but it was simply too hard to hate a piece of wood protruding from the ground, and she had no real memories to serve as better targets for her anger. After Gaalben's grave came his children's, all three of them side by side. The faces of their gravemasts bore no dates, but Ely knew that they had been young when they died, the oldest born just a few years before her. Beyond them, the line devoted to her kin continued, covering almost a quarter of the length of the yard.

This was her family, Ely thought. Or rather, it was the family she should have had. They were the ones she should have rejoiced with last night after a long-in-coming reunion, the ones she should have broken her fast with that morning over the traditional Dedication egg, and the ones she should be standing with even now in the jostle of the cathedral square. But this was all most of them had ever been to her: silent, rigid, untouchable, without even a bit of blowing cloth to add life to their stiff wooden bodies. Even her mother was by now only a thin cloud of features and moments in her memories, a side against which to snuggle, a blurred face and a set of slender, ageless hands. Surely she had spent more time in the company of this wooden post than she ever had in the living flesh of her mother's arms.

Ely was not sure how long she had been sitting there when a shadow fell across her, and she looked up, a tear rolling down her cheek. Unaware that she had been crying, she wiped it away quickly with a brush of her hand, in the same motion stuffing the comb she held back in its bag.

"'Morning, Miss Celundine," the portly man said in a hesitating voice. "Didn't mean to disturb you."

"Good morning, Wharfmaster," Ely said, shielding her eyes from the glare that was outlining the man's bulk. He wore a fine satin doublet with bright abalone buttons that strained at the too-tight fit, and a pair of silky breeches covered his stocky legs. His thick beard was combed and trimmed close to his chin, and his long hair was oiled and pulled back over his scalp in a thick, dark braid. A raw look hung about his cheeks, as if they had recently been scrubbed for the first time in a long while. His hands looked much the same, though one of his large fists was closed tightly at his side, as if hiding something within.

"I suppose you be here visiting your ma and folks," the Wharfmaster said, scratching behind his ear awkwardly with his free hand. He glanced down the row. "I'm here for my wife, you know."

Ely nodded. Lizzadra Abrohl's grave was only a few beyond those of the Monsels – she had been Gaalben's sister-in-law. Maybe that made Ely and the Wharfmaster related somehow, but there was no word for the relation. He was a private man, and always had been. Once his name had been inked next to her father's on the burial agreement that fateful night, it had seemed to the young Ely that he simply vanished for a number of years, leaving her and her father to do their grieving alone despite their shared tragedy.

"Well . . ." the Wharfmaster said with a tight-lipped smile, "tell ol' Barty hello for me."

Ely smiled back politely. "I will." His distance did not bother her as it might have. It comforted her to know she was not the only one who sometimes preferred solitude.

The Wharfmaster walked past, down the line of graves a short way until reaching his wife's. Ely thought to give him some privacy, but even as she purposefully averted her gaze, she caught herself trying to watch him out of the corner of her eye.

Wharfmaster Abrohl glanced over one shoulder, then over the other as he stood before the gravemast where his wife was buried. Furtiveness did not fit his form well – his size made his every move plain, and the posts about him seemed spindles by comparison, offering no concealment. Apparently content that no one but Ely was near, the Wharfmaster crouched in an ungainly fashion, used an index finger to bore a small hole in the dirt at the base of the post, and dropped something small and white into it from his closed fist. After looking around again, he smoothed over the hole and stood up, wiping dirt from his hands onto the legs of his expensive pants. He stepped back, hunching his shoulders and then relaxing them, kicking his feet this way and that, doing his concerted best to look casual. His awkwardness was comical, but unnecessary.

"No one saw you!" Ely called out to him, cupping her hands around her mouth.

The Wharfmaster jumped slightly, and then he turned to look at her, the flush evident in his face even from a distance. Ely rose and walked over to him. They seemed to be the only two people left in the cemetery now, and the growing noise from beyond the cathedral suggested that the Dedication ceremony was nigh.

A nervous chuckle escaped the Wharfmaster's lips. "I did not figure you for the spyin' type, Miss Celundine," he said.

Ely smiled wryly. "That's only because you didn't spend enough time around me when I was growing up," she said. "But I won't tell anyone. It's a stupid rule anyhow."

The Wharfmaster looked down at his tightly laced and smartly polished leather boots with a bobbing nod.

"She deserved better than this," he said quietly.

Ely nodded in agreement. "Most of them did," she said.

"It's my fault too," he said after a moment, not meeting her eyes. "I could have torn up that damn paper and walked out. I could have buried her on a secluded cliff somewhere far away from here, where I could put anything I

. . . ." The Wharfmaster seemed to choke up for a moment before regaining some of his composure.

"But I didn't," he said. "I signed the paper, because she loved this city, and because they all said it would help, that it would be for the best. And maybe it was. Who am I to say?" He shook his head a little. "It sure don't seem like eighteen years, though, that she's been gone."

This was the longest conversation Ely recalled having with the man in years, and she was about to offer words of comfort, but an interrupting cry went up from the distant crowd. The ceremony was starting.

Wharfmaster Abrohl gave Ely a sidelong glance. "Best be runnin' along, miss. Wouldn't want you missin' the show on my account."

Ely noticed a hint of wetness in the Wharfmaster's eyes. "You aren't going?" she asked.

The big man shook his head, causing his braid to swing stiffly. "I've seen it before, sure enough. Better to leave some room for the young ones." He patted his wide hips and shrugged, blinking a few times in quick succession. "More use for me down at the docks, I'll wager. No pittance o' work there, even today."

Ely looked back up at the thick white stones that formed the cathedral's rear wall. Six large, round windows of clear glass stared back at her from their rigid sockets, their corners sparkling with reflected sunlight. The noise of the crowd put a vibration in them, shaking them until shimmering droplets of light dripped down onto the stone below, where they disappeared. That was where she should be, she thought, alone among all those happy families, wallowing in the fact that she lacked what they had. The Wharfmaster might not be exactly family, but he was someone who understood her, if only a little, and it was not fair that either of them should have to suffer for their solitude.

Ely stuck her tongue out at the edifice of the cathedral and made a rude sound.

"What a coincidence," she said. "I'm not going either."

The Wharfmaster's mouth was slightly ajar, but to his credit he did not question her decision. "Well," he said slowly, "you're welcome down at the docks, if you got nowhere else to be."

"I'd like that," Ely said, smiling. It was refreshing for once not to have her decisions challenged. Her father certainly had no qualms about doing so, at least when he was around, and Barty stood in for him quite effectively when he was not.

The Wharfmaster led the way, squeezing through the narrow cemetery entrance, and Ely followed close behind. Neither was sorry to put the rising sound of the crowd at their backs as they followed the nearly deserted streets south toward the ocean, the satchel once again bouncing from Ely's legs as she walked.

•••••

Donvin scowled out over the sea of heads from the top of the cathedral steps. Each one seemed to babble a ceaseless flood of syllables that blended into an almost tangible miasma of suffering for his sensitive ears. What had all these people to talk about, he wondered, when those who were a hundred times their betters were content with silence? Worse than the noise, though, was the heat. The day, like the one before it, was growing unseasonably warm for autumn, enough to be uncomfortable even if he had been wearing nothing but his own skin instead of heavy furs.

A glance over at the other two Masked did nothing to ease his frustration. Neither the crowd nor the rising temperature seemed to bother them, and they stood unmoving in the same way that they had since reaching the site of the ceremony without the benefit of a guide. The Lady Evana had never appeared at the inn, though that did not surprise Donvin given his discovery of the little book that was now hidden safely in the inner folds of his mantle. The memory of her laughter at him bore somewhat less sting now, for he was fairly certain that wherever this day found her, she was no longer laughing. The thought brought a pleasing curl to the corners of his mouth, and for a moment its savored taste obscured the more repulsive ones of sweat and human odor.

As it turned out, Evana's guidance had not been necessary in the slightest. Donvin's mentor had led the three of them easily to the cathedral, where he set about making what minimal preparations were needed for the ceremony. Donvin and Furrow looked on while he sketched the outline of a large circle on the stone landing that led from the top of the wide, shallow steps to the closed cathedral doors, and they complied obediently when he instructed them to stand on either side of it while he stood behind, all three facing out toward the square that had gone from packed to overflowing with people as the noon hour approached. Then, they had commenced the waiting.

Donvin looked over his shoulder as he detected the faint sound of well-oiled hinges in motion. One of the cathedral's doors opened, and an older-looking man emerged, clearly past his middle years but still moving with a firmness and vigor defiant of true old age. He approached Donvin's mentor, exchanged a few words too low to be heard over the mindless babbling of the crowd, and then proceeded to the edge of the steps and raised his hands over his head. As the people below took notice, the din lessened and eventually faded to silence.

Rather than speak now that he held the crowd's attention, the older man nodded to Donvin's mentor, and then returned to the cathedral.

"Blessings upon you, people of Falls Gate," Donvin's mentor said, his voice booming out through the square at a volume that took Donvin by surprise.

The masked man extended his arms. "At this very moment, people all across this land are gathered as you are now, in sun and in rain, in wind and in hail, to honor what binds us as one people. We have come to remind you of your promises and your reasons for making them, for we are all a part of the same pact, and it cannot survive, we cannot survive, without the faith of all."

He paused, allowing the words to settle in the warm air.

"We ask that you now affirm the pact with your own hands," his booming voice rang out, "rather than rely upon the promises made by your ancestors."

This seemed to be a cue, for both of the cathedral's grand doors opened wide and a procession of men and women emerged in three single-file lines. Donvin recognized none of them save for the man who led them: Gillibardo Groundwise, the stablemaster. In the middle of the procession, attached by long, multi-colored ropes to those walking around it, was a heavily painted and ornamented beras, its shell gleaming with pigments in bright whites, blues, and greens. Leading the beras by a short rope attached to its single horn was a youthful woman in stately ceremonial robes that matched the painted colors of its shell, stepping gingerly as if afraid she might trip on their low hem.

Master Gill and the beras attendants led the enormous insect between the Masked and positioned it in the center of the circle drawn on the stones, the stablemaster giving a nod and a wink to Donvin's mentor as they passed. Once the beast was in place, the attendants took firm hold of their ropes and backed away to the outside of the circle, pulling them taut so that the creature could not move. The robed woman then made a show of formally presenting the lead rope to Donvin's mentor, who accepted it with a nod and exchanged a few quiet words with her before she too retreated outside the circle to stand with the other attendants, blushing deeply the whole way.

A few in the crowd whistled or shouted when the beras was presented before them, and a murmur of approval passed from their collective mouths. Even Donvin had to admit that the painting on the shell was expertly done. Various shapes of blue and green suggested land and sea, with puffy smudges of white dotted across them as if the view were one from high above the clouds. The brush strokes were so fine as to be almost invisible, the work of a very patient hand with a very delicate tool.

When the attendants had backed away to a safe distance, Donvin's mentor made a subtle gesture, and the circle around the painted beras flashed with that special light only the trained eye could see. Suddenly the beras was gone, the ropes attached to it severed cleanly where they crossed the line drawn on the stone. The circle was a portal, Donvin realized, though different in form from the ones he was used to.

The crowd gasped. Somewhere among the sea of bodies, a child started to cry.

"Your fathers and grandfathers have cared well for our gift to you," Donvin's mentor spoke to the crowd once again, "your mothers and grandmothers have nurtured it as their own. It gave them the means to survive through the darkest of times, and they honored it as a living symbol of the ancient pact between our peoples. But these are not the days of your fathers and grandfathers. These are not the days of your mothers and grandmothers. We ask of you: will you be as righteous as they were? Will you sacrifice of yourselves to ensure the prosperity of all?" The questions echoed out over the rapt audience. "You who would secure our blessings once again, who would ask with humility and sincerity that this order our ancestors established live on, come before us and make your offerings. You who would ask that our protection of this world continue, bring proof of your commitment to the pact and present it with thanks in your hearts."

A number of those near the front of the crowd immediately began ascending the cathedral steps, forming a makeshift line that others quickly joined. One by one they stepped into the circle where the beras had been and laid an object down on the stones. The first man to make an offering placed into the circle a glass candlestick, made a strange sign by holding the fingers of one hand pointed upward in front of his face, and then stepped back. He was followed by a woman who put in a pair of bone knives, and then by another who offered a roll of fine, wispy yellow cloth.

The line of people carrying offerings to the circle seemed endless, and there appeared to be no pattern to the things they brought. Blades of glass or bone were not uncommon, but so too were items of fresh food and baked goods. One child of no more than three carefully placed a doll made out of yarn within the circle before running back to her waiting mother on the steps.

The endless procession quickly grew tiresome, but there was little Donvin could do other than silently watch the pile of offerings grow higher as the sun slid across the sky above. When at last the final offering had been made what felt like hours later, the pile had reached the height of his head and contained the strangest collection of things he had ever seen.

Donvin's mentor moved around to the front of the pile so that he could still be seen by the crowd at the foot of the steps.

"Your offerings this day are a testament to your faith and love for one another. Through your individual sacrifices, all have earned our blessing and our protection. Behold!"

The masked man threw his arms wide, and a host of glowing threads, invisible to the crowd, poured from his body into the mountain of offerings behind him. The pile began to stir as its pieces rose slowly into the air, only a few at first, then by the tens, and then the hundreds. They drifted apart as they ascended, forming a bizarre cloud of shoes, shirts, fruit, glass trinkets, stone bowls, clay vases, books, earrings, feathers, belts, fish, toys, coins, and even an occasional gemstone that swirled in the air over the heads of the awestruck crowd.

Then the swirling cloud of objects began to compress, growing smaller and smaller as its components swirled faster and faster. The speed grew so great that it generated a wind that pushed back the hair from the thousands of upturned faces watching the dance of the offerings unfold above them. Smaller the cloud grew, and darker and denser, until its diameter was no greater than the length of Donvin's forearm, and still it shrank. It was the size of his head, then his fist, then his finger, then . . . .

There was a flash that forced all eyes to look away, and when the light had faded the painted beras stood once again in the circle, the severed ropes held by the attendants made whole again. The returned beast reared up and thrashed with sudden energy, its six barbed legs straining at the colorful ropes that held it, but the attendants stood firm, fighting its attempts to force its way out of the circle toward Donvin's mentor, who stood unmoving not but a few paces beyond the reach of its lashing horn. Four small holes in side of the creature's painted shell grew larger as flexible plates that covered them shifted aside, and Donvin could hear the faint hiss they made as they sucked in and then expelled puffs of air.

Then, after much struggling, the beast at last fell still, its huge black eyes placidly staring to the sides once more as though nothing at all had happened. Donvin's mentor nodded in acknowledgement to the ring of panting attendants who held its reins, and then he lifted an arm to the sky. Something small and sparkling descended from the air above the crowd, where the storm of offerings had vanished, to land in his outstretched hand.

"This is your Dedication," the masked man's voice rang out as he held the glittering crystal aloft for all to see. "May its light never dim, and may its beauty never fade, through all the days of your lives."

•••••

The suspending ropes creaked and strained as the wooden platform inched lower, swaying in the wind that rushed along the cliff face. Ely gripped one of the taut lines in a white-knuckled hold and did her best to ignore the two hundred feet of empty air that still separated her from the crashing surf below. Wharfmaster Abrohl, on the other hand, strolled easily about on the suspended contraption, checking and rechecking the fastenings of the several crates that were their cargo. He seemed far more at ease here, even dangling as they were with no railing to separate them from a lethal fall, than he had been with his feet on the solid ground of the city now high above.

The lift's descent to the docks was a slow one, controlled by the plodding pace of four beras harnessed to a large wheel winch at the top of the cliff, which gave Ely plenty of time to take in the view. White-and-gray gulls soared about the platform, making their throaty calls and circling back again and again in hopes of scavenging food from open boxes or the hands of unsuspecting humans. Occasionally the wind would shift, peppering birds and passengers alike with a fine spray from the falls, which cascaded in an airborne concoction of foam and mist down the cliffs only half a span to the west. All the way out to the horizon the noonday sun sparkled on the rolling waves of the ocean, dimmed not at all by the few high clouds sliding across the dome of the sky. Somewhat closer, vessels of all sizes could be seen plying the coastal waters, flying sails and banners in countless colors and shapes. There were matching pairs of long-bowed net skimmers, a smattering of squarish, low-floating crabbers, and even several large, many-masted galleons plowing white paths through the swells. The sight was almost enough to make Ely forget about the swaying of the boards beneath her feet and the unnerving groans of the ropes.

This was hardly Ely's first time on a lift, but usually she rode the passenger variety, with plenty of other people and tall railings between her and the precipice. The cargo lifts provided no such luxury. The Wharfmaster had assured her that it was quite safe to ride along with the crates being sent down to the docks, but that did little to convince her hands to ease the death grip they held on the rope.

As they approached the base of the cliffs, Ely ventured a look over the edge. Below, several dockworkers were grabbing the long lines that dangled from the underside of the lift and pulling them this way and that, guiding the platform in for a smooth landing. Its swaying stabilized, and Ely found herself breathing a touch easier for the last few moments of the ride.

A light bump indicated that they had touched down, and the Wharfmaster hopped off with surprising spryness for his size. Ely disembarked more slowly, stepping carefully in an attempt to retain her dignity. Salutatory calls and waves greeted their arrival from the men who were loading and unloading the other lifts, of which there were seven arranged in a line against the cliff face.

The knot of circling gulls that had been following the platform dispersed, mixing with the hundreds of others that strutted about the docks and flew laps back and forth to the distant stone breakwater where many had their nests. Their greenish leavings made the wooden walkways slick in places, leaving Ely wishing that she had worn a pair of more rugged shoes.

As soon as Ely and the Wharfmaster had stepped clear, four well-muscled men set to work on the cargo that had accompanied them, expertly hefting the boxes from the lift into a small waiting cart that was pulled by another pair of equally burly workers. It surprised Ely that there were so many people to be seen here during the Dedication ceremony, though on second thought she supposed that it shouldn't. The docks were large, with a mooring capacity of at least twelve full sized galleons, and the winds that blew in the ships of trade observed no holy days. Even now, a two-masted trader of no small stature was just tying up to one of the nearer berths, and already workers swarmed around it like ants around a candy dropped on their hill. Farther down the docks Ely could make out the crew of a crabber unloading a set of full cages from its flat deck, while next to it a number of much smaller skiffs were loading up with empty ones to scatter out in the open water.

In addition to the usual mess of trawlers and modest traders, there were three ships of truly imposing stature docked at present. One was the familiar presence of the Falls Gatekeeper, a giant of a ship that dwarfed even most other galleons. Four thick masts jutted from her high deck, bound up with so much rigging that it gave the impression of a web spun by a confused and abhorrently proportioned spider. A line of six gun ports ran down the length of her hull, each concealing behind its hinged door a massive iron engine of death. The Gatekeeper was one of a pair of sister ships, the other being the River Guardian, whose home port was the secondary docks on the opposite side of Cliffdiver Falls. Together, they protected access to the city and to the river trade routes, though the mere sight of them was usually more than enough to accomplish that task. More often than not they remained at their respective moorings, setting sail only for certain festivals or important events of state.

The other two ships of notable size were smaller than the Gatekeeper, though still far from diminutive. One was a relatively standard-looking trader of Midcoast manufacture, displaying the characteristic three masts and checkerboard coloration of hull planks. The second was a bit more unusual, and while it too sported three masts, it also had uncommonly high gunwales and a sharp prow made from rich, dark wood. Even more unusual, it openly displayed a large ballista that poked over the side of the top deck.

"You be looking at the Low Tide," Wharfmaster Abrohl said as he approached Ely, a coil of rope slung over his shoulder and a long wooden rod in his hand. "She's a handful, that one. Hasn't docked here in three years, I figure, least not before a couple nights back. Can't say I missed her."

"Why's that?" Ely asked, eyes drifting back to the dark hull.

The Wharfmaster chuckled. "She be a smuggling ship, that's why. Don't ask me to prove it, but it be truth. Her crew ain't exactly the friendly sort, and her captain, well . . . ." He shrugged. "He's a slick one. Got into some trouble with the Council a few years back, but whatever it was, he's still a free man. Figured he wouldn't be too eager to come back, but here he is. If I had my way, he'd never set foot on these docks again. But then, I don't make the law, I just keep it, an' that's the way it is."

The Wharfmaster shook his head in resignation. "Anyhow, how's about we go fishing?" He shook the coiled rope on his arm. "I could use me a spotter, and I'll wager my best trousers the haul will be good today." Indeed, he still wore the same nice clothes as he had up in the city, though the trousers in question had already managed to acquire a smear of grease across one of the legs.

"Fishing?" Ely said, blinking incredulously at the heavy rope.

"Aye, but not for fish," the Wharfmaster said with a mischievous smile that broke his beard. "Come along, I'll show ye'."

The large man tromped across the sturdy wood of the docks, shaking the boards underfoot as he went. Workers and crewmen cleared the way in front of him, often with a friendly wave or shout, and he nodded business-like back to them. Ely followed closely, careful not to be in the way when activity resumed in his wake.

A few short minutes of walking brought them to the more distant berths that were closest to the falls, many of which stood empty save for the gleam of sunlight off of gently lapping water.

"This do look about right," the Wharfmaster said, coming to a halt. He turned and handed the wooden rod he carried to Ely.

Ely accepted it, still confused about what exactly they were doing, and turned it over in her hands. It was not solid wood, she discovered, but instead hollow and quite light, with circles of glass fitted tightly inside at both ends. It looked vaguely like a scope for spying great distances over water, but much longer.

While Ely was examining the strange device, the Wharfmaster was uncoiling the rope, which frayed into many separate strands toward one end. Affixed to each was a small weighting stone, and to each stone were tied several glass fishhooks arranged so that their points faced outward, a configuration Ely had never seen used in traditional fishing.

"Well then," the Wharfmaster said, "go on an' put the scope in the water an' tell me what ya' see."

Ely hesitantly leaned over the edge of the pier and dipped the tip of the rod into the water of the empty berth, holding it at arm's length and trying to look into the end.

The Wharfmaster laughed. "You got to put yer' eye to it, like this," he said, making a ring-shape with his fingers and holding it up to his eye. "An' you'll get a better view if you sit on yer knees. I'd do it myself, but these legs got the aches in 'em more days than not."

Curiosity overcame Ely's desire to avoid soiling her clothes, and she knelt, feeling the roughness of the dock's planks even through the fabric of her skirts. Holding the scope with both hands, she put her eye against one end and lowered the other down into the water.

"Well?" the Wharfmaster said expectantly.

While the strong reflection of sunlight had obscured Ely's vision from above, using the scope allowed her to look past the reflective surface. From this lower perspective, the brightness of the sun aided, rather than hindered, her view, and she was able to make out details quite some distance down, all the way to the rocky shelf some twenty feet below where the pylons that supported the docks were anchored.

"I can see the bottom," Ely said with a smile. Even as she spoke, a tiny fish darted through her field of view, distorted and elongated by the scope's submerged lens. The sudden movement made her start, but she held on to the wooden tube tightly, afraid of letting it slip into the water.

"That's good," the Wharfmaster said. "It's a nice bright day, great for fishing. See anything amiss down there?"

Ely frowned. The length of the scope limited her field of view to a small circle, too narrow to see much of the bottom at once. "I only see rocks, and a fish, a moment ago," she said uncertainly.

"Never mind the fish," the Wharfmaster said patiently. "Keep looking at the bottom."

Ely scanned back and forth slowly with the scope. "Just rocks," she said again, then paused. There was something that looked like a small, fuzzy shadow down there, but with the sun almost directly overhead, there seemed to be nothing to cast it.

Noting that her searching had stopped, the Wharfmaster piped up hopefully. "See something? Where is it?"

Ely squinted, but the distance and the distortion of the water made identification impossible. "I don't know what it is," she said slowly, "but I think it's close to that post, there." She pointed to one of the barnacle-covered pylons that were supporting the planks beneath them.

The Wharfmaster grinned, hefting his length of rope. "Keep watchin'," he said. Holding the base of the frayed end, he spun the weighing rocks over his head and then let them fly out into the water of the empty berth, allowing much of the coiled rope at his side to spool out after them.

Ely watched through the scope as the barbed rocks fanned out and descended slowly through the water. A few of them came to rest on the bottom just a pace or so from the mysterious object.

"That was close, just a bit too far," Ely said.

The Wharfmaster grunted in acknowledgement and gave the end of the rope a slight tug. In the lens of the scope, the barbed stone weights skittered across the rocky shelf, two of them snagging the shadowy shape and dragging it along with them. Clearly it was no shadow.

"You got it," Ely said, pulling her face away from the scope.

The Wharfmaster smiled in satisfaction. "Right, now we see what we caught." His thick arms towed in the waterlogged rope with great speed, and just a few moments later the barbed rocks emerged dripping from the water, several of their hooks embedded in the dark object.

The shadowy blob turned out to be a small bag of black sealskin. A bulb of grayish wax encased its tightly drawn mouth, creating a waterproof seal, but the Wharfmaster crushed it easily and brushed away the bits of wax into the water. Then he upended the contents on the dock.

To Ely's surprise, out of the bag fell a small stream of coins, clinking together as they scattered across the boards. The Wharfmaster gave the bag another shake, and out fluttered a tightly folded piece of paper, which he snatched up before the wind could carry it off. He unfolded it, quickly scanned the message, and then passed it to Ely. All that was written on it were three lines of numbers in extremely cramped penmanship.

"Smugglers' code," the Wharfmaster said, tossing the empty bag to the ground. "This is how the good, honest types who live up there," he said, nodding toward the city high on the cliff, "communicate with the more sordid types moored down here."

Ely pinched her lips together in confusion. "Can't they just come down and talk to them?" she asked.

"Sure, if they want to be seen at it in the light of day," the Wharfmaster said. "But the docks are closed at night, and the sailing crews are banned from the city after dark. So an upstanding citizen comes down here during the day and drops a message in the water when no one's looking, and then a sailor swims down at night to collect it."

Ely thought about it for a moment. "That's really quite clever," she said, "but what's to stop the smugglers from taking the payment and never delivering the goods?"

The Wharfmaster chuckled. "You got a good head on yer shoulders, lass. Smuggling is this close to being a legitimate business." He held up a thumb and index finger a hair apart. "In fact, most smugglers also deal in honest trade, and they'd get quite a filthy name for themselves doin' business like that." He grinned with barely disguised glee. "Which is why these fishin' trips do be so much fun. When we haul up these little baggies ourselves, for all the merchant up there knows, the smuggler pocketed the money and sailed off into the sunset. Plays havoc with their reputations, I'll wager."

Ely smiled too, seeing the humor in it. "But this isn't exactly a lot of money," she said, looking again at the assortment of glass coins and the variety of colored flowers they contained. "Twenty petals at most. Can you really buy smuggled goods with just this?"

"That's the rub, that is," the Wharfmaster acknowledged reluctantly. "Most bags out here are just down payments. It only took a few good days of fishing to teach them that lesson."

"Still, it must add up to a lot over time," Ely speculated. "What do you do with it all?"

"Keep it locked up for expenses, mostly," the Wharfmaster said. "Those dockhands don't pay themselves, that they don't. But I'm proud to say that in fifteen years of managing this place, I've never had to go before the Council beggin' for more funds, not even in hard times. I also hear there's an orphanage down about the Milltown way that's doin' pretty well for itself these days," he added with a slow, obvious wink.

"Anyhow," he continued, "we won't stop no smugglin' just gabbin' about it. Go on, spot me another one."

Ely obliged with a smile, dipping the end of the scope back into the water. In this way they moved from berth to berth, Ely searching and the Wharfmaster casting. Some were empty, but on the whole there seemed to be no shortage of little black bags lurking down below.

After pulling up their fifth of the day, Ely leaned down to put the scope in the water again and felt the strings holding the pouch at her hip loosen unexpectedly. She had been enjoying the work so much that she had almost forgotten it was there. The scope clattered to the deck and rolled away as she seized the pouch with both hands, barely catching it before it dropped into the water. She sat down hard, the rush of adrenaline making her hands shake for having nearly lost it to the deep.

The Wharfmaster stopped the rolling scope with his boot. "You've been carryin' that around with you all day," he said, pointing to the pouch. He hesitated a moment. "Was it to be an offering?"

Ely nodded.

"Something you didn't want to give up?"

Ely clutched the pouch tightly, feeling the hard shape of the comb within. "I suppose so," she said, a bit ashamed.

"There ain't no shame in that, lass," the Wharfmaster said seriously. "Some of us have already given up too much for this city. There be nothing wrong with letting others make this sacrifice."

"My father wouldn't think so," Ely said, her eyes downcast.

The Wharfmaster grunted. "No, he wouldn't, but your father's a man who doesn't know the end of duty. They killed his wife, and to this day he still goes to war for them. Why? Because that's what he's supposed to do, and it will never be over for him until he's dead."

"You're still here too, aren't you?" Ely pointed out. "You're still doing their work, just like him."

The Wharfmaster shuffled his feet a bit. "Well, we do what we know, I 'spect. What good would I be doing anything else?" He paused. "I don't do it for them, that much is truth."

He lowered the casting rope and looked out at the open water. "Workin' by the sea reminds me of her. Could you really expect a man to give that up?"

"No," Ely said, standing and retying the pouch about her waist securely. "I couldn't."

The Wharfmaster looked at her out of the corner of his eye. "You do be growin' into a woman a lot like your mum. She was a serious one too, and smart. Lots of ambition."

Ely flushed a bit. "I don't have much ambition," she mumbled. "Otherwise I'd be married or apprenticed by now."

The Wharfmaster raised his eyebrows at her. "'Tis your father that says that, no?" He chuckled and shook his head. "He always did have both too much sense and not enough, if you get my meaning. If I were a betting man, I'd wager the shirt off my own back against him on that one, and I hardly know ye'." Ely flushed again at his words.

"Ambition ain't all there is to life, though, no sir," he added. "Yer mum was a fine woman, and no one could say different, but she could have used a touch more joy in her days. She could have laughed a bit more. After all, you never know how much time for merrymaking you got left."

The two of them stared out over the water in silence.

"Speaking o' which," he said, looking up at the angle of the afternoon sun, "we had best be headin' back. I got me some practicing to do."

"Practicing?" Ely said.

The Wharfmaster nodded proudly, pointing at his chest with his thumb. "Yer looking at the entertainment for tonight's celebration at the Keep. I got to get my fingers limbered up and my sea drum in tune, you know. You like the sea drum?"

Ely made a neutral sound.

"O' course you do," the Wharfmaster said. "Yer mum liked the sea drum. Everybody likes the sea drum. I hate to cut short our fishin', but I wouldn't want to disappoint the crowds. I expect I'll see you there tonight?"

Ely shrugged. She still did not fancy the idea of weathering any throngs, merrymaking or otherwise. Not today. "Maybe," she said.

The Wharfmaster put a large, heavy hand on her shoulder. "Just because you ain't got family don't mean you got to be alone, Elymia," he said. "I'm sure your friends would miss you if you weren't there. And how's about I play a special tune, just for you? There was one your mum did like a lot. I'll be sure to play it when I see you there."

Ely looked down at the water to hide the trembling corners of her smile and the moisture that had suddenly decided to condense in her eyes. She would like that, she realized. She would like that very much.

•••••

After the main event, the remainder of the Dedication ceremonies took place indoors, under the high ceiling of the Falls Gate cathedral. The interior of the ancient structure did not suggest to Donvin that any sort of Masked worship normally took place there. In fact, none of the stained glass or statuary that filled the grand chapel depicted the Masked at all. Instead, a wide array of sculptures of men and beasts lined the walls, each given its own alcove where worshipers could light candles or leave small offerings. The pantheon they represented was diverse, comprised of effigies both familiar and foreign. Among them, Donvin recognized but a few: the Hunter-on-the-Wind, the embodiment of wanderlust and the seeker's patron, and the Dark Maiden, the woman-as-man who rejected motherhood and choose destruction over creation, the patron of unwed women and female soldiers.

Yet more prominent than any of the other deities, engraved upon each of the support pillars and depicted in a massive statue behind the main altar, was a many-armed leviathan of the sea, in various portrayals supporting countless things upon the tips of its upturned arms. At the base of the great statue was an inscription:

On his arms I am lifted, and by his arms I shall sink;
From his arms I am gifted, with life beyond my years.

It seemed evident to Donvin that these people lived with two separate, parallel faiths: one of abstract gods, and another of practical reverence for their living guardians, the Masked, practiced only rarely.

Donvin's mentor spoke from behind the altar to a crowd which packed the chapel from wall to wall. The people were largely still and quiet, a marked change from the excitement during the Dedication display of the Masked's power. Children made up a greater portion of this audience, many staring with mouths agape at the gemstone born from the people's offerings that glittered silently upon the altar.

"Honored people of Falls Gate, we address you now in the shadow of the Deep One," Donvin's mentor intoned, gesturing behind him to the looming, many-armed statue. "It is fitting that we speak to you here, in his house, for he is perhaps the best symbol of the message we bring to you and the faith we ask you to remember and keep."

Donvin's mentor turned around and joined the congregation in gazing up at the smooth stone of the leviathan's towering visage.

"He is many, and he is one," Donvin's mentor continued, turning back to the audience. "He occupies the darkest depths, lifting us above them even as he sacrifices to them his own body. Your people have had a special kinship to the Deep One for as long as this city has stood, and you understand his ways better than any in all of Altissara. Listen, then, and believe, when we tell you that we of the Mask also live our lives in the way of the Deep One. We too are his kindred."

By their shifting postures and attentiveness, Donvin took it that the crowd was intrigued by this idea.

"We are many," Donvin's mentor said, gesturing to Donvin, Furrow, and himself, "and we are one." He touched the cheek of his bark mask with a finger. "We stand vigilant against the forces that would ravage this world, even as we must give the whole of our lives to fighting them. Just as the Deep One has arms to lift the righteous and unrighteous alike, so too we preserve the faithful and the faithless alike."

"But the Deep One is more than this," he went on. "He is also a symbol of family, of a unity of diverse parts. No arm is the whole, yet the whole would not be complete without every arm. His nature warns us against doing violence to one another, for living as we do upon the tips of his limbs, how are we to know that one who seems a stranger in this life is not, in the depths of his grace, connected closely to ourselves?"

Donvin's mentor took a breath. "To keep the pact that our peoples have made is good, but the pact is a thing of men, and in time the things of men grow weak, or corrupted, or forgotten. But though it is a thing of men, it holds within it the spirit of the Deep One, and carries but a simple message: as we are raised by his divine will, let us all be raised. As we are one in his heart, let us be one in our hearts. And as we all must be summoned back to his watery embrace in the deep, let us send each other on that final journey with compassion, not with hate. Remember these things, and our pact will never die. Hold them as truth, and this world will be safe forever."

His speech concluded, Donvin's mentor stepped down to stand in front of the altar with the other two Masked.

Donvin could appreciate the skill with which his mentor drew on these people's silly religion and used its language to gain their trust, but he cared little for the details of the sermon. What did it matter what they believed? They lived without care, neither understanding the true nature of the world they inhabited nor appreciating the cost of keeping that nature in check. Why were they worth the effort, when they were so fickle as to invent fanciful gods to worship when the true gods, the true source of their continued life, stood plainly before them?

But as mighty as they were, the Masked were not in fact gods, Donvin knew. Their powers were not infinite, and if Lith was right, the boundaries of their strength would all too soon be reached. He, on the other hand, was not so limited. Not only had Lith made him free, but she had also promised him a power even greater than that of the Masked. That memory of her promise awoke an intriguing thought in his mind: once the Masked were dead, as Lith wished, who would remain to protect the world but him? If he alone were all that stood between life and death, between existence and oblivion, would that not make him a god? Or, if these carved images were what passed for gods among these people, would he be something even greater?

Donvin looked with disdain at the upturned faces of the people of Falls Gate. It would not be for them, certainly, that he would preserve the world when that duty fell to him. They certainly did not deserve it. No, they were significant only to the extent that they were able to serve his ends, for they did little else of use with their lives. And they *would* serve him, he thought, in their own way. Though they were not yet aware of it, that service had already begun.

If his mentor's brief speech had proven uninteresting, what followed was nothing short of deadening. The three Masked remained before the altar, Donvin doing his best to remain awake, while a parade of supplicants formed a line between the pews and came before them one by one, this time to ask instead of to offer. Every one of them, it seemed, was eager to blather on about this problem or that, one ailment or another, and when they had finished they were uniformly sent on their way with assurances that the Masked would watch over them, their families, their businesses, their property, their city, and their great uncle Hobb's stubbed toe. The only thing that kept Donvin conscious through the monotony was his knowledge that, thanks to last night's secret work, things were soon sure to get quite a bit more interesting.

At long last, as the light in the cathedral's multicolored windows was growing dim with the coming of dusk, the thing that he had been waiting for arrived. Donvin recognized it as soon as the man knelt before them to make his plea: his eyes were watery, his breath strained, and he moved slightly hunched over. A few small spots of wine decorated the front of his velvet jacket.

"For my wife," the man said, looking at their feet and wheezing. "For my wife to . . . for . . . please bless . . . wife . . . ." Then he clutched his stomach and vomited a smelly liquid mess onto the polished floor of the cathedral. Donvin stepped back just in time to avoid having his moccasins soiled. The ill man fell over on his side and started shivering violently, his arms and legs pulled in close to his body.

The supplicants in line behind the convulsing man drew back from the nauseating spectacle, aghast. This too pleased Donvin. He had chosen symptoms frightening enough to spark the fear of contagion, and it seemed his alterations to the wine were working well.

"Someone help him!" a woman in line cried, though making no move to do so herself. "I think he's dying!"

Donvin scoffed behind his mask. How overly dramatic these people could be. A true plague with all its messy deaths would only interfere with his plans. This was something far more subtle. The symptoms would indeed be terrifying, but they would not prove fatal. They would last only as long as was necessary.

Furrow knelt down and touched the sickly man's face with both hands. The shivering intensified.

"He appears to be getting worse," Furrow said.

"Save him!" the same woman among the other supplicants called out to the Masked. "Please, you must save him!" Similar cries were quickly taken up by the others.

Furrow looked up at Donvin's mentor for guidance, and he received a shake of the head in return. Donvin knew what they were thinking. The Masked did not heal the sick. That was not their purpose, nor was it an approved use of their power.

"Go on, do something!" another voice shouted as the shaking man contorted in the throws of a deep, wet cough. Pinkish spittle dripped from his lips and united with the vomit on the floor. The voices in the crowd were rising in intensity and in tones of panic, and Donvin judged that this was the proper time to make his suggestion, before things got completely out of hand.

"We have to heal him," he said quietly, placing a hand on his mentor's shoulder.

"That is against our code," the masked man said, but the convulsions taking place at his feet had done their work, and the words came without their usual conviction. Furrow too shook his head, although not without a moment of hesitation.

"Of course," Donvin said, sensing victory close at hand. "But if we do not, what will these people think of us? It would be like we killed him ourselves. All our work here today will be undone, and more. They might even blame our presence for sickening him in the first place. You know the things they say our coming portends."

Donvin could almost see his mentor's mind working behind his featureless mask, but he knew the outcome well before acknowledgement came from the other man's mouth. All rules were subject to breaking, under the right circumstances. How easy it was, when he controlled those circumstances, to induce the Masked to break theirs.

"Very well," Donvin's mentor said, nodding to Furrow. "Do it."

Furrow delayed briefly, but it was clear that he too realized the potentially dangerous situation that they were in. "If we must," he said quietly before reaching out with silver threads of power and sending them into the sick man's body, feeling out and annihilating those things within that did not belong. It took hardly any time at all, for Donvin had not intended the poisoning to be difficult to cure. Moments later, the man's frantic shivering subsided.

Almost on cue, there was a scream as a second supplicant, this time a woman, collapsed in a quivering heap about halfway between the altar and the door. Donvin did his best to emulate the confusion that the other Masked were genuinely feeling. They hurried to her and performed the same healing, much to the relief of those onlookers who were still standing. Everything was proceeding exactly as Donvin had imagined.

No sooner had this second victim been healed than a frantic voice calling for help from outside the open doors drew their attention. When the Masked emerged onto the steps outside, they saw that at least three people had collapsed in the square below, their twitching casting horrible shadows in the light of the lamps that ringed the plaza. Donvin could tell that neither his mentor nor Furrow relished violating the code of the Masked, but both realized that now that they had begun, there was no turning back.

"Is this some kind of epidemic?" Furrow wondered aloud.

"It may well be," Donvin said, false concern dripping from his voice. "If it's happening here, it must be happening elsewhere in the city too. We'll get to the victims faster if we split up." That would serve quite well to distract the other Masked from his activities for a time, certainly long enough to retrieve his disguise from the inn and make his way to the Keep.

This time, consensus was easy to obtain – now that the prohibition on healing had been broken, it was the only logical thing to do. Unlike the other two Masked, however, Donvin knew exactly where he was going when he departed the cathedral square, and it was most definitely not to heal the sick.

Chapter 11

The Player and His Instrument

The great hall of Cliffhome Keep was more bustling for the post-Dedication celebration than Ely had seen it in years, filled with the light of hundreds of candles that easily repulsed the growing darkness outside. In the center of the floor, a space had been cleared for dancing to the deep, pulsing sounds of the Wharfmaster's sea drum. He was a gifted musician, and he plucked at the strings on the driftwood neck more nimbly than seemed possible for his thick, salt-toughened fingers. The body of the instrument, a mollusk shell so heavy that it had to rest on the floor while the Wharfmaster stood behind it, echoed the vibrations of the sinew with powerful, undulating tones.

"He never misses a chance to haul out that dreadful old thing, does he?"

Ely turned her eyes from the Wharfmaster to find Tamalina standing by her side. Meticulously curled ringlets of dark hair framed her face, which was squinting as if she were sucking on something sour.

"It's . . . rustic," Ely said as the tune quickened, and the dancers with it.

"It sounds like a turtle, if turtles could sing. And I'm glad they can't," Tamalina said dismissively. "But I suppose that with enough wine, anything sounds passable."

That reminded Ely of the glass in her hand, half full of a wine that was newborn-pink and painfully fragrant. She did not much care for drinks so potent, but she had a feeling she might need it if the Wharfmaster did not tire soon. Clearly she did not enjoy the sea drum as much as her mother.

Tamalina looked at Ely, then blinked.

"What a beautiful comb!" she exclaimed, standing on her tiptoes to peer at the back of Ely's head. "Why have I not seen you wear this before?"

Ely touched the knot of hair that was secured by the white bone comb to check its placement.

"It was my mother's," she said solemnly. "I don't wear it out much." Not at all, in fact, before today. Yet after her conversation with the Wharfmaster, Ely had thought it appropriate that night, even if it did feel a touch shameful to be displaying the very item she had failed to offer in the Dedication ceremony.

"Oh, but you should," Tamalina glowed. "It makes you look so mature, but in a subtle way, I think. I would have chosen some matching earrings, of course, but still . . . ."

Not one who had ever been comfortable having her appearance analyzed, Ely did her best to change the subject.

"I haven't seen your sister about," she said, snatching at the first observation that popped into her head. It was indeed rare to see Tamalina without Eomila close behind.

Tamalina rolled her eyes. "Yes, well, Aunt Evana hasn't been home since yesterday, and Eomila, the baby that she is, is busy worrying herself sick. I told her, 'Eomila, our aunt counts taxes for a living. It would be strange if she did come home on the Dedication.' But no, why should she mind her elder sister?"

Tamalina's face took on a disgusted look. "I swear, now that everyone knows she was the one who painted that ugly bug for the ceremony, she seems to have gotten it in her head that she knows better than I do. Can you imagine?" She scoffed. "Now she's managed to get Mother worked up about Evana's 'disappearance' too, and they've both gone out looking for her. At least father had the good sense to tell them they were overreacting." She ended the story with a dramatic sigh.

Ely was taken aback. Eomila had been selected as the Dedication artisan? The choice was always kept secret until the unveiling at the ceremony, but it had never even occurred to Ely that it might be one of her friends. She wanted to bang her head against the wall at the sudden, deep pang of guilt that struck her. If only she had not skipped the ceremony, she would have been able to see what was surely Eomila's greatest work to date, yet now that chance was gone. She had always thought Eomila should get more recognition for her skill with a brush, and now she had managed to miss it when it finally happened.

Rather than let on her surprise, Ely nodded sympathetically. "Have you asked Remiana about your aunt?" she said. "Her mother and your aunt are friends, aren't they?"

"What is this?" Remiana appeared before them as if summoned by her name, smiling widely and dragging a uniformed man along by the arm. Her red silk gown rippled gracefully as she came to a halt in front of them, its shimmering waves pulling nearly as many eyes as its exceptionally low cut. "You would not be talking about me behind my back, would you?"

"It's nothing. My aunt has gone missing, that's all," Tamalina said with expertly practiced understatement, twirling a bit of hair between her fingers and rolling her eyes yet again for Remiana's benefit. "I don't suppose you know where she is?"

"Missing, on Dedication night?" Remiana gasped, giving Ely a sideways smile and a wink so forceful that it made her golden curls bounce. "I have not an inkling. Though I hope she is not doing anything . . . scandalous."

Remiana certainly seemed to be in a good mood, Ely thought. Perhaps she had been drinking, though unlike most of the people in the room, she held no glass in her hand. Then again, with the lengthy Dedication ceremonies over, did anyone need an excuse to be a bit giddy?

Tamalina snickered, switching instantaneously from mature, put-upon sister to impish co-conspirator. "Oh, I hope she is. And I hope mother catches her at it. That would make her high horse a little lower, wouldn't it?"

Remiana joined her in giggling, while Ely smiled politely and looked away. The man on Remiana's arm did the same, though his gaze seemed fixed somewhere farther off than the walls of the room.

"I don't believe we've been introduced," Ely said.

The man said nothing. Remiana patted his arm with her gloved hand.

"It is my fault, Elymia," Remiana said. "I borrowed him from my mother's bodyguard for the night so I could enjoy myself without unwanted male attention. He is under strict orders to say nothing, just to stand close, like so." She tugged him nearer so that their hips were almost touching. "The men here are not near bold enough to approach a woman with a man already at her side."

"An excellent idea," Tamalina said, nodding sagely. "A shame I didn't think of it before, I could certainly use it."

Don't flatter yourself, Ely wanted to say, but she kept her mouth shut. Tamalina was a fine person, assuming you could corner her alone, well away from anyone she thought was worth the effort of trying to impress. Otherwise, she had the unfortunate tendency to behave like a preening sap.

Ely examined the bodyguard again. He was good looking enough for the role, albeit in a frozen, dutiful sort of way. The military haircut and uniform were dead giveaways, but even if recognized for what he really was, a woman with a bodyguard was just as unappfroachable as one with a dance partner.

"Has it been working?" Ely asked.

"Oh, superbly," Remiana said with a grin as she glanced about the room. "I may consider employing him more often."

"Wouldn't that discourage any real suitors?" Ely said, raising an eyebrow.

Remiana just shrugged, an amused look on her face. "You would not be trying to marry me off and get rid of me now, would you? You would have to fight my mother for the privilege, and my mother is not known to lose. At anything."

Ely smiled a bit. "I have no delusions about my chances in that contest."

"Quite right, quite right," Tamalina interjected. "And speaking of your mother, I suppose I might as well ask her if she has seen Evana about. Is she here?" She touched her hair gingerly as she spoke. Ely imagined that talking to Oridine Aloise with mussed hair was something Tamalina probably had nightmares about.

"Yes, though I believe she is currently taking refuge from that . . . music," Remiana said, casting a glance over her shoulder toward the happily-strumming Wharfmaster. "I will take you, if you like."

"Please," Tamalina said. "Are you coming, Ely?"

Ely shook her head. "I think I'll just stay here." The music was indeed becoming grating, but an audience with the Aloise matriarch was not likely to be much better.

"Suit yourself," Tamalina said. "Oh, and now that the word about Eomila is out, I have been instructed to invite you to a party in her honor at our home tomorrow evening. I think it's all a bit much for one silly painting, but you had best come, else she will be dreadfully upset."

"I wouldn't miss it," Ely said, swallowing a lump of shame.

Remiana gave Ely a farewell nod, then led Tamalina and her silent bodyguard off toward the back of the hall. Ely waited no longer than it took for them to be out of sight to make her own exit, shunning the grand entryway and heading straight for one of the hall's narrower side doors. As nice as a stroll in the fresh air would have been, there would be just as many revelers out in the courtyard as in the great hall, which made the Keep's many hallways a better choice for getting away from the noise and bustle.

With the door shut firmly behind her, the pressure that had been building in her head began to ease. She was not, however, alone in her desire to escape the hubbub. There were plenty of other partygoers scattered about the halls, talking quietly in groups of two or three and taking advantage of the privacy that the great hall could not provide. Even their presence was more than Ely desired, but thankfully a minute or two of brisk walking and several turns chosen at random were enough to put her out of earshot of the worst of the noise. She took a flight of wide, curving steps up to the second floor and then on to the third, and found herself in a long passageway that ran along the outer wall of the Keep lined with tall, open casements.

A cool breeze swept through the corridor, soothing Ely's warm face and hands. Content at being able to hear the sounds of the great hall and the courtyard only faintly, she strolled down the line of windows until she found one not too badly stained by bird leavings and hoisted herself up on the broad stone sill. These third floor windows were not high enough to see over the Keep's curtain wall into the city outside, but that suited Ely just fine. Sitting with her back against one side of the frame and her feet against the other, she let her head roll back against the chilled stone, careful not to damage the comb in her hair, and closed her eyes, taking deep breaths in an attempt to rid her nostrils of the overpowering smell of wine. She had not realized how pungent it hung in the great hall until she could smell the fresh salt air of the sea again, and she resisted the urge to give the glass she still had a little flick and topple it out of the window. With so many people wandering about, it might well land on someone, and she was in no mood to explain why she was bombarding people with glassware.

It was altogether too peaceful, resting there in the window, and Ely was too eager to escape from the dull ache of guilt she felt at having shirked her responsibilities and missed her chance to share in Eomila's joyous day. Sleep laid its soft, comforting hands upon her before she even noticed its approach.

Yet sleep's caress did not linger. It was startled away suddenly by someone brushing past where Ely lay, close enough for the breeze of the movement to still be tingling on her face as she jerked awake. She looked up and down the corridor, blinking to clear her vision but hampered by the milky mix of shadows and moonlight that grayed everything in the hall to a perfect monochrome.

There was no one there, and Ely let out her breath. She had almost returned to her original, relaxed position when she saw out of the corner of her eye the flicker of faint, yellow light. Turning her head again, she saw that it was coming from beneath a door just across the hall from where she sat. Had it been there the whole time?

Turning in place, Ely hopped down from the ledge, collected her wine glass, and crossed the corridor to stand in front of the door. Light spilled onto her feet through the crack at its base, brighter now, as though torches had been lit on the other side. Shadows cast from within the room slipped under the door and entwined themselves about her legs, sharpening their points and edges in the brighter light. This part of the Keep was rarely used, and all of the doors had been kept locked for as long as Ely could remember, so she had scarcely any idea of what sort of room lay on the other side or who might have use for it. Curiosity got the better of her, and she gave the door a slight nudge with her toe, hoping to crack it just enough to peek inside. Instead, the door swung wide open, washing away her vision in a deluge of light.

Ely raised a hand to protect her eyes, peering out from a slit between her fingers. The room was bigger than she had expected, though not exactly large. Three shallow steps led down onto the flat stone floor of the rectangular space, which contained several rows of shelves stacked with books. Oil-burning lamps hung along the walls, their flames safely contained in thick glass housings. Toward the front of the room stood a long table attended by several scattered chairs, and in one of them sat a man giving her the most irritable look.

"And you are?" he said in a near-growl.

Ely slowly lowered the hand from her eyes as her vision adjusted more fully to the light. The man's voice sounded strange, blurred by an accent that was unfamiliar to her. Nor was that the only strange thing about him: he was dressed in stableman's leathers, an unusual sight in itself here in the Keep, but beneath the table she could also see his feet were covered by some sort of moccasins rather than boots.

Suspicions aroused, Ely ignored his question. "I think you are the one who should be explaining yourself," she said in her best imperious voice. "On whose authority are you here?"

The man gave her a long, probing look with unnervingly dark eyes. He was young, Ely realized, younger than he had seemed at first, for the scowling wrinkles aged his face significantly. She could see him carefully taking in the sight of her now-crumpled dress, the strands of hair that had come loose from her knotted braids, and the full wine glass in her hand. His gaze was uncomfortably searching, and it lasted longer than Ely would have liked. Then, abruptly, he pushed back his chair and stood.

"I meant no disrespect, my lady," he said cordially. "I was sent by Stablemaster Gillibardo to fetch several books back to the stables." His demeanor was different, suddenly. The tightness around his eyes was gone, his youthfulness more apparent. Ely suspected he might even be a year or two younger than she.

"Books, to the stables?" Ely's voice was incredulous. She knew Master Gill to be fond of his leisure, but he had never seemed much interested in books. Descending the few steps from the open doorway, Ely stopped in front of the table. Several volumes were stacked on it in a messy pile, but they were uniformly in shambles, with their covers in various stages of rot. "What use does Master Gill have for these old things?"

The stable boy shook his head and shrugged. "I don't know, my lady. I'm just a stable hand."

"And your name?" Ely asked.

"Keth," he replied, adding a belated, "my lady."

It was a plain name, Keth, but it sounded vaguely familiar. Perhaps he really was just a stable hand on an errand, but Ely still couldn't shake her suspicion that something was amiss. "Would you mind telling me what books you're looking for?" she asked.

Keth did not respond immediately. Instead, he just stared curiously at the wine glass in her hand. When his gaze did finally rise to meet hers, he was smiling.

"Of course, my lady. But if I may have the pleasure of your name?" His demeanor had shifted again. His smile was wide and earnest, and a teasing spark had come into his eyes, youthful innocence replaced by practiced playfulness. The suddenness of the transition was disconcerting, but even so, Ely couldn't help but notice how much more handsome his face was when it wore a smile.

"My name is Elymia Celundine," she said, "though I prefer Ely." She put a hand to her mouth, surprised. She had not intended to let him address her so familiarly, but the name had just slipped out.

"Well, Mistress Ely, it would be my pleasure to show you what I'm looking for, though you mustn't hold it against me if you find it boring." Keth gestured for her to come around to his side of the table. When she had, he drew close and produced from his pocket a strip of paper covered in messy scrawl, though the letters were not in any script Ely recognized.

"These are the titles," Keth said, placing the paper on the table and running his finger vertically down the lines of characters. "And these," he said, moving his finger over, "are descriptions."

Ely leaned over the paper, confused. "What language is this? Can you read it?" It perplexed her that, despite considering herself well read, she had never seen writing like this.

Keth nodded. "It is the writing of my people."

She wanted to ask if this was some sort of joke, some way to make fun of people with little learning, but Keth's eyes, now so dark and delightfully entrancing, sucked away her desire to do anything but nod.

He pulled the top book off the stack and set it down beside the list. A few black flakes fell from the peeling covers where his fingers touched the binding.

"See? The title is the first one on the list. " He took Ely's hand and placed it on the letters that were pressed into the book's cover. The touch was wholly inappropriate, given her rank, but it sent a thrill up her entire arm nonetheless. She was not one to get easily flustered by men, but for some reason Keth's closeness was making her heart beat at an increasing rate, and his eyes . . . .

Desperate to break free from the inexplicable spell that was falling over her, Ely grasped the first book that her fingers could reach and knocked it onto the floor between herself and Keth, only hoping the act did not look too obviously intentional. Thankfully, the azure binding of this book was in better shape than that of the first, and it survived the fall unharmed.

"I'm sorry," Ely said, the fluster in her voice only half faked. "That was careless of me."

"Not at all," Keth replied, mercifully turning his ensorcelling eyes from her and releasing her hand as he bent to collect the fallen volume. "These books have endured far worse than that, I should think, though this one seems well off by comparison. It must not have been read often, this 'Eset Dolmon-'" Keth's words stopped abruptly, as if in surprise, and he stared down at the book in his hands.

"What does it mean?" Ely asked, her curiosity aroused at his odd behavior.

"Nothing important," Keth said, rising and turning that disarming smile on her again. "I must have taken this one from the shelf by mistake. I too can be careless sometimes." He reached for her hand again.

"You were not born here, then, if this is your language?" Ely said, needlessly adjusting the comb in her hair in order to avoid his touch.

"You are very perceptive," Keth said, letting his hand fall. "My family lies far away from here, and it was such a shame they could not come for the Dedication. What about your family, Mistress Ely?" He tapped his fingertips on the surface of the table lightly, as if putting points on his words.

His voice was so sweet, Ely thought, while at the same time shaking her head and backing up a step to remain out of reach. Her heart was racing, despite her attempts to control it.

"My father . . ." she said, beginning to answer his question. She wanted to answer, though she was not sure why. "My father is the only family I have. He could not come home. He commands our northern armies still in the field . . . ."

"Oh?" Keth said, cocking his head. "Then you must be very important, as the daughter of such a great man? People must attend you, and listen when you speak? You must have powerful friends who would give heed to your advice? Don't be modest." His fingers tapped upon the tabletop impatiently.

Ely flushed. Her tongue paid little heed to her will. "I . . . I suppose . . . . Some might think that I am . . . ."

"Excellent," Keth said. His fingers stopped their drumming abruptly.

The fog around Ely's thoughts began to clear, and she backed away a few more steps. The heat that had risen in her cheeks dissipated, and she straightened her back, struggling for what composure she could muster. Keth was no longer even looking at her, and instead he had turned his attention back to the list on the table, as if he had gotten from her whatever it was he was after.

"I must be going," Ely said awkwardly, continuing to back away. Even with his eyes focused elsewhere, something warned her against turning her back on this man.

"I understand," Keth said with a nod, still not bothering to look up. "The party is still going on below, if you care to return to it." His voice had lost its alluring quality and was now just flat, almost bored. He settled back into the chair he had risen from and opened the book in his hands.

Ely strained her ears, but in the enclosed space she could not make out any sounds outside the room. Unsure of what to say, she elected simply to make her exit as quickly as her feet would take her to the door.

The whole encounter had left her feeling oddly drained, and as she mounted the steps to the door Ely recalled the glass of wine still in her hand. Her throat was suddenly parched, and for the first time she was glad she had kept it with her. She moved to raise it to her lips, but partway through the motion the glass seemed to twitch. It wrenched free from her grasp, toppling to the floor and shattering into a hundred fine, crystalline fragments. The pink wine puddled amidst the shards and began to drip slowly down the steps.

Ely stared at her empty hand, then down at the floor. Perhaps she was more shaken than she thought. Perhaps the quivering that she felt in her hands had begun before she had dropped the glass, not after. Perhaps.

Ely slipped out of the room with one backward glance at the man called Keth. He had not even bothered to look up at the sound of the breaking glass, yet his fingers were tapping on the cover of his book in time with the drops of wine as they dribbled down the steps and splattered to a final resting place at the bottom.

Tap. Tap. Tap. Tap.

•••••

When the woman had gone, Lith reemerged from the rows of books. "I did not think you were the type to leave witnesses. She has seen you without your mask."

Donvin closed the book with the blue binding and tossed it casually back with the others, face-down so that Lith could not see its title. The chair scraped loudly on the floor as he stood. "And I did not think our arrangement required me to justify my every action to you," he replied. "I found the books. Beyond that, I will do as I wish."

"I know you will," Lith said with a smirk. "It is one of your best qualities. I trust you have some use for that woman in mind. But do not forget, in your eagerness to play with the locals, that you still have one more task here."

"I have not forgotten." Donvin pulled the envelope from his vest and waved it dismissively over his shoulder. It would be impossible for him to forget such an important thing. Too bad that he would not be able to stay to witness the delicious chaos that it would soon trigger. That was the trouble with plans: one always had to be thinking of the future rather than enjoying the fruits of the present.

Donvin rounded the table and strode over to where the fragments of a once-fine wine glass lay scattered on the ground. He knelt to pick up a piece of something small and white, something he had used his threads of power to break in addition to the goblet of poisoned drink.

"Taken to collecting souvenirs, have you?" Lith said.

"In a manner of speaking," Donvin replied with only the hint of a smile, tucking the comb tooth safely into the black silk pouch that hung around his neck.

Chapter 12

Truth, of a Sort

A light breeze rustled the reddening leaves of the canopy overhead, pulling loose a few of the driest in a sign of autumn's tightening grip. For the Masked, the changing of the seasons signaled an intensified gathering and preserving of food in preparation for winter, an activity that spread many of them far and wide from their camp for much of the day. Their absence made it easy for Donvin to enter Boulder's hut unseen.

"Welcome!" Boulder said warmly, setting aside the patch of hide that he had been scraping as Donvin ducked through the low opening. "How went the Dedication in Falls Gate? Rumor has it there was an outbreak of illness. Nasty stuff, they say."

There was barely room for the two of them to sit comfortably on the ground in the tiny space, but the hut afforded a barrier against prying eyes that the woods outside did not.

"That's true," Donvin said carefully. It had only been a single day since he, Furrow, and his mentor had returned from Falls Gate, but already the story of what had transpired there had spread among the Masked. As yet, none had treated it as anything other than an unfortunate coincidence. With any luck, it would stay that way.

"Regrettably, we had to use our powers to prevent it from disrupting the ceremonies," Donvin continued. He scrutinized Boulder's body language as he spoke, looking for hints of sympathy or disapproval, but the other man's opinion was not nearly so hard to read.

Boulder nodded knowingly. "It was the right decision. Sometimes the rules must be bent for the greater good."

"My thoughts exactly," Donvin said with a hidden smile. He had suspected Boulder would see things his way. With that confirmed, it should not prove too difficult to drive the wedge between him and the Masked's doctrine a little deeper.

Donvin's head scraped the ceiling of the hut as he shifted, reaching into his furs and producing two of the books he had taken from the old Cliffhome Keep library.

"Are you able to read these?" he asked. It was just a ploy, of course. Lith was perfectly capable of translating them, and she had already examined the first of the pair to her satisfaction. There were several other books Donvin had pilfered from the Keep on Lith's instructions, most of them filled with pictures that needed no translation, but they were to serve a far different purpose, and Donvin had safely hidden them within a hollow stump deep in the forest. The second book he presented to Boulder, on the other hand, was Donvin's idea alone. He had snuck it from the Keep's library without Lith's knowledge, and he preferred to find someone else who could tell him what knowledge was locked away within.

Boulder leaned forward in the dim light and peered at the ancient-looking books, one bound in brown and the other in blue.

"The old scholar's script of Paviar! Not a real language at all, actually, just a transliteration of a predecessor dialect of our own tongue. It certainly is unusual to see books written in it any more . . . . Where did these come from?" he said, his mask pointing back up at Donvin.

"The people of Falls Gate offered them to us as tribute, but it was too late to include them in the Dedication," Donvin lied. "It would have been rude to refuse."

Boulder nodded, his gaze returning to the books. Donvin had been right about this as well. The explanation needed only the barest veil of plausibility to give Boulder's natural curiosity an excuse to take over. Now the books themselves would take care of the rest.

"Ah! This one is the Endelune o nes Byssus," Boulder said, picking up the first, more decayed of the two volumes and cracking its brown covers carefully. "An old treatise, very old, and even this one is likely a fifth or sixth copy from an original. It's not particularly rare, however. One or two could be found in any respectable library, though its contents are no longer taken seriously by modern thinkers."

Donvin frowned behind his mask. Why would Lith have suggested that he show Boulder such a common book? "What is it about?" he asked.

"The title means 'An Examination of the Nature of the Byssus,'" Boulder said, flipping back to the cover and pointing to the depressed lettering. "That about sums it up, really."

"What is a . . . Byssus?" Donvin asked, the odd word feeling strange on his tongue, a problem that Boulder did not seem to have.

"Well that is the big question, isn't it?" Boulder said, and Donvin could hear a smile in his rumbling voice. "In times long past, people were quite concerned with the precise ways in which the world worked and what exactly it was made of. Obsessed, one might say. As a result, they wrote many books about what forces drove the events they witnessed: why rivers flowed, or why some birds could not fly despite having wings, or what made gold soft and iron hard, for metals were not so scarce in those days. This is one of those books."

Boulder cleared his throat. "But that is a digression; the question was about the Byssus. According to the theory laid out here, a Byssus is a sort of fiber, invisible to the eye, that covers every object in the world. It is by the tangling and untangling of these fibers that matter interacts as it does. Most people today, however, would consider that baseless speculation, no different than many of the other theories back then."

"They make matter interact? How?" Donvin said, trying figure out what about this conversation Lith had thought would be helpful to him.

Boulder thought for a moment, and then he placed the book back on the dirt floor between them. After a second or two of waiting, he said, "Why is the book still on the ground? Why isn't it floating in the air? Why didn't it slide out the door?"

Donvin shrugged. This book was just to get Boulder talking, he surmised, or to remind him of his life before the mask. From the way he spoke, it sounded as if he might once have been one of those "modern thinkers" he had mentioned.

"According to the book," Boulder continued, "it is because the book's Byssi and the ground's Byssi are tangled up with one another, and this entanglement prevents the book from drifting away. The same principle acts upon all things, even people's bodies. It is only through the push or pull of energy conveyed from one object's Byssi to another that the book, or anything else, can be moved."

"So why can't we see these fibers, if everything has them?" Donvin said.

Boulder chuckled. "Again with the big questions. It is precisely because they can't be seen that the theory has been mostly discounted. But, if one were to believe the book, this inability to observe them is because they are more of a concept than a physical thing. They are more like conduits or channels for energy than objects in their own right, paths along which energy could flow. In this way they can be said to connect all things, not just those close to one another like the book and the floor."

Again Boulder paused, formulating another example. "When one sees a hawk circling in the sky," he said, "does the air along the path it might choose to fly look any different from the air everywhere else? No. One path becomes visible when the hawk does fly upon it, but that does not change the fact that there were other paths it could have taken. The book compares these paths, these Byssi, to 'white roads' on which all forms of energy can travel from one object to another, white for their ability to carry all forms of energy just as white light carries all colors."

White roads . . . . Donvin had a sudden memory of the bridge of pure white stone he had crossed on the day he had received his mask. He thought of the silver, infinitely delicate yet powerful strands that obeyed his will. But as similar as they sounded, the comparison was not perfect: the portal created by Point had contained a tree, not a bridge, and those created by the other Masked often contained things equally bizarre and diverse. In fact, Donvin realized, the only times he had seen the white bridge were in the presence of his mentor.

"Our power," he said slowly, "does it come from these . . . Byssi? When we travel, is it these Byssi that serve as our roads?"

Boulder looked straight at Donvin. "It is just a theory," he said carefully. "It is not a thing within our doctrine, for questions such as 'why' or 'how' have no bearing on our work. However, there is one more piece of evidence to consider before judging the theory's validity. The book also claims that all the uncountable number of Byssi attached to all the uncountable number of objects in the world form a web of innumerable intersections. Once this web was small and infinitely compact, but as time passed and matter separated into the universe as it exists today, the web of Byssi connecting it all grew larger and more complex. The book imagines the shape of the web through time as a tree, with its beginnings as a tiny seed and its present and future as an infinitely expanding web of branches. It calls this tree 'Byssalion.'"

"What sort of evidence is that?" Donvin said, confused.

"The book claims," Boulder continued in a low voice, "that the Byssi do not simply connect one object to another across space, but that they also connect each object to itself through time, from one instant to the next. This is how a stone that is hot now will still be hot a moment from now – the heat passes from the stone in the past to the stone in the future along the Byssus that connects its past self to its future self. In the absence of such connections, causes would have no effect, and the past no influence on the future." Boulder paused, allowing his words to sink in. "This also means that, theoretically, if one could control the Byssi, energy could travel backward in time just as easily as it naturally flows forward, appearing to those who witness its arrival as if it were simply created from thin air."

Boulder stopped, crossing his arms and tucking his chin as he stared down at the book between them. Donvin realized suddenly that he had been reciting all of this from memory, for he had hardly even opened the book at all.

"The appeal of the notion is easy to see," Boulder said. "Seemingly limitless energy at one's beck and call . . . . What man would not be tempted by the possibility? Yet such an extraordinarily unnatural act as manipulating the Byssi would of course have consequences. It would create a breach in the order of the future from which the energy was extracted, a place where the normal laws are reversed, a point where energy coalesces rather than disperses as it begins to be drawn backward in time."

"A breach," Donvin said, suddenly making the connection. "You mean the kind we fight."

Boulder nodded. "Yes, if one subscribes to the theory. But it does seem to fit quite well, does it not? We have used our power to contain the breaches for millennia, but they never stop coming. In fact, they only multiply with each passing year. Why? Because the power we use to fight them is the very same one that creates them."

Drawing energy from the future . . . . Was that what those silver threads truly did? "Then why not stop?" Donvin asked. "If the- if we ceased to use our power, then the breaches would cease as well."

Boulder shook his head. "It is not that simple. Even if we were to stop, the breaches would continue. The ones we fight now were born long ago, and those we create today may not be felt for thousands of years. It is too late to simply let them run their course and hope to survive it. We would not. Nor would anything living in this world."

It has been too late for a long time, Lith's voice whispered in Donvin's ear, making him jump slightly. He looked about, but he could see no hint of her in the tiny, enclosed space. Then he remembered the small metal sculpture hidden away within his furs.

Boulder interpreted Donvin's jerk as one of shock. "Fear not," he said, his voice taking on a lighter tone. "We are not on the brink of calamity just yet. Though they are indeed growing stronger, we still have the strength to combat them for some time."

If only he knew how little time remained, Lith whispered. If only he had been there to witness the source of what is coming, he would know how futile their efforts against it would be.

"But they will eventually overwhelm us," Donvin said uneasily.

Boulder sighed. "If one believes all of this, then the answer is yes. It would also mean believing that our mission is pointless, one that was doomed from the very start. There are many among us who find that thought . . . uncomfortable. So instead of searching for the truth, we rely on tradition to protect us in our ignorance, and carry out our tasks without the burden of disquieting questions."

"What about you?" Donvin asked, finally seeing the reason for the conversation. "What do you believe?"

Boulder was silent for what seemed like a long time, choosing his words carefully before speaking. "Evidence is more important than belief," he said finally. "And the evidence that we are only contributing to the eventual end of all things is too strong to ignore as we have been doing for so long. If that is truly why we exist, merely to postpone an inevitable end, then so be it. But we should not be afraid to question, as some are, the methods we have relied upon for generations for no reason other than tradition."

"You mean we should be seeking a way to stop the cycle, a different way to protect the world?" Donvin probed.

Boulder shook his head glumly. "That is nothing but wishful thinking. Perhaps a way to save Altissara exists, but of all people, we are the least capable of finding it. We have lost much since those ancient times when our power was free to all, not hoarded by only a few. It might be true that such freedom was what set us on this road to destruction, but it might also have contained the spark of our salvation if not for our forbearers, who thought they knew better. Whatever the case, we of the mask are incapable of changing the course of the future because we refuse to understand our own nature. Without knowing even that, how can we possible recognize the choice, if it exists, that would lead us to a better end than the one that approaches?" Boulder's voice was full of sadness, and Donvin decided it would be better not to press him on what was becoming an increasingly grim topic.

"What about this other book?" Donvin said, indicating the one with the blue binding.

"Hmm, let us see," Boulder said, perking immediately up as he remembered the other gift that Donvin had brought him. He set the first book aside and gingerly picked up the second, less damaged one.

"This one is unfamiliar. 'Eset Dolmon' – that would be 'The Beginning of Service,' roughly translated." Boulder gingerly turned the dusty blue cover aside, translating slowly as he read. "Part One – Birth from Death-!"

He grunted with recognition. "Ah, this is a book on the Dolmon legend. In that case, a better translation of the title would be 'Born a Servant.'"

Someone has been telling you things that you are not ready to hear, Lith's voice whispered bemusedly. I did not ask you to retrieve that book. It will be of no use to you.

"What is the Dolmon legend?" Donvin asked defiantly. He had known that he would not be able to keep the book from Lith forever, but she had no right to lurk about and intrude on his private dealings. Who was she to say what was or was not for him to know?

"It's an older tale. Grim stuff, if memory serves," Boulder said, flipping through the pages. "Not many illustrations in this edition, gods be praised."

I'm warning you, Lith's voice whispered. Put the book away. This is not the time.

"What's wrong with illustrations?" Donvin pressed, ignoring her.

"Quite frankly, they're sickening," Boulder said, searching out a particular page and then handing the book to Donvin. Taking up most of it was a pen-and-ink sketch of a man cutting strips of flesh from the body of a struggling victim. A cooking pot was featured prominently in the foreground. "It's hard to believe stories like this were once told to children."

Put it away, Lith whispered, or you will regret it.

"Cannibalism?" Donvin said, contemplating the picture. Even though it lacked color, the artist had left no doubt as to what all those puddles and smears of ink were meant to be.

"Ritual cannibalism of the living, actually," Boulder said with distaste. "Even today, some primitives think that sort of vile practice serves some purpose. Thankfully, most cultures have evolved beyond-"

There was a scratching at the hut's entry flap. A second later, it opened partway, and a masked face thrust its way inside. From its smell, Donvin instantly recognized the owner as Bird.

"A word?" Bird said in a low tone. The request was clearly directed at Donvin, and there was no way he could have missed the open book in Donvin's lap.

Donvin hesitated, thinking on how he might be able to refuse, but Boulder made a shooing motion with his hands. "Go on, no doubt there are more important tasks to be about. It's no bother."

Donvin nodded reluctantly, and the masked face withdrew from the hut, leaving the flap swinging in its wake. He closed the book in his hands. "Thank you for sharing your wisdom," he said.

"Of course," Boulder replied. "It's always a pleasure to have another inquisitive mind to speak to."

Donvin rose, his eyes flicking down as he did so to the first book he had brought, which had been shoved into a shadowed corner of the hut. He made no move to collect it, and Boulder did not protest his casual attempt to leave it behind. That was a very good sign.

After ducking outside, Donvin found Bird waiting for him just a few steps away.

"Welcome back," Bird said, stepping forward and extending his hand in greeting.

Donvin clasped it in his own, perplexed by the sudden attention from the man who often seemed too busy and aloof to socialize, but he was willing to play along.

Bird looked down at the blue binding of the book he carried.

"What is that?" he asked.

Donvin thought quickly. The Masked were not permitted possessions beyond their clothing, and the perfunctory excuse he had given to Boulder was not likely to suffice here.

"A book of history," Donvin said, modifying the lie for his new audience. "The people of Falls Gate believed it might be useful to us and presented it as an offering. I was just attempting to see if they were correct."

Bird held out his hand expectantly, and Donvin, not wanting to appear even slightly suspicious, surrendered the book immediately. Seemingly at random, Bird opened it – to the very illustration Donvin and Boulder had been examining.

Bird's voice grew lower. "And were they, in fact, correct?"

Donvin gave a little chuckle. "Of course not," he said. Bird was easy to read. He was a true believer, righteous to the core. His passion for the mask had been evident in the way he argued for the Dedication two months prior. It was not hard to figure out what he wanted to hear. "What purpose would it serve for us? We need no books to remind us of our heritage and our duties. I was just on my way to destroy it."

Bird nodded slowly. "Indeed," he said, "that is correct. Any gifts we receive must be promptly destroyed." Before Donvin could say anything in reply, he turned to the nearest fire pit and tossed the ancient book onto the warm coals. Yellow tongues leapt in excitement at their first taste of the bone-dry pages, and within seconds the covers, text, and bloody illustrations had all been completely devoured.

Bird brushed his hands together as if dusting off unwanted residue. "Now that that is taken care of, there is a more pressing topic we must discuss. Come, let us walk together."

"Oh?" Donvin said, fighting hard not to let the rage he felt filter through into his voice. All his hard work to get that book, and it was gone in so much ash. But he dared not speak out, dared not show even the barest hint of distress. As he himself had said, a faithful masked would care nothing for things such as books. He followed Bird as he strode between the trees, heading away from the cluster of huts. "What topic did you have in mind?"

"The poisoning in Falls Gate," Bird said.

"Poisoning?" Donvin said, hiding his twitch at hearing the word. This was unexpected, and could potentially be far worse than the loss of a single book. "There was a sickness, yes, but we don't know its origin. What makes you think it was poison?"

"Don't be so naive," Bird said harshly as he walked. "Things like this do not happen by mere coincidence. We have no shortage of enemies, those who have let their fear of what they do not understand turn to hate. They rarely organize or speak openly, but in their hearts they would like nothing better than to see the people of Altissara turn against us. Some would even go so far as to hurt their own kind to use the blame for it as a weapon. It has happened before."

Donvin frowned behind his mask. It would be better if he could convince Bird that there was no one behind what had happened at all. He did not need anyone thinking that there was a hidden truth out there waiting to be uncovered.

"But if this was a malicious act," he said, "surely it failed. The people of Falls Gate thanked us for our aid rather than blaming us for their ills. Would our detractors really have made it so easy to turn an attack to our advantage?"

Bird cupped the chin of his mask in one hand. "Yes, it's possible that they miscalculated, but then again, perhaps not. There were no deaths, at least as far as we know. Doesn't that seem odd? Our enemies would have killed as many as possible to provoke the greatest outrage, and even a natural disease would have killed at least one or two of its weakest victims, yet this ailment did not take a single life. It's almost as if it was intended to be stopped."

Donvin's hands began to sweat. "That is very odd," he agreed. "But there's nothing we can do about it now. Without knowing where the sickness started or how it spread, there is little to be done."

"Quite," Bird said. "But we can investigate nonetheless, and we will. With luck we may be able to turn up something that will lead to the source of the poison."

Donvin's fingers dug into his palms. "Is that really the best use of our time, chasing after what might not even have been poison at all?"

Bird patted him reassuringly on the shoulder. "It will not be so taxing a task for those of us with greater experience in these matters. We cannot afford to be anything less than fully vigilant against those who would do us harm. While it may not be our ultimate goal, we must still take every precaution to know our enemies and protect ourselves. We are Altissara's only guardians, and any threat against us is a threat against the world itself."

Donvin nodded, as if in understanding, but he was only just able to keep himself from grinding his teeth. He had enough to do already without having to worry about Bird poking around the places he had been. There was little he could do to stop it now, but he would have to make ready to remove any particularly meddlesome Masked from the picture if they came too close to discovering what he was up to. The spark for the fire that would consume the Masked would be struck tonight, in Falls Gate, but that did not mean the plan was secure. To the contrary, it meant he would have to work even harder to keep the Masked from interfering before the conflagration that would be their doom raged too strongly for them to stop.

Chapter 13

Sparks to Flames

A cloth banner hung over the opulent entryway of the Resposé home, painted with the words "Congratulations Eomila!" Ely gazed up at it uncomfortably while the butler took her coat. Clearly it was going to take longer than a single day for her guilt over missing Eomila's moment of glory to pass, though she hoped her presence at this dinner would at least begin to make up for it.

"This way to the dining hall, Miss Celundine," the butler said, making a beckoning gesture as if Ely had not been in the house a hundred times before. She followed him under one of the entryway's curving flights of stairs and into the expansive east wing of the house. Farther down the long hall, she immediately spotted Remiana and a tall, severe-looking woman with an identical shade of blonde hair walking in the opposite direction. Remiana was looking at the ground and so caught up in thought that she did not notice Ely until they were nearly on top of one another.

"Elymia, so nice to see you on this fine day after the Dedication," she said formally, but her smile was strained.

"And you," Ely said, making a precise curtsey, mindful of Remiana's mother's rank.

If something was disturbing Remiana to the point of distraction, her mother Oridine looked quite the opposite, the corners of her mouth drawn up in a thin smile that seemed genuine even if it did have to struggle awkwardly to gain purchase on a face that had clearly known far more frowns.

"Ah, Elymia," she said, eying Ely up and down with a businesswoman's valuating gaze. "It has been some time. You look very presentable." Coming from Oridine Aloise, Ely supposed that was actually intended as a compliment.

"I am afraid we only stopped by to give the young Eomila our good wishes, and we must be on our way," Oridine said, "but do enjoy yourself." She walked a few steps farther down the hall and then paused again, as if remembering something. "Oh, and Elymia," she said, "I expect you to continue to extend your friendship to my daughter."

Ely, caught off guard, stumbled over her reply. "Um . . . of course, Ma'am," she said. One did not question even the oddest statements of an iron family matriarch.

Remiana gave Ely a pained look, but said nothing.

Oridine's unnatural-looking smile deepened. "Come along, Remiana. Time is wasting."

Despite the command, Remiana lingered at Ely's side for a moment, allowing her mother to get a few paces ahead.

"That was a strange request," Ely said in a soft voice. "Anything I should know?" If she had to guess, she suspected this meant Oridine had finally chosen a husband for her daughter, and that in turn meant it would not be long before the two of them would depart back to the Craghorn. The thought of losing Remiana's company made her sad; despite her occasional harshness, Ely felt a kind of kinship with Remiana that she lacked with her other friends. She understood the realities of the world in a way that Ely admired.

Remiana gave Ely a long look, then shook her head.

"There is nothing," she said, swallowing hard and looking over Ely's shoulder as she said it instead of into her eyes. "Enjoy the party." Then she hurried off to catch up to her mother, her rust-colored dress swirling about her like a falling leaf in the wind. The two Aloise women disappeared into the entryway, Remiana trailing in a subservient fashion uncharacteristic of her usual boldness.

"The other guests have already arrived," the butler reminded Ely gently as she stood in the hallway and watched them go. The exchange left Ely with an uneasy feeling in her stomach, but whatever the cause of the Aloises' unusual behavior, it was not something to be resolved this night.

A bit farther on, the hall gave way to reveal a large, high-ceilinged room, the long oak table in the center surrounded by chairs of blackened wood. On the far side, a wall of windows looked out on house's gardens, which were planted with flowering trees and separated from the street by a half-height fence. Before the windows, a number of well-dressed men and women were standing about chatting, evidently waiting for the meal to be served.

No sooner had Ely set foot across the threshold than Matrice darted up and took her by the arm.

"There you are. A word of warning," she said in low tones close to Ely's ear. "I would not mention the Lady Evana in conversation if I were you. She still has not been found."

Ely made a sympathetic sound. This would mark the second day of Eomila's aunt's absence, which made it a more serious case than Tamalina had suggested last night. "Are they looking for her?" she asked.

"Mr. Resposé has been out since dawn doing just that," Matrice said, "but the family is trying not to let it ruin Eomila's day." She glanced at the back of Ely's head as she spoke. "Oh, that is an exceptional comb. Where did you get it?"

"Mother's," Ely said bluntly. She wished people would stop noticing.

Matrice nodded, knowing not to ask any more.

Ely reached up and touched the carved bone lightly. With her hair entwined about it, it was almost impossible to tell that it was now missing a tooth. She had discovered the damage upon returning home last night, and no amount of searching had turned up the lost piece. She had cried a little out of shame for breaking the one thing of her mother's that she still had, but in the end she had decided to wear it again. Something about what the Wharfmaster had said made her unable to bear the thought of just locking it back up in a drawer.

Scanning the room, Ely saw that most of the attention was centered on Eomila, who stood glowingly at the center of perhaps thirty admirers who were all trying to compliment her at the same time. The only person presently seated at the long table was Tamalina, who was looking decidedly worse for wear. She was wrapped in a plain brown blanket and sipping at a steaming teacup while glaring over the top at her sister's growing entourage. Ely walked around the table and took a seat next to her.

"Feeling all right?" Ely asked.

The twin rubies in Tamalina's ring flashed as she set down her cup. "I had a minor touch of the chills last night, that's all," she said dismissively, hardly looking over to meet Ely's eyes. "It's best to be cautious to avoid worsening an illness."

"I would say it was rather more than a touch," Matrice said, taking the seat on the other side of Ely and ignoring Tamalina's attempt to evade the subject. "According to Eomila, you were shaking fit to bring down the house, and worse."

Tamalina flushed and gave her an angry look.

"There is no need to be ashamed," Matrice said matter-of-factly. "I've heard that quite a few people suffered the same last night. Mother recorded for a brief council meeting on the subject today. They suspect it was due to the contamination of recent food imports by rats."

Tamalina grimaced, looked down into her teacup, and then pushed it away. "Must you talk about these things?" she said.

Matrice bit her lip thoughtfully, considering whether it was, in fact, a necessary topic of discussion. "Well," she said, "from what I heard, all of the cases cleared up by around noon today, so I suppose it's no longer terribly pertinent."

"Thank goodness for that," muttered Tamalina.

Eomila, having noticed the three of them at the table, broke away from her group of admirers and came over to them. Ely rose and gave her a light embrace.

"Congratulations," she said sincerely, wishing again she had been able to see the work for which Eomila was being so praised.

"Thank you so much for coming," Eomila said, her whole face aglow. "It means so much to have my friends here. I do wish Remiana could have stayed."

"You should be thankful someone as important as her made time for you at all," Tamalina said gruffly.

"Oh yes, I am," Eomila said, bobbing her head vigorously for emphasis.

The delicate tinkle of a glass bell drew their attention and quieted the chatter in the room. Eomila's mother entered at the far end of the dining hall, flanked by four serving women in demure whites and grays. Her eyes were red, Ely noted, no doubt due to the unknown whereabouts of her sister, but her voice was steady. As a city official, Nantala Resposé had no shortage of practice in exercising self control.

"I would ask that our guests be seated," she said.

In the shuffling of feet and chairs that followed, Tamalina, looking decidedly uncomfortable, stood, stepped aside, and gestured for Eomila to take her seat.

Eomila flushed. "Oh, I couldn't," she said. "You're the eldest, after all."

"Can't an eldest do something nice for her sister now and then?" Tamalina muttered, clearly not pleased that Ely and Matrice were there to witness her unusual act of kindness.

Eomila continued to blush, but did not protest further, sliding into the seat next to Ely while Tamalina moved to the unoccupied chair on her right.

"In honor of my dear daughter's talent and her undoubtedly bright future, I entreat you all to join me for a night of fine food, merriment, and friends," Nantala said from the end of the long table. "But first, because only the best is fit for my most cherished Eomila, we must begin this celebration in proper form."

She clapped her hands twice, and the serving women moved down the length of the table, placing a rectangular wooden box in front of each guest. Coos of surprise issued forth when they were opened, each revealing a delicate set of slender, perfectly polished steel dining utensils. Ely briefly tried to guess at the total weight of all that steel and calculate its cost, but she stopped when her head started spinning.

"For our daughters, the pride of our lives, we spare nothing," Nantala said proudly, her eyes now red from happiness rather than worry. "So please, share with me the joy of a mother's pride. Now, let us eat!"

Nantala had been extremely serious, Ely discovered as the night wore on. A parade of fiddlers, tumblers, experts at sleight-of-hand, and singers passed through the dining hall in a steady stream throughout the meal and long after, each one performing to the applause of the audience. Wine flowed freely, and even Ely was able to find a subtle white that tickled her usually particular palette in just the right way. The table was moved aside after the plates were cleared to allow room for dancing and some of the more elaborate entertainments, but fresh delicacies never ceased circulating in the form of platters of aged cheeses, spiced sea urchin, and tiny, underdeveloped beras eggs no larger than a pea.

Standing as she was amidst her closest friends and watching an acrobat balance on one foot atop her well-muscled partner's outstretched hand, Ely felt a warmth that she had not felt in what seemed like a very long time. Perhaps it was the wine, but it seemed that Tamalina was being decidedly nicer to her sister than usual, and Matrice was pleasantly chatty, apparently taking a break from her normal stolidity. When it came time for dancing, Ely found herself joining the line of women in a partner-switching, around-the-room-skipping whirlwind and giggling all the while at the fact that she was actually having fun.

When a break came in the dancing, she felt compelled to draw the red-faced, slightly sweating Eomila aside for a moment. The enjoyment she was having was too great to let the burden of guilt temper it any longer.

"I have something to confess," Ely said, eyes downcast. "I was not at the Dedication ceremony. I did not have a chance to see your painting. I missed it, and I should have been there. I'm so sorry, Eomila. Please forgive me."

To her surprise, Eomila smiled as she wiped a bead of sweat from her temple with a sleeve. "It's all right. I'm actually glad, you know?" she said in a hushed voice so that the others who were taking a break from the dance floor would not hear. "It seems like everyone else is only here because they think I'm going to be famous one day. But you came because you actually care about me, not just my painting. Thank you, Ely."

Ely's eyes teared up, and they embraced, tightly this time. She did not know quite what to say.

"Come on," Eomila said, pulling at her hands, "the next dance is starting."

So they danced, and drank, and talked long after darkness fell outside the hall's large windows, the comb in Ely's hair glowing like the pale luminescence of the moon as she spun and smiled and laughed the night away.

When the last of the musicians had finished playing and the last dance had left her breathless and aching, Ely's head was buzzing with a thousand warm emotions that seemed to make their own music for her and her alone. For once, she felt like she was exactly where she ought to be. She was walking with a bounce in her step over to where Matrice and Eomila appeared to be exchanging farewells when a loud noise cut through her fog of bliss.

Several things seemed to happen at once. There was the crash of breaking glass, a few startled shrieks, and a cry of "Fire!" Ely turned in alarm and saw that one of the large windows had shattered and the far end of the table that had been pushed against them was indeed burning. As Ely and the others looked about for water to quench the flames, a second window shattered as something struck it from the outside. A patch of stone floor in the middle of the room erupted in flames, fueled by a puddle of oil amidst shards of broken glass.

"Everyone out!" Eomila's mother shouted to the remaining guests as a third flaming bottle of oil was pitched into the room from the darkness outside, shattering against the wall and setting an expensive silk hanging alight. Thick, black smoke began to fill the room, and Ely was caught up in the human stampede that followed. She lost track of Matrice, Tamalina, and Eomila as she was swept out of the room, down the hall, and toward the front door by a press of panicked bodies desperate to escape the spreading flames.

The flight of the partygoers was halted, however, when they burst forth from the mansion's and encountered an unexpected obstacle in the street. A semicircle of men armed with lowered spears surrounded them, trapping the would-be escapees against the front of the house. Those who had emerged first tried to back up, shying away from the obsidian blades that menaced them, but the press of people still trying to get outside prevented them from retreating back into the house. The ring of armed men began to close about the crowd, grabbing those closest to hand and throwing bags over their heads and binding their hands with rope. The screaming that ensued alerted those still inside that something was amiss, but the doorway remained too jammed for anyone to get through.

One of the armed men grabbed at Ely, but she tripped over someone else's feet in the throng and went down hard on the paving stones. Her assailant leaned over to seize her, but she rolled onto her back and kicked viciously at his face, sending him reeling with a pointed toe to the eye. She rolled several more times to get clear of the melee and all its stamping boots, then scrambled to her feet, picked up her skirts, and ran for her life.

She had no idea what was happening, but she had gotten a good look at the man who had tried to grab her. He had been wearing a uniform of white and gold that stood out from the darkness like the vestments of a savage ghost. White and gold . . . .

The process of finding meaning in the colors was halted by a distant but loud boom from the direction of the harbor. For the first time since escaping the house, Ely stopped running and looked up from the ground in front of her feet. The night was surprisingly bright, but not due to any street lamps. The glow of fires burning in all quarters of the city cast an eerie, orange light onto the underside of rolling plumes of black smoke rising over the rooftops, giving the scene the air of an impossible nightmare.

Terrified, and without a clue as to what she should do in the face of such a horrific vision, Ely did the only thing she could think of: she ran home. Her shoes pounded the cobbles at a furious rate, carrying her faster than she had ever run in her life. They were not made for running, however, and they pinched her toes so painfully that she eventually kicked them off and continued on without slowing for more than a second, her bare feet numbing almost instantly as she sprinted across the night-chilled stones. She did not stop for anything or anyone, not even when she had to run directly past a building that was wholly engulfed in flames and spitting sparks into the street. More uniformed men haunted the side streets in the edges of her vision, but she passed them in a blur. If only she could get home, she thought, Barty would know what to do. He would know how to keep her safe.

Ely ran until she could not run any more, ran until she was crying from the exertion. In the end she almost ran right past her own house, for she hardly recognized it. She stopped half past it in the roadway, panting, and looked up at the column of flames that once had been the place where she had been born. Yellow and red tongues leapt from her bedroom window and from all the others, laughing merrily as they fed upon all the tangible things in the world she knew and loved. The terrible sight held her motionless with shock and despair. This could not be happening, she thought. Things like this did not happen in Falls Gate.

She fell to her knees in the street, not capable of moving another inch and with nowhere to go even if she could. When the two white-and-gold soldiers approached her from behind, she hardly had any strength left to struggle as a black bag plunged her sight into darkness. Her consciousness followed closely after.

Chapter 14

New Order

Ely's eyes opened slowly. She lay on a floor of cold stone that pressed hard against the back of her skull, which was pounding with a regular, painful rhythm. It took her a moment of staring at the ornamented ceiling high overhead to recognize where she was – the great hall of Cliffhome Keep. It was an unmistakable ceiling, covered by a mosaic of colored glass that reflected the light of three massive hanging braziers. Ely propped herself up on her elbows, wincing as the throbbing in her head intensified.

Of the soldiers who had abducted her there was no sign, but the hall was nevertheless packed with people, some looking as though they had been taken directly from their beds. Silk sleeping shifts were common attire, many adorned with no small amount of lace. Streaks of grime marred the greater portion, and a few sported streaks of blood. Several wailing voices could be heard throughout the crowd, adding regular, sobbing punctuation to the backdrop of scared murmurings. The whole place smelled of human filth, and of fear.

Ely slowly realized, as she took in the sight of the crowd, that she recognized nearly all of these people. Some she had seen in this very room at the Dedication celebration the previous night, and most of the rest over the years at one function or another. She hazarded a guess that most of those in the city who claimed any substantial amount of noble heritage were here, though it would take someone like Tamalina, whose penchant for gossip left her with a formidable knowledge of most of the major family trees, to be certain.

Tamalina . . . . A wash of fear skittered across Ely's body, and she twisted her head about, trying to peer through the crowd for any sign of her friends or any of the others she had left behind when she fled the Resposé house. She was not certain whether it would be a relief to see them there or not. If they had not been brought here, they might have escaped the soldiers somehow, or they might have-

Ely's search was interrupted when a mess of curly white hair with a dangling pink tongue darted from around the ankles of the crowd and leaped over her outstretched legs in a single bound. Upon landing, the puppy paused, head turned to contemplate the obstacle it had just hurdled, and then it bounded excitedly into Ely's lap and tried to plaster its tongue across her face. A child of perhaps ten pushed his way through the forest of legs a moment later, clearly in pursuit, and Ely disentangled herself from the flailing paws and handed the dog over to him. The puppy yipped excitedly and struggled, clearly eager to resume the chase, but the boy held its squirming body firmly to his chest.

"Mistress Ely!" the boy cried in recognition, and then he hugged her, squishing the small, squirming dog between them. He pulled back, his tousled shock of brown hair sticking almost straight up, and Ely realized that she was holding Matrice's little nephew, Bermin. The family actually treated him more like Matrice's younger brother, and he was a common sight whenever Ely visited the Pourin home. In truth he was Matrice's brother's child, fathered on a glassworker's daughter just months before he left the city to marry into a merchant house in Quarry Bay. Ely remembered how the young Matrice had cried when she had found out about her brother's indiscretion, sure that the shame would ruin the family. As it turned out, it seemed most people were willing to overlook the child's origins, especially once his sincere personality and wide, infectious smile had come into bloom.

The look on Bermin's face now, however, showed no hint of his usual joy.

"Matty has been worried about you," he said, meaning Matrice. "Everybody is really scared. These men broke down the front door and they had spears and they were shouting and . . . ." He choked up as Ely embraced him again.

"Are you all right? Was anyone hurt?" she asked, running her hands up and down his small form, searching for injuries.

She felt his head shake against her shoulder, and she allowed herself a measured taste of relief. That was something to be thankful for, at least. From the sound of it, Matrice too had managed to make it as far as her own house before being taken.

"Come on then," she said, pulling away and getting slowly to her feet. She brushed at her torn dress out of habit, though the soot stains it had acquired appeared indelible. "Why don't you take me to find Aunt Matty?"

Bermin took her hand and began to lead her through the throng, and the puppy, sensing only one hand holding it, struggled until it broke free. It landed on the ground at a dead run and was instantly swallowed by the crowd, its frequent, shrill barks growing fainter as it went. Some of the people they squeezed past nodded at Ely politely, and a few others spared a quick, tight-lipped smile for Bermin. Clearly no small number of them recognized her. She wondered, suddenly, why they had let her lie there on the floor without aid.

They were somewhere near the center of the large room, stepping carefully around several older women kneeling in a prayer circle, when Ely heard a faint, muffled clattering. She had only seconds to contemplate the noise before doors at the back of the hall slammed open. A startled cry went up, and the crowd shied away from the opening, wedging Ely between a lean, broad-shouldered man in a bedshirt and a frail looking woman whose shoulder dug painfully into Ely's back when she stumbled against her. Bermin's hand gripped hers tightly, and she squeezed back, no less frightened at the sudden surge of bodies than the child.

The clattering intensified, and there were exclamations and gasps from the front of the crowd, but even on her toes Ely was not tall enough to make out what was happening.

"Quiet!" A voice snapped over the sea of heads. There was a scraping sound of something heavy being dragged over the floor, and then the head and shoulders of Oridine Aloise appeared above the rest. Her blonde hair was done up in a neat bun, far too neat for someone who had been abducted from her bed. She wore a close-fitting white top emblazoned with the Aloise gold hammer on both breasts, and she held a wooden rod resting easily on one shoulder. White and gold, Ely realized, finally completing the connection she had been trying to form earlier. The weight of the realization would have made her stagger if not for the press of others around her holding her up.

No sooner had the Aloise matriarch mounted the platform above the crowd than she was joined by two truly terrifying figures: men covered so thoroughly from head to toe in metal that Ely could not see a sliver of skin between them. Even their heads were obscured by rounded helms, and hinged visors hid their faces in shadow. The two were identical in appearance but for the color of those visors, one white, the other red. These men took up positions to either side of their mistress and remained there, still as statues.

"My people of Falls Gate," the Lady Aloise proclaimed in a voice that was not a shout but nevertheless cut through the air. "Let me be the first to welcome you into the new world." She paused, as an orator might when expecting applause. When none came, she pressed her lips together and continued.

"I am sure many of you are confused, and some may even be frightened," she said, adding a smile that was meant to be comforting. "But I assure you that there is nothing to fear. Not now, and, with the birth of a truly unified kingdom, not ever. These small inconveniences you have suffered tonight are merely temporary measures for your own good, and in a short time you will reap their rewards a hundredfold." This stirred the crowd a bit, but Oridine talked over them.

"But first, I owe you all an explanation. Many months ago, you sent men north to join in a noble mission to bring all the divided peoples of this land together under a united banner of peace. Strife between our houses has brought shame and weakness upon all of us for far too long, and thus we took up the sacred duty of bringing them to an end forever by eliminating the differences of name and rule that bring men to war on one another." She raised one hand into the air in a grand gesture. "Together, we dreamed of an era of prosperity for all peoples, one achieved by all and for the sake of all, where no man rises at the cost of his neighbor's fall. It is in the name of this dawning era that I come before you today." Oridine let her words settle, holding an almost gentle smile on her face.

A quiver ran down Ely's back, and she pulled Bermin closer to her.

Oridine's eyes flashed a green that was visible from across the room. "But just as we need mirrors to see our own faces, flaws are easier to find in others than in ourselves. You, the people of Falls Gate, joined our quest for a bright future while still unable to see that the seeds of its failure lay within the walls of your own city." She spread her hands plaintively. "Let me be your mirror! Let me show you your flaws so that together we may wipe them away, for the sake of peace!" Again she paused, expecting something from the crowd and clearly not getting it. When she resumed, her voice was cooler and slower, as if explaining to a child.

"Your city has a noble history, of that there is no question. It was built on ingenuity and strength second to none. For centuries it has stood as a pinnacle of success, a beacon of light for those adrift at sea and a beacon of joy representing the best of what powerful ideals can achieve. For this reason your independence has been well deserved. But in these trying times, the inescapable truth is that independence is the poison of peace." Oridine shook her head sadly, tapping the rod she held lightly against her neck. "To stand apart now that the unification is nearly complete is to drive a thorn into the heels of all those who fight for unity on your behalf. Real unity, true unity, must be total and unconditional. Two ships sailing together will one day drift apart. The fore and aft of a single ship, however, will always sail together, or not at all."

"Aye, and she will make us the aft, all right." The man's interjection from near the front of the crowd turned every head in the hall toward him. Ely tried to place the familiar voice, but Oridine did so for her.

"Councilman Jaff," she said, beckoning with a crooked finger. "I am sure your words will carry farther from up here. Come, if you wish to speak your mind. I, for one, am eager to hear what you would say."

As Benard Jaff mounted the platform, Ely noted that he was one of the few among the audience who were properly dressed. The seafarer's getup was too tight around the belly and the ceremonial captain's stripes hanging over his shoulders looked patently ridiculous, but that was hardly unusual; the man was well known for both his outsized ego and his questionable sense of fashion. Being that he was the youngest member of the council, Ely had had the dubious pleasure of meeting him on more than one occasion, but this was the first time she had ever seen him without a cup in his hand or a woman on his arm, or both. The cup might not have been far off, however, for Jaff teetered visibly as his head bobbed into view, his short beard scruffier than usual and his lower jaw set with a drunkard's practiced concentration.

Once he was atop the platform and within grasping distance of the metal-covered men, Jaff's nerve seemed to wane, but Oridine merely crossed her arms and waited, eying him the way a schoolmarm eyes a reluctant pupil. Jaff rubbed his hands on his trousers and coughed weakly, turning to the crowd.

"The aft, aye . . . ." he said, trying to find his place again. "That's what we'll be when her lot gets done with us. We're doing just fine, ain't we? All her kind wants is our damn money, like they ain't got enough already! They're going to unify us into a great heap 'o taxes, that's what. This is exactly what we drafted the treaties to protect us from!" Having regained his train of thought, Jaff seemed to relax. "We'd have to be blind not to see this for what it is: a power grab by a bunch of hull-scraping foreigners who-"

The rod struck him across the back of the skull with such force that he fell to his knees, dazed. Someone in the crowd screamed.

"Look!" Oridine said, raising the rod again. "Look at the selfishness and corruption that has taken hold of you." She brought the wood down across Jaff's shoulders with a sickening crack, and he collapsed so that the heads of the onlookers blocked him from Ely's view. Some of the men at the front moved forward to intervene, but the now-familiar clattering sound told Ely that more of those metal monstrosities were blocking the way to the platform. The rod flashed down again, and Ely winced as she heard the blows land, one after another. She did her best to cover Bermin's ears with her hands. When Oridine had finished, the room was deathly silent.

"I am here to ease the pain of your transition," she said, wiping a spot of blood from her cheek with her free hand, "but some of you will refuse my help. Former Councilman Jaff was the first, and there will no doubt be others. But have no fear, for I will be your ally, and I will not let this precious city that you love become an agent of chaos in the righteous order that our land deserves. When the interregnum ends and the throne is filled once again, our new ruler will inherit a kingdom that is whole and strong, greater and more glorious than it has ever been. I have pledged myself to that end, and it would be in your interest, as good citizens of the crown, to do the same."

Ely's limbs were quivering. The crush of people around her felt suffocating, and she just wanted to run away, to anywhere where she could breathe and be alone, without Bermin or anyone else there to see her. But she dared not move or make a sound.

"You will all remain my guests here in the Keep for a time, until it is safe for you to return to your homes. Until then, please consider what I have said. The sooner you help me bring this city into the new world, the sooner we can dispense with any necessary unpleasantness." Oridine clapped her hands, and her metal soldiers formed into ranks.

"For all our sakes, please do not attempt to leave the grounds or cause a fuss. Neither will be tolerated." Oridine stepped down from the platform, and her soldiers escorted her out of the hall. Just before the heavy door slammed its final punctuation behind her, however, Ely caught the briefest glimpse through the crowd of a familiar set of blonde curls following in her wake. Then they were gone, leaving the captives to the solace of their own weeping.

But Ely's voice was not among those who cried out in sorrow or fear. What she felt in her chest was deeper, more powerful, and more terrible by half than the sort of lesser emotion that demanded sobs and howls as its tribute. What menaced her heart was the jagged, twisting blade of a friend's betrayal.

Chapter 15

The Iron Family

The metal helmet clanged loudly as Edwin dropped it on the table, and he raised his hand in imitation of a toast. "Hear, hear, another victory for the invincible knights!"

A round of sniggers mingled with the sounds of unfastening clasps as the men around him shed their weighty armor. The smell that was released into the Keep's servants-hall-turned-armory as metal peeled away from flesh was repugnant. It had been a long night, and the morning offered little chance of relief for the weary.

"Can it, will ya? It was old the first time." An unpleasant, jowled face appeared from under a visored helm, flushed and sour. "It's bad enough they suit us up in these damn walking cages to do nothing but stand and look pretty. You don't have to torture us with your stale jokes too." The older man tossed a pair of gauntlets down in disgust and sank heavily onto a bench, which creaked ominously under his weight.

"Speak for yourself, Gulbrathe. You just hate laughin' 'cause the only time you hear it is when someone's laughin' at your gut." Vanbilt, a younger man with short black hair and a madman's grin, grabbed a helmet, stuffed it under his sweaty tunic and lumbered about the room as if supporting a nearly unmanageable paunch.

Edwin joined the chorus of laughs, which only intensified when the enraged Gulbrathe leaned over to snatch at his detractor, missed, lost his balance, and became wedged in the space between the bench and the table by the weight of his own breastplate. Soon the eleven other men were in helpless tears of mirth as Gulbrathe struggled vainly and cursed every one of them in turn. The helmet slipped from under Vanbilt's shirt and hit the stone floor loudly as he doubled over, unable to control himself.

"You're all having a good time then, are you?"

The laughter choked off, replaced by a few scattered coughs and wheezes. Edwin wiped his eyes furiously, trying to bring into focus the blurred, fully armored figure in the doorway of their improvised barracks. The white beard on the face that came into view was like a fuzz of ice crystals, the same color as the man's upturned visor, and the voice of its owner cold enough to match.

"Mayhap I'm lost, because I was looking for the Lode Knights, the elites, the invincible warriors. Surely brave souls like those wouldn't waste their time playing half-clothed games in the keep of a city less than a full day under our control?" Gulbrathe had stopped struggling, apparently resigned to take the reprimand lying down.

"This is a sky-damned fighting unit," the captain snarled, "no matter how many spoiled brats . . ." Edwin stood a little straighter. ". . . prancing clowns . . ." Vanbilt studied the floor intensely. ". . . or over-the-hill sacks of meat are in it!" Gulbrathe didn't so much as blink at the insult. "And the rest of you are no better! Have you lost your minds? Would you like some local farm boy to put a spear in your back while you were just having a little fun? If you think for one second . . . ."

Edwin tuned out the lecture, which was turning rapidly toward well-worn subjects. Ever since joining the Lode Knights, he had become a master of feigned attention. The lengthy ceremonies, the lengthy admonitions, and the lengthy donning and doffing of armor that was heavy enough to make him feel like he were carrying his own twin on his back all made for plenty of opportunities to practice. All in all, it was the most useful skill he'd acquired in the supposedly elite unit. He wondered idly how many more hours he'd spend over the next few days propping up his iron shell to lend force to another's words.

As far as assignments went, there were certainly far worse. He could be digging graves, or scraping barnacles off the underside of a ship, or carrying boxes full of someone else's armor plates. Still, when the air inside his helmet felt too hot to breathe and he could map the contours of his body by the army of sweat droplets marching from his neck to his feet, it was hard not to imagine how pleasant it would feel to instead be outside, a heavenly breeze upon his face while he heaved bodies into a ditch. It was almost enough to make him wish he had never saved the life of that Masked, never accepted that damned commendation, and never felt the weight of a true steel blade in his hands.

A clanking sound brought the room back into focus. The doorframe was empty, the captain having moved on, and the other men were slowly stirring back to life. Someone grabbed Gulbrathe's arm and heaved him to his feet while Vanbilt collected his fallen helmet from under the table. They finished the rest of their disarming routine in silence, each conducting his own obeisance to his second self, the self that when they were finished stood watch from the armor rack, waiting for a living soul to once again inhabit its hard, dead flesh.

Edwin was the last to finish. When at last his suit of armor had joined the eleven others, he went to the small stone box on the table and opened it. Inside were twelve iron keys with blunt teeth and flat, rounded heads, each no longer than the end of a thumb. Selecting one of them, he inserted it into the keyhole on the bracer locked around his left forearm and turned it. There was a grinding click, and the pressure on his arm fell away. He removed the bracer and began to coil up the chain of solid, heavy links that bound it to the squared steel pommel of the sword at his waist. When his hand reached the hilt, it paused, resting gently on the leather wrappings and crossguard.

On a whim, Edwin drew the sword from its sheath. Even in a room containing a king's ransom in metal, the sight of the thing still took his breath away. The sun's light bathed it differently, like a father smiling approvingly at a son. Even here, where the shafts of morning gold from the windows were dimmed by a coating of dust on the high glass panes, the weapon glowed, sending its own blades of reflected radiance slicing sidelong into the shadows. For a moment it was a weapon made purely of light, a weapon without flaw, without age, without weight.

When the sword was sheathed again, the room dimmed, and Edwin placed the bracer and blade in the gauntleted grasp of his iron brother, a figure held up now by poles of wood instead of Edwin's aching back. He patted the suit of armor on the head, and the blue visor gazed back at him coolly. He quickly stripped off his undergarb and changed into the Lode Knight's uniform, alternating slashes of red and gold over a background of white. For the brief moments that he was shirtless, the ring he wore on a thong about his neck swung freely, thudding against his bare chest like a second heartbeat dancing with his own.

Once dressed, Edwin exited the improvised armory into the hall. A steady flow of servants and soldiers passed him in either direction. He retraced the path they had taken when they had escorted Oridine Aloise to and from the great hall, through corridors and archways of ancient moss-stone that marked the oldest parts of the structure. Everywhere the bustle of activity was the same, as it had been since the capture of the Keep what seemed like just hours ago. The city had fallen without much of a struggle, and perhaps for that reason the fortification was proceeding at a frantic pace. Whatever enemies lay hidden among the common folk outside, if they existed, had not yet bled enough to be called defeated.

Occasionally Edwin spotted a lone figure wandering directionless among the workers, head down and frilled garments rumpled. The captive nobles were unconfined, save for their inability to leave the grounds of the Keep, and free to pace the halls and chambers to their hearts' content. There were not enough cells to hold them, and they posed little threat. The shock of the loss of their city would render them helpless as surely as prison walls for at least a few days more.

After a few minutes Edwin found himself in the Keep's central courtyard. One of the green-tinged towers that climbed above cast its shadow over the open grounds, revealing a mild chill in the morning air. When he and the rest of the Aloise forces had departed the Craghorn, there had already been a solid coating of snow on the ground, yet here winter had hardly begun to tease the landscape with his touch. It was as though the warships had carried them backward across the seasons as well as over hundreds of spans of coastal waters.

A scattering of dry leaves crunched underfoot as Edwin crossed the green, heading toward the tall doors of the great hall. He paused as he passed the bodies that hung from the branches of the yard's lone Chesamir tree. There had, inevitably, been fools among the nobles who had not heeded the Lady Aloise's warning, and they had revealed themselves quickly enough.

A lone Impelar, swathed in the traditional red silks and thin veil, leaned against the trunk of the tree beneath the bodies, her scythe propped beside her, presumably to prevent anyone from cutting them down. As the personal protectors and most trusted servants of the iron families, Impelars were exceptionally trained and unfailingly loyal. It was a shame to waste such skill on simple guard duty, and Edwin felt sorry for anyone who gave the woman an excuse to unleash any of her pent up energy.

Edwin climbed the shallow stone steps up to the great hall's entrance and with no small effort shifted one of the massive doors just enough to allow him through. Inside, several rows of tables had been set up in the cavernous space, and the smell of food hovered thick on air warmed by the six large fireplaces. On one side, the room was all shades of red and white and gold, colored by the uniforms of Aloise soldiers and laborers and servants as they ate and talked loudly, while on the other it was a dour rainbow of wrinkled silks and silent, darkened faces of yesterday's nobility and today's bereaved.

The two groups existed wholly apart, neither acknowledging the other, as if the tall doors opened onto two rooms instead of one.

The aisle between them was a lonesome place, and Edwin remained there only until he spotted the other knights boisterously making their presence known at a table near the back of the hall. Edwin picked his way through the seated throng and slid onto a bench beside them.

"Oy, here's the laggard! Somebody get him a drink!" A clay mug was shoved into Edwin's hands, and a platter holding the picked-at carcass of some kind of fowl slid down the table toward him. There was hardly anything left but bones.

Tentaltis gave a lopsided grin from where he sat opposite Edwin. "That's what you get for being late. Birds wait for no man, am I right?" This prompted a renewed round of laughter from the table, and Ten flashed his smile all around. Whatever sobriety had filled these men before was long dead.

Edwin looked down at the platter. A puddle of grease had congealed beneath the ragged skeleton, flecked with bits of pale meat and a few small, downy feathers. He pushed the thing away, scanning the table for something more palatable.

Ten was still smirking. "Ho, our boy Ed here doesn't want any o' the bird! Maybe he had himself his own pretty little bird on the way over here an' that's what held him up!" More laughter.

Edwin smiled wryly as Ables, sitting beside him, gave him a rough but friendly clap on the back. Gulbrathe, several seats down, snatched the last biscuit from a tray as it passed.

"I hear these lowland birds are fine, and easy pluckin'," he said above the din, leaning forward so he could catch Edwin's eye. "Might be I'll try one for myself!"

"Yeah, if you could catch one!" Vanbilt chimed in from beyond Gulbrathe, and then gave a grunt as a half-eaten biscuit struck him in the nose.

"Nah, nah, you all got it wrong!" Malbrand, a solid man with a bristly and food-spotted brown beard, said from farther down the table. "If Ed plucked his birds that quick, he'd be drowning in bastards by now!" That comment earned a few more shouts and even a brief whistle.

Edwin took a bite out of a puffed roll and turned the remainder over in his hands as he chewed. It was easy for the others to forget the fate his name would spell for any bastards he sired. Though the particular line he represented had no inheritance to protect and no lands to keep intact, there were no exceptions to the rule. Not even the smallest branch of a strong tree could be left to fester with corruption. That was the Aloise way.

As Edwin ate, his eyes wandered repeatedly over Ten's shoulder to the backs of the huddled figures on the other side of the hall. Some of them were families, he decided, by the way they leaned on one another, while those who were alone sat unsupported by their neighbors, near but still almost imperceptibly apart. The sound of the soldiers buffeted them, and like buoys on the water they silently absorbed the beating, some by rocking, others by fixing themselves to some hidden bed of strength beneath the swells of laughter.

It seemed that no one but Edwin noticed when one of the nobles rose from the crowded bench where she sat. Like many of other women, her face was smudged with soot, or possibly with blood, and her dress was similarly stained. Her hair, brown or some dull shade of red, fell tangled and lumpy about her shoulders, having largely escaped from the teeth of a white comb that held it up. She looked about, as if confused to find herself on her feet, and then began making her way toward the door.

Edwin watched her progress while the men about him continued to eat and laugh. She must have been unsteady on her feet, for as she moved between the tables she put her hands on those she passed, like a blind woman feeling her way down a passage of human backs. Her touch rippled outward like on the broken surface of a pond, drawing attention as it moved. Soon she had every other noble's eyes fixed upon her. To Edwin it was like watching a play of ghosts, carried out in silence beyond the invisible wall that divided the living half of the room from the dead.

The woman reached the doors and stopped. They were tall and heavy, cut from solid pieces of timber that must have come from trees greater than any found in the modern world, which made it no easy task for even a strong man to shift them. This, however, did not deter the woman. She set her shoulder against them and pushed, her feet struggling for purchase as she tried to brace herself against the polished floor. Edwin noticed for the first time that she was not wearing any shoes.

"Well, have a look at that!" A soldier, with a bird's wing halfway to his mouth, pointed with his free hand. Heads turned to watch the struggling figure pit herself against the unmoving edifice, and a few jeers went up from those seated around Edwin. The wall of silence dividing the room might very well have been one of stone for all the notice the woman took of the taunts, and she carried on without pause.

"Five petals says the door wins!" A howl of laughter was followed by a stream of further bets.

"Three on the girl!"

"That's a good way to lose your money! I'll take it!"

"Eight says she'll start crying!"

In the ensuing commotion, it seemed that the subject of their wagers had been almost completely forgotten until a grinding vibration set the cups and plates rattling on the tables and sent a buzz up the startled men's legs. The door stood open, just a sliver, and the wetness that dripped from the woman's face was sweat, not tears. She gave the stunned and staring men on the other side of the room a level look, her first and only acknowledgement of their presence, before squeezing out through the opening she had made.

In the wake of her departure, the two halves of the room became one again in their joint silence. Edwin smiled a little, half wishing he had wagered on his guess.

Another woman from among the nobles rose, gathered up her skirts, and made for the sliver of grass and sky visible beyond the doors. Others followed, and soon they were all on their feet, pushing the door aside easily as they washed out of the room in a multicolored tide.

The soldiers watched them go with a palpable sense of unease hovering among them. Some elected to follow the odd procession out into the courtyard, but instead of joining them Edwin left his seat and let himself out by one of the back doors of the hall, his meager appetite gone. There was no need to follow, to watch. Nothing that transpired within these walls could change their roles as prisoners and conquerors. Nothing could reshape the will of an iron family.

The hall into which Edwin emerged was clearly in a less-frequented part of the Keep, decorated by dusty hangings and torch brackets that hadn't been cleaned in living memory. He picked a direction at random, uncertain of the shortest way to reach his destination. He climbed stairs whenever he found them and was soon high enough that the windows in the eastern wall looked out over the Keep's bailey and into the city. The air was thick and golden where the sunlight tangled with the still-rising plumes from the night's fires, pushed visibly northward by the wind off the sea. No one was in the streets. The darkened windows of the buildings stared up at the Keep in apprehension, children eyeing a new and untested father.

Three more flights of stairs and Edwin's legs began to burn, for they had not yet recovered from their grueling nighttime climb through the cliff tunnels. In full armor it had taken the better part of an hour to traverse the seemingly endless spiral of those passages, and by the time the knights had hauled themselves to the top, not one of them had the breath to complain that they had fallen far behind the advance of the front lines.

After counting eight floors, Edwin abandoned the stairs and wandered the mostly empty halls until he came across a door guarded by two regulars, both apparently unarmed. Upon seeing him, one of them cracked the door and spoke something into the room, then waved him on with a brief smile. Edwin strolled through the open door without even needing to slow his pace.

The inside was cozy and soft, a stark contrast to the bare stone halls he had left behind. Heavy maroon curtains hung partially drawn over the bedchamber's windows, hiding most of the hazy city beyond. Beside the window leaned an unstrung bow and a quiver of arrows, each one fletched with two red feathers and one gold. A dark rug competed for space with a writing desk and a four-poster bed covered with a thick, ivory bedspread.

On the bed sat a pretty woman, clad in the same tones as the arrow fletchings, with a head of loose blond curls that fell about a face drawn in an intense frown. A bottle of red ink was open and balanced precariously on the quilt beside her, the pen in her hand hovering over a parchment resting on her knees. As Edwin entered, she quickly set aside the pen and paper and stood to greet him. The ink bottle rocked dangerously atop the quilt, but remained upright.

"Ed!" Remiana said, replacing the frown with a smile so quickly that it seemed she had donned a mask. "I did not expect to see you so soon. I trust the voyage was not too hard on you?" Her voice was warm and welcoming, that of a hostess rather than a commander of men in the middle of a hostile city.

"Good afternoon, cousin," Edwin said with a slight bow, using the preferred familial term of the Aloise and doing his best not to let his vague disappointment reach his voice. She was playing the gracious iron daughter with him, one of the many roles that her life had called on her to perform without regard for which she might have preferred. Remiana was good at it, to be sure, but Edwin had seen those eyes and that smile too many times before to be fooled into believing that was really her.

"I trust I'm not disturbing you?" he added formally. "Certainly you have important duties at a time such as this. It wouldn't be right for someone of my rank to keep you from them."

Remiana blinked twice, as though awakening from a walking sleep. Her smile weakened.

"Sorry, Ed. It has become habit, now," she said, sinking back down onto the bed with a sigh and rubbing at her eyes. "I do not have much opportunity anymore to just . . . talk. I think I might be forgetting how."

Edwin grinned. "The day you forget how to talk will be the day the whole world goes mute. I'm lucky my ears still work after all the talking I used to hear out of you."

That brought forth a real smile onto Remiana's face. "It was your own fault for eavesdropping on my lessons. I had to recite the lineage so many times it nearly made me deaf. I still do not understand why you kept creeping back even after being whipped for it."

Edwin moved closer, crossed his arms, and rested his weight on the corner of the unused desk. "Your lessons were different from mine. I was curious what all that rich blood earned you."

Remiana laughed. "A fat lot. I would have gladly traded with you. You took your lessons outside!"

"You don't really mean that," Edwin said. "You're an heiress, and if my mother hadn't been serving yours, I likely would have grown up in a shack with no lessons at all."

"Oh, you exaggerate," Remiana said with a light laugh. "The family never would have let you live so low. Do you forget? 'The smallest Aloise is still a giant.'"

The way Remiana recited her mother's favorite saying, Edwin could almost believe. She certainly did. He wondered, exactly, what type of giant that made him.

The conversation lulled, both of them caught up momentarily in thoughts of the past, and Edwin's eyes drifted to the folded parchment on the bedspread. The black writing was too small to read from any distance, but he could see red marks in the margin. It had the look of a list.

"How's your mother?" Edwin asked in order to banish the growing silence. He had little love for the woman, but his professional interest was more significant than his personal one.

Remiana clasped her hands in her lap. "Busy tending her new baby, I expect." She smirked at Edwin's confusion. "I mean this city, of course. She has hardly spoken of anything else in the past week, so anxious has she been for this day. It was all her plan, you know, everything," she added, no longer smiling. "She never had any intention of marrying me to one of these lowlanders."

Edwin had suspected as much as soon as the deployment order had arrived. Oridine Aloise had a curious power in the family, even for one who was the widow of the late king's brother. Directing a coup was no more, and no less, than he expected from her.

Edwin decided to press a little further. "This has something to do with the succession, doesn't it?" he said. There had been countless hours in which to contemplate the true purpose of their mission as the ships carrying the Aloise troops had made their way slowly along the coastline, and after much thinking, it was the only theory that made sense. Yet even after all that thinking, he could not figure out exactly how it was to work.

"Of course not," Remiana said, her face studiously blank. "What purpose would it serve?"

Edwin shrugged. "That's what I was hoping you could tell me, cousin," he said. "Your house already holds five of the eight iron territories, more than the majority needed to select the new king. Why take a new territory now?"

"Our house," Remiana corrected him sharply. "And it is exactly as you say - we will have more than enough votes in the succession. As mother said, this is about unification."

"Our house, of course," Edwin said absently, frowning at the tone of her voice. House Aloise was many things, but it was not a bastion of idealists. "Unity" was just a word, and it took the promise of money or power to prick Aloise ears. Nevertheless, he did not want to upset Remiana on their first meeting in over half a year, so he nudged the conversation to a different track.

He nodded to the bow and arrows beside the window. "What have you been doing with your time, then, if not searching for a husband? Practicing your marksmanship?"

The answer came after a brief pause, during which Remiana's eyes flicked toward a door in the side wall. It was painted in the same color as the wood paneling around it and had no trim to speak of, causing it to blend in so effectively that Edwin had failed to notice it.

"Nothing important," Remiana said. Her eyes left the door and moved about restlessly. Never did they alight on the paper lying beside her, not even once. The knuckles of her clasped hands were white. "Mother believes this will all be very instructive for me to observe."

Edwin was sure of it now: she was lying, and not just about this, but about the succession as well. He had known Remiana since her days as a sloppy, willful child long before her transformation into a courteous and quick-witted adult. She was the reason he had, as a youth, first begun to doubt what he had been taught about the value of blood, for in her he saw a strange creature who, despite having the highest of all bloods in her veins, stumbled and wept and made a mess of her plate just as he did. And just as he came to have an intimate knowledge of her table manners, so too did he learn to recognize her lies and her half-truths, even those that would fool her tutors and minders. Rank had never allowed them to be as close as they might have been, but he doubted if there was anyone within a hundred miles with whom she would speak more openly than him - including her own mother. If she would not tell him the truth, there would be no prying it from her.

Edwin shook his head sympathetically. "You are a woman grown, cousin. It would be a shame if your mother refused to see that you are fit for more than a place in the wings."

"My mother is right. I still have much to learn," Remiana said. "It will be many years before I am anything like her." These words, at least, were genuinely spoken.

"She's a strong woman, certainly, but . . . ." *It would be a shame if you became like her.* Edwin finished the thought only in his head. There was a limit to what he could say, even here, just among family.

Remiana seemed to have heard the unspoken words, and her green eyes flashed at him like mirrors of his own. "You would do well to think carefully before speaking of my mother. All that she is, all that she does, is for our family. Even you, at the fringe of the Aloise name, should know that. There is no one more deserving of respect, no one I would rather learn from, than her." As she spoke, a shiver ran through her body, either from indignation or from something else. It was so faint that Edwin might have failed to notice it had it not upset the inkpot beside her on the bed. The bottle wobbled and then tipped, spreading a deep crimson stain onto the quilt.

Remiana snatched up the parchment and leapt to her feet as the ink crept toward her dress. Closer now, Edwin could just make out a few of the cramped lines of writing. They were names.

"How clumsy of me," Remiana said, taking a seat on the desk chair and smoothing her dress. She quickly tucked the paper away in the desk's sliding drawer, which was open just long enough to reveal its only other contents: a single envelope, of the size that might hold an ordinary letter. Edwin felt the vibration as Remiana slid the drawer forcefully shut.

He opened his mouth, but was interrupted by a sharp rap at the door, which cracked to admit a woman swathed in red silk, a veil of the same barely leaving a gap for her eyes. It was the same Impelar Edwin had seen in the courtyard, though she now carried no weapon. She slid through the narrow opening like a tongue of flame caressing the wood of the door, which shut quickly behind her.

The Impelar came up short when she saw Edwin, but that did not halt her for more than a moment.

"My lady," she said. "There is a situation that requires your attention."

Remiana folded her hands atop the desk and gave the woman a displeased look. "As you can see, I have a visitor. If you would wait outside, I will summon you when we are finished."

The Impelar raised her dark eyes to meet Remiana's gaze. "It is urgent, and within your responsibilities, so forgive my insistence that you come at once. I would not wish to bother the High Mistress about it."

Edwin cocked his head in surprise. The Impelars were highly respected, most of them being purportedly noble-born themselves, but even they did not presume to command the Iron Blood. Stranger still, Remiana did not reprimand her.

Instead, she turned to Edwin with regret. "It seems we will have to continue this later. There are a few small things that mother has left to my care, and, insignificant as they may be, they are my charge. I am afraid that I will have to take my leave. Unless . . . ."

Edwin could see her mulling something over, for her eyes took on the look they always had when, as a child, he would try to convince her to skip lessons and take their pans and sieves down to the river in search of gold.

"Unless," she said again, slowly, "you would care to accompany me?" There was a note of hope in her voice.

"My sword is yours," Edwin said, keeping his smile inside. Though the rivers around Alomadra had been stripped clean of their glittering treasure centuries before, he had still always loved panning for gold.

Chapter 16
What Remains

The cell was cold, but Ely wrapped her arms about her legs more for comfort than for warmth. She leaned her head against her knees and tried to control her breathing, not wanting to give the guard who she knew was standing just outside the satisfaction of hearing her weep. Her stomach still hurt where the red-clad woman had struck her, stunning her so that she could not struggle while her clothes were cut away and searched for hidden weapons. In their place she had been given a thin, scratchy tunic and nothing else.

Only the meagerest light made its way into the cell through the tiny slit near the ceiling, but it was better that way, Ely thought. It made it easier for her to ignore the dark stains on the walls that looked like blood and the foul-smelling pile in the corner that was attracting flies. Avoiding the details was the only way she could keep herself from being sick, and the only way to hold on to what little dignity she had left. She wondered, for the thousandth time in just a few short hours, why she had been so stupid as to leave the great hall in the first place. She had not been intending to lead the other nobles anywhere, just to get out of that stuffy, sorrow-filled chamber, but that had not mattered to the scythe-wielding woman who had been waiting under the hanging tree. Leading was not her crime. Her crime was being followed.

There was no bed in the cell, no chamberpot, no furniture of any kind. The floor was stone, and damp enough that Ely could feel the moisture pass right through the paltry cloth of her tunic. It made her skin crawl, but being wet and filthy was not the greatest of her worries, nor was the fat, beady-eyed rat that chittered and bared its rotten teeth at her from the corner of the cell. Far more terrifying was the knowledge that she could hope for no rescue. She had been hauled away in full view of a hundred friendly faces, in the courtyard of the Keep where she had played as a child, and no one had so much as raised their voice to aid her.

Ely dug her fingernails into her bare legs, trying to hide her anguish under physical pain. She did not even know what she should be feeling. Anger? Betrayal? Understanding? Would she have done any different, if someone else had been taken instead? Had she made even a peep as she watched Benard Jaff beaten? The fact that she had no right to cast blame only made the tumult of emotions churn even faster. Their mixture produced something akin to rage, but darker: a hatred of everyone and everything, including herself. It was the rage of a caged animal, of a life unwilling to disappear quietly into death, directionless and primal.

Warm blood wet her fingertips, but that gave Ely little pause. What was a little more filth on the outside, she thought, when her guts were twisted as they were with even filthier emotions? Why shouldn't she bleed, when she was just as responsible for her condition as anyone else, all the rest of whom were beyond the reach of her nails and teeth?

Perhaps smelling the blood, the rat that had been eying her began to advance, and Ely kicked at it savagely with her bare feet. Her heel caught it squarely and sent the little creature sprawling into the corner with a squeak, producing in Ely a black satisfaction. She wanted to do more than just kick the rat, she realized. She wanted to pour all the terrible things she was feeling out through her hands and hurt it like she had never hurt another living thing.

On her hands and knees, Ely had crossed half the length of the cell toward the injured rodent when muffled sounds from outside the door brought her up short. The scraping of the bar lifting dispelled all else from her mind. She coiled herself, ready to inflict as much pain as she could upon whoever came through the door, unable to think of anything but revenge against the world that had conspired to wreak havoc on her city and her life.

The door opened with the rasping of swollen wooden hinges, and three figures, not the one she had been expecting, filed into the small room. Back-lit as they were by torchlight from the hall, it took Ely's eyes a moment to be able to make out their faces.

"Remiana!" Ely cried in surprise, trying to stand.

The second figure stepped forward and stuck Ely across the face with a backhanded blow so hard that she fell and hit her head against the far wall. Her vision blurred with a thousands specks of color before refocusing with deadly clarity on her attacker.

"Address the Mistress properly!" the woman in red said. "A traitor has no right to speak her name."

Ely clenched her teeth and glared murder at the Impelar, but Remiana's voice pulled her attention away.

"I am surprised to see you here, Elymia," Remiana said, looking around the cell and lifting a hand to her nose. "I thought you were a reasonable woman, not prone to any sort of foolishness. But now my Impelar tells me that you have been . . . ." Remiana turned to the red woman expectantly.

"Inciting disobedience, Mistress," the Impelar said.

Remiana shook her head in disbelief. "I am ashamed of you. Can it truly be that you want to cause more deaths? Have we not already had enough to satisfy you? Have we not yet lost enough friends?" The flickering torchlight caught flashes of silver at the corners of Remiana's eyes. "I have been working to save lives, to keep the peace, and now I must find that my own friend has been working against me?"

"You're lying scum," Ely said, spitting the taste of blood out of her mouth. Her fingers curled like talons against the stone floor. "You have no friends here, not after what you've done."

The Impelar stepped forward again, but Remiana caught her arm and stopped her.

"I am not the one you should blame for this, Elymia," Remiana said softly. "Believe me, this is not my doing. Nor is it my mother's. If there must be blame, place it with the long history that brought us here. Blame our ancestors, for all the countless years they let the distance between our peoples grow unchecked, not considering the pain that unification would eventually bring. But you are wrong to blame me, Elymia. We are merely agents of the roles we are born into, roles that we have no choice but to fill. With your family's history here, I would have thought you would understand that."

Remiana's words hit her with painful memories, and Ely scowled to avoid letting them show on her face. "So you had to pretend to be my friend, to be a friend to all of us, and then you had to bring your men here to kill us? Did you think that after doing all that, you could expect me to believe any more of your drivel?" She glared as hard as she could into Remiana's eyes. "I hope you die."

Remiana lowered her head, as if in contrition. "I know you do not believe me to be your friend, Elymia, but I am. When my mother-" She stopped for a moment, then looked up at Ely. "I am a friend to all the people in this city, even if they do not know it. But I want to show them. I want them to see that they need not fear me, or us. And for that, I want your help."

Ely almost laughed. "No."

Some part of her knew that she might be playing with her own life, but the overwhelming desire in her to seize any scrap of power she was given and use it against the woman who had lied to her, lied to all of them, superseded rationality. She had found a target for her hatred.

Remiana's face hardened. "There is, of course, still the matter of your insubordination. A wise leader does not let such things go unpunished."

A sneer crossed Ely's face as she looked up at Remiana. "Is that what you're here for? To beat one of your 'friends' while your lapdogs look on? Is that something your whole family enjoys, or is it just you and your mother?"

The words hit their mark. Remiana lurched forward and grabbed Ely by the shoulders, lifting her up and slamming her against the wall with both hands, exhibiting strength Ely would not have guessed she had. The pain of it was far away, however, clouded by a haze of elation at having found those deliciously vicious words.

"Curse me into the depths of the pit," Remiana hissed, inches from Ely's face, "but you will not curse my family." Her fist drew back, but all Ely could do was smile at how deeply her words had cut.

"She didn't do it," a man's voice said from near the door.

Ely blinked in surprise. In her anger, she had forgotten that there was a third person in the room. Remiana turned her head, still holding Ely to the wall.

"What do you know of this, cousin?" she snapped.

Ely observed the man over Remiana's shoulder. His blonde hair was short in the style of a common soldier, but to Ely he looked enough like Remiana that he could have been her brother. His voice bore an accent similar to hers, though his speech was rougher and quicker. At his waist hung a sword, and one of his hands rested easily on its pommel. Ely guessed that made him a knight, though he was wearing none of the knights' armor save for a bracer attached to his sword by a chain.

The knight looked squarely at Remiana. "I was there. I saw this woman in the great hall with my own eyes. She did nothing but go outside for some air. There was a . . . disturbance, but it was not of her making. There is no need for you to punish her."

"With respect," the Impelar said, "my lord may have been in the hall, but he did not see what-"

The knight coughed, rattling the chain on his sword loudly enough to halt the Impelar's speech. He stepped forward and put a hand on Remiana's arm. The Impelar visibly quivered, but held her tongue.

"Just look at her," the knight said. "Punishment for whatever small thing she may have done has already been served. You don't need to do this."

Remiana lowered her fist slowly, then stepped back, letting Ely slide down the wall.

"Of course. You are right," she said, wiping her hands on a handkerchief that the knight produced for her. She turned back to Ely.

"A knight's word is as unfailing as his steel, and he has vouched for you." She paused, looking down at the handkerchief, now a muddy brown from the filth that her hands had collected from Ely's skin. "I should not have been so quick to doubt you, after all this time we have known one another. You have my apologies. You are hereby released and free to return home."

"Home?" Ely said, hardly daring to hope.

"Yes. I shall be releasing all those nobles who are willing to accept the peace my mother offers."

"Who are you going to keep?" Ely asked, suddenly wary.

Remiana turned to the Impelar. "Who else is in these cells?"

The Impelar balked. "Giving that information to a prisoner is-"

Remiana folded her arms. "That is not for you to decide. Tell me."

The Impelar drew herself up straight and recited the list from memory. "The Tullochs, husband and wife. The Jaffs, mother and daughter. The Abrohl man and the older Resposé girl. The-"

The last two names struck Ely like a lash. She had not known they had been jailed as well. "I want them released too," she blurted out. "Tamalina and the Wharfmaster." She was not sure why she felt so bold, barely upright as she was, but her mouth seemed to work on its own.

Remiana frowned. "I think not. Tamalina assaulted one of my soldiers with a knife. He lost an ear, and may yet lose an eye. That sort of crime cannot be overlooked, even for a friend. As for the Wharfmaster, he did a good bit worse. One of our ships is at the bottom of the harbor because of that man, and he will face public execution once things are more settled here."

The thought of Tamalina wielding a knife was unfathomable to Ely, but her surprise would have to wait until later. She pushed herself into a full standing position, using the wall behind her for support. Feeling was returning to her body and reason to her mind, but she was determined to make the most of her boldness while it lasted.

"Then let's make a bargain. I'll tell everyone you treated me well. Like a friend, even," she said. "But only if you let them go. Right now, with me." It pained her to make the offer after suffering such betrayal, even if it was a lie, but the reward would be worth it.

Remiana looked her up and down, and Ely felt suddenly vulnerable in her stained tunic. "A prison cell is no place for striking bargains," Remiana said. "Nor do I have any assurance that you will uphold your end once freed." She tapped her foot on the ground, thinking.

Ely held her breath. All the carelessness and rage had fled her, leaving her hollow and tired, wanting more than anything to be out of that dismal cell and in the air and sunlight again. If Remiana refused, she would not have the strength to argue.

After what seemed like a long time, Remiana spoke. "I will accept your offer, but only for Tamalina, not the Wharfmaster. That is, provided you swear to it the way we swear. Your sword, cousin."

The knight drew his blade, which flashed brightly in the dimness of the cell. He presented it to Remiana, though the chain connecting it to the bracer on his arm prevented her from taking it far.

"On your knees," Remiana said to Ely, pointing at the ground before her with the blade she held in both hands.

Ely dropped to her knees, wincing as skin scraped against stone. As much as she could not abide leaving the Wharfmaster behind, she knew she had no choice.

"Put your hands on the floor," Remiana said.

Ely put her palms down in front of her. Her hands seemed so much older than they had that morning. They were covered with grime, hiding the true pallor of her skin, and blood had dried into their cracks and folds like a web of old riverbeds muddied and splitting after a rain. They looked like hands capable of terrible things.

"Lower your head," Remiana commanded.

Ely obeyed, but there were tears in her eyes that none could see as she stared down at the ground. She felt the cold tip of the blade in Remiana's hands settle on the back of her neck.

"Now swear," Remiana said. "Swear your friendship to the Aloise name. Swear your friendship to me. Swear it."

Ely's eyes flicked up. Beyond Remiana's shoes, which even in the squalor of the cell smelled like fresh, new leather, a glint came from the darkened corner. Two bulbous, rodent eyes gleamed back at her, an evil fire burning within them.

Kick me, they said, *kick me, and kick me again, until I am bloody and broken, but that will not stop me from hating you; and if my teeth should find your throat in the night, then plead, plead, and plead again, but that will not stop me from killing you.*

Ely's eyes remained locked with those of the rat. The words burned like acid in her throat as she retched them up, but still she said them.

"I swear."

Chapter 17
Sowing Doubt

Donvin waited until most of the other Masked had turned in for the night before approaching the fire in front of Point's hut. It was a small flame, hardly large enough to heat the clay pot over it and certainly not enough to dispel the chill of the darkened woods, but night after night Furrow never built it any bigger. As usual, Point and Furrow were seated together, and Donvin took a seat across from them. What he had in mind for this night might not be as entertaining as the events unfolding in Falls Gate at that very moment, but he knew it was of equal importance.

"Welcome," Point rasped happily, joy evident even through the coarseness of her speech. "Well?" It was the best greeting she could manage.

Donvin nodded at her. "I am well," he said. "And you?"

Point gave a little shrug, her charred mask turning down to look at the fire between them. "Same," she rasped. She coughed, and Furrow handed her a scrap of cloth which she used to wipe her mouth behind her mask.

"Don't talk," he reminded her as he went back to grinding leaves between two stones. "The tea will be ready soon."

Point nodded, the firelight causing the blackened edge of her mask to glisten in the darkness. She kept the cloth balled up in her hands when she had finished with it to hide the bloodstains that Donvin knew it held. This was the worst time of day for her injury, since by now it was usually aggravated from a day's worth of struggling attempts at speech.

Furrow kept his eyes on the leaves he was preparing, his hands twisting the grinding stones with a fierce intensity. This was the time of day when he too was at his most vulnerable. It was the time when he was reminded how little he could do for the woman who sat beside him and endured her pain without complaint.

The water in the pot began to boil, and Furrow brushed the crushed leaves into the boiling water and waited a few moments before removing it from the flame and pouring some of the mixture into Point's battered clay mug.

"We have only one cup," Furrow said apologetically to Donvin as he set the pot on the ground to cool. Point sipped at her tea, shoulders hunched, self-conscious at being the only one to drink.

"I don't mind," Donvin said. "I'm only here to see how the two of you are faring."

Furrow nodded and sat back down.

"We are managing," he said. "It is a kindness to enquire after us."

"Great kindness," Point added between sips, her body exuding a strong odor of appreciation.

They seemed to be in the right mood for it, so Donvin moved ahead with his plan.

"I never apologized to you," he said to Point. "I never apologized for the part I played in what happened to you. If I hadn't been distracted by those soldiers, if I hadn't let the others get distracted, we might have noticed the breach before it-"

"No," Point interrupted with a vigorous shake of her head. "No fault."

"But I-" Donvin protested.

"No," Furrow concurred. "There is plenty of fault to go around, but none of it can be found in this company. The blame lies with those coastmen, and with the . . . ." He balled his fists, but allowed his sentence to trail off. The gesture brought a smile to Donvin's concealed face. These two were so easy to read, but still, he would take it slowly.

"Yes," Donvin said reluctantly, "I suppose you're right. It's those soldiers who were to blame. If they hadn't come at us, we would have been ready to meet the breach and no one would've been hurt. But having someone to blame can't make for much comfort these days, I imagine."

Point shook her head, finishing the contents of her cup, and Furrow reached over to pour her a second.

"Not matter," she said. "No blame."

Donvin hung his head. "I only wish there were something we could do to help you, some way we could ease your suffering," he said.

Neither Point nor Furrow said anything, but the tension in Furrow's shoulders told Donvin everything he needed to know. It was time to bring in a second angle.

"There was something else I wanted to tell you," Donvin said, this time addressing Furrow. "It's about the illness we treated during the Dedication. Some suspect that it was the result of poison."

Furrow looked up sharply. "Poison?"

"Yes," Donvin said. "Apparently there are those who have been known to poison their own people to create ill will against us."

Furrow's voice was full of disbelief. "What kind of people would do that? Even the worst kinds of men still look after their own."

Donvin shook his head. "I couldn't believe it either, at first," he said. "But I have it on good authority that this is not the first time this has happened. After what we saw in the north, their willingness to attack us, I am willing to believe it."

"What does that mean, then?" Furrow said, suppressed anger in his voice. "We broke our code to heal people who poisoned themselves?"

"We had to do it," Donvin reminded him. "The others agree. It was not a true breaking of the code because it was necessary for the Dedication to serve its purpose."

Furrow leaned the forehead of his mask on his hands.

"Ridiculous," he said, his fingernails scraping the bark. "We have no qualms about healing the wounds of traitors' spears, no problem healing schemers who poison themselves to turn others against us, but we won't heal-!"

"Not mean that," Point interrupted, putting a calming hand on Furrow's arm. "Code important." Her voice sounded slightly better after drinking the tea, at least enough to eke out an extra word or two at a time.

"But he's right, you know," Donvin said to Point. "There hasn't been a day since what happened that I haven't felt guilt for being healed while you were not. I know why it had to be so, but try as I might, I can't convince my heart that it's right." He turned to Furrow. "But she's right too. You know why we don't heal injuries from the breaches."

"Respect," Point said, running a finger lightly down the crack in Furrow's mask. "Already know this."

"Respect indeed," Donvin said. "Those we protect must never imagine that our service causes us no pain, or that we make no sacrifices for it. We must bear our scars proudly to remind them of the cost we pay for their lives, not use our powers to heal in ways that don't further our mission. That is what the code commands."

"So we reward those who hate us, those who are filled with the worst kind of evil, while at the same time torture ourselves for their benefit?" Furrow asked, anger now seething openly behind his words.

"That is what the code commands," Donvin repeated with a sigh. "I only wish it were not so." A regret-filled silence fell between them.

"Sleep now," Point said, tugging on Furrow's furs and trying to break his gloomy contemplation as he stared into the fire.

"A good idea," Donvin said, rising from where he sat. "We all need our rest. I didn't mean to upset the two of you. Please forgive me."

Furrow nodded a farewell in silence, and Donvin slipped away into the night. As he walked, he heard behind him the violent kicking of dirt onto the coals of the fire he had left behind. Anger was good, Donvin thought to himself. With enough of it, all he had to do was prepare the noose, and then he could watch as the Masked walked into it willingly.

Chapter 18
Sea Dog Surrender

Ely stared at the ball of dough lying on the breadboard in front of her. It slumped unevenly to one side, resisting all of her efforts to smooth it.

"Looks lovely," said Alnina Pourin, swooping in to scoop up the ball and replacing it with a fresh, unshaped lump.

Ely's flour-coated hands moved automatically, rolling and folding and rolling again. She still could not believe that so soon after being a prisoner under Cliffhome Keep, she was standing in the Pourins' kitchen making buns with Matrice's mother as if nothing at all had happened. It was almost possible to believe that all the terrible events of the past few days had occurred in a dream. The Pourin house was every bit the refuge Ely had prayed to find after Remiana had turned her and Tamalina loose with nothing but the clothes on their backs.

The thought of Remiana made Ely shudder, and she put a hand to the back of her neck, sending a dusting of flour down her collar. For a moment she was back in that dark, rancid cell, with all the light and smells of the afternoon kitchen reaching her only faintly through that tiny slit near the ceiling. Hatred bubbled in her gut, but she pushed it down again through sheer force of will. Matrice and her parents had done their best not to press her for details, but that did little to keep the memories from welling up like black oil to foul the well of her mind.

"Don't go freezing up on me now," Alnina said as she pulled a tray covered with buns from the oven. "There are so many people to feed, you'd think I had the only working kitchen in the city." The lightness of her voice hid an ugly truth. Ely's had not been the only home to burn that first night.

Alnina's presence was comforting in a way Ely could not quite describe, so she did not mind being put to work in the kitchen. Matrice's mother made everything seem so simple, so normal. She looked exactly as she always had: brown hair up in a neat bun, a book under her arm, and a well-worn smile on her face. Today, that book was one filled her own heavily annotated recipes. While baking would have been Ely's last concern under the circumstances, Alnina set about it with all her usual enthusiasm, and Ely began to change her mind as soon as the house filled with the smell of warm bread. The frantic urge to do subsided, replaced by something more like the calm it seemed she had not felt in ages. And, like a flame attracts moths, the steaming chimney and spreading smell attracted people, and with people came information.

Even though they learned much from those drawn by the promise of food, there was still much they did not know. They heard that the Aloise had sealed the port and the gates, cutting off all routs of escape from the city, but not whether anyone had gotten out beforehand. They knew that there were nine Aloise transport ships moored in the harbor, though not how many troops had been aboard. Worst of all, they heard countless reports of deaths as the Aloise troops swept through the city, yet the names of the dead seemed to change by the hour, as did the even larger list of the missing. In all the confusion, learning the fate of a particular person was practically impossible, and though Ely had asked time and time again, no one had been able to tell her what had become of Barty. Try as she might, after the cruelty she had witnessed from the Aloise, she could not help but fear the worst.

Matrice poked her head around kitchen door. "Are those buns nearly done? More of the Council has shown up, and they'll be starting any minute."

Alnina scraped the last of the buns onto a serving platter, arranging them into neat stacks of five. "Almost ready," she said. "I'll have Ely bring them in a moment." She looked over at Ely's dough-covered hands. "You had better wash up, dear. I can manage the rest here."

Ely moved to the wash basin and dipped her hands in the lukewarm water. The dough clung stubbornly to her skin, coming free only with much scrubbing.

Matrice beckoned impatiently from the door, but that did little to motivate Ely to move faster; a Council meeting was one of the last places she wanted to go. From the youngest of ages, she had never been able to face that body without silently wondering which of them had given the order that robbed her of her family. It made no difference to her that by now only a few of its members were the same as in those days, nor did their official denials of responsibility persuade her. Could there be such a thing as an accidental massacre? Ely did not think so.

Drying her hands on a rag, Ely watched as Alnina sprinkled a pinch of salt over the top of the stacked buns.

"Perfect," she said, smiling as Ely hefted the large serving platter in both hands. She turned to Matrice. "Elymia shouldn't be the only one helping out around here. You can at least carry the tea."

"All right, but let's hurry," Matrice said. She hefted the large clay jug in her arms, making no attempt to keep it from rubbing on the front of her dress.

Ely followed her out of the kitchen and into the hall, which was like stepping from placid shores into a swollen stream. They twisted and wove their way through the multitude of people, many of them strangers, who packed the rooms and corridors of the spacious residence. According to Matrice, the gathering had begun slowly, but now the place seemed close to bursting. The house had already been uncomfortably full when Ely and Tamalina had appeared on the doorstep, disheveled and hungry, but the Pourins had taken them in without a moment's hesitation. There had been no place for them to sleep but on folded blankets on the floor of Matrice's room, but the want of space had not slowed the new arrivals.

Watching their feet to avoid tripping over a family who had made camp right there in the hallway, Ely and Matrice wormed their way to the formal dining room. It seemed mercifully empty inside, though only by comparison. At least forty people stood around the edges, trying to avoid crowding the table in the center. As she approached, Ely noticed that the high backs of its chairs were still covered with a thin layer of dust from disuse.

Matrice planted her jug on the table with a thud, rattling the thin-stemmed glasses and small plates that sat before each chair, while Ely set the platter of buns down as gently as possible. Their smell had already gotten the attention of the spectators, but the food was not for them.

Ely's hand was barely off the platter when the low murmuring of voices died and the door opened to admit a short line of six people. Her jaw tensed. She had wanted to be long gone by the time the Council started in earnest.

The first into the room was Councilman Orndas. Ely recognized him immediately despite the stubbly beard that had begun to shadow his face. She knew him better than any of the rest, for he had been a frequent guest of her father in the years before the war. As the representative of the smiths' guild, he was the nominal chairman, though it was historically a position without much clout. Falls Gate had always been a locus of trade more than of crafts, so the metalworkers played second or third fiddle to the shippers and minters and merchants who were the lifeblood of the city's prosperity.

Following Orndas were other members Ely knew less well. There was Councilman Alm of the seafarers, with a tall face and prematurely white hair that hung past his shoulders; Councilwoman Shima of the glaziers, whose father had been one of the best glass spinners in decades; Councilman Glabara of the bankers; and Councilman Haime of the weavers. The woman bringing up the rear of the line, however, came as a surprise: Tamalina.

She looked nothing like the mute, morose, inconsolable girl Ely had left in Matrice's room that morning, still wrapped in a blanket and staring blankly out the window just as she had since their release from prison. She stood straight, and her hair, which to Ely's shock had been hacked short during her brief time in captivity, was worn openly without shame, its reduced length revealing a ruby choker that Ely recognized as Tamalina's mother's.

That thought gave Ely pause. Tamalina's mother was the mistress of the census, which was a position on the Council. Ely looked around the room for a second time, but doing so only confirmed that Nantala Resposé was not hiding among the onlookers. Her absence put a sinking feeling in Ely's stomach.

The six approached the table, and Matrice pulled Ely out of the way, leading her back toward her father, who had entered on the heels of the council and barred the door behind them. Ely swallowed hard. She wanted to demand that Aldan Pourin stand aside and let her out, but she quailed at the thought of drawing the attention of the whole room to her. With reluctance, she found a small unoccupied space beside Matrice and watched the Council take their seats.

The table was much too large for only six people, but instead of sitting together, each of them seemed to have a chair already picked out. The resulting arrangement was sparse and awkward. None of them looked particularly happy to be there.

When all had been seated, Gerard Orndas looked up and down the table.

"What a sorry Council this is," he said. The streaks of white in his chestnut hair flashed as he once again looked left and right. Ely could see him recounting the empty chairs.

"What a Council, indeed. Still, it gives us a place to begin. A grim one, but necessary." Gerard pushed his own chair back and stood. The seat to his left was empty, and he moved to stand behind it, placing his large, creased hands on its back.

"Where is Councilman Drum?" The words landed, dead and still, upon the table with an almost audible thud. The silence that met them was unyielding.

Gerard looked down at the chair and gently patted its wood. His voice was low, but it carried. "Missing. What I wouldn't give for one of your famous pints now, old friend. No doubt you feel the same." He moved to the next empty seat, passing over the one in which Elster Alm sat.

"Where is Councilman Tulloch?"

Again, silence. Painful, awkward silence. The people in the room wanted to know, yet at the same time were afraid that someone might speak a horrible truth.

Ely was caught off guard by the question, for she actually knew the answer. She had the sudden sensation of being squeezed, unable to exhale without words coming out along with her breath. Before she knew it, her mouth was opening.

"Imprisoned," she said, her voice ringing unnaturally in the stillness. Almost all the heads in the room turned to look at her. She fought a sudden surge of panic, some part of her brain protesting that her body had acted before her mind could stop it.

Councilman Orndas looked up to where Ely stood by the door, recognition softening the lines of his face. "Elymia," he said. "It's a relief to see you safe. We had heard terrible things. I doubt any of us would have been able to face your father had they proved true."

Ely's throat tightened. Where had those sentiments been when she was taken? "What you heard was not all wrong," she said, trying to hold her voice steady. "I was freed, but Councilman Tulloch and his wife are still locked under Cliffhome Keep, just as I was. Nor are they the only ones. The Jaffs too, and the Wharfmaster." She tried not to let the words dredge up any more memories than absolutely necessary. She sought Tamalina's eyes, but the other woman was staring straight into the table, looking no more alive than a corpse.

"You saw them there?" Councilman Orndas said.

"No," Ely said, focusing again on him, "but I heard it from the mouth of Remiana Aloise herself." That brought a murmur from the rest of the onlookers.

"Damn those Aloise!" hissed Councilwoman Shima between her teeth, not that doing so made her curse any less audible. She had the arms of her chair in a white-knuckled grip and looked ready to tear them off entirely.

Councilman Orndas turned a tired eye on her for a moment, then shifted it back to Ely.

"Forgive me, Elymia," he said, "but there has been a great deal of . . . misinformation lately. The fact that you are standing here with us can attest to as much. What's more, I can only assume that this is exactly how the Aloise want it. I have no doubt you speak truthfully, but to put much faith in what you heard while in their custody would be a mistake."

Ely's nails dug into the palms of her hands. "It's the truth, I swear it. Tamalina was held in the same place; doesn't that prove there are others? And with so many missing, where else could they be?" Ely suddenly found herself trying hard not to answer her own question. She looked to Tamalina for support, but once again got only silence in return.

Councilman Orndas' mouth tightened. "What your ordeal proves," he said, "is that the Aloise bitch has spawned a whelp with an equally twisted delight in betrayal. That she singled out her former friends to be captives in her own special dungeon is revolting, but it speaks of a personal vendetta, nothing more." The councilman looked about at the others who were seated at the table, many of whom were busily averting their eyes. "Something grave has surely befallen those who are not with us today. But whether they are held under the Keep or have found their rest under some ignoble patch of earth, words heard from the mouth of a traitor like Oridine Aloise's daughter cannot be trusted."

Ely wanted to reply, but she felt a prickling on the back of her neck. A clot of barbed, black emotion formed in her throat, so thick it threatened to choke her if she tried to speak. She clenched her teeth and was quiet.

Councilman Orndas addressed the rest of the room. "Are there any here who can speak with certainty to the fate of the absent councilors?" Silence answered him.

"Then as our first order of business," he said, "those seats should be filled. The more troubled the times, the more plentiful the minds that should rise to meet them."

A wave of nods swept around the table, though Tamalina continued to appear dead to all around her. Ely wondered bitterly why she had even bothered to come to the meeting if she refused to speak, even to bolster the word of a friend.

Councilman Orndas continued. "I suggest first that Mr. Pourin be seated. It is by his grace and in his home that we meet. It would be wrong to deprive a man of a voice under his own roof."

Aldan Pourin stepped forward. He was solidly built, closer to short than to tall, with a bristle of graying hair that made a neat circle on his scalp. His white, knitted shirt revealed the modest bulges of one who was aging in comfort.

"You honor me," he said, "but I have no head for these things. All my life I've been a man of the mints, and I know my trade well. Governing, I do not know. These times call for greater wisdom than mine. Thank you, but I must decline."

"Nonsense," Councilman Orndas said. "All of us here know you to be a good man, and more, a wise man. And, as a Mintmaster, you have as much right as any other, and more than most. Your city needs you, Aldan."

A cloud passed over Mr. Pourin's face. "Then let this wise man make it plainer for you, Gerard. My family needs me more." He reached out and grasped Matrice's hand, pulling her forward to stand beside him. "You all know this meeting will be punished if word of it reaches the Aloise. Maybe the rest of you are willing to risk your loved ones for your small rebellions, but I am not. I lend you my home because I owe you that much, as a citizen and as a friend, but I will not sit with you and damn my family."

Aldan Pourin turned and stalked out of the room, leaving Matrice standing there rigid and alone.

A wave of unease traveled through those who remained. Aldan had said nothing they did not already know, of course. The peril they faced was likely the reason no one had objected to the absence of Matrice's mother, the city recorder. No one wanted to leave behind tangible evidence of their meeting. Still, the reminder was not a welcome one.

"Then perhaps I should ask, who is there who still has the courage to serve his city in this time of need?" Orndas said, his eyebrows raised in question.

Councilwoman Shima thrust herself up from her chair, her ring-adorned hands splayed on the table. "I too ask, who here is brave enough to serve her city by casting out the foreigners and thieves who wish to take it from us?" The male councilors shot cool looks in her direction, but she seemed not to notice.

Ely, like the others, looked about for anyone who might be preparing to speak up. It did not take long to find one.

"What man could resist such a noble, plaintive cry?" Gillibardo Groundwise, the Stablemaster, strolled forward from where he had been lurking in the far corner. The shine from his bald scalp was so pronounced that Ely wondered how she had missed him before.

"I humbly offer to lend my considerable experience, Councilors," he said with a bend of the knee.

Gerard exchanged glances with Shima over the table.

"Master Gill," he said deliberately, "your offer is a generous one, and we would of course accept were it not for your considerable duties as Stablemaster. Now more than ever, our beras must be preserved if we are to recover and rebuild after this is all behind us. We would not wish to distract you from that even more important duty."

The Stablemaster's mouth turned down in a grimace. "That excuse won't work this time, Gerard, much as I wish it would. The stables are in the hands of the Aloise now."

Councilwoman Shima made an unidentifiable sound. She was quivering, and her ears were turning red.

Gerard Orndas did not look nearly so surprised, but when he spoke, some of the life had gone out of his words. "What happened?"

Master Gill wrung his hands and began to pace. "They've had their eyes on my stables all along, obviously. I should have known this would happen when poor Keth turned up dead after the Dedication. That boy was one of my gate watchers. No doubt he saw something he shouldn't have, and they killed him before he could warn me, warn all of us, about this . . . ," Master Gill glanced about the empty seats at the table. ". . . this travesty."

Ely was surprised to hear Keth's name. Wasn't he that strange young man she had met in the Keep? Had he somehow gotten involved in all of this?

Holding up his hands, Councilman Alm interjected. "I'm sure you have suffered, Gill, much like the rest of us. But our order of business now is to seat a Council and move forward, not count and recount our losses. I move that we seat the good Stablemaster and get on with it."

Reluctant nods from most of the other Councilors signaled their agreement. Master Gill's face brightened considerably.

"Well, shit," a voice said from across the room. "If losing some stables is all it takes to get a seat, a lost galleon should be more than enough."

Councilwoman Shima straightened, glaring daggers at the man who had spoken.

"Jonner Ceer," she said with strained dignity, "you are not welcome here. Leave us in peace."

"I missed you too, Tallomi," he said, pushing away from the wall and giving her a toothy grin. "Not enough to stay, I'll admit, if I had any other choice, but a man can't sail without a ship. So long as I'm stuck here, a Council seat seems as good a place as any to park my buttocks."

"Your problems are your own, not ours." Shima pointed to the door. "Now get out, before we throw you out."

The man called Ceer raised his hands in an exaggerated shrug, making the fish bones that formed a dangling frill on his shirt click as they knocked together. "Just as hateful of outsiders as ever, I see. But even if you are deaf to the sufferings of this poor foreigner, might I instead offer a trade? I've always found this city eager for commerce, both in the marketplace and . . . elsewhere."

Shima turned as deep a shade of red as it was possible for a human being to turn. Councilman Alm, perhaps wisely, took over the conversation before she could overcome her indignation.

"What trade would that be?" he asked.

"Weapons," Ceer said simply. He pulled a short dagger from his belt and tossed it on the table. The distinctive glint of steel was visible as it clattered to rest. "A bit of steel, plus more obsidian than you have hands to wield."

"And what would you be seeking in return?" Councilman Orndas asked.

Ceer shrugged, grinning widely. "Oh, not so much, really. For the moment, I'll take a seat on your Council. Once the city is freed and the Low Tide is returned to me, it'll be lands, a title, and moorage for any vessels I see fit."

"This man is a smuggler!" Councilwoman Shima fumed. "We do not do business with smugglers!"

Ceer raised his arms, still smiling. "You have me there, my sweet. I am indeed a smuggler, but I don't see any well-heeled proprietors of armaments about to make you a better offer. I'm afraid you'll have to make do with me."

Councilman Alm interrupted. "Your offer is duly noted, Mister Ceer, but we decline."

A murmur went around the room, and the smile dropped from Ceer's face.

"We can ill afford anything that would create more violence," Alm continued. "Arming ourselves would be the surest way to provoke a full scale war in our own streets."

There was more murmuring, and louder. Ely could hardly believe what she was hearing.

"Are you saying you don't intend to rescue everyone who's still captive?" she blurted out, her mouth once again outpacing her brain. The thought of the others remaining in that dungeon, waiting for help that would never come, was unbearable.

Councilman Alm looked at her sharply. "We will secure the release of any prisoners, if they exist, through negotiations, not force of arms."

"Negotiations?" Ely said, her voice growing shrill. "The Aloise negotiate with steel! Were you not here two nights past? They can take anything they want from us without a second thought! What could you possibly offer them?"

"That is a matter to be determined during the negotiations," Councilman Alm said coolly.

"What kind of plan is that?" Ely exclaimed in disbelief. She turned away from the table toward those at the edges of the room. "Are you blind? This is our chance to take back the city! Do the rest of you honestly think people like the Aloise are just going to let their prisoners go if we don't make them?"

"Enough! You are out of line, Elymia!" Councilman Orndas shouted. "You are embarrassing yourself. Even your father knows better than to think every problem can be solved with war! Councilman Alm is right. We must not provoke a fight with the Aloise in the streets of our own city; the destruction and the cost would be far too great. Acquiring arms would only give their troops an excuse to lay waste to everything we have built here."

Ely was speechless. The cost? From the way he spoke, she could tell he did not mean lives. How could they be thinking about the cost when people were suffering and dying? She looked around at the carefully guarded expressions of the councilors. Shima's was perhaps more rigid than the rest, but not one of them moved to object.

That was it, Ely realized. That was the true reason they turned down arms, the reason they did not want to believe the worst of what was being done by the Aloise. These were the representatives of the merchants, the traders, and the craftsmen, and the foe they faced was perhaps the wealthiest power in the world. They weren't afraid of what armed resistance would do to the people. They were afraid of what it would do to their profits.

Councilman Orndas pointed to Jonner Ceer. "Your offer is noted and rejected by the will of this council. Now leave us in peace."

Ceer shook his head, a look of pity on his face. "I always knew this place was governed by fools," he said, "but fools this big I never guessed. If you change your minds, I'm sure you know how to find me. If not, then when the

Aloise butcher you, I'll be sure to put shells on all your graves." He stalked out of the room, and the door slammed shut behind him.

"He's right," Tamalina said unexpectedly, uttering her first words since the meeting began. Her voice was cold, like the groan of timbers under the weight of winter ice. "You have no idea what those monsters will do. What they did to my mother, what they did to my sister . . . ."

Ely stiffened, tears welling up in her eyes as the confirmation of what she had already feared hit her harder than Remiana's fists ever could. Eomila . . . . Ely's sudden memory of her embrace brought agony rather than comfort. All that warmth, all that light, gone as if it had never been. It took all her strength just to remain standing. She wondered how Tamalina, whose loss was so much greater, could bear to speak at all.

And the Council was condemning even more to the same fate by abandoning them to their captors, Ely knew. If no one acted to stop it, more houses would soon be as empty as Tamalina's . . . and her own.

"You're all cowards," Tamalina said. "Every single one of you. You make me sick." She stood, her chair scraping loudly against the floor, and followed Ceer out of the room. A long silence followed.

There was no further talk of weapons that day, nor of prisoners. Ely sagged against the wall, barely conscious of what was going on around her. It did not seem to matter any more. She apologized in her mind to Wharfmaster Abrohl and Councilman Tulloch and all the others who would suffer and die because she didn't have the words or the power to convince the Council to save them. She apologized too to Eomila and Nantala, tears flowing silently down her cheeks, for running away and leaving them to face their fate alone. Then she apologized to Tamalina, her heart burning as she formed the words in her mind, for not throwing herself on Remiana and tearing out that murderous traitor's throat with her bare hands when she had the chance.

•••••

The events of the council meeting left Ely feeling dazed even hours later as she prepared for bed. She flipped the the wooden box on the desk before her open and closed as she stared morosely out the third floor window of Matrice's bedroom. It was still early, but with the port sealed and no way of knowing when it might be reopened, even basic items like candles and oil had to be conserved, meaning that the time to turn in was dictated largely by the falling of darkness.

The box she toyed with contained her comb and Tamalina's ruby ring, the only two objects that had managed to survive their imprisonment. The ring had suffered the worst of it: one of its twin rubies was cracked, and the other was missing entirely. Nevertheless, Ely would not have expected Tamalina to abandon it, yet she had not returned since disappearing from the dining room earlier in the day.

"She isn't in the house," Matrice said, closing the door carefully behind her to avoid upsetting the candle she carried on a saucer. "No one has seen her in the last few hours."

Ely snapped the lid of the box shut and stood up from the desk.

"Don't even think about going out to look for her," Matrice warned, snuffing the candle and returning the room to dimness. "You'll never find her in the dark."

"You want to leave her out there alone?" Ely said harshly. "She needs us, after what happened to . . . to . . . ." Even now, she could not bring herself to say it. "We can't just leave her."

"No," Matrice agreed, "but going after her now won't help anyone. We can search for her tomorrow, when it's light."

Ely knew Matrice was right, but that familiar feeling of helplessness still made her angry. Once again she had been left behind, with nothing to do but hope and pray and wait. Now Tamalina was just like the prisoners of the Aloise, distant and unreachable, beyond Ely's feeble power to aid. She hated it more than she could stand.

"I know all this is difficult to abide," Matrice said, sensing Ely's distress, "but we aren't soldiers or Councilors. We can't choose what's best for everyone. We can't have everything we want." She climbed into bed and stared up at the ceiling. "Trying to resolve things peacefully with the Aloise might end up being for the best."

Ely looked back out the window. Matrice had been there in those first horrifying minutes of fire and fear. She did not have to see the other woman's face to know that the sentiment was but a fleeting hope rather than an honest prediction.

Chapter 19
Harvest Time

"It has only been two days, and already these lowlanders are behaving no better than animals," Remiana said, passing the looking glass to Edwin.

Leaning against the side of the ditch where they hid, Edwin lifted the scope to his open visor and surveyed the farm in the weak light of dusk. Smoke was rising from behind the barn, and though the fire and the people around it were obscured by the building, their voices carried well enough to betray their presence. The only movement he could see was a shifting of shadows in a nearby stand of apple trees, but closer examination showed nothing more than branches bobbing in the breeze.

A clattering beside him drew Edwin's attention, and he hissed at the other soldiers for silence. They were no more than twenty all told, crouching in the ditch in a rough line. The one who had slipped in the mud gave Edwin a shameful look, then put his head back down and worked on extracting his backside from the ooze. Edwin found himself glad that he was the only one of the Lode Knights who had come along on this excursion. A fall like that in full plate could be dangerous on top of embarrassing, and metal footwear made for very poor traction.

The Impelar standing with Remiana gave Edwin a sneer that he could see even through her veil. She had been watching him with suspicious eyes ever since yesterday, when he stopped Remiana from beating that poor girl in the cell. Impelars enforced the iron law with particular zeal, and Edwin could not help but think that this one was contemplating a way to punish him for interfering. He did not even know the veiled woman's name, yet it seemed they were already enemies. He stared back coldly at her sneer, determined not to give her the satisfaction of a reaction.

Remiana, for her part, was so intent on the scene before them that she noticed neither the commotion nor the staring contest going on behind her back. She carried her own bow and quiver of red-and-yellow arrows slung across her back, having rebuffed Edwin's suggestion that she let one of the men hold them for her. He had hoped that if he could separate her from her weapons for just a few minutes, he might be able to arrange for them to go missing until the danger was past. Unfortunately, it seemed that months of confinement within Falls Gate had driven Remiana to jump at the riskiest opportunity that came along, and at that moment she would probably no sooner give up her weapons than her life. Edwin had even gone so far as to reminded her what would happen should her mother discover that she had personally led this deployment without permission, but not even the looming threat of Oridine's displeasure had been enough to dissuade her.

"This is the place?" Edwin asked of the ill looking man who was crouched in the ditch behind him.

The farmer nodded. "They had us locked up on the second floor, me an' my wife an' my sons," he said, pointing to the farmhouse. "That's where they put us when I tried to stop them killin' our herd. I got out the window at the back by jumping to the roof of the latrine. Please, you got to save my sons, sir, they're just babes."

Despite the farmer's disheveled appearance and the slur that marked him as either extremely uneducated or mentally deficient, Edwin had sensed that this man would bring serious trouble as soon as he had stumbled into Remiana's noontide audience. He was dirty and exhausted, as if he had been running the whole way from gods-know-where, and it took little prompting for him to begin spouting wild stories of banditry and killing and theft. Within minutes, Edwin had found himself being sent to round up troops and arms for an expedition outside the city walls. Remiana had seemed all too eager for the distraction, content to have any reason at all to get out of the confines of the Keep and away from whatever unknown duties her mother had assigned her.

A small movement brought Edwin's attention back to the field. A man appeared from behind the barn, carrying something bulky in his right hand and swinging it back and forth as he walked. Just a few paces into the grass, he stopped and heaved the object into the air with an underhand swing. As it flew, Edwin caught a glimpse of horns and tufts of pale hair before it dropped out of sight. The man then proceeded to fumblingly unbutton his trousers, reveal himself to the soldiers lying concealed in the ditch, and urinate onto the ground.

Remiana made a sad sound, as if it had been her own goat that had been decapitated and roasted by drunken bandits. She probably did consider it to be her goat, actually. If Falls Gate was now an Aloise fiefdom, as seemed to be more the case with each passing day, its territory was as much hers as the stony walls of Alomadra Fort or the cobweb of mining tunnels beneath, and lawbreakers found little comfort in lands ruled by iron law.

That thought reminded Edwin of the question he had been struggling with for days: Why? What was Remiana hiding from him? Why did they need this land at all? If Oridine had waited until the unification campaign ended, Falls Gate would have come willingly into the fold, bringing all its riches with it. Why was it, then, that house Aloise needed these lands now, and desperately enough to take them by force?

Edwin would have scratched his head had his helmet not prevented it. No matter how many times he tried to reason it through, it always came back to the succession. Controlling a sixth territory, especially one as valuable as Falls Gate, might secure an additional vote at the conclusion of the interregnum. But having a sixth vote seemed pointless – a majority was all they needed to choose the new king, and the Aloises' five existing holdings would have sufficed.

Edwin gave a mental sigh and tried to refocus himself on the present. A battlefield was no place to wonder about the why of anything.

The man urinating in the field had apparently had a great deal to drink, for he showed no signs of stopping. Not only had there been time for Edwin to lose himself in thought, but there had also been plenty for Remiana to remove the bow from her back, nock an arrow, and take careful aim. She stood to her full height in the ditch to get a good draw on the bow, which would have made her visible to the urinating man if he had bothered to look. Edwin tensed, but he held his tongue. Remiana had been trained far better than this, but it seemed she was intent on being reckless. Still, he knew better than to point it out in front of her troops.

Remiana had always been a good shot, but the distance from the ditch to the far edge of the field was significant, and she was several months out of practice. The loosed arrow struck the man high on the shoulder, spinning him halfway around before sending him to the ground. The yell of pain came almost a full two seconds later, greatly delayed by senses that must have been absolutely swimming in alcohol.

Remiana sighed, lowering her bow in disappointment.

"You had best go finish him off, Ed," she said, unhurriedly pulling another arrow from her quiver. "I expect the others will be coming soon."

The Impelar interrupted. "I would be honored if you would give me this task, mistress," she said, hefting her war scythe in both hands. Unlike the farming variety, the weapon was straight-hafted and its blade only gently curved, designed for hooking, tripping, and pulling foes off balance. Perhaps the most useful function of its shape, however, was intimidation.

"You will stay until I tell you otherwise," Remiana said sharply. "This is my command, and you will not question it."

"Yes, mistress," the Impelar said, deferring with her words if not entirely with her tone.

"There were about ten of them, I think," the farmer spoke up from behind them in a wavering voice, trying to be helpful. "Great burly men with all sorts of weapons."

Edwin snapped his visor down to hide the irritation on his face. He wished Remiana had been persuaded to change her mind. Her Impelar likely had fewer qualms about killing without investigation of guilt or innocence.

Edwin scrambled up the embankment alone, armor rattling loudly in his ears. His feet slipped back several times on the loose earth, but with a great heave he was able to pull himself up over the edge and stand erect, already panting, at the edge of the field.

The act of standing up, exposed to the eyes of the enemy, still filled him with fear despite his metal plates and the row of archers hidden at his back. It was a sensation he had not felt in a long time, not since joining the Knights, when his duties had been reduced to putting armor on and taking armor off. The fear was heavier by far than his armor, but Edwin had been trained all his life to carry heavy things, and it was a skill he had long since mastered. He took one step toward the farmhouse, and then another.

Three figures appeared on the far side of the field, attracted by the pained yelling to where the shot man had fallen. At least one was carrying a pitchfork, though the other two looked unarmed. They were still at some distance, but Edwin flipped up his visor and called out to them.

"In the name of the iron law, lay down your weapons and --!"

A red and yellow blur flashed past Edwin's head, streaking out and striking one of the unarmed men in the chest, and he dropped like a sack of grain to the ground.

Edwin spat out a curse and looked over his shoulder. Remiana was holding her bow with perfect form, hand still poised by her ear where it had released the arrow. She smiled at him and gave a little wave. Edwin wanted to throttle her, but turning back now was out of the question. He began a slow, lumbering jog toward the remaining two men.

Several more arrows arced over him as he ran, giving him the clearance that Remiana's should have, but they buried themselves in the soil short of their targets. The bandits responded just as Edwin feared they would: they turned tail and ran. Shouts of warning rang out, and faint shadows cast by the fire scattered among the buildings and sheds.

Edwin slowed to a walk. Now the element of surprise would be the enemy's if they chose to remain and fight. Cursing Remiana's recklessness again, he slid his sword from its scabbard and waved it in a wide arc over his head, signaling for the soldiers in the ditch to advance with caution. They would do no good firing blindly over the top of a barn.

Blade readied, Edwin moved toward the building that was blocking his view of the fire. The doors were shut and barred, and the windows much too high to reach, so he doubted any of the bandits had taken refuge inside. Just behind it, however, would be an excellent place to ambush an attacker who expected the enemy to be on the run. An ambush meant close range, close enough to touch, and Edwin hoped that would give him a chance to end this without any more bloodshed.

As he moved cautiously alongside the barn, Edwin passed the still-blubbering victim of Remiana's first shot. He had crawled some distance back toward the fire, but by now had run out of energy to do anything other than make pitiful noises. Despite Remiana's instructions, killing him and silencing his cries would only give away his location to the bandits who still lived. Edwin decided to leave him be and proceed as quietly as his clunky armor would allow.

Reaching the end of the barn wall, Edwin paused, readying himself an ambush. Prepared for the worst, he stepped around the corner and into the open. Immediately something hard rammed into his breastplate, threatening to push him off balance. Then there was a crack, and the pressure yielded. The bandit wielding the pitchfork had just enough time to look down at where the tines of his weapon had broken off against the metal plate before Edwin swung with the flat of his blade, catching the man on the arm hard enough to shatter the elbow.

The bandit dropped his broken weapon, and in one motion Edwin grabbed him with a gauntleted hand, threw him to the ground, and planted a heavy boot upon his chest.

"Surrender! You are outnumbered!" Edwin shouted at the other buildings, though he saw no hint of movement. Mere sight of the Lode Knights in their shining armor could halt battles in full swing, or so Edwin had been told. He hoped the same tactic would work here, although the mud of the ditch had done away with the 'shining' part quite handily.

The bandit on the ground wheezed under Edwin's boot, but no other response seemed forthcoming.

Then a flying rock pinged off the side of his helmet, making Edwin wince at the piercing ring. In the half-open doorway of the stables he spied a figure twirling a sling, and seconds later another rock whizzed by, clattering off the barn behind him.

Edwin clenched his fist around the hilt of his sword. These men seemed hell-bent on throwing away any chance of survival. In the Iron Kingdoms, attacking an Aloise was a crime punishable in ways not fit for decent conversation. Even so, he might have been able to fudge the facts to spare them had Remiana's Impelar not rounded the corner of the barn just in time to see Edwin on the receiving end of the attack.

He could feel the Impelar's eyes upon him, watching like a falcon circling on high. She was looking for weakness, he sensed, for hesitation, for anything she could use against him. It was the same gaze he had endured all his life, the one that none who shared his name could escape. Though he could hide the ring that symbolized his heritage, it was not that bit of iron about his neck that made him its target. In the end, it was his own body that betrayed him, for he could not hide his hair, his eyes, his face. Together they formed the unmistakable mask of an Aloise, and under the unspoken threat of that gaze, he had no choice but to act the part.

"Sorry," Edwin whispered. He raised his sword with both hands, looked away, and drove the point downward through cloth, flesh, and bone. The bandit with the sling screamed, and another rock bounced harmlessly off Edwin's breastplate with a low ring that sounded like the toll of a bell. His chest hurt as if it had struck home.

He took one step, and then another toward the open door of the stables, deflecting the next stone with the flat of his blade and sending a pair of faint sparks falling to earth. Each step added to his speed, and within ten paces he was moving as fast as the bulk of his armor would allow, sword trailing, no longer bothering to guard against the stones that rained upon his head and shoulders like stinging hail.

The bandit saw the charge and slammed the door of the stables against it, but it was a futile gesture. The wooden hinges splintered under the onslaught of metal as Edwin crashed into the door at full speed, breaking it into pieces and knocking the terrified bandit on the other side sprawling in a rain of splinters. For a moment, all was stillness as the dust settled in the light of the setting sun.

In the moment of calm, Edwin got his first good look at the bandit on the floor. He was hardly more than a boy, with thick arms that spoke of long hours in the fields. His clothes were threadbare, suited more for battling brambles and bugs than blades and arrows. Teardrops sparkled on his cheeks, catching and reflecting the fading light like tiny stars. With his sling lying out of reach, he raised his hands in surrender.

Edwin shook his head. "You don't want to do that."

The boy's face took on a look of uncertainty.

"This land belongs to an iron family now," Edwin said, his voice flat inside his helmet. "Do you know what the iron law holds for captives charged with banditry and assault of a Knight?"

The boy shook his head.

"It's better that way." Edwin drew the dagger from the sheath at his hip and tossed it to the floor. "Pick it up."

The boy did not move.

"This is the only kindness I can do for you now. Pick it up," Edwin repeated.

"He was my brother," the boy said, eyes fixed on the blood that stained the end of Edwin's sword.

Edwin's heartbeat thundered in his ears. "Then for your brother's sake, pick it up. He wouldn't want you to suffer what will happen if you don't."

The boy's eyes stared into Edwin's visor for a long moment, making him glad that with the setting sun behind him, he must have appeared as no more than a glimmering shadow.

Then the boy nodded. Slowly his fingers reached out, seeking the cold, uncompromising touch of Aloise-forged steel.

•••••

Remiana's soldiers were swarming over the farm when Edwin emerged from the stables, the fighting already ended. Remiana herself was stepping out of the farmhouse, holding one young boy in her arms and leading a frightened-looking woman who held another. The farmer ran to meet them, arms outstretched and tears on his cheeks, so overwhelmed with relief that he collapsed in a near faint upon reaching them.

In the center of the yard, the remaining bandits were being corralled beside the fire. Three were dead: one by Remiana's arrow, one by Edwin's sword, and one, with an arrow still protruding from his shoulder, whose head had been neatly severed by a scythe. Two more were alive and restrained under the watchful eye of their captors. A nearby pile of their weapons contained nothing more than one broken pitchfork, an obsidian knife covered in goat's blood, and a hefty stick that might have been serviceable as a club. Oddly, there were no bottles or other traces of alcohol anywhere.

Edwin shook his head in disgust. These men were not professional bandits. There was no reason any of them needed to die.

He stalked over to Remiana and took her by the arm, interrupting the praise being heaped upon her by the farmer and his wife. He pulled her into the farmhouse and slammed the door in the Impelar's face when she tried to follow.

"Tell me why we're here," he demanded.

Remiana looked confused. "There were bandits att-"

"Don't play dumb with me," Edwin cut her off, pulling off his helmet so that she could see his eyes. "Tell me why we're here."

Remiana's face took on an annoyed look, and she crossed her arms. "You well know, Ed. The unification-"

"Don't lie to me!" Edwin shouted, drawing his sword. Remiana took a step back, bumping into the farmhouse's rough-hewn dining table.

"Look at it," he said, holding it up so she could see the dried blood on its blade. "I've killed for you, killed a man who didn't deserve it and broken a brother's bond, and now you're going to tell me why!"

Remiana looked uncomfortable. "Do not ask this of me, cousin. Mother has forbidden-"

"Damn your mother!" Edwin said. "You are your own woman, and I'm asking you for the truth."

Remiana stared at the blood on the sword for a long moment. Edwin did not want to think of what he would do if she refused him. He did not want to believe that the girl who had been his only friend during those long, cold years at Alomadra had truly slipped away. He could not bear to imagine that he had lost his only –

Instead of backing away, however, Remiana drew closer.

"It is for the succession," she murmured in a low voice.

Edwin was not sure whether to feel relief at her admission, or anger that he had been right all along. "Your mother can't be that stupid. She already has the votes to choose the next king."

Remiana looked at the floor, refusing to meet Edwin's eyes. "She does not wish to select a king," she said, barely above a whisper. "She wants to select a queen."

Edwin's sword slid home in its sheath with a soft hiss. Suddenly it made sense.

"There is no suitable male heir in the main Aloise line," Remiana said. "At least, none my mother finds suitable. I have no brothers, nor did her sister have any sons."

"So rather than give the throne to a lesser branch of the family . . . ." Edwin said.

Remiana nodded. "Yes. She would instead change the iron law to permit a woman to claim the throne."

"Which requires two-thirds of the territories," Edwin finished.

Remiana nodded again. "Falls Gate will be our sixth. Out of nine."

Edwin's head was spinning. "But won't the other families refuse to recognize Falls Gate as a voting territory?" he asked. "Surely they have no desire to see Oridine on the throne."

"They cannot refuse," Remiana replied. "Falls Gate was chosen carefully. It is prosperous and powerful, more than the equal of some of the other holdings. But more than that, it has an army already in the field. If Falls Gate were treated as a conquest instead of an equal, it would mean total war against an already deployed and powerfully motivated force. The troops' absence made Falls Gate easy to capture, but it also makes it a dangerous asset for the families to hold without granting it full rights, including a vote in the succession."

She looked up at him, her green eyes meeting his. "And I am the one my mother plans to put on the throne."

•••••

Donvin smiled to himself as he watched the Aloise troops overrun the farm. Their tight quarantine of the city might have slowed the news of the coup from spreading, but tidings of soldiers wearing Aloise colors marching from Falls Gate would spread fast and far. It surely would not take long to reach the city's troops deployed abroad.

His usefulness at an end, Donvin released the farmer from his controlling threads, letting him crumple to the ground mid-step. It was a truly delightful application of his power, Donvin thought, and just one of many the books he had acquired from Falls Gate hinted at. With the knowledge those volumes contained, a touch in the right places could move the tongue, eyes, and mouth almost as convincingly as their true owner. So long as those to be fooled did not know the puppet well, a slight affect to the speech would be easily overlooked. Even better was that Donvin found the technique to be only a small drain on his strength, making him wonder what other, grander marvels he might be capable of. It stirred in him a hunger for more, and for the fulfillment of Lith's promise of an even greater power that, so far, she had failed to deliver.

As for the "bandits," Donvin had freed them as soon as the fighting started; their instincts had served to control their actions well enough after that. Except, that is, for the boy who had fled from the rear of the stables carrying a new steel dagger. Donvin could not fathom why the Aloise had let one of their enemies escape, but he saw no reason to intervene. A survivor would only spread the story faster.

How easily his ruse drew them out told Donvin that the Aloise were hungry for a real fight, which fit his plans perfectly. He would make sure they got their fill, and more. He turned and stepped through the glowing curtain behind him. After a brief return to the forest of the Masked, it would be time to once again call upon a certain young woman in the occupied city of Falls Gate. The seeds of war had been sown, and now it was time to teach her how to tend them.

Chapter 20

Accusations

Night had fallen in the forest when Donvin emerged from the gateway just outside the Masked encampment, and he hoped he could be about his business and gone again before his presence was noticed. In that, however, he was mistaken.

"Greetings again," Bird's voice said.

Donvin turned to see the masked man leaning against a tree, clearly waiting. Their meeting was no accident.

"Greetings," Donvin replied warily.

Bird detached himself from the tree and approached. Donvin could see he was carrying something in one hand, though the gloom of the moonless night prevented him from making out more than a blobby outline.

"The Listeners did not hear a breach tonight," Bird said, the veiled question no better hidden than a dagger sheathed in a silk stocking.

"I was visiting the site of an earlier breach," Donvin lied. There were not many excuses for leaving the camp, especially not for traveling by means of the power. "I feared it might not have been fully contained."

"Even though the Listeners said otherwise?" There was a pause. "And was anything amiss?"

"No," Donvin admitted. Lying about something verifiable would be stupid, and it was better to be thought foolish than deceitful.

"Why not trust the listeners? It is our way to go where they bid us."

"They have been wrong before,"

"And that means we are not to trust in the ways of protecting this world passed down to us?" Bird probed.

"That's not what I said," Donvin countered. Bird was testing him, he could feel it. What bothered him more, though, was that he did not know why.

Whatever Bird had gleaned from his questioning, he kept it to himself.

"The source of the poison in Falls Gate," he said in an abrupt change of subject, holding up the object in his hand. It was a half-full bottle of wine. "It has been found."

Donvin cursed his bad luck, but made a show of curiosity about the bottle.

"Is that it?" he asked.

"It is," Bird said. "It seems Falls Gate was subject to a coup in recent days, just after the Dedication, which made this difficult to find. Nevertheless, here it is." He cradled the bottle in both hands, making the contents swirl inside.

"It was indeed poison," he continued, "but a strange one. Not unlike the kind in Memory flowers, yet rendered nonlethal."

"Do you know who might have done it?" Donvin asked, silently cursing himself again. It had not been intentional, but creating a poison that mimicked something as unique as the Memory flower had been a terrible mistake.

Bird shook his head. "None of our detractors are capable of it. The flowers are rare, much too rare to provide the amount of poison that was used. And then there is the matter of its alteration. To do this would require great knowledge . . . ." He looked up at Donvin. "Or great power."

Donvin said nothing.

"One who wields our power would have been able to do it, and perhaps no other," Bird said.

"But that's absurd," Donvin replied, glad that Bird could not see his face. "None of us would have any reason. Could it have something to do with the coup you mentioned?" He hoped very much that Bird believed him.

"Absurd it does sound," Bird acknowledged, "but that is what the evidence tells us." He drew closer to Donvin, his voice dropping to a whisper. "It tells us that there may be a deceiver among us."

Donvin wondered if he could get away with silencing Bird right then, but knew that he did not dare. They were but feet from the Masked camp, and in the darkness he could not be sure that there were not others about to witness.

Bird sniffed several times, his face hovering over Donvin's shoulder.

"That smell is one of . . . worry," he said, his mask tilting slowly toward Donvin's own. "Is there a reason for worry?"

"I'm only worried that you may be jumping to conclusions," Donvin said in a tense whisper. "There could be another explanation." He had not wanted to rush the plan quite so quickly, but it looked like he would need a scapegoat a bit sooner than anticipated. It was risky, but at this rate Bird would expose him if he didn't act.

"It could be that others have acquired our power," Donvin said. "They could be using it in their petty squabbles, like the coup in Falls Gate."

Bird shook his head. "Unlikely," he said. "How would they have taken it without our knowledge?"

"Even if it's unlikely, we can't ignore it," Donvin said. "Like you said, we should deal with all threats seriously. Even if the chance is small, we must make certain."

"That has the sound of an excuse," Bird said, his voice growing dangerous, "and a poor one at that."

"Do not be so quick to dismiss the possibility," a third voice said as Donvin's mentor stepped out of the darkness. "These are the same misguided coastmen who have already attacked us once. It would be a mistake to underestimate them."

Bird stepped back from Donvin to consider the new arrival.

"It's impossible. Such a thing has never happened," Bird said. "It is a baseless claim, meant to distract us from some other truth. That is what it smells like." He looked at Donvin and sniffed the air again for good measure.

"But if it's not?" Donvin's mentor challenged. "It is a serious thing to accuse one of our own of deception. We should eliminate all other explanations first, should we not?"

"It will be simple to test," Donvin spoke up. "All we have to do is watch the Listeners. If they sense activity in Falls Gate when all of us are here, then we will know I'm right."

Bird cocked his head, as if hearing something unusual.

"Say that again," he said slowly.

"I said the Listeners will be able to tell us if I'm right," Donvin said.

Bird reached up and scratched under his chin, contemplating. "That they might," he said, turning toward the camp. "Shall we go and see them?"

Donvin's mentor stepped into his path. "Not now," he said. "Most are sleeping. We will begin at dawn, when the others wake. A few hours will make no difference."

Bird looked between Donvin and his mentor.

"Very well. But you will be there to watch with us," he said to Donvin. It was not a request.

"Of course," Donvin replied. He would indeed be there. A few hours more would be all he needed to ensure that this test proved his innocence.

Chapter 21
The Offering

Ely's eyes snapped open. The sheets beneath her were damp and cold, and beads of sweat quivered on her bare skin. Her strained breathing eased as the room came into focus and the dream that had been stalking her receded into the sea of shadows that blanketed the ceiling. Her grip on the corner of her pillow slackened, and she grimaced at the vile taste in her mouth.

A draft at the window moved the filmy curtains, sending a ripple through the shadows that crowded the room. Matrice twitched slightly in the bed, reminding Ely with a minor startle that she was not alone. She was not used to sharing a bed, but with Tamalina gone it was only the two of them in the room now, and the floors of the old house were cold. Even more than she wanted warmth, however, she wanted not to be alone.

Ely's eyes drifted shut again. She felt the dark dream slip away from the other shadows and steal up to the foot of the bed, reeking of shit and mold and damp, stagnant air. She felt it place a wet, filthy hand on her foot as its yellow rat eyes rose like twin moons from the horizon of the footboard.

"So good to see you again, Elymia," they hissed.

Something powerful wrapped itself around her neck, choking off the scream that was about to push its way out. Her wrists and ankles, too, were suddenly restrained. Her eyes were open now, she was sure of it, but the force that was holding her did not flee as a dream upon waking. The shadow at the end of the bed turned its head toward her.

"Quiet now," it said in a shockingly familiar voice. "Your friend is sleeping."

Ely's eyes strained wide. "Keth," she managed to squeeze from her constricted throat. Dots of color were welling up at the edges of her vision, splashing the walls with putrid ochers and lurid reds.

"Am I?" said the shadow.

The force holding her throat eased, and Ely sucked in a huge gasp of black night air.

"Keth is dead," she whispered.

The shadow nodded, its outline barely visible against the moonlit windows. "Yes," it said, "he is. And he suffers less than many who are still living."

Ely shuddered. For a moment she could again sense cell walls closing in around her, the air growing damp, the skittering of crooked nails coming toward her . . . . Then the vision faded, and she was once again in Matrice's bedroom, blinking furiously to clear the tears from her eyes.

The shadow turned toward Matrice, who still slept, oblivious to the nightmare sitting upon the foot of her bed.

"Don't touch her," Ely said with alarm.

"She is your friend, is she?" The shadow leaned in closer. "A true friend? Or a friend like your friend in the tower, who relaxes in comfort while you huddle in fear, afraid to be alone even in sleep?"

Anger swelled in her chest, but Ely still could not move.

"I can see it burning in your eyes," the shadow said, speaking with the voice of a dead man. "I can see the lust for revenge."

"You're just a nightmare," Ely said, her voice stronger now that her fear was lessening. The rational part of her knew that this could not be real.

"If I am a dream," the shadow said, "then consider me a dream of things to come, of paths that lurk beyond the sunset. Of your future, and of the revenge you so desire, know this, Elymia: you will not have it. You are nothing but an ordinary woman, and ordinary women do not get their revenge. They suffer, they weep, and they die with hatred soaking their bones, but they do not get their revenge."

Tears were welling up in Ely's eyes, from a source unknown even to her. Even in a dream, the words hurt. "No," she said.

"No?" the shadow mocked. "Why deny it? You know you are nothing. You have no power to make your desires come true. You are just a scared little girl, too frightened even to fall asleep alone."

Ely squeezed her eyes shut, not wanting to acknowledge the truth of those words.

"Then why are you here?" she said in a quavering voice.

"I am here to change all that," the shadow replied.

Ely's eyes opened again. Forgetting momentarily that she was speaking to a dream, she asked, "How?"

"I can give you the power to deliver justice. I can return to you the power stolen from your ancestors by an arrogant few."

"Why me?" Ely said.

"Power I can grant," the shadow said, "but the will to use it, I cannot. So many of your kind are weak and selfish, and they will make any excuse to avoid the pains of doing what is right."

Ely's face pulsed hot as she remembered how the Council had turned down Ceer's offer and damned their kinsmen to captivity and death.

"But not you, Elymia," spoke the shadow again. "You have righteousness in your blood. You are the daughter of a warrior. You will not let the wrongs committed against your people slip from their place on the anvil of retribution. You will be the hammer that pounds this crooked world straight, if you will let my power forge you."

This could only be a dream, Ely thought, or something that walked the twilit border between dream and nightmare. There was no harm in indulging a fantasy in a dream. In her sleep, at least, she did not have to live in fear.

"Name your bargain," Ely said.

"Bargain?" the shadow said. "There is no bargain, for it costs nothing to be a servant of justice. Use these three gifts I grant you as your heart demands: free your friends and strike down those who oppress you. And if your heart should falter and shy in weakness from what must be done, consider this a reminder of the mercy of your enemies."

Something small and dense dropped onto Ely's chest, making her wince, then slid off to land on the floor with a thump.

"What is-" Ely started to say, but a soft knock on the door interrupted her, followed by the sound of the latch being raised.

"Aunt Matty?" a quiet voice said from the doorway.

"Mmm? Bermin?" Matrice mumbled, stirring under the quilt. Ely had pushed herself up in the bed, about to shout a warning, when she realized with confusion that there was nothing holding her down.

"I heard funny noises," Bermin said in a sleepy drone, shuffling into the room to stand by Matrice's side of the bed. He was holding his drooping-eared puppy over his shoulder, its limp body showing as much drowsiness as its master's. Ely scanned the room, but none of the shadows were anything other than ordinary. She reached down carefully beside the bed where the small object had fallen, but felt nothing other than cold boards under her fingers.

Matrice yawned. "I'm sure it was nothing, Bermin," she said with her face half buried in a pillow. "The house is full of people. It was probably just somebody snoring. We didn't hear anything, did we, Ely?"

"Nothing," Ely said weakly. It had been a dream. Of course it had been a dream.

Evidently unpersuaded, Bermin climbed over Matrice and into the bed, curling up with the puppy in his arms between her and Ely. Matrice, clearly too tired to protest, groaned, rolled over, and was asleep again in seconds.

Ely sat upright in the bed for a while, but the longer she stared at the dark corners of the room, the more foolish she felt. As terrifying as it had been, part of her wanted the dream to be real. Yet no matter how hard she listened, none of the shadows spoke to her. She wondered, her thoughts dulling in a drowsy blur, whether the nightmare she would wake to in the morning would not be worse than the one that had visited her in the night. Sleep took her at last, one arm still hanging off the bed in a half reach toward something that was not there.

•••••

The smell of hot bread tickled Ely's nose, coaxing her gently to wakefulness. For a few blissful moments, she felt nothing but the sun's light falling on her skin and thought of nothing but that enchanting aroma that filled the house.

Reality, not content to give her more than a moment of peace, was swift to intrude. The faint smell of smoke wafted in on a breeze, and on its heels came the memories: Eomila. Nantala. Barty. Ely's bones ached with loss, and her appetite withered and died. As much as the pain urged her to stay in bed, thoughts of Tamalina ultimately forced her out. No matter what she was feeling, it could not be half as crushing as a sister's loss.

Shaking herself to loosen the hold of those unpleasant memories, Ely stood and tried to stretch the soreness from her muscles, feeling a tension in her body uncharacteristic of sleep. She noticed that neither Matrice nor Bermin was in the room, presumably having been drawn downstairs by the smells of the kitchen. She did not blame them for letting her stay abed. In Matrice's place, she would have done the same.

As she had the day before, Ely dressed herself from Matrice's closet, this time picking out a green traveling coat and pair of matching leggings that would hold up well for as long as needed when they went out to search for Tamalina.

Her hair was a mess, but Ely paused as she reached for the wooden box that held mother's comb. The comb was there, but it was resting on top of the box, not inside it. She was sure she had put it away last night. Had Matrice taken it out again? She put her fingers out to touch the smooth bone, but pulled them back sharply as it gave her a small jolt, like a discharge of static that made her whole hand tingle. A second touch revealed that whatever energies had filled it were gone, for now it felt just as it always had, its worn contours comforting against the palm of her hand. She frowned, but found nothing else out of the ordinary. Perhaps Matrice had borrowed it that morning. Yes, that must be it.

After dressing and fixing her hair before the tall mirror, Ely remade the bed, and she was just folding down the final corner when the tip of her toe touched something unexpected under the hanging edge of the quilt. It had just been a dream, she reminded herself, but nevertheless she could not keep from holding her breath as she knelt and lifted up the fringe to look underneath.

Her breath came out in a disappointed sigh as she saw that what her foot had touched was just a little book, no doubt fallen from the table on Matrice's side of the bed that was piled high with them. Ely picked it up and rose to her feet again. Matrice had probably not even noticed it was gone. Granted, it did not quite look like Matrice's usual reading material. Its title was only a single letter, and its binding far more worn than typical of the pristine collection that the Pourin family kept, but before Ely could open it and look inside, the door to the room burst open and Matrice rushed in, grim lines written across her face.

"They found Evana," she said.

•••••

When Ely and Matrice arrived on the scene in the quarter of the city known as Milltown, they found a large knot of people already gathered in the street with their necks craned upward. Shielding her eyes, Ely followed their gaze up sheer brick walls to where several men were balancing on the steep incline of roofing tiles. One of them she recognized by his distinctive white hair as Councilman Alm, whose long limbs and gangly shape helped him move with relative ease across the roof. The other two were of a younger sort and stockier build, dressed in the thick, water-resistant leggings favored by dock hands. Each had a coiled length of rope wrapped about his waist.

The three men made their way along the roof to the thickest chimney of brick and paused to untie their ropes. Councilman Alm said something and motioned with his hands. Then the three of them knelt, disappearing from Ely's view. A moment later, the councilman's head poked out over the roof's edge.

"Clear away!" he shouted down at the people in the street, making a sweeping motion. The crowd backed up a few paces, jostling and bumping as it went.

The veil of white hair disappeared again, and then a long, cloth wrapped bundle tied with ropes was rolled up to the brink. Even from a distance, there was no mistaking what it was. Many heads turned away as the thing was lowered down the front of the building, twisting and bumping awkwardly into the brick wall. Watching that descent did more to disperse the crowd than Alm's warning had, and by the time the ropes touched ground, Ely had no trouble reaching the front to confirm the awful truth with her own eyes.

The body was not fresh, and the birds had been at work for days before their activity had been noticed. Yet even through the damage the scavengers had done to the remains, the blow that had killed Evana Respose stood out clearly: a long, cleaving stroke from shoulder to hip had left a great chasm through which the birds had removed the majority of the internals.

"Sink me, I've never seen a wound like that," a man in the crowd said, holding a handkerchief over his mouth and nose. The smell was indeed revolting, but Ely's senses were mostly numb.

"It's a sword wound."

Hearing the familiar voice, Ely tore here eyes away and looked up to see Tamalina, swathed in a rough-spun cloak, staring at the body. Her tone was unaffected, as if her aunt's disfigured corpse were no more remarkable to her than that of a feral cat.

"I saw what blades of iron did to my mother and my sister," Tamalina said. "This is their work." She thrust out a hand, pointing toward the tower of Cliffhome Keep.

"This is their work," she repeated, "and still the lot of you do nothing. You just cower and pray that the next one won't be you." The words were chilled as they slipped from her mouth, not hot with passion as they should have been. The fires of anger in her eyes had burned out, leaving something black and malformed among the ashes.

"I'll put a stop to it," she said. "And once my mother and sister and aunt are avenged, I will draw the price of their blood from you who cared too little to help." The gray cloak swirled like a choking mist about her body as she turned and stalked off down the street, leaving a trail of frightened stares in her wake.

Ely wanted to call out to her, to follow, but she realized now, after looking deep into her friend's eyes, that the gesture would be pointless. She was powerless against the evil that held Tamalina in its clutches. She could not bring back Eomila, or Nantala, or Evana, and nothing else in all of creation would be enough to ease Tamalina's pain.

"That's no sword cut," a man's voice said, breaking the spell of stillness Tamalina had left behind.

Jonner Ceer, the smuggler who had been ejected from the Council meeting the day before, was kneeling over the body in the street, closer than any had thus far dared.

"A man would need the arm of a giant to do this in a single blow," he said. "I've seen plenty of metal blades in my time. They're strong, but they aren't magic. No, this looks like it was done by a boras horn, or something like it. Still . . . ." He looked up at the rooftop, from which Councilman Alm and the other two men were descending on their ropes. "A boras didn't put her up there, that's for damn sure."

"Then who do you think did, Mister Ceer?" Councilman Alm said as he hopped lightly to the ground from the rope.

Jonner Ceer rose and backed up a step, lifting his arms in a shrug. "I haven't spent time here in years, so my guesses aren't worth much. But her job never made Evana Resposé a popular woman, and nobody puts a body on a roof if they're looking to hide it. Seems to me like someone wanted to send a message. If she was still keeping that little book of hers as scrupulously as she used to, half the businessmen in the city have probably wanted to kill her at one point or another."

Something tickled Ely's memory. *And if your heart should falter and shy in weakness from what must be done, consider this a reminder of the mercy of your enemies.* The book she had found under the bed . . . . What letter had been on the cover?

Ely slowly drew the small book from her pocket, suddenly glad she had brought it with her in their rush out of the house, and looked at the title. The swirling fragments of thoughts in her head began to come together, forming a picture both frightening and wonderful. She did not have to just wait and hope any longer. There was finally something she could do.

Ignoring the stares of the onlookers and the other woman's objections, Ely grabbed Matrice by the wrist and dragged her away, back toward the

Pourin house. What she had experienced last night had been more than just a dream. Something was waiting for her in that room, she was certain of that now, and for the sake of the Lady Evana and all the others who had suffered and died at Aloise hands, she was going to find it.

Chapter 22

The Chosen Few

"It's not that I don't believe you," Matrice said an hour later, standing near the windows in her room and flipping through the pages of Evana's small notebook. "It's that you are clearly in shock, and you need to rest until you're thinking rationally again."

Ely did not pause as she pulled another drawer from Matrice's dresser and upended it, sending a flood of carefully folded undergarments spreading across the floorboards.

"He said he gave me three gifts," she repeated, doing her best to ignore how crazy the words sounded as she tore the room apart in search of something that remained, as yet, undiscovered.

"I believe you had a nightmare, and with all you've been through, I'm sure it seemed very real," Matrice said patiently, "but this book hardly proves anything. It could have gotten here any number of ways, and I'm sure that no one else was in the room last night except for Bermin. You need to stop before you hurt yourself."

Ely gave up trying to pry a wooden shelf off the wall and stood surveying the wreckage she had made. Every drawer had been emptied, every shelf cleared, every corner scoured and every dress in the closet shaken upside down, and still there was nothing. She might have been able to accept that she was delusional if not for the fact that the shadow had alluded to Evana's murder hours before the body was found. But what did that matter, if all the rest had been a lie?

Seeing Ely's fervor subside, Matrice stepped over a pile of clothing and took Ely's hands in hers. "You need to relax," she said calmly. "If you promise to lie down, I'll go make you some tea with extra honey, and then you can drink it nice and slow and we can talk about this reasonably. Agreed?"

Ely smiled sheepishly. "I've been acting a fool, I know," she said, looking down at her hands, which were red and abraded from their frantic searching. "And I'm sorry about your room, I really am. I suppose I could do with a bit of rest, and some tea."

"That's right," Matrice said, gently guiding Ely to the bed. "Now just breathe deeply, and I'll be back with that tea before you know it."

Ely released Matrice's hands and sat down onto the bed, and immediately she heard a dull *clink*. Matrice, having only just turned toward the door, froze in mid-step. Body tensed, Ely leaned over and lifted up the pillows.

Beneath them, lying innocently on the plain white sheets, were three identical glass vials, each with a dark amber liquid held inside by a cork stopper. Ely felt a rush of relief. She knew she had not imagined it all.

"Is that proof enough?" she asked, turning to look at Matrice.

The other woman had her lips pressed together and her gaze locked on the three vials, and Ely could almost see the wheels of her mind spinning quickly, searching for traction on a road where the familiar ruts had suddenly disappeared beneath them.

Ely reached out and scooped up the vials. The liquid inside was clearly thicker than water, and a few flecks of sediment swirled slowly at the bottom. The color, a deep amber at first glance, took on a more reddish tint when held up to the light. Whatever it was, it was not a substance Ely knew.

Matrice sat down on the bed beside Ely, a carefully neutral look on her face. She held out her hand expectantly, and Ely passed her one of the vials. Matrice polished it deliberately on her sleeve, as if some speck of dust might hinder her analysis, before holding it up to her squinting gaze.

"Any idea what it is?" Ely asked as Matrice turned the vial this way and that. There was no doubt that Matrice had far more knowledge of things bizarre and unusual; the bookshelves of the Pourin house proved that beyond any argument.

"Not yet," Matrice said, cocking her head. All skepticism had vanished from her voice.

"So you believe me now?" Ely asked.

"Since I don't have a better explanation for how these came to be under my pillow, I'm willing to accept yours, for the time being. Though I think consulting an alchemist would help us sort that out."

"No," Ely said quickly. "No one can know about this, not if want to keep the element of surprise for when we use them." The certainty in her voice surprised even her. Still, it felt good, for once, to be the one with a plan, the one in control.

"Use them?" Matrice said, raising an eyebrow. "Use them for what? I don't see how we can possibly use them without knowing what they are."

"It's something that can free everyone the Council wants to abandon," Ely said, recalling the shadow's words. "It can get justice for Evana and all the rest."

"And you'd believe this on the word of a creature you saw in a dream?" Matrice asked.

Ely nodded. She no longer cared about seeming a fool. Perhaps she had finally cracked and was succumbing to madness, but it really did not matter to her if she was. She needed this to be real. It was her chance to escape her helplessness, and she would not let it slip away.

Matrice made a thoughtful sound. "I've always known you to be trustworthy, Elymia, so I'll trust you in this as well. But that hardly resolves our problem. We can't come up with a plan without knowing more about what we possess."

Ely stumbled over the retort she had been preparing. "You . . . think we should use it too?" she asked in surprise.

Matrice fixed Ely with a critical stare. "I was in the street this morning, just as you were," she said. "Just because I don't faint or have hysterics dosn't mean that I don't care about what happens to my friends and my city." She made a fist around the vial, tight enough that Ely feared the glass might break.

"We've been terrorized, tortured, imprisoned, and killed, while our own Council throws away the chance to drive out our enemies. And now you've managed to convince me that there's someone on our side with the power to help. How could I not want to use it?" There was danger in her eyes. "How could I not want to kill every last one of those-" She caught herself before going any further, and her usual, controlled expression returned.

"Then you think Tamalina was right about what happened to Evana?" Ely said, unsettled by Matrice's rare loss of poise, but understanding it nonetheless. No one could face the things they had seen and remain unmoved.

"I trust her more than some bilge-drenched smuggler," Matrice replied. "Even if she's wrong, the ledger was red with blood long before Evana's name was on it." She sighed. "But none of it matters if we can't figure out the nature of the gift you've been given."

"No alchemists," Ely said firmly. If they would take a coin to identify the liquid, they would readily take a hundred to identify the people who brought it in to their enemies.

Matrice nodded reluctantly. "So be it, but that leaves few options. Is there anything else you remember from your dream?"

Ely thought for a moment. "He called it a kind of power," she said, "something from long ago that was stolen away."

Matrice put a finger to her cheek thoughtfully. "That's not very helpful," she said. "Why didn't you ask for more details?"

Ely blinked, her mouth open. More details? Did Matrice expect her to have calmly interrogated a shadow creature that was holding her hostage in the midst of a nightmare?

"No matter," Matrice said. "We can make do without the alchemist, if we must." She used her thumb and forefinger to delicately loosen the cork and wiggle it free from the top of the vial, then passed it back and forth under her nose.

"It smells like . . . ." Matrice's nose twitched, and she closed her eyes. "Old leaves," she said finally, opening her eyes again, "and a touch of fruit – berries, I think."

"Does that mean anything?" Ely said, sniffing cautiously.

Matrice shrugged. "Not much, but enough for the next test." With one quick motion, she tilted the vial back and poured its contents into her mouth.

Ely was too surprised to stop her. When she did manage to separate the vial from Matrice's grip, it landed harmlessly in the mouth of an upturned slipper on the floor.

"What do you think you're doing!?" Ely shouted. "That could be poison!"

"Not likely," Matrice said without concern, wiping her mouth on her sleeve. "If it was poison meant to kill you, it would have looked much more appetizing. And if it was poison to use on someone else, it wouldn't have had such a strong smell or color. What's more," she added, counting her reasons on her fingers, "three vials is too much if the goal was to poison only you, but too little to poison all our enemies. So, it only makes sense that the vials aren't poison."

Ely sputtered. "That doesn't mean you should just drink it!"

Matrice shrugged again. "Well, you were the one who refused the alchemist, and this was the next best way to . . . ." She trailed off, putting a hand to her throat.

"Matrice?" Ely said, alarmed. "What's wrong?"

Matrice just stared straight ahead, as if seeing something that Ely could not. "It burns," she whispered, sounding suddenly dazed. As she spoke, she slumped forward, and Ely barely managed to catch her before she fell off the bed. She pulled open the high collar of her coat, but her throat looked perfectly normal.

"Damn it!" Ely cursed at the semi-conscious woman. "Why did you have to be so stupid?!"

"Burns," Matrice moaned, and beneath her half-open eyelids Ely could see a disturbing amount of red.

Ely did her best not to panic, but all thoughts of secrecy fled.

"You're going to be all right! I'm going to bring help!" Ely said, clambering over Matrice's to get to the door as quickly as she could. A hand caught her ankle, almost sending her face-first into the mess that littered the floor.

"Don't," Matrice croaked out, tears leaking from the corners of her increasingly crimson eyes. "Don't leave me."

Ely pulled her leg away and scrambled to her feet. "I'm going to help you, please hold on!" she said, hardly able to look as her friend contorted weakly in pain. She dashed to the bedroom door and yanked it open, revealing for a brief instant a startled-looking woman standing just on the other side, arm outstretched as if she too had been reaching for the latch.

"DON'T LEAVE ME!" Matrice screamed.

The door tore itself out of Ely's hands and crashed shut with such force that the whole house shuddered, and all the furniture in the room traveled an inch or two across the floor. A large crack appeared in the wall before Ely's eyes, dancing its way up to the peak of the ceiling.

There was a sound of shattering glass from somewhere below, and then the vibrations faded and the house fell curiously silent. Then the shouting began, followed closely by the sound of feet pounding heavily on the stairs.

"Are you all right in there?" a male voice called from the other side of the door. "We heard a scream. What happened?"

"We're fine," Ely lied unconvincingly, though given the muffling of the door and the many panicked voices from below, it probably did not matter. She pulled on the handle, but the door refused to budge. "But I think we're stuck," she added. The shock of what had happened, whatever it was, seemed to have shaken the terror right out of her. Even so, she still had trouble taking her eyes from the door that had come alive in her hands.

Over on the bed, Matrice was now quite still.

Something heavy struck the door from the outside, followed by a muffled exclamation of pain.

"It's jammed good," the voice on the other side said, biting off a curse. "Don't worry, we'll get you out." There were more heavy steps on the stairs, and Ely could hear the rumblings of a conversation start up in deep, concerned voices.

Not seeing anything she could do to aid the men outside, Ely returned to the bed to check on Matrice. The other woman's body was limp, but she was still breathing, and her eyes were closed as if in sleep. The skin of her face and arms was flushed a bright red, as if she had spent too much time in the sun. It was hot to the touch as well, but the change in color had come over her too quickly for a fever. Whatever was happening to her, it seemed that the worst had passed, at least by the standards of what came before.

At a loss for what to do, Ely just sat on the bed, holding one of Matrice's unusually warm hands in hers, and waited. The sounds from outside the door continued, punctuated by a thud every time another man thought to test the unyielding portal. Not one of the voices seemed to be able to go more than a few seconds without asking where in hell's tide the violent shaking had come from.

As Ely waited, she became aware of another, more curious noise coming from above. Matrice's bedroom was on the top floor of the house, and Ely swore she could hear the faint clicking of roofing tiles moving across the ceiling. The sound reached the edge of the roof, and then it stopped. Ely was ready to dismiss it when suddenly a window slammed inward and a human form tumbled through, landing awkwardly amid the debris on the floor.

The intruder pushed herself up, and Ely recognized her as the woman who had been just outside the door when it had sealed itself so violently. She was older than Ely, perhaps by as many as ten years, and she wore a civil service tunic turned inside out so that no insignia was visible. Her brown hair was loose but for a single braid that hung over the right side of her freckled face, and her eyes blazed with determination.

"Give me the book," she said to Ely in a dangerous tone. There was no question of the one she meant. "I know you have it. I saw you with it in the street." She did not appear to be armed, but her voice carried all the threat of a weapon, and more.

"Who are you?" Ely asked, glancing about the room for anything she could use to defend herself.

The intruder bristled at the question, but she answered it. "Maewell of Southwater is my name. Now hand over the . . . ." Her words trailed off as her gaze fell to Matrice. "What in the deep is that?"

Ely looked down and gasped. Tiny wisps of smoke were issuing from Matrice's reddened skin, curling upward in lazy white lines. Ely reached out tentatively and touched Matrice's hand, only to recoil in pain as something stung her flesh. Matrice's hand was moist, and something in the sweat burned at Ely's palm until she rubbed it vigorously on her trousers.

Then, even as they watched, the smoke lessened and then stopped altogether, leaving the two women to stare in awkward silence, wanting very much to disbelieve what they had just seen. Then Matrice opened her eyes.

They were terrifying eyes, there was no denying that. Nothing remained of their whites, so intensely bloodshot had they become, leaving them a sickening medley of black and red. As Ely stared, Matrice slowly sat up, wincing as she did so.

"What?" she said, her voice a touch raspy but still far too normal for her monstrous visage. "What are you looking at?" She turned to look at the intruder.

"Mae?" she said with surprise, but also recognition. "What are you doing here?"

Maewell of Southwater stood frozen, looking into those horror's eyes. She might have been trying to speak, but nothing came out.

Ely touched Matrice lightly on the shoulder and pointed toward the mirror.

". . . Oh my," was the exclamation Matrice chose, an understatement if ever there was one. She reached up a hand to her face, but jerked it away quickly when it touched the raw, red skin of her cheek.

"How long?" she asked Ely, turning those bloody orbs once again toward her.

"What?" Ely said, her mind working slowly under the burden of that alarming gaze.

"How long was I unconscious?" Matrice said.

A loud crack came from the door, making all three of the women jump.

"We found a hammer!" a man's voice called from the other side. "Stand back, we're going to knock it down!"

Matrice looked at Ely questioningly. Ely tried to explain, but to little avail.

"When you passed out," she said, "the door, it . . . ." None of the words that came to mind seemed helpful. "It . . . got stuck."

Matrice nodded slowly. "We can sort it out later. But for now, we have to get out of here before those men get through the door. Yes, you too, Mae," she said, giving her a stern look. "And for the gods' sake, Elymia, hide those vials."

Ely blinked, looking down at the two remaining vials still in her hand, then quickly tucked them into a jacket pocket.

The door gave another loud crack, but showed no signs of caving just yet.

"Now hold on here," Maewell said, shaking her head vigorously. "You're obviously sick, Matrice, and I'm not going anywhere until you see a doctor. And as for you," she said, pointing an accusatory finger at Ely, "you will not set one foot outside this room until you hand over the Lady's book and explain yourself, or I'll report you on suspicion of murder."

"This book?" Matrice asked, pulling the small tome from beneath her and holding it up. "You can have it, but only if you take us out of here the same way you came in, which I'm assuming was not by the door. A doctor is precisely the last person who must see me now, and if those men outside see me like this, they'll take me to one by force."

Maewell's eyes narrowed when she saw the book in Matrice's hand. "A conspiracy then, is it?" she said. "You knew that this woman had the book, and you didn't report her?"

Matrice rolled her eyes, a rather gruesome gesture. "Report her to whom, exactly? And besides, Mae, you know perfectly well that neither Elymia nor I is a murderer. Now if you help us, I'll explain everything once we get somewhere more private."

Ely, having had enough time now to organize her thoughts, stepped between the two of them, holding up her hands.

"You're in no condition to be going anywhere, Matrice," she said. "A doctor is exactly who you need to see. What will your father and mother think if you go missing after what just happened here? What will Bermin think?" She could see Maewell nodding in agreement out of the corner of her eye. She might be the sort to climb roofs and break in through windows, but at least this Mae person did not seem completely out of her head.

"They will think I'm dead, probably," Matrice said unemotionally, "and you as well, at least for a time. That's a price I'm willing to pay. Besides, being thought dead will prove useful to our plan, if you hadn't considered that fact. Remiana and her mother won't be expecting a visit from dead women."

"Our plan?" Ely said in disbelief, throwing up her hands. "What plan? You nearly just died after doing perhaps the stupidest thing ever. There is no plan!" She paused for breath. "And why in the deep's name can't you see a doctor?"

"Because," Matrice said, lowering her voice, "we have what we wanted now, Elymia, and for the next few minutes, we're the only three people who know it."

A thin crack appeared in the surface of the door as another blow from the hammer tore into the other side. Ely found herself at a loss for words, not knowing if she should believe Matrice or restrain her until help arrived.

Matrice turned to Maewell.

"Mae, if you guide us out of here right now, without a single objection, I can promise you something that no one else can."

Maewell crossed her arms in defiance. "And what is it you think I want badly enough to let you risk your life for it?"

Matrice did not miss a beat. "To avenge Evana's murder."

The words seemed to rekindle the fire in Mae's eyes. It took her mere seconds to consider before she spat out a foul word and motioned for them to follow. She turned, put her foot on the sill of the window, and climbed outside.

Chapter 23

The Bait

Donvin squinted down at the metallic discs of the Listeners in the blue glow of the underground chamber. *Move*, he thought, *move!* But the rings of the three devices remained still.

Donvin closed his eyes and listened to the sounds of the other Masked moving about the cave. They were not happy to be there, he could sense. They had been incredulous when Bird had rounded them up and herded them down to the Listeners' chamber at dawn, and they were growing more restless with every passing hour. So far there had been no open dissents – Bird was well respected among them – but their patience was wearing thin.

Donvin looked down at the Listeners once more. Why was it taking so long? He had left the vials of Scarwood sap with Elymia in the early hours of the morning, and now it was nearly noon. Had he misjudged her? Would she, in the end, prove too timid to use them?

"Unsteady nerves?" Bird said smugly from the other side of the Listeners' pedestals.

Donvin cursed under his breath. With every passing minute, Bird was growing more and more confident. If something did not happen soon, he might announce his suspicion of Donvin's involvement in the poisoning at Falls Gate, and if that happened, Donvin's chances for leaving the room alive would grow dangerously slim. He needed a backup plan.

"I need to stretch my legs," Donvin said. "We've been at this for hours."

"By all means," Bird said, as if granting quarter to a wounded foe. "But we can't have anyone wandering off alone and getting lost in the tunnels, can we?" He nodded, and another Masked stepped up to Donvin's side. It was Limp.

"Come on. If we're going to walk, let's walk," Limp grunted. Donvin fumed that Bird would presume to assign him an escort, but he did not argue. Even if he could not go alone, a walk would at least give him time to think.

Donvin wove his way though the throng of loitering Masked, Limp trailing close behind, and headed toward one of the many tunnel exits. He fingered the black pouch that hung from his neck beneath his robes, feeling the shard of bone that had once been the tooth of a comb within. What would he do if Elymia did not come through for him?

"This is all a load of dung," Limp complained, interrupting Donvin's contemplation. "Coastmen with Scarwood sap using our power? Hah! They hardly know how to find their own asses with their hands in the dark." The scorn in his voice made him sound even grumpier than usual.

"But no," he continued sarcastically. "Some of us think they have the right to order the rest around like servants, as if we didn't have more important things to do." He was talking about Bird, Donvin realized. That gave him an idea.

"This whole thing is really my fault," Donvin said, leading them into one of the darkened tunnels.

"Eh, how's that?" Limp grunted, following.

"Well, you know the way it is, how . . . certain people like to be in charge," Donvin said. "If I didn't know better, I'd say he was keeping us down here all day just to punish us: me for doing what he couldn't, and you for questioning his judgment. You remember what I'm talking about, don't you?" It had been quite a while since that day in the snow fields, but Donvin suspected Limp would not be quick to forget. "I undermined him by putting out that fire without his help, and he's been waiting for the chance to remind the rest of us that he's still the one in control. Why do you think he's making you follow me around like a bodyguard?"

"That's an ugly accusation," Limp said, though the disapproval in his voice was mostly perfunctory. "That was months ago. We aren't savages like those coastmen. We don't carry grudges."

"We shouldn't carry grudges," Donvin said, lowering his voice, "and I'm sure someone like you never would. But you've seen how he behaves like he's better than the rest of us. He's only waited until now to do this because he needed an excuse like this 'poisoning' in Falls Gate. I don't know about you, but he never let me examine that poison he found. How do we even know it's poison at all?"

Limp was quiet for a moment, which told Donvin that he had been right: Bird had not allowed anyone else to check the poisoned wine.

"He could have made up the whole thing as a way to put us in our place," Donvin whispered. "He could even be trying to set himself up as some kind of . . . leader."

Limp froze. "That would be against the code," he said slowly.

"Yes," Donvin agreed. "No one has the right to command the Masked or set himself above us."

Limp sounded wary. "But the chances that one of us would be willingly violating the code are . . . ."

"Greater than the chances of some backwards coastmen learning the secret of our power."

Limp's mask lowered in thought. It was working.

"If that's really what's going on here," Limp said deliberately, "then it can't be allowed to continue."

"I agree," Donvin said, "but there's nothing someone like me can do. I'm still new to the mask, and few would trust my word over his. Only someone more experienced, someone the others already look up to, could expose this farce."

"Someone the others look up to . . ." Limp repeated, savoring the words.

"Anyone who stood up to him would be doing us all a great service," Donvin said slyly. "Such a person would earn a great deal of respect for their courage and selflessness."

Limp's mask bobbed in the almost total darkness of the tunnel.

"The first thing," Donvin whispered, "is to show him that we don't take orders from him, or from anyone."

Limp looked over his shoulder, back toward the dim blue light of the main chamber.

"There's no need for an escort down here," he said abruptly. "Most of the tunnels don't go very far anyhow. Go on, take your walk." He turned back toward the main chamber, a new vigor in his limping steps.

Donvin smiled. Perhaps he did not need Elymia's help after all.

"Aren't you the clever one," a voice said from the darkness behind him. Lith.

"What do you want?" Donvin said, recalling their last encounter in Boulder's hut with bitterness. "If you're not going to help, then stay out of my way." He peered into the dark, but Lith did not reveal herself.

"I merely wished to warn you," she said. "Cleverness is good, but you should be careful not to be too clever. A cornered enemy is more dangerous than one who thinks he has the upper hand. If you provoke the one you call Bird too much, he may choose to deal with you directly."

"Oh, I'm counting on it," he said. If it could have, his mask would have grinned.

"And you think you can best him?" Lith asked.

"Yes. Because you'll help me."

Lith gave a light laugh, a chime of bells in the night. "That's rather presumptuous, isn't it?"

"I'm growing tired of your games," Donvin said. "You've been holding out on me, and not just about Dolmon, whatever that is. I'm the one risking my life for this plan of yours. It's time you gave me those powers you promised."

"You can't rush fate, Donvin," Lith said. "The time will come when it comes, not when it pleases you."

"I don't think fate has anything to do with it," Donvin said disdainfully. "That's just an excuse for you to keep me on your leash. I intend to call your bluff."

Lith laughed again, though there was something darker in it this time. "You want me to believe you'd risk your life against Bird just to pry these secrets from me?" she said. "Hardly. I created you; I know you value your life too much to gamble it."

"Only if I thought you might actually let me lose," Donvin said with a devious smile. "Don't forget, Lith, I know what you value too. If I lose, then so do you."

Lith was silent for a moment. "There are some things you are just not ready to know. On this, you must trust me."

Now it was Donvin's turn to laugh. "Trust you? Trust is the last thing a fool does before he dies. Thankfully, you did not make me a fool."

No reply came from the depths of the tunnel, so Donvin could only assume that Lith had vanished again. There was too much she was still keeping from him, far too much to consider her a true ally. Yes, she had led him to the books that had revealed some of the finer points of his power, but there was so much more she wasn't telling. Dolmon, for one. Someone out there wanted him to know the meaning of that word, but for some reason Lith did not, and that was reason enough not to trust her fully. If risking his life was what it took to force those secrets out of her, then that was what he would have to do. And once he had them . . . . Well, what further need would he have of her?

Rising voices from the Listeners' chamber reminded Donvin that he still had much to do before that contest could happen. He headed back toward the light, hoping that Limp would prove to be just as arrogant and self-aggrandizing as he seemed. He was not disappointed.

". . . And we've all had about enough of this," Limp's voice greeted Donvin as he entered the cavern.

"The test is not finished," Bird replied. "There could be a traitor among us, and we will wait until we know the truth, however long it takes."

Limp snorted. "Then why not hand over that bottle so the rest of us can be sure we're not just wasting our time?"

"That sounded like an order," Bird said, his voice icy and crystal sharp.

"An order?" Limp said. "And who among us would know about those? One who issues them himself, perhaps, and expects the rest of us to follow? Well, we're tired of following, and it's time we had the chance to decide for ourselves whether there's any good reason for this 'test' of yours."

"That would be unwise," Bird said. "Each time we test the poison with our power, a bit more is destroyed. If we all test it, there would be no evidence left."

"How convenient," Limp spat. "How convenient for one who wants to keep us all in the dark, who wants our obedience based on his word alone."

"Be careful," Bird warned, "before making accusations. Disrupting the harmony of our union is a violation of the code as surely as lying."

"Then why don't we see which of us is the violator?" Limp said, holding out his hand. "Hand over the bottle."

Donvin, who had made his way through the onlookers as Bird and Limp were arguing, stepped between the hostile parties.

"Let's remain calm," he said soothingly. "Remember, we're all on the same side." He could smell the heat of Limp's anger for having interrupted the confrontation that he himself had suggested, but he did not give him time to speak.

"If there is a question about the bottle," Donvin continued, "let a neutral party hold it until the dispute is settled." He held out his hands to Bird.

"Treachery!" Bird declared. It was evident he knew what Donvin was up to, but that would not help him now. He had not aired his suspicions to the others, so the rest of the Masked had no idea of Donvin's personal interest in the matter. Making those accusations now would only seem like evasion. "This is a plot!"

Limp was quick to spy the advantage being presented to him. "That seems like a reasonable suggestion. Surely we can agree on that?" He looked around at the other Masked. "Let a cooler head help us sort out our differences." He nodded at Donvin, and several of the other Masked nodded with him. Donvin's mentor, lingering near the edge of the cavern, was among them.

"No," Bird said, anger rising in his voice. "No one must touch this bottle until the test is finished, especially not-"

"Be careful," Limp said, mimicking the tone Bird had taken with him. "Those sound like the words of someone with something to hide."

Donvin felt a light hand on his back, and suddenly Point was at his side.

"Please," she rasped imploringly at Bird and Limp. "Not fight. Be reasonable. Give. Trust." She patted Donvin on the arm. The other Masked started making noises of agreement. Donvin found himself glad for having visited her and Furrow the other night.

Bird growled, but it was clear the weight of opinion was against him. "This is a mistake," he said, but he nevertheless pressed the wine bottle stiffly into Donvin's hands.

One touch was all it took. With his hands pressed against the dark glass of the bottle, Donvin's glowing strands were hidden as they flicked out to render the poisoned liquid inert. To any who examined or drank it now, it would be wine and nothing more.

"There, that wasn't so hard," Limp said. "Now, might we ask our impartial arbiter what he makes of the contents of the bottle?"

Donvin looked around at the many masks that were now focused on him. The bottle, free of its potential for incrimination, felt noticeably lighter in his hands.

"It is not for one of us to speak and the others to follow," he declared. "Each of us has the right to know what he wishes for himself. We are equals, and we must treat each other as such. It is what you think that matters, not I." He set the bottle on the ground and stepped back. Nods of approval met the gesture.

The first silver strands to reach out and probe the bottle's contents were, predictably, those of Limp, but several of the other Masked followed suit quickly after. The Listeners whirred and clicked, their rings spinning and locking in as they detected the activity, but no one paid them any mind.

"The wine is clean," Limp stated triumphantly after just seconds of examination. "There is no poison in that bottle."

"Impossible!" Bird said, but the others too withdrew their silvery strands and turned their heads away from him.

"It seems we know who the liar is," Limp smirked.

"He did this!" Bird snarled, pointing at Donvin. "He destroyed the poison when he touched the bottle!"

"Without alerting the Listeners?" Limp scoffed. "Please. Your lies are getting more desperate by the second. Perhaps you should shut your mouth before you do any more damage."

Bird leaned close to the Listeners, but not a single one of their arrows was pointing at Donvin. He straightened slowly, humiliation and rage pouring off of him in waves.

"I think you've mistaken me for something I'm not," Donvin said to him, his voice dripping with innocence.

Bird stepped close to Donvin so he could not be overheard.

"There is no mistake," he hissed. "Your very words betray you, deceiver. One day soon, you will understand how dangerous it is to meddle with forces beyond your control."

"I'm looking forward to it," Donvin hissed back.

In the commotion of the argument and its aftermath, no one was watching when the Listeners' rings spun and locked in facing south, in the direction of Falls Gate.

Chapter 24

Three

Ely poked her head out the window, gulping as she surveyed the escape route Mae had plotted for them. The ledge outside was narrow, a lip of stone left protruding when the third floor of the house had been built, and the alley below looked wholly unforgiving of jumps or falls. It was paved with cobbles and had nothing like the carts of hay that were always present in children's tales.

As Ely watched, Mae, with Matrice in tow, shuffled along the ledge toward the brick chimney protruding from the backside of the house. The thump of a hammer hitting the door behind her urged her to hurry and follow, but Ely took a moment to grab a cloak and gloves from the messy floor before making her exit. If Matrice didn't want her new appearance noticed, they would need to cover her well.

Gathering her courage, Ely eased out of the window, shutting it behind her. The three story height suddenly seemed much higher, and she teetered for a moment before digging her fingers into the cracks between the wall's stone blocks. Then she shuffled after the other two women, keeping her face toward the wall. Inch by inch, she slid sideways, trying to avoid looking down.

When all three of them had reached the chimney, Mae led by example. She stuck out her foot and used it to feel around on the near side, eventually catching a loose brick and pushing it inward to create a small toehold, then did the same with a hand. In this way she began to lower herself, moving one limb one at a time to probe for purchase.

Grateful that she had chosen to wear something practical that morning, Ely waited her turn on the improvised ladder, lending Matrice an arm to help her shift from the ledge to the handholds in the brick. She guessed that it would only be a minute or two before the door back in the bedroom gave way and their absence discovered.

Mae proved again to be quite nimble, hopping to the paving stones below just as Ely was taking her first tentative steps down the chimney. Following

Matrice was slow going, and Ely's fingers ached with the strain of gripping the bricks, but at least every step was bringing her closer to the ground.

Blood was oozing from scrapes on her hands by the time all three women reached the bottom, but Ely was just glad to be on solid ground again. The cloak and gloves she carried she passed to Matrice, who put them on without question and pulled the hood forward as far as it would go. Hopefully it would be far enough.

Once Matrice was settled in her makeshift disguise, Mae took the lead again, hurrying them eastward, toward the city center. As they fled, Ely glanced back one last time at the third floor window they had escaped, but she saw no searching faces pressed against the glass.

They stuck to shadowed alleyways until just a few blocks from Cliffhome Keep, where they were able to join the sparse foot traffic on the thoroughfare without notice. Ely scrutinized the other pedestrians as they walked, watching to see if any took an undue interest in Matrice's cloaked form, and also to steer them well away from the occasional Aloise patrol. She had just avoided one of the latter, in fact, when Matrice elbowed her in the ribs and nodded over her shoulder.

Ely risked a quick glance, but at first she did not see what Matrice was trying to point out. The soldier they had avoided was walking casually, crossbow in one hand and the other gesturing conversationally to a woman who followed at his side. She was wearing a brown half-dress, the sort that commoner women made at home in imitation of richer styles, and showing no small amount of leg beneath. It took Ely's confused eyes several full seconds to recognize her as Tamalina.

Ely's feet stopped moving, bringing her to a halt in the middle of the road, but Matrice jerked her forward by the wrist.

"Don't," Matrice whispered.

"What does she think she's . . . ." Ely trailed off, no longer trying to hide her stare. Tamalina looked completely different than she had just hours ago: her clothes were changed, her hair was washed and combed to a shine, and a smile graced her face.

"Do you want to get thrown in prison again?" Matrice hissed. "Because that's what'll happen if you try to drag her away from a soldier who has other plans for her. That's if you're lucky. And in case you forgot, we have bigger problems at the moment."

Ely resumed walking, though she continued to watch behind her until Tamalina and the soldier turned onto a side street. Matrice was right of course, but after the way Ely had seen Tamalina act in Milltown, so full of terrible coldness, she hated to think what she might do if left to wander the city alone. It could easily be something that might get her killed, if flirting with Aloise soldiers was any indication. But if she chased Tamalina now, it would mean abandoning Matrice to this stranger Mae, and that was not something she could bring herself to do.

The road they followed was a wide thoroughfare just south of the Keep, with offices of trading companies and guilds lining its sides. Beras-pulled carts were usually a common sight here, but today only a few plodded the cobbles, and even they were light of cargo. Mae stopped them before one of the taller buildings, all five stories of its edifice constructed from the same ancient, weathered blocks sporting eaglehead motifs. A set of double doors faced onto the street, above which were carved the shapes of a pen, a coin, and a ship – the symbol of the city registry, where the Lady Evana would have had her offices.

"Isn't this a bit conspicuous?" Matrice asked. Ely glanced about to ensure that they were not drawing attention, but no one else in the street was close enough to overhear.

Mae just pushed open the front doors and went inside. With little alternative, Ely and Matrice followed.

The smell of parchment and chemicals struck Ely as she passed through the doors. The atrium they entered was tall, and when she craned her neck, she could see balconies for each of the higher floors overlooking it from above.

It was immediately clear that all was not well in the house of the registry. Stray papers rustled and skittered across the floor as the women entered and shut the doors. At the foot of the stairs that led to the upper floors, it looked like someone had dumped a whole armload of books from one of the balconies above.

Mae put her hands on her hips as she surveyed the damage.

"Come out, you cowards, it's just me!" she yelled, her voice ringing in the confines of the building.

A head of straw-colored hair popped up from the second floor balcony, and the slender man attached to it made double time down the stairs to greet them. Like Mae, he too was wearing an inside-out tunic, though his showed its age with ink stains and fraying seams.

"Have any soldiers been back since I've been away? And where are Dubble and Tailorship?" Mae demanded, crossing her arms.

The man bobbed his head meekly. "No soldiers since yesterday, ma'am. There's hardly anything left for them to take. As for Dubble and Tailorship, they went home."

"They went home? What gave them the idea that they had the day off? Why didn't you stop them?" Mae said angrily.

The man looked at his feet and shrugged. "Everything is ruined, and we can't do any work without our books. They didn't see any point in staying."

"That's absurd talk, Lewmas, and you had best get it out of your head," Mae said with crisp authority. "I expect tea in my office in five minutes, and then I want you to start copying out new ledgers to replace the old ones." A growl issued from her throat. "By the deep, how could they think there was no work to be done?" Ely could almost hear her teeth grinding.

Mae motioned for Ely and Matrice to follow her up the stairs, but the man called Lewmas interrupted them.

"Did you find out?" he asked, his deferential tone shed in favor of genuine concern. "Is it true?" His eyes focused intently on Mae, wide with question and with hope.

Mae stopped and made a face like she wanted to spit, but refrained from doing so on the polished floor.

"Aye," she said. "It's true."

A tear came to Lewmas' eye, but he blinked it away and bowed his head. "Poor Lady Evana," he said. "But she is resting in a better place now, may the gods receive her with grace." He made the sign of the tree, closing his eyes and touching his forehead with the middle finger of his splayed hand.

Mae whirled on the stairs, that now-familiar rage back in her eyes.

"She's dead, that's all there is to it, so shove that crap and get back to work!" she snarled, though there were tears in her eyes too.

Not waiting to see if Lewmas would follow the order, Mae stormed up the stairs, leaving Ely and Matrice to trail behind. They did not have far to go, for they left the stairs on the first floor and took but a few steps before Mae opened a door and ushered them inside.

The room, which Ely took to be an office of some kind, had bookcases of dark wood lining the walls, though they were mostly empty. A long desk stood across the far wall in front of a narrow window, but most of its contents appeared to have been swept onto the floor.

Neither Ely nor Matrice was eager to be the first to speak, for Mae was still fuming as she stalked across the room to perch herself on the corner of the desk, ignoring the chairs in front of it. Ely busied herself helping Matrice remove her cloak and gloves.

"How is it that you know this woman, exactly?" Ely whispered, tugging on the fingers of Matrice's glove.

"I met her during my apprenticeship under Lady Evana," Matrice whispered back. "She's been Evana's best accountant for years. Loyal, if a bit . . . rash."

Ely paused, the second glove only half off Matrice's other hand. This was not an apprenticeship she had heard about before.

Matrice, sensing Ely's curiosity, looked away. "It was very short," she added, "and I was young."

Ely moved to lift the cloak from Matrice's shoulders. It was not surprising that there were times of Matrice's life she did not like to discuss – there were certainly times in Ely's own she would sooner forget – but few things seemed able to genuinely embarrass Matrice. Not even of the most lascivious talk made her flush, yet of this she seemed ashamed. Ely shook her head slightly, behind Matrice's back. As much as she thought she knew her friends, in many ways, it seemed she did not.

"We can trust her," Matrice whispered, unprompted.

"And what makes you say that?" Ely asked, wondering how much Matrice could possibly know about this Maewell person from such a short time so long ago.

Matrice sniffed loudly, as if offended by Ely's doubt. "She wants what we want," she said.

"How can you be so sure?" Ely asked. "She was spying on us. She broke into your room, for heaven's sake! What's to say she won't try to turn us over to the Aloise?"

Matrice sniffed again. "I just know, that's all," she said.

"If you two are done holding your little whisper council over there," Mae interrupted from across the room, "I think we have some business to discuss. Take a seat." She gestured to the chairs in front of her. When the other two women hesitated, she added, "Don't worry, we won't be found here. The Aloise have already come and gone, and they took most everything we had with them. I very much doubt they'll be back."

"What were they after?" Ely asked, picking one of the chairs.

"Better to ask what they weren't after," Mae said, scowling at the empty shelves. "They wanted information on most everything about the city: population, taxes, prominent businesses, ship moorings, and more. They carted off almost all our books rather than risk leaving anything behind."

"Why would they want all of that?" Ely asked. "Not that those books aren't important, of course," she added hastily when Mae's hackles went up, "but those aren't the sorts of things an occupying army would need. They should be looking for weapons and food, things like that."

Mae shrugged. "Think what you like, but I tell you, they were determined to get all of our records, and quickly."

"Perhaps that was why they abducted Lady Evana?" Matrice speculated, seating herself next to Ely.

"Perhaps," Mae said, her gaze hardening. "But I think you know more about what happened to her than you're saying. Why don't you start by telling me about these?" She reached into a pocket and produced two glass vials of amber liquid.

Ely clasped a hand to her jacket pocket and discovered that it was empty.

"Looking for something?" Mae said, wiggling the vials between her fingers. "Now that I've helped the two of you flee from your own families for gods only know what reason, it's your turn to help me. Tell me what these are, what you're planning, and how in the deep you got your hands on Evana's book, and I might not turn you in."

Ely glared at her. "We don't even know what's in the-"

"Scarwood sap," Matrice interrupted, "and I would appreciate not being threatened, thank you. I also suggest you give those back, or I will have to take them from you."

Ely choked. Since when did Matrice know what was in the vials? And since when was she the kind to make threats?

"Never heard of it," Mae said, leveling her gaze at Matrice. "And I'd like to see you try to make good on that threat."

"If you insist," Matrice said.

The two vials tore themselves free of Mae's grip, floated through the air, and landed in Matrice's lap. Mae frowned at her now-empty hand, while Ely's mouth hung open.

"That's a fancy trick," Mae said, being the first to recover. "But if I'm supposed to be intimidated, you'll need to do better."

"Very well," Matrice replied. She put out her hand, and the desk leaped two feet off the ground, forcing Mae to scramble for purchase. Ely jumped to her feet in surprise, knocking over her chair as she tried to back away.

"Saltspit!" Mae cursed, hopping off the edge of the levitating furniture and staring back in shock. "That's solid beachgrove! Put it down before you break something!"

Matrice furrowed her brow, and the desk settled back to the floor with a thud.

"How in the great seas did you do that?" Mae said, prodding the surface of the desk as if looking for hidden strings or hinges.

"As I was trying to explain," Matrice continued, holding up the vials, "this is Scarwood sap."

"You knew what it was?" Ely said. "Since when?"

"Well, I didn't know until I tried it myself," Matrice said, "but I suspected before that."

"And you didn't tell me?" Ely said angrily. "I thought you were dying!"

"I just wanted to be sure," Matrice said coolly. "Anyhow, I'm shocked neither of you have heard of it. Did you never read Flora Remembered?"

"Spare us the academics," Mae cut in. "Just tell us what it does."

"It's thought to be what gives the Masked their power."

There was a pause.

"Thought to be?" Ely said.

"You can't expect the Masked to confirm it," Matrice said, "but it seems obvious. They eradicated the last known Scarwoods a few centuries ago, and before that it was a crime to grow them. It's also well established that Masked are initiated rather than born, so their power clearly comes from an external source."

"But if Scarwoods are extinct," Mae said, "where did this sap come from?"

Matrice looked to Ely. "I think you can explain better than I."

Ely did her best to pare down the story of how they had found the book and the vials to its essentials, hoping that would make it sound a bit more believable. It didn't. Nevertheless, Mae picked up the gist quickly.

"So you have a Masked helping you," she said in summary.

"That was my guess too," Matrice said with an approving nod.

The shadow had hardly acted like a Masked, Ely thought, but who else besides the Masked had that kind of power?

"So now that you know what you have," Mae said, "what are you planning to do with it?"

"Get our revenge, of course," Matrice said, a grim smile on her face. "And yours."

Though Ely had thought the very same thing, somehow it shounded worse coming from Matrice, the bookwormish recorder's daughter. She shook her head.

"There's something more important," Ely said. "We've got to free the Aloises' prisoners. No one else is going to do it."

"You have a plan for this?" Mae asked.

"Well . . . ." Ely glanced over at Matrice. "We're working on it."

"I see that," Mae said skeptically, also looking at Matrice. "And so far, you've planned yourself out of your own bedroom and into a nasty rash. Bravo. I suppose you think you're just going to walk into the Keep and free everyone by lifting up a few tables?"

Matrice frowned.

"And what about money?" Mae continued. "You didn't bring anything more than the clothes on your backs, did you?"

"Money?" Ely asked. "Why would we need money?"

"So you really were planning to go in there with just the two of you?" Mae said. "How thick could you possibly be? No matter how many tables you can lift, the Aloise would fill you both full of arrows before you'd finished pissing yourselves. You won't even be able to get inside without a good distraction, and the only way you'll convince any man to help you with something that boneheaded is by paying him enough to make him forget how stupid it is."

Ely felt suddenly foolish. She had not considered any of that. As much as she thought she had learned about tactics from her father, this sort of thing still felt new to her.

"Are you saying you can help?" Matrice asked.

"You already have everything you need," Mae said. "It's right there in your pocket."

Matrice's hand went to her jacket pocket and came out with Evana's little book. She opened it, but most of the writing inside was made up of unrecognizable characters.

"Evana kept a copy of everything in that book," Mae said. "Unpaid taxes, outstanding loans, even the location of a certain storehouse for confiscated goods." She smiled. "Too bad she kept it all written in code."

Ely looked down at the ciphered pages, then back at Mae. "You know how to read it, don't you?" she said.

Mae's smile grew wider. "I might. For the right compensation."

"What do you want?" Ely asked, but she had a feeling she already knew.

"I want the vengeance I was promised," Mae said, the deadly tone returning to her voice. "I want the Aloise to pay in blood for what they've done.
I want one of those." She pointed to the vials in Matrice's hand. "Give me
that, and I'll ensure you have all the coin you'll ever need. But as for finding
men dumb enough to take it, you're on your own."

"Don't worry about that," Ely said, an idea popping into her head. "I know
how we'll be able to spend it." She smiled at Mae, feeling the satisfaction,
for the first time in days, of something finally going right. "I think we might
just be able to make a deal."

Chapter 25

To Be a Queen

Remiana took a moment to compose herself outside the audience chamber, lightly touching the ribbons in her hair and straightening the shoulders of her coat. She wore an officer's uniform rather than a dress, a prudent choice, Edwin thought, for the meeting to come.

Edwin knew he was little more than a pawn in this game, but he could not rightly leave Remiana to face this audience alone, especially not with the way things in the city seemed to be taking a turn for the worse. Hours earlier a patrolman had been found in an alley, his throat cut, with his pants around his ankles and his body mutilated in a way that made Edwin cringe. There had been no sign of a struggle. It was the sort of death that made the rest of the men uneasy, and so far they had found no hint as to who was responsible. This audience, though, was about a different problem.

When Remiana was ready, Edwin knocked sharply on the chamber door.

"Enter!" a woman's voice called out.

Remiana locked eyes with Edwin, her gaze showing both gratitude and fear, before giving him the nod to proceed. He opened the door and stood at attention as Remiana brushed past, her face now a perfect mask of poise, all hint of emotion scrubbed away.

The room they entered was light: fresh candles burned on the walls, and floor-to-ceiling windows looked out over the courtyard of the Keep and the mostly leafless branches of its Chesamir tree. A small, square table at the room's center was its only furniture. Between the table and the windows stood a lone figure, her blonde hair up in a tight bun and her arms folded behind her back.

Oridine Aloise turned to face them, and Edwin made a stiff bow, allowing the door to swing shut behind him. Though the full length of the room separated them, Edwin's heart beat a little faster. Oridine was a dangerous woman, and she looked every inch of it today.

"Acknowledge me, daughter," Oridine demanded, and Remiana fell to one knee. Those of the highest blood did not demand such displays from one another except in the direst circumstances.

Oridine stared at her kneeling child for several moments before considering Edwin.

"Why have you brought him?" she demanded, lifting her nose as if at an offensive odor.

"He is my escort, mother," Remiana replied, her eyes on the rug at her feet. "It is the right of every heir to be guarded by-"

"Do not lecture me about your rights," Oridine snapped. "You came from my loins; your rights are my rights. If I wish him to leave, he shall leave. Is that clear?"

"Yes, mother," Remiana said.

"However, I desire that he stay," Oridine continued, pinning Edwin to the wall with her stare. "He played a part in this, and he will share in its consequences."

"Thank you, mother," Remiana said. Edwin, on the other hand, was not feeling particularly gracious just then.

Oridine turned back to the windows. For a long while she just stared out at the overcast skies and the reddening leaves still clinging to the Chesamir's branches. Many had already fallen, creating a growing crimson patch around the trunk.

"Do you remember why I had you taught how to use a bow, child?" Oridine said, breaking the silence.

Remiana nodded. "It was because-"

"Stand when you address me, girl," Oridine said sharply. Remiana stood and put her shoulders back proudly.

"It was because you told me that having power was like shooting a bow," Remiana said.

"Yes," Oridine said. "Come closer. Tell me the rest."

Edwin followed Remiana protectively to the center of the room. The little square table that sat there, hardly more than a block of rough wood with legs, looked decidedly out of place against the rest of the decor.

"Our actions are like arrows," Remiana recited. "We must aim every action precisely and with purpose."

"So you do remember," Oridine said, leaving her spot by the window and coming face to face with her daughter across the table. "You took twenty soldiers from my city yesterday. Why?"

"To restore the peace," Remiana replied. "I had received a report of banditry."

"And you thought that was a prudent decision?" Oridine asked.

"Yes," Remiana said unflinchingly. "Lives were at risk, and it is our responsibility to protect the people who live beneath our banner."

"Tell me," Oridine said, "did you consider what the consequences would be?"

This was the real reason Remiana had been summoned, Edwin knew. He had done his best to warn her, but she had been unswayed. Nevertheless, seeing her reprimanded for it brought him no joy. He felt, rather, the guilt of his own inability to stop her.

Remiana remained silent, and Oridine continued. "Did you consider what might happen if word of our soldiers' presence here spreads too quickly? If the army of Falls Gate catches wind of it too soon?"

Remiana looked straight ahead. "I did not, mother."

Oridine clicked her tongue. "We are so close, child. The application for annexation is nearly prepared, and the city council has offered no resistance. They are content to be strung along with a few worthless promises and negotiations. In that, at least, your judgment was sound. Silencing the ones you identified has made the rest easy to manipulate."

Oridine's words of praise seemed to weigh heavily on Remiana's head, bending it toward the floor.

"But then you go and do something like this," Oridine said. "With our victory so near, did you truly think the lives of a few lowland peasants more important than your future throne?"

"No, mother." Remiana said quietly.

"Then you are telling me you were simply behaving like a careless, thoughtless child?" Oridine pressed.

"Yes, mother." Remiana said, her jaw stiff.

"Good," Oridine said. "Unlike stupidity, carelessness can be cured. I do not wish to think on the possibility of having bred a stupid daughter." She raised her voice. "Bring them in!"

A side door opened to admit one woman and two men: the Impelar and the two bandit captives from the farm.

The prisoners were bound with blindfolds and gags, their wrists and ankles tied so they shuffled and hunched. The Impelar prodded them forward with the butt of her scythe.

"The Impelars serve us in more ways than one," Oridine said. "You should thank this one, child, for making your foolishness known to me so that it might be corrected."

Remiana looked at the red-swathed figure, but said nothing.

"Did you not hear me?" Oridine said, an edge in her voice.

Remiana twitched her head in the tiniest possible nod. "Thank you," she murmured. Behind her veil, the Impelar smiled widely as she made a low curtsey.

"Putting aside the problems your actions may cause us," Oridine said, "we have before us the more immediate fruits of your mistakes. It is my understanding you wish to petition for leniency for these men?"

"That is correct, mother," Remiana said.

This had been Edwin's idea, though Remiana had needed little convincing after seeing the sorry state of these "bandits" for herself. While they had indeed killed six goats, it was unlike any case of banditry Edwin knew. The survivors were the farmer's own cousins, who had been working the very same farm they attacked. They swore up and down that they had been under a fit of madness, and their lack of motive or preparation seemed to bear it out. Indeed, the farmer's wife said it was she, not the bandits, who had locked herself and the family in their bedroom when the men had begun acting strangely. As for why the farmer hadn't related any of this, he too blamed a spell of madness.

"Remove their blindfolds," Oridine commanded, and the Impelar used her scythe to cut them away. The strips of fabric fluttered to the floor, revealing two pairs of brown eyes clutched by terror. Silent tears dripped down into their beards, but even their sobs made not a sound.

"I will grant your petition," Oridine said. "You have done the right thing by acknowledging your failure, so I am prepared to give you what you ask."

"Thank you, mother," Remiana said, not betraying any surprise. They had not actually expected leniency, anticipating that Oridine would demand the worst kind of penalty to punish Remiana for her misjudgment.

"Release their gags," Oridine instructed, and those too were cut loose. "Speak your names, prisoners."

"Stekar is our family name, high mistress," the taller of the two men stammered. "I am Tay and my brother is Luwil."

"Tay and Luwil," Oridine repeated, looking not at them but at Remiana. "Your sentence of death is commuted."

The two men's postures slacked to those of relief, but the ease of it gave Edwin a bad feeling.

"However," Oridine said, "as you were so keen to observe, daughter, these men have still committed crimes under the watch of our banner." She looked with distaste upon the brothers' filthy clothes and tear-stained faces.

"They will receive the lesser punishment for common thieves: the loss of one hand."

Luwil's terrified moan choked off as he was clocked soundly by the haft of the Impelar's scythe.

The captives might have been surprised, but Edwin was not. It was still worse than they deserved, but Oridine was not known for her mercy. At least this way they would keep their lives.

Remiana, too, still seemed to consider this a victory.

"That is most gracious of you, mother," she said.

"Not at all," Oridine said. "It was your actions that brought them here, and it is your actions that spare their lives. They should be thanking you for only losing a hand, not me."

"I . . . I suppose so," Remiana said. It was clearly not the line of reasoning she would have preferred.

"And since that's the case," Oridine continued, "you should be the one to grant this mercy to them. Personally." A slender bone dagger appeared in her hand, and she placed it on the table between them. Edwin felt his blood go cold.

Remiana stared at the blade, taken aback. "You jest," she said, her voice quavering for the first time since entering the room.

"I do not jest, child," Oridine said. "A queen must take responsibility for her mistakes. I have warned you before that a time would come when you must carry your own burdens. That time is now."

"I . . . I cannot," Remiana said, unable to look at the silent brothers.

"You were the one who asked for this pardon," Oridine said, raising her eyebrows at her daughter. "If you have changed your mind, it can be rescinded." She nodded, and the Impelar raised the blade of her scythe to Tay's neck.

"No!" Remiana cried.

"Which is it, child?" Oridine demanded, slamming her hand down on the table and making the dagger rattle. "You are going to be queen, and yet you cannot make such a simple decision?"

Remiana's eyes were wide. "This is . . . . I've never . . . ."

"No one will accept a queen who can't bear the consequences of her choices!" Oridine hissed, her eyes harder than any steel. "The only way to survive is to be stronger than your enemies, strong enough to end their lives before they end yours! Hesitation is no better than death! If lives as meager as these distress you, then you are not fit to be queen, or even my daughter!"

Tears leaked from the corners of Remiana's eyes, the first time Edwin had seen her cry since they were children. He could not let this go on any longer.

"I will-" he started to say.

"I'll do it," Remiana said in a throaty voice, putting out a hand to stop him.

"You mustn't," Edwin said, grabbing Remiana's wrist as she reached for the dagger. "Let me."

"I think not," Oridine said. "Did you not come back yesterday light of your dagger, a steel dagger at that?" Edwin had no reply.

Oridine sneered at him. "It seems you too are in need of a lesson. She will mete out punishment for both prisoners. You will do nothing but watch."

Edwin looked back to Remiana, but she refused to meet his gaze.

"Let go, Ed," she said softly.

"Cousin, you don't have to. . . ."

"I do." Remiana lifted her eyes, and he saw that they were cold again, rocky stream beds empty after the flood had receded. She was wearing her mask, the mask that protected her from what it meant to be an Aloise, but it would not be enough to protect her from this.

Edwin released her wrist, and Remiana took the bone blade in her hand. It was a yellow paler than her hair, which even now gleamed prettily despite the dark thoughts that must have been stirring beneath. Edwin longed to save her from them, longed to take that blade and cast it from the highest tower in the Keep, but he knew it was futile. This was what she was born to be, and no amount of longing could pry her free from the twisted clutches of her name.

Chapter 26
Gathering the Threads

Ely looked over her shoulder in the noisy bar, but there was still no sign of the man she was to meet. Mae and Matrice were keeping watch together at a table by the door, hooded and cloaked as usual. Though their eyes and skin had recovered somewhat in the two days since dosing themselves with Scarwood sap, they still did not look like anything approaching normal.

Despite it being midday, the bar was crowded. With the city sealed, all the traders who had been inside during the Aloise coup were trapped, with nowhere to go and nothing to do but drink their coin away. The same went for the many craftsmen whose shops had fallen idle for lack of materials and customers. At the rate things were going, the city's supply of alcohol would dry up long before the patrons' coin.

Ely sipped at her drink, ignoring its repulsive taste to avoid arousing suspicion. She was busy staring at the bottom of her cup and wondering how long she could make the dregs last when the chair opposite her scraped across the floor.

"Ho, here's the little firebrand from the council meeting. Elymia, was it?" Jonner Ceer dropped into the chair and crossed his legs casually.

"You're late," Ely said coolly.

Ceer grinned and leaned closer. "What're you gonna do about it? Spank me?" His breath made Ely's nose crinkle, but she did not shy away. She had Matrice and Mae at her back, with orders to make things unpleasant for him if he tried anything foolish, and she had seen more than enough of what they could do to be genuinely sorry for him if it came to that.

"I'm afraid you would only enjoy it," Ely said. "But enough of that, we have business to discuss."

Ceer leaned back and looked her over. "What makes you think I'd do business with you? You aren't on the Council."

Ely, Mae, and Matrice had spent hours guessing what questions Ceer might ask, and Ely had practiced answers ready for all of them.

"My name is Elymia Celundine," she said. "You might recognize it."

"Celundine," Ceer said, tapping his chin. "That makes you the daughter of old Celundine the Grayfin, I'd reckon."

Ely nodded. "But you already knew that, or else you wouldn't have agreed to meet in the first place. You know the power my father wields, and what it could get you."

Ceer switched from tapping his chin to stroking it. "All right then, what do you want?"

"Weapons," Ely said. "The weapons the Council turned down."

Ceer slapped his knee and let out a hooting laugh, but the bar was loud enough that no one noticed. "What's a pretty little lady like you want with a bad ol' smuggler's weapons?"

Ely gave him a hard look. "Sell them to me, and I'll tell you."

Ceer shook his head. "The price has gone up, missy. It'll take a council seat, a title, land, free mooring, and all the cannons off that big lug of a ship you got down there in port – you know the one I-"

Ceer cut himself off as the noise in the bar dwindled. Ely looked over her shoulder and saw that two men had just entered, both wearing Aloise uniforms.

"Two of your best beers, and snappy," one said, strolling up to the bar. He looked around the room menacingly, but when the beers arrived, he and his companion did nothing more than settle down at the bar and drink them. The other patrons watched them in silence for a minute, but once it was clear nothing dangerous or exciting was about to happen, the drone of conversation returned.

"It looks like we'll have to cut this short," Ceer said. "I don't fancy dealing under the nose of the law."

"Don't be absurd," Ely replied, thinking quickly. "Walking out now would only make you look suspicious. Besides, there's nothing more natural than a stranded sailor enjoying his idle days with a local woman."

Ceer did not look fully convinced, but he did not leave his seat either.

Ely used the lull to recall the things he had asked for. They hadn't guessed he would want cannons, but that was really no worse than all the rest.

"I can promise you everything but the Council seat," Ely said, trying to restart the conversation. "At least, I can't promise you a seat on *this* Council." That got his attention.

"This Council?" Ceer said.

Ely cradled her mug and took a slow sip, making him wait.

"When my father returns with his army," she said, "do you expect the Council who let the city fall so easily, who let his daughter be imprisoned, will keep their seats for long? They'll be lucky if they keep their heads. When the time comes to choose their replacements, my father will look favorably on anyone who aided me in my time of need."

Ceer gave Ely a thin smile. "You make sweet promises, little girl, but you are in no position to fulfill them just yet. You'll have to make me an even better offer if you expect me to risk my ability to collect on your father retaking the city."

Ely looked down at her fingernails as if bored. "My father won't be the one doing the retaking," she said casually. "But if you need a little extra, I can offer you something unique: a suit of Lode Knight armor." Ceer seemed a man who was fond of his weaponry, and his request for cannons had only confirmed it.

Ceer's eyebrows climbed. "How, pray tell, do you plan to get something like that?" There was doubt in his voice, but also a hint of greed. Ely knew she had him.

"Sell me the weapons," she said, "and you'll find out."

Jonner Ceer stared at her for a moment, and then held out his hand. "You tempt a man into risky waters, Miss Celundine, but I do believe the price is right."

Ely had never negotiated for anything before, and her heart was beating hard in her chest at her success, but her work was not finished. She ignored Ceer's hand. "We're not done bargaining, Mr. Ceer. I also want to hire your crew, and any others of the right . . . disposition you might know. Ten wheels a day per head sounds fair, to be paid to you for their service."

Ceer's eyes narrowed at the sizable sum. "What in the deep are you up to, girl?"

Ely pulled a piece of parchment from her pocket. "I'll also need the items on this list," she said, pushing the paper across the table. "I'm prepared to pay five hundred wheels for the lot of it."

Ceer picked up the paper and scanned it quickly.

". . . animal skins as well? You're asking a lot. This much won't be easy to find within the walls of the city."

"An extra hundred wheels if you have it all by tomorrow night," Ely said. Drown him in coin, Mae had told her, and he won't put up a fight.

Ceer folded the paper and tucked it into his coat.

"I do none of this without an explanation," he said.

Ely nodded. She had never expected to avoid giving one. "Very well, smuggler. But know that if you think to turn on us for profit, you'll be hunted to the ocean's bowels by the Grayfin himself."

It was an hour before the plan was explained and all the details hammered out. By the end, Ceer could not stop grinning.

"Even if I tried to sell you out," he chuckled, "not even a madman would believe me." As he stood, he gave Ely a small bow. It was a mocking bow to be sure, but a bow nonetheless. "We'll meet again tomorrow, as agreed. And if what you say is true, then I hope those Aloise sleep soundly tonight. They're going to need it."

No sooner had Ceer departed than Mae and Matrice joined Ely around the table. Their hoods were pulled forward, but there were looks of anxiety on their faces.

"Look at the soldiers," Matrice hissed.

"There's no problem," Ely said, still riding the high of her achievement. They had made a plan, and now she was making it happen. "They didn't hear-"

Matrice reached across the table and grabbed Ely's hand. "Just look."

Ely looked. The soldiers were on their third or fourth pints, but they had not bothered anyone. They were, however, no longer alone. Between them sat a slender woman with brown hair cut just below the ears. It was Tamalina. Again.

"Don't stare!" Mae hissed. "And for the gods' sake, don't show her your face!"

Ely turned away quickly. "She hasn't seen us?"

Matrice shook her head. "She never did more than glance in your direction."

"And we need to keep it that way," Mae said. "You're both supposedly missing. If we're recognized and found by one of your families, the whole plan could fall apart. We're leaving. Now."

Ely stole a glance back at Tamalina. She and the soldiers had left their seats, and she was leading them toward the back door.

"Again? What is she doing?" Ely whispered.

"Not our problem. Let's move," Mae said.

"But she might need help!" Ely said, struggling to keep her voice a whisper.

"Then she can find her own," Mae said harshly. "We've got bigger things to worry about than one girl who's too stupid to keep her legs together." Matrice looked away, but she did not protest.

Ely hated to admit it, but Mae was right. If only Tamalina could keep herself safe until tomorrow night, everything would all be all right, she told herself as she watched her friend leave on the arm of one of the soldiers. If things went to plan, tomorrow night would put an end to all this and send the Aloise fleeing to the hills with their tails between their legs. It would also, as Mae's eagerness made plain, offer them their first true taste of revenge.

Chapter 27

Revenge

Edwin rolled on his cot, pulling the blanket tighter around him. The tiny room he shared with three other men had once been a larder, and the lingering smell of spices made his nose tingle through the night, rendering sleep elusive.

But as much as he wished to blame his nose for his sleeplessness, that was not truly what kept him awake. Whenever he closed his eyes, all he could see was that knife in Remiana's hand. He was a stranger to bloodshed; he was, after all, a soldier. But what kind of mother could demand such a thing of her own child, then stand back and watch with satisfaction in her eyes? Was anything, even a throne, worth the price Remiana was paying for it?

Even when Edwin did manage a few moments of sleep, his dreams were troubled and restless, filled with memories of his own mother. She lay on her bed in the basement of Alomadra manor, quietly coughing blood into a yellow handkerchief; he felt her weak hand pulling at his childhood locks of blonde hair; he heard her pleading, desperate words.

"Never tell," she whispered in his ear. "Be one of them, and live. Your sister will protect you. Stay close to her. I could not bear to lose two sons."

Then he would wake in a sweat and lie still in the silence, fingering the ring about his neck as he remembered. A day after his mother had spoken her final words, Oridine had sent him away to be trained as a soldier, even before the burial. Be one of them, and live. And he had been one of them, and he had lived. He wondered, now, after all he had done, if that too had been worth the price.

A snort and grumble came from Vanbilt's cot as he twitched in his sleep, and the comatose lump that was Gulbrathe retorted with an audible release of gas. Edwin groaned and sat up, rubbing his eyes with the heels of his palms. There was no rest to be had tonight, not here.

Thud.

"Shaddup, 'm tryin' to sleep," Gulbrathe groaned through his pillow.

Edwin looked around for the source of the noise. The only light in the room was the trickle coming in under the door, reducing everything within to indistinguishable shadowshapes. Nothing was moving.

Thud.

"I'm going to tear someone's goddamn head off if they don't stop that," Gulbrathe growled, sounding more awake and more angry with each word.

Edwin squinted into the darkness. "I don't think it's coming from-"

THUD.

The vibration shook the floor of the room. Something fine and dusty fell onto Edwin's head, and he brushed the stuff out of his hair. He stood and immediately bumped into Ables, who had risen from his cot at the same moment.

The sound of grinding stone made them both look up, only to spit and curse as dust cascaded down into their eyes and mouths. Edwin made a blind lunge for the door, fumbling the latch and then ramming it open with his shoulder. Both he and Ables tumbled into the hallway on their knees, coughing and rubbing at their eyes.

"What the hell?" Edwin heard Vanbilt's drowsy voice say behind them. "Who put rocks in my bed?"

THUD.

This time the vibration was followed by several closer crashes as stone blocks fell from the ceiling and split on the floor of the corridor. One impacted just a few feet away, sending razor fragments pinging off the walls and enveloping Edwin in a cloud of dust. There was a crunching sound, and the door frame behind them cracked and caved, pouring a deluge of smaller stones and dusty mortar into what had been their sleeping quarters. Vanbilt let out a high-pitched scream.

Two white-clad soldiers dashed past at full tilt, lances in tow, not bothering to stop for the pair of dirty, half naked men outside the caved-in doorway. Edwin tried to call out to them, but his throat was so full of dust that all he managed to do was spasm with coughs.

"Get up!" Ables shouted at him over the now constant rumbling. He grabbed Edwin by the shoulders and hauled him to his feet, hitting him on the back roughly as he continued to cough.

"Attack?" Edwin managed to rasp.

"Sure as shit!" Ables yelled in his face, the only way he could make himself heard over the noise. Still holding Edwin's shoulders, he whirled him about and pointed down the hall.

"I'll help Gul and Van; you get to the armory and bring us whatever you can carry! Go!" Ables sent him off with a hard shove, then dove onto the pile of debris like a man possessed, flinging rocks behind him with such force that they broke against the opposite wall.

He could hardly see where he was going, but that did not stop Edwin from running as fast as his choked lungs would allow. It seemed like every other torch in the hall had been knocked from its bracket, leaving dangerous patches of blackness in the passageways where a single wrong step on the broken stones could mean a shattered ankle, or worse. Even where the lights still burned, a fog of dust had descended so thickly that visibility was hardly better than if there had been no light at all.

The path from their sleeping chamber to the armory should have been simple, but the way seemed utterly foreign now. In places the walls had simply crumbled, revealing rooms that Edwin had never seen before, throwing off his sense of direction. What siege weapon could do this? he wondered as he ran. It would take a hundred catapults to do this much damage to a fortification the likes of Cliffhome Keep. And that rumbling . . . .

Edwin felt something familiar, something that brought him to a dead stop. It was like invisible movement all around him, a unique sensation that he had felt once before. He had barely enough warning to throw himself flat before the left wall exploded in front of him, showering him with stinging pebbles. The right wall followed suit a second later. Then the roar of breaking stone quieted, but Edwin remained motionless, watching.

Several figures crossed the hall from one freshly made hole to the other. More followed. Edwin tried to count them, but only some were carrying torches, and they moved quickly. Still, he caught glimpses of animal pelts dangling from their bodies as they darted past. The sound of more explosions discouraged Edwin from following, but he guessed there might have been as many as forty in the party. What he was sure of, though, was that all had been armed.

The dust from the shattered walls began to settle, and Edwin extracted himself from beneath the rubble. The two holes in the walls stood like mouths of rotten teeth, each showing a throatfull of blackness. Despite their ugliness, however, their breath was salty and clean. Somewhere down there lay the outdoors, and freedom.

Edwin hesitated, gazing into the darkness. A short run would take him outside, away from this madness and the ancient structure that seemed ready to crumble down around his ears. The thought was alluring. If his senses could be trusted, there were Masked about this night, and no armor or sword in the world would matter anyway.

Then he thought of Remiana. She was still in the Keep somewhere, and he could not simply abandon her, not even if staying meant facing down the Masked.

With an effort Edwin turned away from his escape and continued toward the armory. The ring around his neck pounded on his chest, heavy and cold, as he ran once more into the darkness.

•••••

Ely covered her mouth as the dust from the ruined wall settled around her. Mae had smartly tied a handkerchief around her face, while the fur-clad men behind them choked and coughed. They had breached more than ten walls already, and Ely prayed that they had not become lost in twisting, darkened corridors of Cliffhome Keep.

"Wharfmaster?" she called out into the corridor before them. "Mr. Tull-och? Madam Jaff?" There was no reply. Ely was doing her best to direct Mae toward the prison where she had been held, but in those conditions it was still largely guesswork. She could only hope that the prisoners were still there.

"We need to keep going," Mae said through her handkerchief. "We can't give them time to regroup."

"I know, I know!" Ely said, trying to keep her nerves in check. They were close, she could feel it. If only she could find something that looked familiar! It was then that she noticed a stirring in the darkness before them.

"Hello?" Ely called.

A gray-uniformed man came charging out of the shadows, the spear in his hands aimed straight at Ely's heart.

Ely fumbled for her blade, a long iron dagger she had picked from Ceer's stash, but Mae was faster. An invisible force lifted the running soldier off the ground and smashed him into the ceiling, then down into the floor, where he shuddered and lay still.

"Thanks," Ely said after getting her breathing under control. She swallowed hard, trying not to look down as she stepped over the body. The reality of watching men die turned her stomach in a way for which her father's stories had not prepared her.

But this was what she wanted, she told herself as they moved forward. They deserved it for what they had done to Eomila, to Nantala, to Evana, to Barty, and to Keth. Yet it had been plain from the moment she had watched that first soldier die, a spear lodged in his gut, that she did not love it, that she could not love it. In their screams, all she heard was more pain. It had come as a shock, how much and how deeply she hated it, but still she struggled to cling to her purpose and her anger, to keep her feet moving forward. This had been her plan, and no matter what it took, she had come too far not to see it through.

"You should be more careful," Mae said, following on Ely's heels. If the killing nauseated her as it did Ely, she did not show it. "This wouldn't happen if -" She stopped abruptly.

"What is it?" Ely said.

Mae cocked her head. "Can you hear that?"

Ely listened, but all she heard was the distant rumbling of Matrice carrying out her assault on the northern side of the Keep, shredding stones and flattening walls to provide cover for Ely and Mae's more focused infiltration.

"I don't hear anything," Ely said.

"Someone's calling for help," Mae said, looking down at the debris-strewn floor. "Below us."

"Then what are we waiting for?" Ely said. She still could not hear what Mae was talking about, but she took her word for it. Like Matrice, Mae seemed to have developed uncanny senses.

"Spread out and defend this spot!" Ely shouted to the twenty men who were still following them, emulating her father's commanding bark. There had been closer to sixty at the start of their assault, but she had released many of them to loot what they could from the damaged Keep, hoping their scattering and their Masked disguises would sow even more confusion among the Aloise.

"Ready?" Mae said to Ely.

"Whenever you are," Ely replied, fighting the urge to close her eyes.

Mae knelt and touched the floor beneath them, and suddenly the stones under Ely's feet gave way. Before she knew it she was tumbling off balance, plummeting down into the room below in a rain of crumbling mortar. She landed awkwardly on her hands and knees, and Mae landed beside her, grunting at the impact.

"Like trying to open a letter with an axe," Mae grumbled, picking herself up and offering Ely a hand.

"You didn't kill us, that's a start," Ely muttered, grasping Mae's hand and hauling herself up. Matrice and Mae's abilities were impressive, but both seemed to lack finesse when it came to controlling their powers.

Ely called up to the men they had left above, and one of them dropped a torch down to her. The room they had fallen into was quite small, smaller than she had expected it to be in the darkness. In fact, it looked like a cell.

"I can hear that voice again," Mae said. "Behind this wall."

"How about making a small hole this time?" Ely said.

"I'm doing the best I can," Mae growled, raising one hand and blasting an opening. It was indeed smaller, though Ely still had no trouble slipping through it.

"Hello?" Ely said, raising the torch over her head again.

"By the Deep One, is that you, Elymia?" a rough voice replied from beyond the edge of the light.

"Wharfmaster!" Ely exclaimed, rushing to the large man who was tied to the wall.

The torchlight revealed that he was in a sorry state, spattered with grime and rent in places where a whip had cut through cloth and flesh alike. Spittle flecked his beard and his hair was matted, but beneath it all his eyes still glittered with the light of defiance.

Ely felt her throat tighten, but she had no time to cry. In an instant she had drawn her blade and cut the Wharfmaster down, and he slumped forward onto his knees.

"The other prisoners," Ely said, putting her shoulder under his arm to help him up. "Are they here?"

The Wharfmaster looked at her out of the corner of his eye. "You're a damn fool girl," he said. "You shouldn't have risked yourself for me."

"Tell me about the others," Ely repeated. "You can yell at me later."

"Not here," the Wharfmaster said, shaking his head. "Not any more. That Aloise woman offered them rooms in the tower if they'd cooperate. They all did."

Ely felt a weight greater than the Wharfmaster's body settle on her. Cooperate? How was that possible?

"Something's wrong," Mae interjected, poking her head through the hole in the wall. "Listen."

The distant rumbling of Matrice's attack had stopped, but it was much too soon. The Aloise forces should have been in utter disarray, too scattered and surprised to coordinate. So what had happened to Matrice?

"We follow the plan and get out while we still can," Ely said. They had agreed: if either prong of the attack failed, both would retreat. "There should be some stairs at the end of the hall outside the cells. We can take them up, collect the men, and retrace our path back outside." She gave a nod to Mae. "The door?"

Mae mumbled something about taking orders like an errand girl, but she knocked the door off its hinges just the same. The three of them left the cell and headed toward the stairs, moving as fast as the Wharfmaster's weakened legs would allow.

"You there, stop!" a man's voice shouted. The light of several torches illuminated soldiers coming down the stairs ahead of them, crossbows in hand.

"Down!" Mae shouted as several bolts whizzed in their direction, and Ely and the Wharfmaster dropped to the ground. Mae waved her hands, somehow stopping two of the projectiles in mid air, but one got through, grazing the hood of her cloak. As the soldiers were reloading, Ely and the Wharfmaster retreated back into the cover of the doorway.

This wasn't supposed to be happening, Ely thought desperately as a second volley whizzed past. She had been sure the soldiers would flee when faced with what looked like Masked!

"Can't you do something about them?" Ely yelled to Mae, who was taking cover in the doorway opposite.

"They're too far!" Mae shouted back. "Are those stairs the only way out?"

More Aloise troops were flowing down the stairs every second. Even with Mae's powers, there was no way they were getting through that.

"Not if we make our own," Ely answered.

"Matrice's attack is done," Mae said. "If we start blazing a path now, the noise will tell every soldier in the Keep exactly where we are."

Ely looked to the Wharfmaster, but he just nodded.

"Well," she called back to Mae, "then I hope you're ready for a fight."

•••••

By the time he arrived at the door to the armory, Edwin was convinced that the situation was even worse than he had thought. Parts of the hall behind him had collapsed as he ran, making a return trip impossible. If he was going to make it back to Ables, Gul, and Van, he was going to have to find a different way. Worse than the damage to the Keep, however, was what had been done to the men within. He had passed more than one body covered in furs, and even more wearing the Aloise white and gold. In the face of such destruction, the reasons behind it no longer seemed important. What mattered now was staying alive, and helping others do the same.

Edwin reached for the door handle, but before he could grab it the door burst open and a cold, hard hand closed on his throat.

"Shit," a hollow-sounding voice said. The hand loosened, and Edwin's hazy vision cleared to reveal a Knight whose armored bulk nearly filled the whole doorway. He flipped his yellow visor up, revealing an ugly but familiar face.

"Damn it Ed, what the hell are you doing running around half naked? I thought you were one of them!" Tentaltis snarled, pulling Edwin into the room and slamming the door behind him. The ceiling of the armory was only partially intact, Edwin noticed immediately, and some of the armor suits were lying crushed under rubble.

"Them?" Edwin said, putting a hand gingerly to his throat.

"Who do you damn well think?" Tentaltis said. "Those bastards dressed like wild men sticking spears in people!" He slapped his pauldrons with a clang, pointing out the thin trail of blood leaking from a joint in the plates.

"Don't worry, it ain't bad. Him that did it got a whole lot worse." There was definitely more blood on Tentaltis's sword than on his armor.

That gave Edwin pause. "You killed one?"

Tentaltis leered. "Who said anything about one?"

That was some comfort, at least. Those fur-clad figures could not be Masked if a normal man could kill them. But if they were not Masked, then what was that power they were using?

"What the hell are you waiting for? Suit up! I ain't plannin' to hang around here all day," Tentaltis said, and the walls rattled with another explosion as if to punctuate his words.

Donning his full suit of armor was no quick task, so Edwin settled for the essentials: breastplate, sword, and gauntlets. His helmet stared forlornly at him from the stand, its blue visor drooping, but Edwin knew that restricting his vision in the already terrible conditions could prove lethal. He said as much to Tentaltis, but the other man shrugged it off.

"I gotta protect my pretty face, don't I?" Tentaltis said. "If you want to get an arrow put in yours, I ain't gonna stop you. Just hurry up."

Feeling slightly more secure beneath a layer of steel, Edwin snapped on the bracer that was chained to his sword and took up the blade in both hands, leaving the sheath behind.

Seeing that he was as ready as he was going to be, Tentaltis opened the armory door again and hefted his sword onto his shoulder.

"It's time to teach those bastards what it means to face a Knight," he said, eagerness thick in his voice. Edwin followed him out and closed the door behind them, hiding the remaining armor from view. There was no sense in giving the enemy any help pilfering their equipment.

Back in the hall, Edwin realized that the rumblings that shook the Keep had grown quieter. Instead of coming from all around, they now sounded as if they were originating somewhere down the corridor to the left. Tentaltis, however, was already moving off to the right, where the clamor of clashing weapons echoed between what remained of the stone walls.

Edwin was about to follow when a flash of something yellow to his left caught the corner of his eye, something that looked alarmingly like torch-light on blonde hair. He wanted to believe that Remiana was not foolish enough to descend into this mad melee herself, but he was not about to take any chances. He called out after Tentaltis, but the other knight was already gone. Cursing, Edwin turned and went the other way.

It did not take long to run into trouble. The next crossing hallway came up quickly, and Edwin slowed as he approached, realizing that he was not alone. Two fur-clad men were on their knees where the passages crossed, going through the pockets of several soldiers on the ground. Upon seeing Edwin and his sword, one of the pair immediately fled, stumbling over rubble and bodies in his haste to get away. The second, perhaps noticing that Edwin was not fully armored, stood and hefted a javelin instead.

"Yer one of them knights, ain't ya?" the man called out. "I be likin' that shiny sword o' yours. How bout you give it here?"

Edwin said nothing. Closing in slowly, sword in a guarding stance, he sized up his opponent. The man was taller than he was, and while the dangling animal pelts made it hard to gauge his true size, his speech was that of a sailor, and no one made a livelihood of sailing without plenty of stamina and strength.

Seeing that Edwin was not going to surrender, the sailor dropped into a crouch, his javelin held high for stabbing. Edwin continued to advance slowly, weighed down as he was with no small amount of steel.

When he was close enough, the sailor took a quick step forward and jabbed with his javelin, a move intended to make Edwin overreact and lose his balance. Edwin read the attack correctly and took a small step back so the weapon merely brushed his breastplate.

The sailor darted in again, this time aiming low at Edwin's unarmored legs, but a sweep of Edwin's sword forced him back. Edwin advanced, and the sailor retreated. Together they moved down the hall, weaving around fallen stones and bodies as they went. This was good, Edwin thought. He was moving forward and his opponent back, meaning that every step they took was another opportunity for the sailor to trip over an unseen obstacle, giving Edwin a chance to strike the finishing blow.

Such a chance seemed to come when the sailor's foot twisted awkwardly under him, and Edwin realized an instant too late that it was a trick. He had already lunged, sword outstretched, too committed to regain his balance. The sailor spun to the side, using the balance that he had never really lost, and stabbed down at Edwin's unprotected neck. Edwin barely deflected the blow with one gauntleted hand, using the other to swing his sword around and-

The wall beside the two fighting men exploded, pummeling them with flying chunks of stone. Edwin took one to the breastplate hard enough to knock him against the opposite wall, crushing the air from his lungs and leaving his vision spotted. He struggled weakly to stand, but the touch of a blade at his throat made him freeze.

"Looks like we'll be bringing back that armor you promised Ceer after all," a woman's voice said. "Don't need what's inside it, though."

"Wait!" another female voice said, this one somehow familiar. "I know him!"

"What? How?" The pressure on Edwin's neck eased.

"I'll explain later. Just pick him up and let's move," the familiar voice said. "We're nearly out."

"You're mad!" the first said. "I can't carry him and still-"

"I'll carry him," a third voice rumbled. "This be no time for arguing."

Edwin felt two strong arms lift him off the ground, and then the roar of another wall exploding rattled his body and knocked his feeble consciousness into oblivion.

Chapter 28
He Who Seeks the Truth

The fire crackled as it consumed the moist wood, throwing orange light across the forest floor in a wide, flickering ring. It was a large fire, larger than the Masked usually built, and it had already burned through their small store of wood and was being fed with wetter, newly fallen logs. Still, it was good at dispelling the frigidity of the night air, and that was what Limp seemed to care about.

"Unbelievable," Limp grumbled, leaning forward to hold his hands out to the flames. "Just unbelievable." Being awoken in the middle of the night had put him in a foul mood.

A fur-draped figure emerged from the night and jogged up to where Donvin, Limp, and many other Masked were sitting about the bonfire. "It's still happening," he said in a breathless voice, standing close to the flames and rubbing his hands vigorously. "All three Listeners agree."

Limp waved the messenger off, not giving him a chance to warm himself properly. "Don't dawdle. Go back and keep watch, and report again if there's any change. Hurry!" The messenger dashed off toward the Listeners' chamber even more quickly than he had arrived.

The other Masked were silent, but it was not difficult to tell what they were thinking. What the Listeners were detecting was not a breach. Someone was using their power, and a lot of it at that.

"If nothing's changed, then the coordinates the Listeners are giving are still fuzzy," a female Masked said from across the fire. "Maybe it's just a defect in the Listeners themselves. Maybe nothing's happening out there at all."

"Or they're sensing multiple sources," Donvin replied. That would give them something to chew on. He had, after all, left Elymia with three vials, and the Listeners were clearly pointing toward Falls Gate.

The Masked stirred restlessly. Thinking about one was bad enough, but the possibility of several using their power unchecked was downright mortifying.

"So what do we do?" asked a male Masked on Donvin's left.

Limp continued staring into the fire with his shoulders hunched, smelling like an old badger who had just been poked with a stick, so Donvin spoke up instead.

"Until we know exactly what's happening," he said, "we need to exercise care. We should treat the area around the anomaly as dangerous until we know otherwise."

"Let's not ignore the obvious," Furrow's voice cut in from beyond the firelight. "We all know who's responsible for this." Donvin turned to watch his approach. He was coming from the direction of Point's hut, as usual.

"Do we?" Donvin asked. He did, of course, but there was no reason any of the others needed to know.

"There's only one of us who's not here now, isn't there?" Furrow said. "There's only one of us who was caught in a lie involving the same place the Listeners are now pointing."

Donvin smiled to himself. He had been waiting for someone to mention Bird. The more focused they were on Bird, who had left the camp shortly after his humiliation at Limp's hands, the less likely they were to suspect the real culprit.

"We should not jump to conclusions," Donvin said. "Blaming one another shouldn't be our first reaction." He paused. "But it would also be foolish to deny that one of our own could be involved."

The silence that followed was broken only by a guttural noise from Limp. "More wood," he barked, and two Masked hurried forward to throw more green branches on the fire.

"He's aiding those damn coastmen," Furrow said angrily, staying on the edge of the shadows, the crack in his mask a finger of darkness reaching down to stroke his face. "Maybe he even ordered the attack on us that prompted the Dedication! He certainly argued hard enough for it." The quietness of the Masked betrayed them: they had already contemplated these possibilities. In the silence, the fire hissed and spit steam from the moist logs like a cornered animal.

"Again," Donvin said, "speculation does not help us. We need more information if we are to decide what action to take."

"But how will we gather it?" Boulder's voice rumbled into the conversation. The flames were so high that Donvin had not noticed when he had joined the group, nor could he even see him through the dancing tongues of yellow and red. "This is neither a breach nor the Dedication. The code says we may only use our power to travel for those purposes. Going by foot could take weeks."

Donvin nodded. "That's true." He took a deep whiff of the air, gauging the mood of the group. It was worried, hesitant, uncertain. "But at the risk of sounding unfaithful," he continued, "I don't think I'm the only one who has realized that the code bends when it must bend, and yields when it must yield." There were mutterings of confusion, and a few slight nods of agreement.

"Hear me out," Donvin said. "I believe we stand on the brink of a very important and dangerous decision, one that may decide our very survival." That was true enough, though not in the way the others would understand it. "It's possible . . . likely, even, that one of our own has abandoned the code and plotted with the coastmen, the same men who attacked us unprovoked." He rose from his seat, allowing his hand to go briefly to the scar on his side. "If true, it means we face an enemy unconstrained by our morals and laws, one that we have an obligation to the world to contain. But how can we meet that obligation if our code denies us the tools?"

The scent in the air shifted as some of the Masked began to see the direction of Donvin's argument, but he continued to drive the point home, sensing their minds were winnable.

"For years our code has guided us," Donvin said. "Our adherence to it has kept the world safe. But if one of our own has rebelled against it, then it has failed in its purpose. It is meant to keep our basest desires in check so we can handle a power that would corrupt normal men, so we can use it for the benefit of all. Yet if one of us can flout its decrees, then it has proven flawed. As soon as one of us abandons it, it becomes an impediment to our ability to counter that one's corrupt intent."

"That sounds like a proposal to abandon the code entirely," Boulder said. "That would be unprecedented. Radical."

"I'm not saying that the code is pointless," Donvin said. "But we must recognize that this situation is beyond it. We were never supposed to turn on one another or need to fight against our own kind, but that is the reality we face. To do what's right, a few of us must be willing to go beyond the strictures of the code. To seek out a traitor, for example, and bring him to justice."

"Then who decides which of us can do these things?" Furrow asked, the hunger in his voice clear.

Donvin turned his head sharply. "I think you misunderstand," he said. "Casting off the constraints of the code is not a privilege. It is a risk, a step down the path of temptation that might lead to you being hunted as a traitor. Think on that before wishing for something that might destroy you." There were nods all around, and Donvin caught a whiff of embarrassment from Furrow.

"But to answer the question," Donvin said, "no one has the right to tell a Masked what he can or can't do. The only voice we must heed is that of our own conscience." He watched his audience slyly from behind his mask. "With that said, it would of course be foolish to make such decisions without consulting the wisest and most experienced among us." He looked pointedly at Limp, and the other Masked followed his gaze.

Limp shifted in his seat, saying nothing at first, but Donvin knew him far too well to mistake what he would say. He would not pass up the authority that Donvin was laying at his feet.

"Consultation is good," Limp said. His shoulders lost their hunch as he began to see the prospect for his own gain. "Very well. Advice on this matter will be given to those who seek it. And let it be known that it would be . . . unwise to ignore the code without first seeking that advice. Doing so might be seen as a sign of a desire to betray rather than aid our cause."

The other Masked seemed agreeable. They had not known what to do in these dire circumstances, and the answer Donvin provided for them was naturally appealing. They would not be so accepting, Donvin knew, if they had even the slightest inkling of what the result would be. They were fools to think that once the door was open, even a crack, to the kind of freedom he was proposing, that what followed could be controlled. There would be no return to the self-tyranny that had kept them in line for thousands of years. Once they believed that they not only had the right to think for themselves, but also the right to use their power accordingly, there would be no more Masked. There would be only the chaos of conflicting morality, disparate hopes, and contrary ideals.

"Since I was the one to propose these risks," Donvin said, moving on to the next step of his plan, "it is only fitting that I be the first to face them."

"Alone?" Furrow said. "Let me-"

"No," Donvin said, cutting him off. "If this idea proves ill conceived, then I will be the one to suffer for it, and no one else." He turned to Limp. "If I am permitted, I will immediately travel to Falls Gate, locate the anomaly the Listeners have detected, and find out what I can. I expect this to take several days, and during that time I propose all others follow the code vigorously, as they always have, while remaining out of danger. I humbly ask your advice on this proposal."

Limp made a show of mulling it over, but the reasoning was obvious. If the plan was successful, he would, as the one who blessed it, gain much respect. And if it failed, he would be hailed for having the foresight to limit the experiment to Donvin alone.

"It is a noble man who risks himself for others," Limp said finally. "It would be wrong to trample on such nobility of spirit. Here is the requested advice: go forth and do those things, setting aside the code when it is absolutely necessary. The rest of us will wait for your report. Before we know the dangers of the temptation we will face, we must proceed with caution."

Donvin bowed his head, smirking as Limp parroted his proposal back to him. Limp wanted power, but he did not have the strength to wield it effectively.

"I thank you for your advice," Donvin said with as much graciousness as he could muster. "It will be followed."

Chapter 29
Hostage

"No," Ely said for the third time, her temper wearing thin. "Absolutely not."

Mae scowled from behind the chair where she was checking the ropes that secured the captive knight's wrists. He was slumped, head bowed toward his knees, still unconscious some six hours after their escape from the Keep.

He was definitely the same man from the cell, Ely noted, the one who had spared her from the worst of Remiana's punishments. With his face illuminated by the light from the warehouse's dusty windows, his resemblance to Remiana was striking. He was an Aloise, there was no doubt of that, and that made his life far more valuable than the steel they had stripped from him. Maybe valuable enough to make up for the otherwise minimal success of their attempted rescue.

"Leaving a prisoner armed is the stupidest thing I've ever heard," Mae said, tugging ineffectually on the chain that connected the sword on the floor the unconscious knight's wrist. "If you'd just let me try to cut it . . . ."

"We're not barbarians, Mae," Matrice said from her seat atop a wooden crate, her shoulder wrapped with linen bandages. "You know we don't have the control for fine work that, and we can't afford to take off his hand by accident." She absently twirled the arrow that had come out of her shoulder, for some reason unwilling to part with red and yellow fletched shaft that had come within inches of ending her life.

"Who said it would be an accident?" Mae murmured under her breath. Ely gave her a sharp look, and Mae shrugged back at her.

"Matrice has the right of it," Wharfmaster Abrohl said, setting down the bowl of stew in his hands. "If you hurt him, you can forget about a prisoner exchange. The Aloise don't take kindly to the maiming of their people. I do know it for a fact." The Wharfmaster looked more alive now that he had been fed and bathed, but there were still cuts and bruises on his face that it would take more than a little warm water to erase.

Ely rubbed the back of her neck as she looked down at the sword and chain. She could sympathize with Mae; she was not happy to see that blade either, but she owed the man attached to it at least the same courtesy he had shown her. There had been more than enough bloodshed already, and there would be no more if she could help it.

As she watched, the man's eyelids fluttered. The chair scraped on the slate floor as he tried to move and found himself bound to the seat.

"I'll handle this," Ely said, shooing Mae away and pulling up an empty crate in front of their prisoner. She found herself relieved that his unconsciousness had proven only temporary.

"Where am I?" the knight groaned, his eyes searching, unfocused, about the room.

"You're safe," Ely assured him, putting a soothing hand on his knee. "My name is Elymia Celundine, and you are my prisoner. Please don't struggle. I'm not going to hurt you."

This, of course, prompted the knight to test his restraints, but the ropes were tight – Mae had made quite sure of that – and he ceased struggling quickly. Then he gave Ely a good look for the first time.

"You?" he said in surprise. "You're the girl from . . . ."

"Yes," Ely said. "I never had a chance to thank you. If not for you, I might still be locked up in that cell, or worse. Would you tell me your name?"

The knight grunted, head tipped down as he examined the cords that held him. "Edwin," he said, his mouth crooked as if he found something funny. "Touching as your gratitude is, I didn't do it for you, and I don't suppose your thanks is enough to set me free anyhow."

"Her thanks saved your life, you ungrateful-" Mae started, but Ely's glare silenced her. There was a reason they had decided Mae was not the best person to speak to their prisoner when he awoke.

"Your name is Edwin Aloise, isn't it?" Ely asked. Edwin just stared at her in silence, admitting nothing.

"There's no use trying to hide it," she added. "You look too much like Remiana for that."

Edwin's head cocked. "You and my . . . cousin," he said. "What is there between you?"

"I though I was her friend," Ely said, judging there was no harm in answering. "That is, until she betrayed us." Could it have been only a week ago that she and Remiana had shared tea together? It seemed so much longer. An age. A lifetime.

"Yet before she released you, you swore that you were still her friend," Edwin said. "You swore it under my blade."

Ely looked away, fighting the urge to touch the back of her neck. She did not care to be reminded, and her answer came out harshly.

"I'm still the friend of the Remiana I knew," she said, "but that traitor who kills and tortures and lies is not her. The Remiana I knew wasn't a bad person, but I haven't seen her since the day the killing began."

"Maybe you haven't," Edwin said, leaning forward the small distance the ropes would allow. "But I have."

Ely met his eyes, and she saw with surprise that they were full of sadness.

"What?" she said, caught off guard. "What do you-"

"Enough," Mae cut in, putting her hands on her hips. "We shouldn't believe anything he says, or tell him any more than necessary. He's an Aloise. He'd say anything, or cut your throat in a second if it got him what he wanted. That's what they're like, all of them."

Ely gave Mae a stern look, but she ignored it.

To Edwin, Mae said, "You're our prisoner, and we're going to trade you for the rest of our people. The condition we send you back in depends on how well you cooperate. Try to play us, and I'll break you like a twig."

Edwin looked up at her, and for a second there was silence. Then, he laughed. It was a forced, mirthless sound.

"What's so funny?" Mae demanded.

"You want Oridine to give up her prisoners in exchange for me?" Edwin asked.

"That's right," Mae said, eyes narrowed, "and you should count yourself lucky that you're alive at all."

Edwin shook his head. "That's not going to happen. She would never trade anything for me."

Mae snorted dismissively. "How noble of you. But we know you're an Aloise, and that's all we need to know. Save the family loyalty drivel for someone who cares."

Ely did not know this Edwin well—in fact, she hardly knew him at all—but it did not sound as if he was bluffing. Their conversation was interrupted, however, by a pounding on the warehouse door.

"I thought you said this place was a secret?" Matrice said, pointing the arrow she held at Mae. "That no one outside the Registry would have any reason to come here?"

"It is," Mae said, "and they wouldn't. It's in the records only as a waste depository. No one should have any business here but me, now that Lady Evana is . . . gone." She glared daggers at Edwin as she spoke the last.

"It sure sounds like someone wants to get in here to me," the Wharfmaster said as the pounding continued. "Shall we see who?"

Ely nodded. "Mae, you answer the door," she said. "You're the only one who would have a reason to be here. We'll stay quiet behind these boxes. Just tell them you're busy and send them away." The pounding on the door was getting louder. "If they won't go, you might have to be . . . forceful."

"I'll do what I have to," Mae said, rounding a stack of boxes and disappearing. Matrice gave a single approving nod.

Ely shook herself. She had just condoned hurting another person without even a stutter, and one of her best friends had done the same. A week ago that would have been unthinkable, yet now it felt like nothing at all. She had felt ill watching those Aloise soldiers die, but even so, she had accepted that as the price of what she wanted and moved on. What was happening to her?

Ely turned to Edwin, suppressing her concerns for another time. "I don't want to have to threaten you," she said quietly, "but I would appreciate it if you were quiet for now. Can I trust you?"

Edwin nodded. "I wouldn't want to cause a friend of my cousin any trouble."

His assuming reply irked Ely, but she did not have time to respond. The sound of Mae opening the front door made her snap her mouth shut and listen.

She heard Mae's voice. "Can I help-. Hey!" There was the sound of the door swinging wide with a bang, followed by the sound of Mae's protestations. "You can't just barge in here, this is the property of-"

Gerard Orndas was the first to round the corner into view, trailed closely by Tallomi Shima. Both wore dire expressions. Ely stood reflexively and immediately wished that she had not. She was no child to be intimidated by the Council, she thought, but her body did not seem to agree.

The first two councilors were followed by Aldan Pourin, Matrice's father, who looked nearly floored with relief on seeing his daughter alive. After him came Master Gill, or as he was now, Councilman Gill. It was the fifth newcomer, however, whose appearance made Ely's heart leap into her throat: Barty. He was alive! Despite his long absence, he looked exactly as he always had, businesslike and well-groomed, with nothing more than a few extra wrinkles and a missing button on his vest to indicate what had become of him over the past week.

Mae was the last around the corner, fury written across her face as she was escorted by no less than five well-muscled men. They wore plain clothes, but Ely suspected they belonged to whatever remained of the city watch.

Councilman Orndas's hard eyes took in Edwin's seated, bound form, the metal breastplate and gauntlets on the floor a short distance away, Matrice's bandaged shoulder, and the Wharfmaster's marred face in one furious sweep.

"I have half a mind to turn you in to the Aloise myself," he said, his gaze settling on Ely. "I did not want to believe the things I was hearing, that you three were the ones responsible for last night's madness, but now I find you hidden away here with an Aloise man as your prisoner. Do you have any idea what you've done?" His challenge brought all Ely's suppressed anger from the council meeting surging back.

"What we've done?" Ely said. "We've been protecting our city and the people you abandoned to rot!"

"You don't know what you're talking about, child," Councilwoman Shima said, but she was silenced by Orndas's raised hand.

"What you've done," he said, "is destroy any chance we had at peace. Did you bother to find out, before wreaking havoc like a mindless savage, that we had already met twice with Oridine and secured a promise of humane treatment for her prisoners? Did you bother to learn that she had agreed to open the port to trade?"

Orndas hardly paused for breath. "And did you even consider the response your deplorable tactics would provoke? The attack on the Keep was bad enough, but cold blooded murder? Mutilation? I wouldn't have thought you capable!"

Ely was stunned. She had not, in fact, known about the meetings with Oridine, nor was she sure what to make of them. And what was this about murder and mutilation? As she struggled to collect herself, it was Matrice who answered.

"No matter what concessions you gain through negotiation, they won't bring justice to the people who died for Aloise greed. And they definitely won't make us free," she said, remaining seated with the poise that Ely wished that she, too, could have maintained.

Orndas was livid. "And spilling blood will, is that what you think?"

"You know what the Aloise are like," Matrice replied. "The only way we'll ever get justice from them is by taking it. Whether or not the price is blood, that's up to them. But if we submit, if we give them what they want, then everyone we've lost will have died for nothing."

"Enough!" Gerard shouted, the lines on his face like ridges in carved granite. "I will not have ignorant children dictating the policy of this city! Whatever you think you're doing, it ends now! If this city is going to survive, we can't afford to deal with the Aloise with a pen in one hand and a blade in the other."

"He's right, girls," Councilwoman Shima said, eliciting a grunt of offense from Mae, who was perhaps only five years her junior. "It's not your place to make decisions that will affect the rest of us without going through the Council."

"I couldn't have said it better myself," Councilman Gill said in an overly flattering tone. Shima gave him no more than an annoyed look in return.

"And when you make blockheaded decisions, it isn't for us to question?" Mae said angrily, elbowing her way through the men who surrounded her. "When you ignore murder, we should just accept it because you know best? Are we supposed to forget the honor of our dead because you say so?"

Shima looked critically at Mae's dusty clothes and frizzy, unbrushed hair, seeming to miss entirely the dangerous look in her eyes.

"It's not as simple as that," she said. "You served under Evana; you should know that matters of governance seldom are. We're responsible for securing this city's future, not for dwelling on the grievances of the past. If that means arranging a peace with the Aloise, even someone like you should understand that we must be willing to accept-"

"Someone like me?" Mae said, jabbing a finger angrily at her freckled face. "You mean someone who wasn't born into nobility, or even into your precious city? Tell me, have you always hated us, or did you only start after bedding Ceer?"

"You dirty little-" Shima snarled, turning a bright shade of red, but Orndas's hand on her arm prevented her from going after Mae.

"It's time to put these squabbles aside," he declared. "I have not come here to fight or negotiate, but to offer clemency. I've brought with me members of your families. Agree to give up this pointless troublemaking, and you can go home with them right now, and we'll forgive what you've done."

"Pointless, you say?" the Wharfmaster said, pushing himself up onto his stocky legs. "Glad to see I mean so much to you, Gerard."

"Mr. Abrohl," Orndas said, inclining his head and lying for the sake of politeness. "Forgive me. I did not see you there."

"Just like you didn't see me when they were flayin' off my living hide in that dungeon, I 'spect. Was that the humane treatment you negotiated?" Before Orndas could protest, the Wharfmaster held up his hands. "I know, I know, 'twas for the greater good that you left me, and I told Elymia she was a fool to save me. But you can't deny, reckless as it was, that she pulled it off, and better than you lot could have."

Orndas frowned. "While I'm glad to see you safe, Mr. Abrohl, we can't have our people taking rogue actions based on nothing but their conscience. Lives have been lost because of her, and more likely will be before this is through. I don't know how these girls were able to do what they did, nor do I want to know. It makes no difference to the fact that for the sake of this city's survival, it's time to give up this foolishness."

Orndas pulled an obsidian dagger from his belt and offered it to Ely, hilt first. He nodded at Edwin, still bound to his chair and watching the conversation intently.

"Free your prisoner, Elymia," he said. "Demonstrate that you understand the error of your ways and let us return him to his people. Perhaps it's not too late to repair some of the damage you've done."

Ely looked down at the knife. Its blade was a glistening black, so polished that she could almost see her reflection in it.

"If you don't," Gerard said grimly, "you have no right to call yourself a patriot of this city. Nor will you have any right to call yourself a Celundine, for the people of that name have always put the welfare of their homeland before their own."

"Elymia, think of your family," Barty spoke up for the first time. "Think of your father. He's a reasonable man. He wouldn't want you putting yourself in danger or making trouble like this." Hearing his voice made Ely's throat tighten, bringing back memories of all the comforts and normalcy of home. That home seemed so very far away now, part of a life that had burned to the ground, never to rise again.

"Think of your friends," Aldan Pourin said pleadingly, tearing his eyes away from his daughter. "Please, don't drag them down with you."

Ely looked over at Matrice, whose bandages were beginning to show some red spotting. She had thought they were partners in this, but if Matrice lost her life, as she nearly had last night, the weight of that loss would have no shoulders to fall on aside from hers.

"Think of your city," Councilwoman Shima said. "Think of all its grandeur that will come to ruin in war. Your family has protected it for generations. You can preserve it, if only you free this man."

Ely looked back to the knife. It was so dark and alluring, dark enough to hide her from the responsibility for what she had done and might still do. It was a chance to go back, perhaps the only one she would ever have. All she had to do was reach out and take it, and she could once again be Elymia the girl-child, Elymia who minded her father and her elders, Elymia who put her faith and loyalty in words like 'city' and 'family' and 'country.' Gone would be Elymia the deceiver, Elymia the killer, Elymia who believed she did not have to wait on others to change the world. Gone would be the pain of knowing that people were dying because of her. Gone would be the pride of fighting for something that was worth that price.

On the other hand, there was that one remaining glass vial, the one which Ely could feel even now pressing against her from inside her pocket. She could take that instead and use it to inflict a terrible wrath on any who dared to question her loyalties, who dared to tell her what was or was not her place. She could kill Oridine, kill Remiana, bring the whole Keep down to the ground and wipe every trace of the Aloise from the face of the world. She could tear down the Council and all its cowardly, false patriots and replace it with something better, something that would rise rather than cower when its people were threatened. No one could stop her. If they tried, she could wash the streets with their blood.

Ely blinked, and the visions of power and death faded before her eyes. Was that what she really wanted? Even more of the killing that so sickened her? If Orndas' knife was the way back, was more suffering the only way forward? Had the shadow from her dreams been right? Was bloody vengeance the only way to bring the crooked scales back into balance?

Even if she did not know the answers to those questions, Ely did know one thing: it would be easier to do what Orndas asked, but that did not make it right. Even if she was not ready to take that next step down the path of destruction that her shadowy benefactor had shown her, neither was she willing to turn back.

"No," Ely said, her voice steady. "I will not."

Shima's eyes opened wide. "This is treason, girl!" she hissed. "Open treason!"

"No," Ely said again. "The only treason here is yours, for thinking you still have the right to speak for us. You're so caught up in protecting the city that you've forgotten about the people who live in it."

"Mind your words, Elymia," Master Gill said. "We are the duly appointed representatives of the Guilds who speak for the city and its people in accordance with the law."

"Exactly," Ely said. "You can speak for the smiths, or the weavers, or the glaziers, or the shepherds, but what of it? What do the smiths care if a few people die so long as the ingots from the iron lords continue to flow? What do the glaziers care so long as their foundries still stand? You're all afraid to fight because of what you stand to lose, and you'd sacrifice anyone in order to keep it!"

"That's preposterous!" Master Gill said. "Our first task has always been to look after the people!"

"If you cared about the people," Ely said, "then you'd be thankful for what I've done. I've shown them that they have a choice. They can choose your path, and bow to murderers to preserve your precious profits, or they can choose mine, and fight for the people they love. I make my choice now, and this is my answer: no."

Shima's mouth worked open and closed in unarticulated shock, but Orndas' face had grown even stonier during Ely's speech.

"If you defy us, Elymia, then I will have no choice but to place you under arrest, to stand trial for treason."

"Do what you must," Ely said, her mind made up. The blood pounded in her veins like molten glass, full of fire and flashes of sparkling potential. "But know that I will not surrender. If you want me, you'll have to kill me, just like you did my mother."

Orndas froze, the unexpected words cutting through anger. "Elymia," he said, tone suddenly softening. "You don't mean that. Your mother . . . . That was never supposed to-"

"It was just an accident then, was it?" Ely said. "She and her brother dared to challenge the Guild rule, dared to suggest that the Council should stand for something more, and someone accidentally assassinated them? Were they only supposed to be tortured a little? Maybe you only meant to burn their houses, or threaten their children, and things just got out of hand?"

"The Council did not order those things, Elymia," Orndas said. "You know that."

"Does it matter?" Ely said. "They happened. But you know what? All it did was prove them right. And when you kill me, you will only prove them right again."

"No one is going to be killed here today," Barty interrupted, raising his hands and stepping between Ely and Orndas. "This has gone far enough. I do not agree with Elymia's methods, but it is clear to me that her intentions are good. What she needs from us is our wisdom and our guidance, not threats and violence. Even a fool could see that she has managed something remarkable here. I, for one, will stand against any who would harm her." He crossed the room to stand by Ely's side. His height was comforting beside her, like the shade of a tall tree, and Ely quivered, the boiling mix of emotions within her no longer identifiable by name. There was relief, yes, but also pride and defiance buzzing through her nerves like lightning through a stormcloud.

"I stand with her as well," Matrice said, finally rising to join Ely and Barty. "You may not believe me, father, but this battle can be won, though it never will be if no one is willing to fight." Ely saw that there were tears in Aldan Pourin's eyes, though of what kind she could not even begin to guess.

Mae stomped over to the growing group and turned, glowering at the councilors and their guards. "Lay a finger on us and I'll take it off," she said, her voice full of knives.

Wharfmaster Abrohl gave Orndas a wide grin. "If we're castin' our chips into the pot, mine don't take much thinking." He walked over and clapped Ely on the shoulder. "I'd watch myself, Orndas. She's a quick 'un, like her mum. She might have your job afore long."

Aldan Pourin ducked his head as he walked past Orndas to join Ely's growing entourage. "Sorry," he said to the confused-looking councilman, "but my daughter comes first, and she always will." He took Matrice by the hand and held on tightly, and she gave him a genuine smile in return.

"Well then," Orndas said, collecting himself and surveying the ragtag but determined group arrayed against him. "I see that you've all made your choice. I can only pray to the gods for wisdom, for it seems there is none left in the realm of men. I hope you live long enough to realize the mistake you're making, but to be frank, that doesn't seem likely." He turned on his heel and walked out.

Master Gill sighed and shrugged before following in the chairman's footsteps. The five men who had been escorting Mae left with him, leaving only

Tallomi Shima behind. She did not look happy, but there was something else in her gaze as she eyed Ely.

Whatever it was, it did not last long, for a glare from Mae sent her scurrying after the other councilors, leaving the rebels alone once again in the warehouse. Matrice and her father shared a happy embrace, and Ely threw her arms around Barty's neck.

"Where in the Deep were you?" were the first words from her mouth. "I thought you were dead!"

Barty patted her gently on the back. "I was doing what I was trained to do, once upon a time when I served with your father. Reconnaissance. I might be a bit rusty, but I knew he'd need it when he returned. There's no such thing as retirement once you've served under the Grayfin's command."

"You really think he's coming back?" Ely said, drawing back from the embrace.

"Whether he is or not, it's my job to be ready," Barty said. "I made this for him, but I think you're in a better position to use it." He produced a sheaf of papers and handed it to her. "You're not the only one who would cast out these invaders, Elymia. I've collected a list of those who stand ready, like you, to fight for their freedom, names your father will be able to count on when the time comes to retake the city. I believe you'll be able to count on them too."

Ely clutched the papers to her breast. In that instant, they felt more valuable to her than gold. Yet something was bothering her. "Do you really think . . ." she said hesitantly, looking away. "Do you really think he would call all of this foolishness?"

Barty turned her head back toward him with his hands. "Your father was never one to let a talented soldier languish in the rear, Ely. He believes that people's gifts are meant to be used. That's why he stayed in this city even after losing your mother, because even though it pained him, he couldn't let his talents go to waste when they might be able to keep good men alive. The choice of how to use your gifts is what defines a person's life, what reveals the nature of their soul. I am certain your father would not want to interfere with yours."

Ely blinked tears from her eyes. "Then why did you say . . . ?"

Barty gave her a solemn look. "Because you mustn't choose by whether your father approves. You mustn't choose by whether the Council approves, or whether I approve. If you are to be a good leader to these people, they must know that you are choosing from your own heart. A good man who lets others steer him is not a man who should lead. They already know you are a good person, Elymia. Now they must know that they can count on you to let that goodness be your guide."

"Lead?" Ely said, drawing back. "I'm not leading anyone."

Barty gave her a slight smile. "No?" he said. "It was you who spoke for them. It was you they rallied around. It was clear as day, in fact, as soon as I set foot in this room. Even Orndas, blind as he is in some ways, saw it."

Ely tried to deny it. It was true that she had devised much of their plan, but Matrice and Mae had been invaluable. She could not have done anything without them. Surely that meant that she was not their leader? Hearing Orndas's name, however, reminded her of something he had said, and it gave her an excuse to put the uncomfortable question of leadership aside.

"What did Orndas mean?" Ely asked, frowning. "About murder and mutilation?"

"You haven't heard?" Aldan interjected, leaving Matrice's side for a moment to join the conversation. "I don't suppose you would have, holed up in here like this. Bodies of Aloise soldiers have been turning up behind taverns and the like, at least three so far, with their throats cut and . . . other things done to them. After what you did at the Keep, the Council assumed it was you lot behind it." He looked a bit uncertain.

"Father," Matrice said with a frown. "You can't think that I would take part in something as wrongheaded as that." She exchanged glances with Ely and Mae. "Or that any of us would, for that matter." Mae snorted, but said nothing.

"Of course not. I knew it couldn't be you," Aldan said quickly, though he looked visibly relieved.

Matrice gave her father's hand a squeeze, though she shot Ely a meaningful look at the same time, a look that confirmed they were thinking the same thing. Behind taverns? Ely prayed she was wrong about what that meant, but if Matrice had made the connection too . . . . It did not bear thinking about.

"But I suppose this means there's at least one other person on our side out there who's trying to help," Mae said.

Ely frowned harder. "That sort of thing isn't going to help us."

"How's that?" Mae asked. "Fewer Aloise soldiers means fewer for us to deal with, right?"

"It runs against our plan," Ely said. "We were supposed to shock the Aloise, make them afraid of what they're facing. We might not have driven them out, but that doesn't mean we've lost. Attacking the Keep was about projecting strength as much as rescuing prisoners, and we did manage to give them a good taste of what we can do. If we can convince them we're strong enough, retreat will seem their best option, and they'll never learn our true strength or numbers." Ely paused. "But small ambushes, murders, mutilation . . . those are tactics of desperation, of people who are too weak to fight their enemies outright. They tell the Aloise we aren't as strong as we want them to think."

The Wharfmaster nodded. "'Tis only the small fishes that bite at your toes. The real monsters will take you when they please, even if they have to bring yer whole boat down to get you."

"That may be," Matrice said, "but what's done is done, and we gain nothing by debating it. We should be focusing on our next step, on actually getting the Aloise out of the city."

"Agreed," Ely said. "And for that, we need to arrange a meeting with Oridine. Proposing a prisoner exchange should be the quickest way. It'll give us another chance to convince her that she's outmatched if she stays."

"So glad I can be of service," Edwin said sarcastically, breaking his long silence. Mae growled, but Ely ignored him. She did note in the back of her mind, however, that he had kept his word and remained quiet in the Council's presence.

"Are we in agreement on this?" she asked the others.

Matrice nodded at once. Mae looked back and forth between Edwin and Ely before giving a shrug. "All right," she said, "but he'd better be worth something if you expect us to put up with him in the meantime." The Wharfmaster, Barty, and Aldan simply stood by and watched, as if whatever Ely decided would be good enough for them. It irritated her, but they had more important things to do than waste precious time while she tried to convince them that she was not in charge.

"Then it's settled," Ely said. "I believe that means we have a letter to write."

Chapter 30

The Hammer of Aloise

"Didn't you assure me that we had the blessing of the Masked?" Oridine fumed at Remiana, whose arms were burried to the elbow in a box of papers and personal effects.

They stood in Remiana's bedroom, or what remained of it. The floor sloped unevenly to one side, and fist-sized chunks of the ceiling were scattered everywhere. The wall bowed inward around the hole that had once been a window, and shards of glass littered the floor and bedspread.

Remiana moved over to her closet. The doorframe was cracked and sagging, forcing her to tug several times before it finally opened. It was empty save for a single saffron dress dangling lonely among four other, empty hangers. Remiana looked at the solitary garment for a long moment, unmoving.

"Answer me!" Oridine demanded.

The Impelar beside Oridine, the only other person in the room, leaned upon her scythe casually and smirked. Since snitching about Remiana's excursion, she seemed to have gained Oridine's favor, and it was rare now to see them apart.

"Yes, mother," Remiana said in a low voice. She lifted the dress out of the closet and placed it gently in the box next to her bow and her quiver.

"Is that all you have to say for yourself?" Oridine asked. "Fifty-one dead, twelve missing, at least one escaped prisoner, half our fortifications in ruins, and the best you can muster is 'yes, mother'?"

Remiana's anger flared. "You saw the letter they left for us on Dedication night just as well as I," she said. "I couldn't have known this would happen. After endorsing your plan, it makes no sense that they would turn on us."

"What makes sense to you does not concern me," Oridine snapped. "I have a hundred reports describing Masked in the Keep last night. You are making me doubt your fitness for the throne, daughter, if you cannot even assure me of the meaning of one simple letter."

Remiana's hands tightened on the fine fabric of the dress.

"He's missing, mother," she said with pain in her voice. "How can you talk about letters and thrones when Edwin is missing? Don't you even care?"

Oridine's fingers twitched, and one corner of her mouth turned down. "Do not use that tone with me, child," she warned. "Queens do not have the luxury of love or grief."

"He grew up in our home!" Remiana exclaimed.

"As did a dozen other servants' children," Oridine replied. "Does it suddenly concern you what happened to all of them as well?"

In the corner of the room, a shadow stirred. Donvin, having grown tired of listening to the squabble, decided it was time to make his entrance. He released the illusion that concealed him, making his fur-clad form seem to coalesce before the eyes of the three women. His suddenly appearance stunned them for an instant, but their shock did not last long.

"You! Traitor!" Oridine cried as soon as she could draw breath, pointing her finger as if it were a blade at Donvin's chest. "You dare to offer us your blessing and then betray us? You will learn what it means to cross an Aloise!" She turned to the closed door and shouted, "Guards! Enter and seize this enemy of the throne!"

Even as Donvin readied himself to face an attack, however, he felt a familiar presence on the other side of the door. *Flicker.* It was followed by two muffled cries, and then by the sound of two heavy objects hitting the floor. The door remained closed.

Donvin smiled. Though Lith might think she could keep him in the dark about everything, including that ephemeral phenomenon that seemed to follow him wherever he went, he was nevertheless beginning to understand something of its nature.

Seeing that no aid was coming, the Impelar at Oridine's side took up her scythe in both hands, but the lightest flick from Donvin's strands knocked her into a wall and instantly unconscious. Her scythe clattered to the floor, and the room was still once more.

"It's unfortunate that you jump to such unflattering conclusions, Lady Aloise," Donvin said, smelling with satisfaction the waves of fear rolling off both mother and daughter. Remiana's hands were resting on the bow protruding from the box of her belongings, but being unstrung, it was useless as a weapon.

"What do you want, Masked?" Oridine said rigidly. "Why come here after breaking your word to us?"

"I believe you're mistaken, my lady," Donvin replied. "No word has been broken. What was promised to you remains true. I am only here to ensure you apportion blame as it is due."

"Spare me your weasely talk," Oridine said. "There is no arguing that your kind participated in the attack here."

"I assume you refer to the reports of your men seeing Masked," Donvin said, "but the truth is that you have fallen victim to a clever ruse."

"A ruse?" Oridine said.

"A staged assault," Donvin answered, "to make you think that the Masked had become your enemies. It wouldn't take more than a few animal skins to fool a common soldier in the dark of night, would it?"

Oridine was a harsh woman and quick to anger, but she was far from stupid. "What power did they wield against us, then, if not yours?"

"Oh, it was indeed our power," Donvin said, "but I can assure you, it was not under our sanction. It seems your enemies are more resourceful than you imagined."

Oridine glowered at him. "If it was your power," she said, "then it is your duty to control it. Is that not part of the compact you Masked ceaselessly remind us of?"

"You're right, of course," Donvin said. "But you must understand, direct intervention in the affairs of men is forbidden by our code, and we have never before faced a situation like this. Even once we are certain of your enemies' wrongdoing, it will take time to prepare a response. Still, we are mindful of our promise of support, and of our shared belief that strong, unified leadership is what this land needs. For the time being, we would offer you some . . . indirect assistance."

Donvin reached into his robes and produced five glass vials, each filled with an amber liquid.

"What is this?" Oridine demanded, while Remiana looked on warily.

"Something to tip the balance of power," Donvin said. "It would be such a shame if a few short-sighted rebels thwarted our shared vision merely because my people could not agree to stop them in time."

Oridine looked hungrily at the vials in Donvin's hand, and he could smell the anticipation leaking from her pores. The greedy were easy to manipulate, and the angry even easier. Judging by the state of the Keep, Elymia has performed admirably in fueling the latter emotion. Donvin could not help but be impressed by the level of destruction a mere three vials of Scarwood sap had been able to inflict. Soon enough, his intervention would no longer be needed. The city would boil and rupture under the pressure of its own violent energies, and into that roiling torrent he would cast the Masked to their final destruction.

"It may be that I did not give you enough credit," Oridine said, taking the vials from Donvin's hand. "You can rest assured that I will use this aid to bring swift justice to those who would upset our infant peace." Remiana, rather than looking at the vials, was looking at her mother's vengeful face.

Donvin nodded to her. "I have no doubt that you will." At least, he had no doubt she would try. She would need to fail, of course, for such a promising conflict could not be allowed to end so quickly. It would need careful nurturing until it could reach the height of its destructive potential.

Having delivered what he had come to deliver, Donvin was preparing to depart when there was a rapid knocking at the door, and the man who rushed in did not even wait for permission before entering. In the brief moment that the door was open, Donvin caught a glimpse of the hall outside. It was empty.

Oridine turned on the heavily breathing soldier while quickly concealing the vials she held behind her back. "Explain yourself!"

"Forgive me, mistress," the man gasped, dropping to his knees and holding out a folded sheet of paper. "It's a message from those who attacked us. They offer an exchange of prisoners."

Oridine snatched the paper from his hands, but did not unfold it. "You opened a missive directed to your superiors?" she said.

The soldier pressed himself even lower to the ground. "No, mistress," he said. "The letter came under no seal. Several of the men read it before it was determined to be for your grace."

"Who delivered it?" Oridine demanded.

"It was . . .," the soldier hesitated, still staring at the floor. "It was no one, mistress. The letter flew in through the window of the guard tower by the front gate. The third floor window."

Oridine turned to look at her daughter. "It seems your marksmanship is not as good as you claim."

Remiana clutched the wood of her bow, but said nothing.

Oridine unfolded the letter and scanned it silently while the messenger waited. When she was finished, she passed the document to Remiana, whose eyes grew wide with relief as she read it. Then her breath caught in her throat as she reached the last line, and the signature.

"A prisoner exchange," Oridine said thoughtfully, "to be held tomorrow, here in the courtyard of the Keep. They must be quite confident to willingly come again into the heart of our power."

Donvin allowed a smile to enter his voice. "I trust you know how to handle the situation appropriately."

Oridine gave him a condescending look. "We will accommodate their request, of course." She waved the messenger out of the room and then turned to Remiana. "It seems your cousin is missing no longer. Draft up a letter of safe passage for our enemies so that they can bring him to the exchange, child. Then find me thirty of our best marksmen."

Chapter 31

The Wages of Mercy

Ely smoothed her dress as she approached the imposing gate of the Keep. From this angle the structure showed little sign of the devastation they had wreaked upon it just two nights ago.

"You'e being a fool," Edwin murmured over his shoulder to Ely, low enough so that Mae and Matrice, who followed her, could not overhear. "I told you they won't bargain for me. I don't know how to make it any clearer that this can only end with both of us dead."

"It's not a prisoner's job to worry about his captors," Ely said dryly, plucking at the ropes binding Edwin's wrists. Another rope bound a cloth-wrapped bundle to his back, one that every so often clinked when he took a step. Having been unable to safely confiscate his sword, they had opted to tie it to him where he could not easily reach it.

"Don't think that my presence is going to protect you," Edwin said. "Oridine wouldn't think twice about killing me to get to you. And personally, I'd prefer not to die just because you made a mistake."

"I know what I'm doing," Ely said, giving him a light shove between the shoulders. "Keep walking." She wished she felt as confident as she sounded. This meeting could still be productive even if Oridine did not want Edwin back, but from the way Remiana had spoken of her family, Ely doubted they would leave one of their own in the hands of the enemy.

Five guards held positions in front of the closed gate, armed with spears and supported by archers in the windows of guard towers.

"We have a letter of safe passage," Ely said as the soldiers lowered their weapons at the approaching group.

The lead soldier glanced between the three unarmed women and one bound man, searching for threats and finding none. "Hand it over."

Ely produced the letter. She had been surprised, upon reading it, to recognize Remiana's flawless penmanship.

"You are expected," the soldier said. He turned and waved up at the guard towers, squinting against the sun. There was a grinding sound, and the heavy gates began to part.

"Walk straight through to the far side of the courtyard. Don't go anywhere else. You will be watched," he added.

Ely took the lead as the four of them passed under the outer wall and into the bailey of the Keep, letting Edwin walk at the center of the triangle formed by the three women. Dry leaves crunched underfoot as they crossed the green and halted before the steps up to the doors of the great hall.

As expected, Oridine was waiting for them atop the steps. As her entourage she had brought two of the Lode knights, one with a white visor and one with a yellow, an Impelar dressed in her usual red silks, and her daughter, Remiana. Behind them stood a nervous-looking Councilman Tulloch and his wife, Councilman Jaff's wife and daughter, two men whose names Ely did not know, and . . . Tamalina?

Ely kept her face neutral. Neither Barty nor Aldan had heard anything about this. Ely hoped against hope that she was wrong about the reason for Tamalina's captivity. At least the prisoners all looked reasonably healthy, displaying none of the marks of torture that had been so evident on Wharf-master Abrohl's body.

After tallying the captives, Ely assessed the opposing delegation while avoiding Remiana's eyes. Edwin had not been shy with the details of what he had witnessed in service to the Aloise in the past week, perhaps hoping that they would unsettle Ely, who claimed to have once been Remiana's friend. It made for grim listening, despite Mae's warnings that Aloise mouths spread nothing but lies. She knew she should have been elated to hear of how Remiana too was being made to suffer, yet she found herself unable to derive any pleasure from it. The thought just made her feel . . . empty. And the fact that Remiana was to be queen . . . . She could not quite bring herself to believe it.

Ely bit her lip hard, trying to quiet her mind and focus on the present. She needed to stay clearheaded for any of this to succeed, and she could not let the words of an enemy unnerve her.

To her dismay, it was Remiana, not Oridine, who descended the steps to speak to them. It seemed there would be no avoiding her after all.

"I have been granted authority to hear your offer on behalf of the house of Aloise," Remiana said, her shoulders back and head high, every angle of her uniform pressed and perfect. "With whom will I discuss terms?"

Ely stepped forward, unable to avoid meeting Remiana's gaze any longer. When it had come time to decide which of them would speak to the Aloise, there had not been much debate. Between herself, Mae, and Matrice, Ely's name was the one Oridine would be most likely to respect. That, and her father's army.

"I speak on behalf of the people of Falls Gate who resist your occupation," Ely declared. *What few of us there are.*

Now that she was closer, Remiana did not look well, Ely saw. Her eyes were shadowed and her lips pale. Despite her sickly appearance, however, Remiana's voice was hard as she moved closer.

"I trusted you, Elymia," she said in private tones. "I trusted you, and this is twice I have looked the fool for it."

"I did what I had to do," Ely said stiffly. "You had no right to expect loyalty from the people you betrayed. Now, do you want your cousin back or not?"

Remiana turned her gaze to Edwin, who flashed her a brief, apologetic smile. For a fraction of a second, Ely thought she saw Remiana's eyes soften.

"He is unharmed?" Remiana asked.

"Of course," Ely said, unable to keep the bitterness from her voice. "I don't mistreat my prisoners."

Remiana let the jab pass unacknowledged. "What offer of trade would you have me convey to my mother?"

"Your cousin's life for the release of the female prisoners," Ely said, "and his sword for the release of the men." She reached up and unwrapped the top of the bundle strapped to Edwin's back, revealing the hilt of his blade.

Remiana thought for a moment, sharing another look with Edwin. "You ask seven things in exchange for two. Is that all you have to offer?"

"No," Matrice said, catching Remiana's eye. "There is more." She pulled down the sleeve of her dress to reveal her bandaged shoulder. "If you will ask for it, I will also offer my forgiveness."

Silence followed. Remiana opened her mouth, then closed it again as she stared at the bandages, a dark flower of understanding blooming behind her eyes as she recognized the wound. For the briefest of moments, her face revealed her heart, and Ely had to look away to keep her feelings in check. How could it be that she harbored even the tiniest bit of sympathy for this woman, this torturer, this murderer, after all she had done? What was wrong with her? People like Remiana deserved no compassion!

"I . . . I think we can reach an agreement," Remiana said, blinking quickly as Matrice straightened her dress. "I will recommend that this offer be accepted." She turned, but a word from Ely stopped her. She had wanted to speak this message directly to Oridine, but in Remiana she saw, momentarily, a receptive ear. Besides, she could not just let her walk away.

"We can't go on like this, Remiana," she said. It was harder to say than it should have been. "Things can only get worse from here. You've seen what we can do. The next time, there won't be anyone left to trade. We returned your cousin as an act of goodwill to prove that we'll let you depart our city unharmed. But if you don't withdraw, if you choose to fight us instead, then you will die, each and every one of you. We have the power to see this finished, and one way or another, we will have justice."

Remiana turned back. Suddenly, as clear as day, Ely recognized her friend again in the other woman's face, glimpsing her as if spying a child peeking from a treasured hiding place.

"It's not up to us, Elymia," Remiana said quietly. "We can't change how we were born. If our roles demand it, then we can go on, and we must." Then just as quickly as she had appeared, the old Remiana was gone.

Mae and Matrice drew closer to converse while Remiana ascended the steps to relay their message to her mother.

"There are archers hiding atop the southern wall," Mae whispered. "At least ten of them."

"And up there, in those windows," Matrice added, nodding toward the main structure of the Keep in front of them. "I don't know how many."

Ely watched as Remiana approached her mother and whispered something in her ear. The hidden soldiers were no surprise. Had their roles been reversed, Ely would have done the same.

"Keep an eye on them, but stay calm," she said. "They're probably just to make sure we don't threaten Oridine."

"Not that it matters," Mae said. "She's too far away anyhow."

She was, Ely realized. Mae and Matrice's powers had a severely limited reach, no more than ten feet at the most. Oridine was standing at least thirty feet away at the top of the steps, and she had made no move to come closer. That was curious. Ely struggled to remember her conversations with Remiana on those warm summer evenings what seemed a lifetime ago. Was it typical of iron lords to negotiate by proxy like this?

At the top of the steps, Remiana had finished her report, and Oridine cleared her throat.

"Here it comes," Edwin murmured.

"I have heard your proposal," Oridine said loudly, her voice like an arrow with the wind behind it. "But I find it lacking."

"What?" Remiana said from beside her, a look of shock slapped across her normally controlled face. Ely, too, felt something unpleasant stirring in her gut, though surprise was not its name. The opposing delegation was not standing at that distance just for show.

Oridine raised one arm, and the hidden archers revealed themselves. There were far more than Mae had guessed, peering down at them through windows and around crenellations and doorframes. Even Mae and Matrice's power could not stop that many arrows.

"That you have come here at all shows you are not lacking in courage, daughter of Celundine," Oridine said. "But the only thing of yours that I want, child, is your life. Consider this my counteroffer." She gestured toward Tamalina. "Bring the girl."

The knight with the yellow visor seized Tamalina's arm and dragged her forward to Oridine's side.

"You know this one, correct?" Oridine said. "My men detained her last night, shortly after she lured two of them into an alley and tried to cut their throats. Just as she has done before."

Ely's heart hammered in her chest, and she felt Matrice stiffen beside her. She did not want to believe, but the words did not shock her as they should have. "That's a lie," she said, barely loud enough for Oridine to hear.

"She does not deny it," Oridine said, "do you, girl?"

Tamalina thrust her head forward and tried to spit at Oridine's face, but the knight wrapped a plated arm about her neck, making her choke instead.

"There you have it," Oridine said. Her eyes narrowed at Ely. "You say you will have justice, child. Well, so will I."

The knight forced Tamalina to her knees.

"Let me tell you something about justice," Oridine said. "Justice can be cruel, or justice can be kind. And those who invoke it cannot stand exempt from judgment. I will have justice for the murder of my men. I will have justice for the destruction and terror you have sown upon us, the ones who come to bring you peace. What kind of justice I exact is for you to decide." At her command, the knight drew his sword and handed it to her.

"Surrender yourself to me," Oridine said to Ely. "Call an end to your petty resistance. Declare for all to hear that you were wrong to fight us. Do this, and the justice you face shall be kind. You and your friend will be executed according to the ways of civilized men, but those you deceived into aiding you will be spared."

Oridine let her declaration sink in for a moment. The air in the courtyard creaked with taut bowstrings. "But if you refuse," she said slowly, "there will be no civility, and there will be no mercy. I will extract the cruel price of justice from your friend's flesh while you watch. Then I will let my men do the same."

Ely's mind whirled, and she felt dizzy, strangely detached from her body. How could things have gone so wrong? Oridine was not even the slightest bit afraid of them! How was that possible, after what they had proven they could do? This should have worked! Out of the corners of her eyes, Ely saw that Matrice and Mae were similarly frozen.

Oridine swung the sword with both hands, striking Tamalina across the shoulders with the flat of the blade, knocking her onto her hands with a gasp of pain. The blow pierced through Ely's mental haze as if she had been the one struck.

"Surrender!" Oridine demanded, inflicting a second blow on the same spot. At Oridine's side, Remiana looked upon her mother's violence as if dreaming, her eyes glazed and unfocused.

Tamalina grunted, but she did not cry out. She did not sob. She just turned her head slowly to meet Ely's eyes.

What dreadful things Ely saw in those eyes, those inhuman eyes, eyes that remained dry as the blade continued to rise and fall. Even facing death, the only pools that formed in them were bottomless oceans of hate.

Ely wept in Tamalina's stead as the blows continued to rain down, accepting the burden of the pain that Tamalina could no longer feel. She wept too for her own weakness, knowing that no amount of Scarwood sap or any mystical art of the Masked had the power to make Tamalina smile again. No bloody revenge could repair the friendship that had once existed between them. No final victory could undo what had been done in its pursuit.

Oridine paused after bringing down another blow, perhaps because her arms had grown tired from the weight of the blade. "Have you had enough, child?" she demanded of Ely. "Do you see, now, why you must submit?" Tamalina, mercifully, seemed to have slipped into unconsciousness at her feet.

Ely felt every eye in the courtyard turn to her. So many eyes, all watching, waiting, wondering what she would say. So many, yet it seemed like even more: she could feel her father's stern eyes as well, and the critical gaze of Gerard Orndas and the rest of the Council. She could feel Barty's eyes, and the Wharfmaster's, and those of little Bermin Pourin and his puppy. She even thought she could feel her mother's russet eyes, eyes that had been closed for the greater part of her life. So many people were waiting on her. They waited, she knew, because what she did next would be more than her decision alone. It would be theirs as well, for fate had not given them a chance to choose. Ely was the one who had been offered that privilege, and they wanted to see if she would speak not just for herself, but for them.

Ely wanted desperately to protect the people she loved, and she ached to spare Tamalina from even one more ounce of pain. Had she been alone, she would have gladly given herself up for their sake. But she was not alone. She was not alone, and she could not bear to snuff the last gleam of hope, of dignity, that she could see shining from all those innumerable eyes.

"Yes, I see," Ely agreed, lifting her head and letting the tears stand out proudly on her face. "I see why you can never be allowed to rule us." A thousand eyes twinkled like glorious stars smiling down at her, and her mother's brightest among them.

Oridine's face was stone. "If that is your choice."

"It is."

Oridine nodded. "Then I will take your lives as they are." She raised her hand again, motioning to the bowmen.

"Wait! At least make the exchange!" Remiana pleaded, suddenly animated again. "Surely there's something worth keeping in what they offered us!"

"They have brought me nothing of value, daughter," Oridine said. "I have blades beyond counting, and bastard children are worthless to a family with proper honor."

"Mother!" Remiana cried out, astounded. "Edwin is no bastard!"

"You are in no position to know," Oridine snapped, and at her gesture the second of the knights seized Remiana's arm. "I am. Allowing his birth to go unremedied might have saved face for the family, but it does not give his life value in trade."

"No, you mustn't do this!" Remiana yelled. "Edwin is still fam-"

"That misbegotten spawn can die with the rest of them," Oridine cut her off. "I have had enough of you associating with such filth. This is for the good of your throne, daughter. I declare it for all to hear: that bastard is no family of ours, not now, not ever. He has no right to die with the honor of the name Aloise!"

Ely felt a stirring beside her as more frozen figures came to life.

"If anyone's going to die here, it's you for what you did to Evana!" Mae shouted up at Oridine. At her command, a sizable boulder burst up from the grassy ground, leaving a ragged hole in the turf. "You may think you're safe up there, but I can throw a lot farther than that!"

Oridine looked down her nose at Mae's snarling face and the levitating boulder. "Evana? I have no idea what you are talking about."

"Like the Deep you don't!" Mae shouted.

"Then kill me, girl," Oridine said, spreading her arms. "If you can."

"Mae, the prisoners, don't-!" Ely said, but it was too late. The challenge proved too much, and Mae launched the boulder with all her might straight at the opposing delegation. There was a boom like rolling thunder, one that shook Ely down to her bones and blew her hair back in a blast of air. The branches of the Chesamir tree whipped and swayed in the violent wind, the last of its dying leaves ripping free and dancing upon the air in whorls the color of blood.

When the winds subsided and Ely opened her eyes, Oridine stood as she had before, unscathed, a look of triumph on her face. To her right, the red-clad Impelar had one hand raised, and the remains of the boulder were disintegrating into sand in front of her. It could not be, but it was.

"No longer will you terrorize my people with your ill-gotten powers," Oridine said. "You are an offense against the order of this world, and I have been given the means to restore it. Now, you die. All of you."

"No, mother, please!" Remiana begged, but a knight's gauntleted hand clamped over her mouth, muffling her cries.

Ely looked to Mae and Matrice, but a single glance told her that they had no more to offer. They were beaten, but at least they had not yielded, and Ely found some comfort in that. Strangely, only Edwin seemed unaffected by their certain death. He was standing oddly straight, and his eyes were even closed.

"You were wrong, mother," he said under his breath, so softly that Ely was not sure she heard him correctly. "She could not protect me. And I could not protect her."

Oridine dropped her hand, and the whistling of arrows filled the air. Remiana shrieked and fought viciously, but the knight's iron grip held her fast.

"Get down!" Ely shouted, some tiny part of her still wishing to fight, useless as it was. She did the only thing she could think of: she threw herself at the still-standing Edwin, tackling him to the ground. Yet suddenly there was no ground beneath them, just an infinite, gaping hole, and the two of them tumbled through it together on a long fall into darkness.

Chapter 32
The Third Meeting

Edwin landed roughly on his side, hitting his head painfully against the hard ground. A second later, another body fell on top of him and rolled off in a sputtering tangle of fabric and hair. He struggled to get to his feet, but the ropes around his wrists and ankles foiled him. He took several deep breaths, trying to calm himself as he squinted against the intense brightness of the sky overhead. There was a high-pitched ringing in his ears, but his body felt remarkably intact considering how many arrows had been flying at it a moment ago. Somehow, he was alive.

He lay there for a minute, just feeling the rise and fall of his chest, drinking in the blessed sensations of life. Then a shape stirred in the corner of his vision. He lifted his head and saw a dazed-looking Elymia, her reddish hair now loose about her shoulders, raising herself into a sitting position with her hands. She was staring past him, her mouth open slightly, looking just as surprised to be alive as he was.

"A little help?" Edwin said, squirming against his restraints and feeling the sword tied to his back press awkwardly between his shoulder blades.

For a moment it seemed that Ely had not heard him, but then her attention refocused. She moved clumsily to stand, nearly falling as her ankle twisted on the lumpy white stone they had landed on. Recovering, she grabbed Edwin by the arm and helped him to his feet.

"What happened? Where are we?" He asked as he steadied himself. Ely just shook her head dumbly and pointed over his shoulder.

Having grown up in the mountains, Edwin was not one to be frightened of heights, but the scene he beheld made him feel suddenly nauseated. The two of them were standing on a bridge of white stone spanning a gap of impossible depth. Compared to the mountain peaks it connected and the vast nothingness over which it hung, the bridge seemed little more than a single strand of silver hair stretched out to span the entirety of an ocean.

Perhaps it was not the fantastical sight that made the bile rise in his throat, Edwin reconsidered, but the strange smell. The shock of their fall had numbed his senses at first, but now he noticed that there was something subtly evil on the air, something both ephemeral and vile being raked across his nostrils by an aggressive wind.

"How did you do this?" Ely demanded, interrupting Edwin's contemplation. "How did you bring us to this . . . this place?"

"Me? I didn't do anything," Edwin said, squinting at her. "What about your two friends? I'm not the one who can toss boulders around like dinner rolls. Why don't you ask them?" He squinted harder. Why was it so damn bright when he could not see the sun anywhere in the perfectly clear sky?

Ely glanced around again, but she and Edwin were still alone. Of Mae and Matrice, there was no sign.

"But you weren't afraid," Ely said, unwilling to let the issue go. "You knew we weren't going to be hit by those arrows."

"Did I?" Edwin said, amused by her certainty. "If so, it's news to me."

"Then why weren't you scared?"

Edwin looked away from her, scanning their unearthly surroundings for anything familiar, any hint of where in the world they might be, and finding nothing. "It doesn't matter," he said. There was no way she could understand what he had felt when facing his final seconds: failure, yes, but also, shamefully, freedom. "But since we are alive, we should be more worried about finding a way out of here. I don't exactly see any signposts." The place might look like strange enough to be the afterlife, but Edwin was certain they were not dead.

Ely joined him in searching the distance, trying to shield her eyes from the light but finding the gesture unhelpful.

"We'll have to go across," she said finally. "Wherever this place is, whatever it is, staying here won't do us any good."

"My thoughts exactly," Edwin agreed, grateful that she had not lost her senses under pressure. Though if she could keep her head in the face of Oridine's brutality, he didn't suppose there was much that could rattle her.

"But I'm going nowhere like this," he added, kicking a leg against his binding ropes. The bridge was perhaps four paces wide, but between its bumps, the strange wind, and his bindings, one trip could be enough to send him over the edge.

"You want me to untie you?" Ely said, incredulous.

"Either that, or you can go out there alone," Edwin countered, nodding to the white span that narrowed to a pinpoint on the horizon. "Your choice."

Ely's eyes followed the length of the bridge as it stretched out across the unbelievably wide chasm, and she shivered a little, brushing her hair over her ear as the wind tossed it about. Then she froze.

"My comb," she said, putting both hands to her head as her hair fluttered around her like a tattered flag. "Where is it?"

"Is that really important right now?" Edwin said. "We've got bigger things to worry about here, in case you hadn't noticed."

Ely glared at him, then dropped to her hands and knees, searching across the stones at their feet. She ran her hands over the bumpy surface, but it was bare.

"This isn't the time, Elymia," Edwin said more forcefully, but that did not stop her seeking. After a minute or two more, he grew frustrated.

"Look," he said. "If you untie me, I'll help you find it. We can't just stand out here like this forever. If it means we'll get moving faster, I'll help."

Ely looked, hands splayed across the white stones. "Supposing I do free you, what's to stop you from trying to kill me?"

Edwin gave a laugh at her serious expression. "Have you looked at where we are?" he said. "Fighting here would be suicide. We'd both go over the edge in a second. But if it helps, I'll give you my word. No tricks."

There was a slight pause before Ely replied. "The word of an Aloise knight doesn't mean much."

Edwin sighed. "No, I guess it doesn't," he said. "But what reason do I have to fight? I'm not much of a knight at the moment. Nor much of an Aloise." The words came out with surprising ease. He had expected them to hurt as he said them, but instead they felt . . . liberating.

Ely locked her gaze with his. Her eyes were the deep brown of rich soil, the kind you had to stray far from the mountaintops to find, the kind that grew fruit so succulent it made even the iron men of the highest peaks dream, for a day, of being farmers.

"All right," Ely said. "But this doesn't mean I trust you. Turn around."

Edwin complied, and Ely set to work on the complicated knots of his restraints.

"I suppose that means it's true, what Oridine said," Ely said over his shoulder as she worked. "You're a bastard."

Edwin saw no point in lying any longer. "I am."

Ely's hands did not slow. "You should've told me. I would have thought better of trying to trade you had I known, and we wouldn't have ended up in this mess."

Edwin could not help but chuckle. "You wouldn't have believed me. Or rather, that Maewell character wouldn't have let you. A real charmer, that one." Ely made a faint sound that might have been the beginnings of a laugh.

"But even if you had," Edwin said, "you must know what the Aloise do to bastards. Why would I trust you with a secret like that? And if you had known, would you have had any reason to keep a useless prisoner like me alive?"

The knots holding the sword to his back relaxed, easing the tension on the ropes around his chest.

"Don't assume that I'm as callous as your people when it comes to killing," Ely said curtly. "Frankly, I'm surprised you survived this long. I didn't think the Aloise made exceptions."

"They don't," Edwin said. "The price for my bastardy was paid in full, just not by me." He hesitated.

Ely's hands stopped. "You don't mean . . . . They killed the wrong . . . ?"

"When my mother was accused of infidelity," Edwin said, "she had two young sons, not even a full year apart. One looked properly Aloise, and the other didn't. It seemed an easy choice." He shook his head, remembering all the times he had looked in the mirror and felt nothing but guilt. Why was it suddenly so easy for him to speak of these things now, things he had never once uttered to another living soul? Why was it so easy to shed the armor he had been wearing his entire life?

"That's terrible," Ely said, resuming her work on the knots. "Barbaric."

"They might have thought twice," Edwin went on, "had the identity of my father been more widely known. But for some, like Oridine, the mistake was convenient. It left no need to explain why the bastard child should look more truly Aloise than the trueborn one. So the lie was allowed to become the truth. At least, until it proved inconvenient."

Ely was silent for a while. "It must be awful," she said as she released the ropes about Edwin's ankles, her voice quiet, "to lose the whole of your family so suddenly. To be abandoned, alone."

Edwin snorted. "Hardly. I've always been alone." Alone, with one exception, and now he had lost even her. At least he had gained some measure of freedom in exchange. She would gain nothing but sorrow.

Ely drew back in surprise. "You had hundreds of family!" she exclaimed. "Everyone with the Aloise name was your kin, all branches of the same tree lending strength to each other – isn't that what the Aloise believe?"

"Were they my family?" Edwin said sharply. "We may have shared a name, but they hated what I was. Even if they didn't know it, I knew. Being one of them was never more than a lie, a mask I had to wear to stay alive. That was all." His mouth twisted in a grimace. "No, they weren't my family. Not even my mother. All she could give me, for the brief years that she lived, was fear. Fear of being caught, fear of being killed. She was so afraid for me that there was no room left between us for love."

"But you share blood with all those people . . . ." Ely said.

Edwin laughed bitterly. "Is that what a family is? Blood?" He turned, the final bindings falling from his hands, leaving only raw, red lines. "Can you look at me, Elymia, and still believe that?"

Ely did look, though Edwin was not sure what she saw. An Aloise? An enemy? Or just a man, feeling the touch of air on his face for the first time after the mask had fallen away?

Now free from his bindings, Edwin unwrapped the bundle that hid his sword. In the intense light of that strange place, the blade shone like white fire, making it difficult to look at and warm to the touch. Edwin used it to cut a strip of fabric from the wrappings and held it out to Ely.

"For your hair," he said, as the wind pulled wild strands across her contemplative eyes and mouth, weaving them over her skin like shadowed canyons in a noontide desert. She took the cloth wordlessly tied back her hair. Then, after giving him another searching look, she returned to picking over the ground for her lost comb, and he stooped to join her search.

With both of them looking, it did not take long to cover the area around where they had fallen, but neither of them found so much as a pebble atop the bumpy surface of the bridge. Despair colored Ely's expression when she realized there was nothing to be found, but she did not indulge in the feeling for long.

"That's it then," she said, straightening. "It's not here. We'd best be moving on." Edwin could tell that she had lost something precious to her, but was not going to let it slow her down. She carried herself like a soldier, one who was used to accepting losses and moving on. It was a quality she shared with another woman he knew, another woman who felt it was her duty to bear her suffering in silence. As an Aloise he had been able to stand by her, but now, cast out from the family, he was useless. . . . Or was he?

"You are like her in many ways," Edwin said to Ely.

"Who?" Ely said, eyes flicking up at him.

"Remiana," he said. "It's not hard to see. *You're both charging forward because you can't go back, fighting because it's what you think your families demand.*"

"You don't know anything about me," Ely said tersely, "and you're wrong. I have no family in Falls Gate. I fight because it's the right thing to do. Remiana and her kind fight for greed, not caring who they have to hurt. I don't see how we could be more different."

"Really?" Edwin said. "In just a few days I've seen men face down their lord for you and women march into the jaws of death at your side. You wouldn't call those people your family?"

Ely shook her head. "That's not the same."

"Is it only shared blood, then, that lets a person feel another's suffering?" Edwin asked. "Is that the only thing that would make one person fight for another?"

Ely had no reply.

"And as for Remiana," Edwin said, "do you really think she relishes the things she's done? Do you think they don't cause her pain, alone in the dark with no one to see?"

Ely set her jaw. "How would I know?"

"Because you know her," Edwin said. "As much as you deny it, she's not a different woman. The only difference is the circumstance, and that is of Oridine's making, not hers. If things were reversed and it was your father who planned to make war on the Iron Kingdoms, would you have been able to stop him?"

"I would have tried."

"And you think yourself so superior to her that she didn't do even that?"

That gave Ely pause, and she was silent for what seemed like a long time. When she spoke again, her voice sounded tired.

"What do you want, Edwin?" she asked. "Why do you care what happens between us?"

Edwin was not entirely sure of what he was going to say until the words emerged from his mouth. "I want to save her," he replied.

"Save her from what?" Ely asked.

"From her mother. From her name. From herself."

"But why? Why do you care so much about her when you claim to have no love for the Aloise?" Ely pressed.

Edwin took a deep breath. More words were gathering inside him, words that, like Remiana, he had never dared to think might one day be free. But things had changed, already more than he could have imagined. He was speaking to a woman who had defied the Aloise twice and lived. What had been impossible now seemed within his reach. "Because she's my sister," he said. "And because she's the only real family I have."

Ely's eyes grew wide.

"But I can't do it," Edwin said, holding Ely's gaze. "Not alone."

There was a long pause, with nothing but the constant, swirling wind to fill it.

"I think," Ely said slowly, "that this is a discussion for another time."

"Then later," Edwin said. "Once we're out of here. All I ask is that you hear me out. After that, you can do what you want with me."

Ely nodded. "Help me get out of here, and I'll owe you at least that much."

Edwin smiled. At least for a short while longer, they would not have to be enemies, and he felt an unexpected comfort at that thought.

"Then allow me to take the lead," he said. He turned and set out across the bridge. Ely followed after a moment of hesitation, and together they took up a swift marching pace, moving as quickly as the poor footing would allow.

As they walked, Edwin realized that the faint ringing in his ears had not faded with time. If anything, the noise had only grown worse, and he used his free hand to massage his temple, hoping it didn't mean he had hit his head harder than he thought.

"Do you hear that?" Ely said from behind him, her voice distorted and roughened by the wind.

"Hear what?" Edwin said over his shoulder, unable to hear much of anything over the roaring gusts and that damnable ringing.

"It's like a tone," Ely said, "It was so faint before, I thought I was imagining it."

Edwin stopped and looked back.

"You hear it too?" he said, relieved. "Can you tell where it's coming from?"

Ely cocked her head, listening. "No," she said with a shrug, "but we should press on."

Edwin nodded and resumed the march, but the shrill sound only continued to grow louder the farther they went.

It was then that he happened to look down at the sword in his hand. At a glance the edges of the blade appeared slightly blurry, as if seen through sleep-weary eyes. Then he realized, suddenly, the shrill noise's source.

"Why have we stopped?" Ely asked. Edwin turned, sword raised in one hand, and she took an inadvertent step back.

"It's coming from the sword," he said, holding it out. "Look."

She was indeed looking at it, he saw, though it took a moment for the flash of fear in her eyes to turn to confusion. "It's . . . vibrating?" she said.

"Ever since we got here, I think, but stronger now." Edwin said, holding the weapon up to his ear and noting how the sound grew louder.

"What's causing it?" Ely asked.

Edwin shrugged. "How should I know?"

"You were a Lode Knight, weren't you?" Ely said impatiently.

"So?" Edwin said. "We wear iron, we don't study it."

Ely frowned. "Do you think it's dangerous?"

"Sure hope not," Edwin replied, "because even if it is, I'm stuck with it." He tugged on the chain connecting the sword to the bracer locked around his arm. That was when he realized that the links of the chain, too, were vibrating. It was slight, but just strong enough that he could feel it as the faintest tickle on his skin.

"What is it?" Ely asked, responding to the thoughtful look on his face. He did not answer, but instead pulled out the ring that hung around his neck and held it on his palm. The Aloise hammer insignia gleamed brightly in the light, displaying the fine craftsmanship of the artisan who had cast it. Ely looked at the ring curiously, but did not interrupt Edwin's contemplation. He suspected it was now obvious to her why he did not wear it on his finger.

"All the metal is resonating," Edwin said. The ring was smaller than the links of the chain and its vibration weaker, but it was there. "The farther we go, the stronger it gets, like we're approaching . . . something." He could not, for the life of him, imagine what that something might be. Ely, on the other hand, had no such trouble.

"Something like that?" she said, pointing down the bridge.

The span had been utterly featureless so far, yet now, on the horizon, Edwin could see some kind of object standing up from its surface. It was much too distant to make out details, but it was different, and that was all he needed to know.

"Let's go," he said, tucking the ring back inside his leathers. "Whatever it is, there's no point going back."

Once more they pressed forward across the white, bumpy ground. The object ahead of them, which Edwin had figured to be at least five spans distant, grew visibly nearer with each step in a way that should have been impossible. Soon he was able to make out that it too was composed of some sort of metal.

By the time they reached it, what it was had become apparent: it was a door of solid steel, unadorned by even so much as a handle. It would have been a perfect picture of impregnability if not for the fact that it stood freely in the center of the bridge, with ample room to walk around it on either side.

Edwin stepped closer to the freestanding portal to get a better look, but found that there was little to see. The metal he carried, on the other hand, reacted strongly. His sword was humming so intensely it made his teeth ache, while the chain and the ring had begun to express audible tones of their own.

"A steel door," Ely said in awe. "Who could even conceive of such a thing?"

Edwin put his hand against the steel frame. It was warm.

"Actually," he said, "There's a rumor that each iron lord's manor has one, used to lock away his most valuable treasures, but I've never seen one myself."

"How could a door like that be opened, even by an iron lord?" Ely said.

"With a steel key, the same way I would open this bracer, if I had one," Edwin said.

"But this door doesn't even have a . . ." Ely's voice trailed off. The door, once utterly featureless, now had a keyhole. The vibration in Edwin's sword jarred his arm with renewed force, forcing him to back away.

"Be careful," Edwin said as Ely reached out toward the new shape on the door's face. "Who knows what could be in there?"

Despite the fact that the door was attached to nothing and could not logically lead anywhere, Edwin had no doubt that it might, in fact, lead to someplace else entirely, given the unearthly nature of that strange land of bridges and mountains. Nor did he doubt that it could easily prove more dangerous than its simple shape would suggest.

Ely stopped, her fingers inches away from the keyhole. "Aren't you curious?" she said. "Maybe this can get us out of here." She had a point, but that door still made Edwin uneasy.

"At least look before you go putting your fingers in there," he said.

"All right, I will," Ely said. She knelt, pressed the palms of her hands against the door, and put her eye up to the keyhole.

"What do you see?" Edwin asked.

Ely just stared for a long moment before answering. "Light," she said softly. "So much light."

As soon as she said it, Edwin could see it too, leaking out around the edges of the frame, pouring like liquid gold through the keyhole and scattering into the air. It seemed to gather Elymia up in its arms, working its way into her hair and clothing to make them shimmer with radiance. It behaved like no light Edwin had ever seen, yet it was still enchanting, and beautiful beyond description.

"Get away from there!" a stranger's voice growled.

Ely jerked away from the door, shock and recognition on her face. Edwin turned to see a masked man standing just a few paces away, his furs rippling about him under the foul touch of the persistent wind.

"You!" Ely exclaimed.

The masked man did not advance on them, but there was something threatening in his presence, something that made the hair on the back of Edwin's neck stand on end. His hand tightened on his sword.

"You disappoint me, Elymia," the masked man said. "I granted you power to right the wrongs committed against your people, not waste time bargaining with enemies who would sooner see you dead. Were it not for me, your corpse would be full of arrows on the cold stones of Cliffhome Keep."

"You saved us?" Ely said in surprise, though it quickly turned to worry. "What about Matrice? Mae? Tamalina?"

"They live," the masked man said, "though I could do nothing for the prisoners. Nor can you."

"But we can still save them!" Ely said. "Just like we saved the Wharfmaster!"

"You speak as if that idiocy were something to be proud of," the masked man said. "All you did was waste your chance at annihilating the Aloise for nothing more than a single man's life. And now, in return, they've done their best to take yours. You would repeat that same mistake?"

"But we can't just leave-"

"Those people are as good as dead! Plan your vengeance instead of wasting time on thoughts of rescue!" The masked man's voice was angry. "Had I known you would be so slow to learn, I would have chosen another to be my agent of justice. The one you call Tamalina certainly understands what's necessary, but you still refuse to see it. The Aloise deserve no mercy! They've murdered and tortured and burned, but clearly that wasn't enough for you. You thought they could be reasoned with. And even now, after they've done their best to kill you, you fraternize with one of them as if he were not your sworn enemy!"

The masked man stalked toward Edwin, who raised his sword in defense only to have it swatted away as the masked man's hand closed around his throat. Its grip was monstrous, full of a strength that lifted him off his feet as if he weighed nothing. The sword dropped from his stunned hand and dangled from its chain.

"No blade of steel can protect you from me here," the masked man growled. "You have no idea what it means to confront me in this place." He turned and held Edwin's struggling body over the edge of the bridge.

"Stop!" Ely shouted in panic. Edwin tried to tell her to run, but not even the tiniest trickle of air could escape his throat.

"Why should I stop?" the masked man asked. "He is your enemy, and he must be killed! The Aloise show you no mercy, and you must show none to them! Have you forgotten the promise you made to me? Have you forgotten all the suffering that you alone have the power to avenge?"

"I . . . I . . ." Ely stammered.

Edwin's vision was growing spotty, his ears full of a ringing that he knew had nothing to do with the singing of the steel. If they ever found his body, at least it would be clear that it had not been arrows that killed him. At least Remiana would know that it had not been her fault.

"I need him!" Ely said in anger, staring down the masked man with new determination. "He knows everything about the Aloise, too much to simply kill. Surely you know that they wield your power too. The only way we can beat them now is through cunning, and to do that we need what he knows. We can't afford to waste any assets, no matter how repulsive."

The masked man shook Edwin's body contemptuously, making his limbs dance like a doll's.

"Do you think he will talk and betray his own kind?" he said. "He won't, not without the sort of convincing that you are clearly too soft for. Better to be rid of him." Edwin felt the grip about his throat ease, and the void yawned below, hungry and waiting.

"I think you misjudge me," Ely said, her voice taking on an edge. "I may not have any . . . formal training, but I do know my father's technique for loosening a man's tongue."

"And what's that?" the masked man said.

"An inch of flesh for every unanswered question," Ely said, meeting the masked man's empty gaze, "and an inch of bone for every spoken lie. It's extremely effective when applied to certain areas of the male body."

The masked man cocked his head. Then he laughed.

"Now that's the proper way to treat your enemies," he said, tossing Edwin to the ground at Ely's feet. "You know they would give you no better."

Edwin curled up in a ball, coughing deep, wrenching coughs.

"Is that all you came for?" Ely said, sounding almost bored. "To see that I still intend to make Aloise blood flow? If so, you could have saved yourself the time. Don't misunderstand, I would prefer it if all their prisoners survived, but I won't let that stand in the way of what the Aloise have coming to them."

"Good," the masked man said. "But I also came to deliver a warning: the Masked have sided against you."

"What?" Ely said in alarm.

"They see you as an agent of chaos, bringing war where your enemies would promise peace," the masked man said. "They value the corrupt stability of the Aloise over the justice that you represent. It matters not that I know better; I can't make them change their minds. Already they have lent their power to the Aloise to deal with you, as you have seen. But since that effort to kill you has failed, they will undoubtedly become involved more directly."

So this was how Ely's friends were able to do what they did, Edwin realized as he listened, continuing to wheeze on the ground. They had the secret aid of one of the Masked. There was something in this Masked's voice that Edwin did not trust, however, but he could hardly muster the strength to move, and Ely at least seemed to believe what he had to say.

"Then what are we to do?" Ely said. "We don't have the strength to stand against the Aloise and the Masked together."

"You won't need to," the masked man said. "The Masked are but a weapon, and any weapon can be turned to your purpose if you know how to wield it."

Ely frowned. "What does that mean?"

"I'll tell you," the masked man replied, "but first you must make a promise. Promise me that you will seek no more peace with murderers. Promise me that you will offer them no parley. Promise me that, when the day I decree for your retribution arrives, justice shall slake her thirst on rich iron blood."

Ely gave a snort, putting her hands on her hips. "That day will make our first attack look like a child's game." From her expression, it looked as if she planned to be drinking that iron blood herself.

"Good," the masked man said. "Then listen well. If you want to survive to see the righteous emerge victorious, bring all the strength you can muster to Crossing Grove at dusk in three days time. You know the place. Dress your people in Aloise colors. When night falls, a Masked will appear before you, and when he does, you will kill him. I'll take care of the rest."

There was a blur of color and a strong gust of wind, and the masked man was gone. What was more, Edwin and Ely found themselves inexplicably at the far end of the bridge, a plain stone archway rising up before them and the steel door nowhere to be seen.

Ely knelt and helped Edwin to his feet.

"That's some ally you have there," Edwin said, wincing at the pain in his throat. "A rogue Masked? What made you accept the aid of someone like that?"

"Desperate times make for desperate deeds," Ely said, stealing a glance at Edwin's sword. He thought he detected a hint of something odd in her voice. Shame?

The way she had changed so completely when talking to that Masked was remarkable, Edwin thought. He had not realized how close to the surface that seething anger must have been for her to be show it so easily. And even if she had only been telling that masked monster what he wanted to hear, she sure sounded like she meant every word of it. Perhaps she had.

"About that 'technique' of your father's . . . ." Edwin said awkwardly.

To his surprise, Ely winked at him, the grimness of her face gone like smoke on the wind. "I made it up," she said. "Though it does sound effective, doesn't it?"

By the peaks, Edwin thought as he followed her through the archway, she was even more like Remiana than he thought!

Chapter 33
Forward and Back

The tea in the porcelain cup was thin and weak, but Ely drank it just the same. It was amazing how quickly things like good tea became hard to find when trade was halted. She had hoped it would do something to counter her tiredness, but at such feeble strength, that seemed unlikely.

There had been little time for sleep since she and Edwin escaped that strange, bright land of mountains and bridges, for they had quickly learned that Aloise had been scouring the city for them since they had disappeared from the Keep. Thankfully, the city's size had so far allowed them to stay one step ahead of their pursuers.

"This tea is awful," Mae said, scrunching up her face. Matrice, on the other side of the table, gave her a level look over her cup as she took a long, deliberate sip.

Ely just shook her head. She had been relieved beyond words to discover Mae and Matrice had also escaped alive. When she and Edwin had popped out of thin air into the Registry warehouse, both were already there waiting for them. Even more remarkable was what else was there: the missing tooth of her mother's comb, its paleness standing out plainly against the slate floor. The masked man had placed it there for her to find, she was sure of it, though she had no idea why.

As it turned out, Mae and Matrice's story was eerily similar to Ely's own, though it differed on a few details, such as the appearance of the strange steel door. To them, it had seemed nothing more than a blank slab. Yet since their return to the natural world, Ely had found herself thinking often of that door, that light, and that glimpse through the keyhole.

"I said, this tea is awful!" Mae repeated, louder. The door to the kitchens flapped wildly as the man Lewmas rushed into the common room of the inn, an apron tied over his tunic and a pained look on his face.

"So sorry, mistress, I'll have it rebrewed right away," he said, snatching up Mae's cup and disappearing back into the kitchen. Now that Evana was gone, it seemed Mae had inherited much of the loyalty she had once commanded. Whether that was a good thing, Ely was unsure.

"What?" an irritated woman's voice rose from the kitchen. "I absolutely will not brew her another cup! That's all we have, gods preserve us, so if she doesn't like it, she can have a cup of my-!"

Lewmas slammed the kitchen door loudly as he returned, drowning out the rest of what his wife Losha had to say. His face was red, but he maintained his composure admirably.

"I'm afraid we're out of tea," he said with an apologetic bow. "Might I interest you in some spicecake instead?"

Mae grunted and waived her hand. "Whatever."

Lewmas backed his way out of the room, bobbing all the while.

Ely had half a mind to chastise Mae for the way she treated him, but it was an argument she did not need at the moment. She had more than enough problems already.

One of them was Tamalina's impending execution. Notices had been posted all over the city, and the news that a daughter of one of the city's prominent families was to be publicly beheaded was not going over well with the people. That would be good for recruiting, Ely caught herself thinking. The whole thing stunk of a trap to draw her out, but she couldn't just ignore it. At least it was still a week away, which gave her time to figure something out while dealing with even bigger problems first, though the fact that she could have problems bigger than that made her want to scream.

"This is the whole list? Absolutely everyone?" Ely asked Barty, who was keeping watch by the door.

"Everyone who would give me an answer. There are more who might join us when the moment comes, but for now they aren't saying." Barty gave a half smile. "They might be the smart ones."

Ely looked down at the list, a thick stack of pages piled up on the table in front of her. Even including the names Barty had brought earlier, the number was not what she had hoped. Only five hundred people she could count on to take up arms, if it came to that. On one hand, it was pathetically few. Out of a city of tens of thousands it was but a tiny fraction, fewer than the Aloise would be able to field. On the other, it was a near miracle that Barty, working alone and in secrecy, had been able to secure so many to their cause.

"The numbers aren't what worry me the most," Matrice said. "It's what you've suggested we do with them."

"I'm in agreement there," Wharfmaster Abrohl said, taking a full bite of the spicecake in his hands and shedding crumbs into his beard.

Ely nodded. She had relayed the masked man's instructions, and they had not been popular.

"I don't see what the problem is," Mae said impatiently. "This is war, and in war you do what it takes to win. We can't afford to sit around moralizing while the Aloise dig in deeper!"

"Attacking a third party unprovoked is how wars are lost," Matrice cautioned. "Slaying a Masked, as we've been told to do, is risky."

"That's what the fake uniforms are for, isn't it?" Mae said, irritated at having to explain the obvious.

Matrice sighed. "I imagine that's the idea, at least. By doing the deed dressed as the Aloise, we would bring the wrath of the Masked down on them instead of us. But even ignoring the chance that the Masked will see through it, the plan is costly. It requires some of our people die so that the uniforms remain on the field to be seen."

"So?" Mae said. "Soldiers die all the time. Do you really expect to fight a Masked without casualties?"

"Expecting death is one thing," Matrice said. "Intending it is something else. What sort of leader sends her troops to the field hoping for their deaths?"

"The girl makes a good point," the Wharfmaster chimed in, and Barty nodded silently from the doorway.

"So what should we do?" Ely asked. "The Masked are against us. Unless we divert them, we don't stand a chance."

"Our odds would be better with three of us using their power instead of two," Mae said, eyeing the pouch at Ely's hip that contained the third vial of Scarwood sap.

"We've been over that," Ely said, her voice hardening. "It was given to me, and I'll decide how and when we use it." She was not about to let Mae bully her into such an important decision. Besides, it was not as if she had not thought about using it. By the Deep, she never stopped thinking about it! But something kept her from it, something that had been lurking in the back of her mind ever since her first meeting with the shadow from her dreams. Despite the value of his aid, she still did not trust their Masked benefactor.

"We could try to negotiate with the Masked," Matrice suggested.

Ely nodded, though she knew that was unlikely to get them anywhere. If the rest of the Masked were anything like the one helping them, she would have an easier time negotiating with a hungry shark. Edwin had experienced a negotiating tactic that had nearly killed him. No, it was better not to reveal themselves to the rest of the Masked and risk another, similar encounter.

Ely looked up at the dusty ceiling of the common room, reminded of Edwin tied up in the room above. Over Mae's objections, Ely had insisted that they keep him close. She had not told them what had transpired between them while they were separated, and she was playing for time while she tried to figure out what to do with him. Learning that he was Remiana's brother, or at least half-brother, had been a shock, and it was something she suspected even Remiana herself did not know. That made the decision that much more difficult.

"Other suggestions?" Ely said. She wished Aldan Pourin were there, but he was acting as a lookout at the end of the street. Matrice's father was not a soldier or a strategist, but he had a solid head on his shoulders.

"We could flee," Barty said. Ely knew he did not personally favor that option, but it deserved to be aired. "If we weren't here, the Masked would have no reason to come into the city, and there would be no more bloodshed with the Aloise."

"You mean cut our losses and run?" Mae said contemptuously. "The coward's way out."

Barty shrugged. "Sometimes it's best to leave the field and return when conditions are more favorable."

"Indeed," Ely said. "Any others?"

"Send a fast ship for help," the Wharfmaster said. He nodded to Mae and Matrice. "With these two, snatching a ship from the harbor would be easy, then we could sail over to Turnwash or Quarry Bay and bring back aid." It was a scenario that would end in a siege, Ely foresaw grimly, one that would last long enough for the Aloise to receive reinforcements. And it would do nothing to help them against the Masked.

Ely sighed. She had half a mind to go upstairs and ask Edwin what he thought. At least he had some formal training, unlike the rest of them save for Barty.

"You know what I would do," Mae said, crossing her arms. "That Masked clearly wants us to win, and he knows how to make it happen. He gave us this power, and he saved our lives. Without his help, we're nothing. Why are you all so eager to ignore him now?"

Mae was not wrong, Ely had to concede. Despite her misgivings, that Masked had done nothing but help them. But the way he had spoken to her, and this plan . . . . Something about it rubbed her the wrong way. It was devious, yes, but so had been their midnight attack on the Keep. She had no problem with using subterfuge to secure victory. But it was more than that.

This plan was cynical. It was one thing to send her men to die for a cause, but to do it just for show?

Ely put her head in her hands. Since when had she started thinking of them as her men, anyway? And why was she the one who had to decide? Mae certainly wanted the job more, and Matrice would probably be better at it, so why her? Why were they putting all the responsibility on the one person who didn't have any idea what to do? She had no shortage of plans before her, but not a single one felt right.

You're both charging forward because you can't go back, Ely heard Edwin's voice say. Fighting because it's what you think your families demand.

Maybe that was why she could not choose a plan. Maybe it was because she did not want to fight at all. *But who does? she thought.* Every one of them wished they had never been given a reason to fight. In reality, they had all too many reasons.

None of the plans would make their situation any better, Ely knew, and most would make it worse. Even if she followed their secret ally's instructions and turned the Masked against the Aloise, they would merely have enlarged the conflict. It seemed that no matter what she chose, it would only bring more violence, more hate, more death.

Isn't that what you want? a voice inside her said. The death of all Aloise? For the first time, Ely was forced to acknowledge that it was not. What she wanted was her house back, her friends back, her life back. What she wanted was to feel normal again. *And because you can't have those things, that's what makes you fight and kill?* Did she really have any choice? Was it not either to fight to the end, or surrender and dishonor everything and everyone they had lost?

There is always a choice, the voice said to her. You just have to be able to recognize it. It sounded like something her father would say, though he believed more in duty than in choice. Or perhaps duty was his choice.

It also sounded a bit like something the masked man had said, Ely remembered. The Masked are but a weapon, and any weapon can be turned to your purpose if you know how to wield it. If the Masked could be a weapon, Ely thought, anything could. Even Matrice, one of her best friends, was being turned into a weapon, a weapon that she daily contemplated how to put to the best use. Even Ely herself was a weapon, organizing and directing men against the enemy.

That thought sent a chill down her spine. Was that what the masked man saw her as? A weapon? A weapon that would kill the Aloise? He certainly seemed intent on that end, and he had known just what to say to play upon her helplessness and rage. Was it possible that she had been consumed by thoughts of killing because that was what he wanted? Could it be that the reason she could not abide his plan was because it was really for his benefit, and not for hers?

"Elymia?" Barty said, concerned at her extended silence.

Ely raised her head from her hands. She would not let herself be used like that, not when the lives of her friends were at stake. If that Masked was clever enough to make people, events, and even whole cities into tools for his own end, whatever it was, then so was she. And in her hands, not every tool needed to be a blade.

"None of those," Ely said.

"Excuse me?" Mae said.

"None of those plans are acceptable," Ely repeated. "I won't spend our people's lives like coin, nor will I run away or rely on others to fight for our freedom."

"Then what do you propose?" Matrice said.

Ely turned to Mae. "Do we have any of those skins left over from what Ceer brought us?"

Mae's eyes narrowed. "A few."

"Good. We'll need a skilled woodcarver too," Ely said, "because we have one, and only one, false uniform to make."

•••••

Once Ely had detailed her plan and set the others about their tasks, she climbed the stairs to the inn's second floor and entered the first room. Edwin was there, on a chair facing the door. His hands and feet were once again bound, though Ely guessed that if he really tried, he could have gotten free of those feeble knots in under a minute.

"Have you thought on what I said?" Edwin asked.

"I have," Ely said, looking down at him.

Edwin simply waited.

"I think," Ely said, "that Remiana has done terrible things. Evil things."

Edwin nodded. "She has."

"She lied to all of us. She betrayed her friends. She was complicit in their deaths."

"Yes," Edwin replied. "She did all those things."

321

"Then what makes you think I'd do what you ask?" Ely said.

"Because she's your friend," Edwin said, "and she needs your help."

Ely snorted. "She hasn't asked for it."

"Hasn't she?" Edwin said, tapping the blade of his sword with a finger. The weapon lay bare across his knees, but for some reason Ely no longer saw any menace in it. "She asked you the only way she knew how, the only way she has been taught."

Ely clenched her fists. "She treated me like a slave in that cell!"

"She spared your life."

Familiar anger bubbled up in Ely's chest. She could smell the rancid stench of the prison again, feel the cold point of the sword pressing down on her neck . . . .

"She still didn't have to do what she did," Ely said, spitting out the words as if they had a vile taste.

"Maybe not," Edwin said, "but her strength is different from yours. Where you see choice, she sees fate. In her mind she is bound because she never learned how to be free."

"That doesn't mean she deserves mercy," Ely said.

"Maybe not. But this isn't only about her, is it? It's also about you."

There was truth in those words, Ely knew. If she was leading the resistance against the Aloise, then what happened to Remiana was her responsibility. Even if she gave no orders, the results would still be of her making. Would she feel proud if Remiana's body ended up hanging from the walls of the Keep? Ely closed her eyes, imagining, but the thought only made her sick. Maybe it was because she knew too much. Remiana was no longer an abstract evil, if she had ever really been one.

"What would you have me do?" Ely asked, turning her gaze back to Edwin. It seemed she could see things in him now that she could not before. There was confidence in the way he sat, determination in the wells of his eyes. It came from having a purpose, she could see now, a purpose that gave him more strength than any armor.

"Spare her life," Edwin said. "Speak to her once more, as a friend. Give her a chance to choose, like her mother never did. That's all."

"And if she chooses to fight?" Ely said.

Edwin bowed his head. "Then at least you will know, whatever comes after, that she was beyond your power to save."

There would be many who would not like it, Ely knew, many who would see any mercy for the Aloise as weakness. But she also knew they could not matter to her. They might be angry, but they were not the ones who would carry the burden if time proved her choice to be the wrong one.

"I'll do it, on one condition," Ely said. She drew her dagger and severed Edwin's bindings. "You help me bring this conflict to a close. Help me find the chance to save your sister, and I'll take it."

Edwin rose from the chair, a full head taller than Ely even when she stood as straight as she could manage. She did not step back.

In one practiced motion, Edwin dropped to one knee, bowed his head, and held out his blade on upturned palms.

"My sword is yours, Lady Elymia," he said.

Chapter 34

The Jaws of Fate

"And this was yet one more thing I didn't need to know?" Donvin growled, staring at the steel door that rose from the white stone bridge.

"Is it that important?" Lith asked, her voice playing at innocence they both knew was a lie.

"Of course it's important!" Donvin snapped. There was a door on the bridge, on *his* bridge, and he had not even known what it was until Elymia had touched it. Before, it had been nothing but a block of stone, yet for her it had become a portal of steel. For her, and not for him. It was infuriating, almost as infuriating as discovering that Lith was keeping more secrets. "You've been lying to me!"

"I'm hurt," Lith said, putting a hand to her breast. "It is true I haven't spoken about the seal, but that's because it has no bearing on your mission."

"Your mission, you mean," Donvin corrected her. "And that's how it always is, isn't it? You tell me only what pleases you, and try to keep me from learning anything else! You think I'm some tame animal!"

"I'm only looking out for your interests," Lith said. "I'm keeping you focused, free of distractions."

"Enough!" Donvin said. "I've had enough of being your pet. You're going to stop holding out on me. Now."

"Oh?" Lith said. "Why is that?"

"You know why."

Lith's face creased in disapproval. "I have warned you against this, Donvin."

"And you're a liar and a thief," Donvin said with contempt, "which is why I'll do it anyway. So give me what I want, or get out of my sight."

In the space of a blink, Lith had vanished.

"Typical," Donvin muttered. In an instant he willed himself from the center of the bridge to the exit archway. Beyond lay the greatest risk he had yet taken, but also, hopefully, his greatest reward. He was done being manipulated. If Lith wanted her plan to move forward, it would do so his way, or not at all.

The smell of rotting leaves greeted Donvin as he stepped from the portal into the woods. The fauna of the forest had already bedded down for the night, leaving the air silent but for faint hooting from the branches above. Owls were not the only avian hunters about that night, Donvin suspected, which was why he had arrived where he had, out of earshot of the Masked camp but with no attempt to hide his presence. If you wanted to lure a hunter, you had to give him something to hunt.

Donvin counted the seconds under his breath as he waited for the trap to spring. One, two, three . . . . Of all the parts of his plan, this was by far the most dangerous. His quarry was too smart, too wary to be drawn in by anything other than assured victory. Four, five, six . . . . To get Bird where he needed him, Donvin would have to give him exactly what he wanted. Seven, eight, nine-

Cords of force coiled themselves about Donvin's throat, lifting him off the ground. Donvin struggled, calling upon the glowing threads of his will, but for every one he summoned a second rose to counter it.

"At last you make a mistake, heretic," Bird's voice said from behind him. "You were a fool to travel alone." Donvin tried again to break free, drawing on all the power he could muster, but Bird was stronger. The threads around his throat tightened.

Bird walked around Donvin's kicking, helpless legs to stand in front of him, surveying his handiwork.

"Your treachery is impressive," Bird said, "but no lie can last forever. No matter how smart you might think yourself, there is always someone smarter."

Donvin hung there in the air, struggling for consciousness, unable to answer. All he could do was stare straight ahead, gasping for breath. He had known this would happen, had wanted it to happen, but now that he could actually feel the life being squeezed out of him, the plan he had laid out suddenly seemed very far away.

"The others might be in your pocket," Bird said bitterly, "but your power to twist the thoughts of the weak doesn't work on all of us. Still, by compromising our unity, you have put the whole world in jeopardy. Perhaps that was even your goal. But that doesn't matter now. Tonight, we right the wrongs you have committed. Then, you die."

The gnarled bark of the Scarwoods looked like stone in the light of Bird's threads. Even the carving on the trunk behind him, a boy and a girl holding hands, looked as if it had been etched into a cave wall a million years before, waiting to be unearthed and marveled over by historians who knew nothing of their lives or promise of friendship . . . .

"This is not the time to be dying, my Donvin," Lith's voice whispered in his ear. "That is not part of the plan."

But he was not going to die, Donvin knew as his sight blurred and darkened. Even if he failed in calling Lith's bluff, he had an ally that Bird did not. *Flicker.*

Though Donvin could not see it, he felt movement ahead of him in the trees. He was in need, and it had come, just as he had known it would. He did not know why, but it was always with him, watching, keeping him safe.

"It seems your friend has joined us," Bird said in a cool voice. "The better to dispose of you both together." He did not sound even slightly surprised.

Any moment now, Donvin thought, the thing would surely be able to distract or injure Bird enough for him to break away. Any moment now . . . .

There was the sound of a brief struggle. Too brief. Donvin felt a flash of panic as he sensed a second bound figure rising to hang beside him in the air.

"Your depravity is truly astounding," Bird said, not even sounding breathless, "to inflict such desecration on the one who cared for you most deeply. Such vile arts were thought lost to the ages. It's deeply troubling that you somehow found a way to revive them."

Donvin strained to turn his head, to see the thing hanging in the air beside him, but he could not. It made no sound, but it had a smell. It smelled of hair, sweat, and blood. It smelled of dirt and death, of neglect and decay. But beneath all that was a smell that tugged sharply on Donvin's mind, trying to drag a memory the size of a mountain through the tiniest keyhole in the prison that held it confined.

"It is not time to be remembering just yet," Lith's voice whispered. "You have a plan. Follow the plan."

"I can't," Donvin said. Everything was fading, his senses ceasing their tired struggle. " He's too strong, and he was expecting her." Her? Why had he called the thing beside him "her"?

Lith sighed. "I warned you. I warned you, and you would not listen. So now you force my hand. You will get what you want, but I promise you that you will not enjoy it. I will show you the power that doomed our people, the power that made the tyranny of the Masked a small price to pay for the right to live on, if only for a while longer. I will show you the power that you have always been destined to wield."

Donvin felt a cool hand touch his chest. "Reach not out, but in," Lith whispered. "Reach not forward, but back. Let me guide you."

No longer sure whether he was still conscious, Donvin found it easy to yield control to Lith's comforting hands, letting the awareness of his body fade away while Lith assumed all the difficult tasks of thinking, breathing, and living. What remained of his awareness turned inward. He was floating on a lake of glass, reclining peacefully inside himself without a care for the world outside. The air above was still and pure, while the water below churned with sediment in a current that was confined to the depths, unable to break the surface. There was something down there, he knew, something dirty and dark and painful, something that would only ruin the peace of the air should it manage to escape. Why was it, then, that he desperately wanted to set it free?

There was a door in the surface of the lake, a door of steel that appeared in response to his desire, the same one that had appeared for Elymia. Something precious of his was trapped on the other side, something he could not live without. He knew that it would not open, but he had seen Elymia look through the keyhole to catch a glimpse of what lay beyond. Perhaps he could do the same. He needed to know what was down there.

Donvin pressed his eye to the keyhole, searching the shadows that lurked below. There was something solid floating in the murky water. A body? Had someone drowned? As it floated slowly toward the surface, Donvin realized that not only was it a body, but that its face was his. A bit softer and rounder, maybe, but still his.

Then the corpse blinked.

"It is time," Lith said.

Suddenly Donvin was back in his own body, his real body, his senses alive as if on fire. In his chest he felt a burning hole, a searing cavity that led elsewhere, and a unique agony that felt both foreign and familiar. Instinctively knowing what to do, he reached deeply into that darkened pit, and pulled.

A black tendril erupted from his chest like a serpent of void and thunder, cleaving a wide arc through the lesser darkness of the night. The gossamer threads of Bird's power yielded like silk to a knife, dropping Donvin to the ground, while the surrounding trees swayed and crashed, shedding severed limbs and caustic sap in the wake of the energy that sheared through them.

Donvin had a portal open almost before his feet touched ground, and into it he dove away from the staggered and disoriented Bird. He could have killed him instantly if he had held on to that awful power a second longer, but every instant he wielded it had been torment, like turning his own body inside out with his bare hands. And besides, killing Bird there was not the plan.

Donvin hurtled along the white bridge as fast as he was able, the bumpy stone blurring beneath him at speeds impossible in the real world. He looked back only to confirm that the hunter had taken the bait. Bird had joined the chase, his furs blowing out behind him as if he were falling horizontally along the bridge rather than running. The corner of his mask had been sliced off and droplets of dark sap glistened like blood on its face, but its narrow eyes were determined.

Good, Donvin thought as he barreled toward the exit archway and the trap he had instructed Elymia to set. It would not do to have Bird lose commitment now, for this was to be the final blow. After tonight, the grand tree of the Masked, which he had been slowly but surely undermining, would be ready to fall at the slightest touch.

Chapter 35
Tides of War

Battle was coming. Edwin could smell it even over the salty wind off the ocean, a cool wind that whistled against the bluffs and rustled through the grass of the cliff gardens. The sun hung low in the west, stretching his shadow to monstrous proportions. Somewhere in the city to the north, blocked from view by the trees of Crossing Grove, the echo of another boom spoke of battle already joined, an opening fanfare for the symphony of destruction poised upon the air.

The men waiting nearby shuffled nervously, clutching a variety of weapons in wind-chapped hands. Clumps rather than ranks defined their formation, and many looked dressed for the foundry or the warehouse instead the battlefield.

Mae noticed Edwin looking at them. "You'd best watch yourself, boy," she said. "If you think to turn that blade of yours on us, you'll be begging to be tied up again after I'm through with you." Aside from a short knife at her belt, Mae herself was unarmed, but she needed no weapon to be dangerous.

Edwin did not reply. Mae had been against freeing him, and nothing he could say now would change her mind. Of the core group in charge of the rebels, only Ely and Mae were there with Edwin on that side of the grove. Wharfmaster Abrohl, Aldan Pourin, and Barty led the contingent on the far side, while Matrice was busy luring the Aloise forces toward the trees between them. The stand of cultivated evergreens was not exactly large – Edwin had been able to walk its width in under two minutes – but it was enough to hide the second rebel force from view.

Three booms echoed in quick succession, closer this time.

Edwin gripped the hilt of his sword, though he was hoping not to have to use it. The reason he was taking part in this mad scheme was not to kill Aloise soldiers, but to protect Elymia. If she died here, he doubted anyone who took her place would be willing to uphold her end of their deal and show Remiana mercy. If only for that reason, he had to keep her safe.

"Come on," Ely murmured as the sounds of battle grew near. If the Masked they were expecting did not appear before the Aloise soldiers reached the grove, things were going to get very, very ugly.

"Ready arms!" Mae shouted, as if the waiting men were not already aware of how soon they might need them. Hands tightened on spears. The faint whispers of nervous conversation fell silent. Edwin raised his blade and stepped in front of Ely.

Then there was movement in the shadows of the trees. Edwin watched as a fur-robed form tumbled out of thin air, hit the ground and rolled through the coating of fallen needles. The air around him shimmered, and he vanished from view again. A second later another, similarly clad figure popped into existence, this one landing firmly on his feet. A chunk was missing from the bark mask that covered his face.

Edwin moved to signal that their target had arrived, but Ely had been faster. A low horn call rang out over the city, alerting Matrice that it was time to bring the quarry home.

"Where are you hiding, deceiver?" the visible Masked called out, taking no notice of Edwin and the others at the edge the grove. "You can't hide. Your stink fouls the air!" The voice told Edwin that this was a different Masked than the one he and Ely had encountered on the white bridge, an encounter whose bruises he still wore.

"You are perceptive to see me for what I am," a smug, familiar voice answered, though it came from no visible source. "But the only reward you will earn is death."

The visible Masked made a sound of derision. "An empty threat. You don't have the strength, not without the surprise of your wicked arts."

"I don't need it," the hidden voice replied. "I'm not the one who will do the killing."

It was then that Matrice came barreling through the grove, shedding her disguise as she ran. Furs flapped to the ground, and a wooden mask flew through the air as she flung it away. She dashed straight past the confused Masked under the trees to join Ely, Edwin, and Mae, panting after reaching the end of what must have been a long and harrowing chase.

The vanguard of the Aloise forces followed seconds after. They had been pursuing and exchanging fire across half the city with what looked like a Masked, and it was a Masked they now saw standing before them. An arrow hissed out, striking the robed figure in the arm before he could turn to defend himself. Edwin's eyes widened in amazement. A part of him could not believe Ely's mad plan had actually worked.

Several spearmen charged forward, the fastest runners among the pursuing troops, but they got no closer than ten paces before the ground exploded beneath their feet, sending them flying into the surrounding trunks.

"Coward!" the Masked man shouted, whirling this way and that, searching for something he could not see.

"Victor," the invisible voice replied.

More Aloise soldiers poured into the grove, quickly forming ranks of bowmen behind a wall of spears. There was a lull as arrows were readied and bows pulled taut.

"This is the end, impostor," a man's voice called out from the Aloise ranks. "You rebels might have fooled us once with that Masked disguise, but not again. Now you have nothing but the cliffs at your back and nowhere to run. Archers, take aim!"

The commander's orders were interrupted by the sound of muffled laughter. The wounded Masked straightened as he surveyed the weapons arrayed against him, a beast facing his hunters without fear.

"Do you think this means you've won?" the Masked man called out to the silent treetops. "Do you think arrows and blades are enough to put an end to us?" There was no reply, but his words seemed to temporarily halt the Aloise attack.

The masked man raised his hands to the sides of his head. "Keep your silence, evil one, but know this. You can kill the man beneath, you can strip the flesh from his bones and grind them into dust, but you'll never have the satisfaction of killing a Masked." He lifted the mask of bark from his face and let it drop to the ground.

The now-unmasked man was looking away from him, but Edwin could still see part of his face in profile. It was a face neither remarkably old nor unusually young, with a modest beard of wiry brown hair and cheeks sunken in the manner of a man who worked too hard and ate too little. A shockingly normal face.

A deep intake of breath made the furs covering his body swell and deflate, and a strange smile cracked his face.

"I stand before you now as nothing more than a man," he spoke into the air, "the owner of a single, insignificant life. If you still desire to take it from me, then come and try. A Masked might refuse to strike down those he has sworn to protect, but I am just a man."

"We won't be tricked by your lies!" the Aloise commander shouted. "You are no Masked! Archers, fire!"

At his command, a cloud of arrows screamed death between the trunks. Shafts buried themselves in trees and earth, buzzing with the force of their strikes, but when their angry hissing quieted, the fur-clad man still stood, unscathed. Somehow, every arrow had missed. Edwin was unable to suppress his awe. Mae and Matrice could stop a few arrows, sure, but this was something wholly different.

The wind rustled the unmasked figure's furs, and he cocked his head as if listening.

"I warned you," he said softly. "Now you will learn what a man unrestrained is capable of."

A pelt fell from his mass of furs to the ground. It was a wolf pelt by the look of it, mottled white and brown like the color of dirty snow. But it did not remain on the ground for long. The hairy thing began to wriggle and swell as something pressed out on it from the inside, acquiring a form as if being pulled tight over a mold. There were teeth in that pelt, Edwin could see now, teeth and claws of pearl white and charcoal black. Four corners elongated into legs, and between them a vicious head took shape, snarling and snapping with life where moments earlier there had been nothing but dead skin.

When the transformation was complete, the creature that had taken shape was too large to be a wolf, though its appearance suggested one. Even so, it lacked many true wolf features: its tail was nothing more than a stub, and it had no eyes at all. Yet there was no denying that this thing, whatever it was, was a predator.

Another pelt fell, and then another as the Aloise soldiers looked on, aghast. More terrifying creatures rose to fill those empty skins, masquerading as bears and deer and other fauna, but moving with a subtle menace that was anything but natural. By the time the pelts had finished falling, the unmasked man stood naked in the center of a horde of nature perverted, a collage of wild beasts repurposed into monsters. Edwin could sense what was coming next, and he drew closer to Ely, planting his body between her and the creatures.

The naked man raised his hand, pointing at the soldiers frozen in fear, and his malformed minions surged forward in a howling tide, crashing into the ranks of the Aloise with savage violence. Fangs tore through boiled leather with ease, ripping men limb from limb before they had time to scream. The archers loosed a second volley of arrows into the oncoming wave, but even where their glass tips penetrated the beasts' hide, they seemed to have no effect.

"He attacked them," Ely said softly, disbelief in her voice. "How could that be, unless . . . ."

Mae seemed not to hear Ely's words. "By the gods," she whispered, rendered nearly speechless by the carnage they were witnessing.

The Aloise soldiers were well trained, and even after being scattered by foes as terrifying as these, they managed to reform their lines and press back against the beasts, a wall of spears guarding their archers from the enemy. The tactic almost worked. The beasts had no fear of the soldiers' weapons, but sticking them with upwards of fifteen spears at once did slow them down. It seemed, for a moment, as if the soldiers might regain the upper hand. Then, under the incredible strain, their spears began to snap.

"Should we-?" Matrice asked, but Ely held up her hand.

"Not yet," she said. "Just a minute longer. I need to be sure." Edwin could see in her eyes that she knew waiting meant condemning men to die.

The Aloise line crumbled as their weapons broke, this time not to reform. Lumbering bears broke through the ranks and rampaged among the archers, sending men screaming and running, trying to climb the trees only to be dragged back to their deaths. Wolves lunged, spraying blood when they found their targets. A gigantic buck with gore dripping from its horns trampled soldiers underfoot as they tried to evade the lashing of its antlers. If Ely waited much longer, Edwin thought, there would be no Aloise force left to save.

"Now!" Ely yelled, waving her men forward. "Attack the beasts! Protect the men!"

The creatures immediately turned their heads, somehow aware that new combatants were entering the field. A horn sounded to begin the charge, and from the opposite direction Edwin could hear the rebels' second force closing in, moving to execute a pincer attack and take the battle from both sides.

Edwin remained by Ely's side, letting their men rush past him with cries of "Falls Gate!" and "Celundine!" He spotted Mae and Matrice near the head of the charge, relishing the opportunity to put their powers to use. Or perhaps they had sensed they might be the only ones with a chance of defeating those savage, perverted monsters.

The Aloise troops seemed to have reached the same conclusion. Edwin saw one of the wolf-beasts lifted into the air by an invisible force, struggling and howling until it was torn in two and reverted to a shredded pelt of hair and dried skin. A red-clad shadow knelt to confirm that the thing was truly dead before being swallowed up again by the melee.

Soon more beasts were being shredded, pummeled, and dismembered by unseen powers as the rebel fighters swept into the battle, adding their shouts and screams and cries to the already roaring din. Yet despite their small victories, for every beast they pinned down and destroyed, ten men, Aloise and rebel alike, fell to crushing blows and rending claws. They were not working fast enough. By the time they obliterated all the creatures, everyone else would be dead.

"It's that Masked," Ely said to Edwin, pointing directly into the mass of bodies that was surging back and forth beneath the trees. "He's there, in the center, controlling the beasts and making them fight. If we could get to him, we could-"

As Ely spoke, a wolf broke off from the fray and lurched toward them in an unmistakable beeline, its feet blurred with awful speed. Its wrinkled, eyeless face was twisted in a toothy snarl, mouth open in anticipation of the kill. Three broken spears protruded from its back and its shoulders were peppered with arrows, but the creature moved without sign of pain or injury. Edwin's heart beat faster. He tried not to think about what little hope he had of defeating such a monster. Whatever his chances, he still had to try.

"Get behind me!" Edwin shouted to Ely, hoping she had the good sense to obey. He squared his stance and raised his blade, facing the charging wolf head on.

The beast lunged high for his throat. Edwin ducked low, then pushed up as hard as he could, catching its belly with his shoulder and hind leg with his sword. The impact sent the snarling creature flipping over both his and Ely's heads and onto its back behind them.

Edwin whirled, but the wolf was already getting to its feet, jaws snapping angrily.

"Look!" Ely said, pointing with her drawn dagger, a steel blade almost long enough to be a short sword. "The leg!"

Edwin would not have noticed, so closely was he focused on that toothy maw, but the wolf's hind leg looked thin, almost empty, as if it had no bone or muscle inside. He had only to blink, and it seemed to become whole again. Had his steel actually hurt it?

He had no time to ponder. The wolf charged again with a speed that nearly caught him off guard, and his reaction was more reflex than plan. He thrust the chain connecting his sword and bracer between the creature's jaws, letting them clamp down on the metal links instead of his flesh. The beast growled and strained forward, its sightless, breathless face inches from his own. The links began to crack.

With a something between a scream and a battle cry, Ely leaped on the creature and plunged her dagger into its exposed flank. It reared and thrashed in some approximation of pain as her blade pierced it, disengaging its teeth from the weakened chain. Her attack had done real damage: the flesh around the dagger was sunken and deflated, as if part of its insides had been sucked out.

Edwin needed no more of an opening than that. He lunged forward, driving his sword deep into the monster's breast and yanking upward as hard as he could. Where steel touched skin, it was as if the forces animating the beast fell away. The fur became weak, allowing the sword to cleave smoothly through it, splitting the wolf's head and torso down the middle. The next instant the wolf was gone, replaced by a torn skin lying on the ground with spears, arrows, and Ely's dagger bristling from it like a miniature forest of weaponry.

"The metal," Ely said, sounding dazed as she knelt to reclaim her dagger. "Something about the metal . . . ."

Their men had discovered the same thing, Edwin noted as he glanced back toward the fighting. Those few steel spears the rebels possessed were at least giving them a fighting chance, and even the surviving Aloise were providing support to their wielders. For all their wealth, the Aloise furnished steel only to those of the highest ranks, and there were precious few officers among those dying beneath the trees.

Edwin took an unconscious step toward the battle, but he stopped himself. He could not leave Ely undefended.

"It's all right," Ely said. "They need your sword more than I do. I can take care of myself." She wiped the blade of her dagger on the ground, though the dying wolf had left no blood upon it. "Get to that Masked and stop him."

Edwin found himself nodding. As much as Remiana's life mattered to him, and by extension Ely's, his sword had the potential to save far more lives than just two.

"Promise me you'll stay back," Edwin said.

"You know I can't," Ely said. "I brought these people here. I have to protect them any way I can."

Edwin eyed her dagger, wondering whether he could disarm her so that she would have no way to fight, but he dismissed the idea with regret. He had not been able to take Remiana's bow, and he would do no better with Ely. He was beginning to wish that they were not so similar after all.

"Fine," he said as he turned back toward the fray. "Just don't do anything stupid!"

Ely gave him a wry smile and said something, but the noise of battle was already too great. It took but a few steps toward the melee for the shouts and screams and bestial howls to overwhelm all else, clashing for dominance in the air just as their owners clashed on the ground. With the arrival of Ely's rebels, the Masked's creatures were surrounded, but they showed no signs of yielding. They were fewer now, but those that remained battled tirelessly.

Edwin waded into the fight, striking from behind at a bear menacing a huddling group of spearmen, only one of whom had a weapon of steel. His sword bit deeply into the animal's backside, and both of its hind legs went limp. It turned to growl at him, but the spearman seized his chance and planted his weapon deep into the bear's face where its eye would have been, and it deflated back into an inanimate pelt.

"With me!" Edwin shouted to the survivors, waving his sword aloft. The man who held the metal spear was an Aloise soldier, he noticed with surprise, and its haft was greased with blood that probably belonged to its first owner. Nevertheless, the man was guarded by several rebels with lesser weapons, some of which were clearly Aloise army issue.

Edwin led the group deeper into the fray. He slashed at any creature that came within range, the flashing of his sword in the dimness drawing other survivors to his side. A gargantuan bear reared up to maul him, but a sweep of his blade severed one of its massive paws, turning it into a scrap of fur on the breeze. Two spearmen darted in to finish the job with consecutive thrusts.

Sweat flew from Edwin's arms with every swing of his sword, and his muscles ached from lifting the heavy weapon again and again, but he could not stop. More twisted beasts fell before him, and more men followed behind, protecting his back while he charged ahead. He was the tip of a surging spear, piercing through the enemy's armor of unnatural flesh toward its heart.

Suddenly there was a break in the horde, and Edwin refocused his eyes to see a naked man standing just ahead, his sun-starved skin seeming to glow with pallid luminescence. His eyes were closed, undisturbed by the chaos that raged around him.

A wolf lunged at Edwin's side, and he had no time to ready a strike. Instead, he swung his arm, heavy with the metal of his bracer, at the creature's face. The blow landed squarely, jarring Edwin's shoulder but knocking the creature aside. It spun past him, hitting the ground and bowling over several men before reversing course almost without slowing down, coming at him a second time.

This time his sword was ready, and Edwin swung with all his strength, timing the blow to take the beast as it lunged. But the attack did not come. Edwin was fully committed to his swing when the creature's charge stopped dead, just outside his reach, and his sword sailed harmlessly past its throat. He felt a stab of fear, realizing he was exposed. The wolf seemed to grin.

Two paws raked Edwin's side, nails tearing through his leathers as if they were silk. He suppressed a cry and let the momentum swing carry him around for another strike, but once again the wolf was outside the arc of the blade, darting back and forward again almost faster than his eye could follow. A paw raked across his back, stripping off the last remnants of his leather vest and showering the ground with his blood.

Edwin staggered, his Aloise signet ring swinging free against his bare chest on its thong. The wolf's second strike had not been a killing blow, despite being against his exposed back. The beast was playing with him. He turned, seeing now that the wolf stood between him and its master, its leering jaws mimicking the smile on the naked man's face. Edwin's eyes burned. People were dying, and this monster was having fun?

Edwin roared, rushing forward with a downward cleave, but the wolf knocked his blade aside with a swipe of its paw. The strike was so powerful that the weakened chain snapped, sending the weapon spinning off under the stamping feet of the men and beasts still fighting around them. The wolf was suddenly behind him, and a headbutt sent Edwin sprawling at the naked man's feet.

"You can't win," an amused voice said from above him. A pair of jaws grabbed him by the leg and rolled him over so he could stare up at those still-closed eyes and sadistic smile.

"You can't win, but you've made this more fun than I expected," the unmasked man said. The wolf moved to stand over Edwin, its bared teeth hanging just above his face. "For that, you can have the pleasure of watching the other weaklings die."

"You're an animal," Edwin spat up at him.

"Aren't we all?" the unmasked man said with a chuckle. "I have no more reason to deny my nature, no reason to resist the sweet pleasures of power. Call me what you like, but all that is in me is in you, too. We are both men. We are both the same."

Edwin had to chuckle too. "We're not the same at all," he said.

"How are we different?" the unmasked man asked.

Edwin smiled up into the wolf's dry jaws. "I'm not stupid enough to give my enemies a second chance." He raised his elbow and slammed it down on the naked man's bare foot.

The unmasked man's closed eyes snapped open in surprise. For a second, all the monstrous beasts froze in place, dolls suddenly abandoned by a distracted child. Without giving himself time to think better of it, Edwin tore the Aloise signet ring from his neck and shoved it down the giant wolf's waiting throat. He had to bury his arm almost to the shoulder before the metal did its work and he was able to kick the limp, empty wolf skin off of him.

The look in the unmasked man's eyes was turning from shock to anger, but Edwin was not about to give him the chance to retaliate. A flick of his wrist wrapped the broken chain of his bracer around the man's ankle, and a hard tug sent him sprawling to the ground.

"Edwin! Your sword!" It was Mae's voice calling, Edwin realized, and he turned to see her hurl the gleaming weapon toward him from beyond the edge of the surrounding melee. She was not weak, but neither was the sword light, and Edwin's heart fell as the weapon thudded into the earth, blade first, three paces shy of him. He scrambled for it, yanked it from the ground, and made it two steps back toward the unmasked man's fallen body before something invisible caught and bound him in place.

"Delightful," the unmasked man said, lifting his head, his hair full of needles. He still lay on the ground, but the creatures were moving again. "So weak, yet still so eager to fight. The animal urge is strong in you."

Edwin was held so completely that even his jaw was frozen shut. The unmasked man was only an arm's length away, but he might as well have been at the bottom of the sea for all Edwin could do to reach him. A wave of hopelessness, tall and dark, loomed up within him. He had failed. He hoped Ely would still honor their agreement even after he was dead.

"No tricks up your sleeve this time?" the unmasked man said mockingly. "Well then, let me take your advice about second chances."

Edwin felt a great weight pressing down on every inch of his body, slowly trying to crush him inward into a ball. The pain was excruciating, worse than any wound he had ever taken, the whole of his frame crying out at being strained to the breaking point. At least, he thought with the tiniest satisfaction, he had upset the man enough to have earned a painful death.

A lare shadow fell across the unmasked man's body, still on the ground.

"The boy do give good advice," the shadow said.

The crushing force around Edwin's body withdrew, but not quickly enough. Before it could stop him, the Wharfmaster slammed a massive mollusk-shell maul down on the fallen man's skull with such force that Edwin could feel the blow travel through the ground and up his sagging legs.

Edwin dropped to his knees, letting his sword fall beside him. His mind could only form one coherent thought, and it repeated itself again and again: it was over. All the many gods be blessed, it was over.

The end of the battle was abrupt, and the grove fell suddenly, strangely quiet in the absence of its angry roar. Upon the death of their master, the life in the remaining beasts vanished as if it had never been, returning them to just a few scraps of fur fluttering to the ground among a mass of bewildered fighters. The growls of bears and the howls of wolves were replaced in an instant by the soft rustling of wind in the branches and the faint, curious twittering of a few inquisitive duskdipper birds as they circled and dived above the treetops.

•••••

Ely nearly had to pry her fingers loose from the hilt of her dagger to return it to its sheath. The battle had ended, and in their favor, but she still could not stop her limbs from quivering. She leaned against a tree at the edge of the grove, too relieved to care whether any of the men saw her momentary weakness.

Just ahead, a bit deeper in the trees, the survivors on both sides had begun reestablishing order. The living were freed from the tangles of the dead and their injuries tended, regardless of the colors they wore. Lanterns were lit against the deepening darkness, and flasks were shared freely. Most of the men seemed too dazed to realize that they were working side by side with others who might have wanted to kill them a mere hour before.

Ely closed her eyes. She did not need to see to know that despite their victory, the price had been great. Bodies littered the grove, in the worst places two or three deep. At least two thirds of the fallen wore the Aloise uniform, but the people of Falls Gate had watered the trees with their share of blood as well. There were easily two hundred dead between both sides, a mountain of lives to weigh against that of a single Masked. And if killing that one man had been the battle's only reward, Ely would have called it a waste. But as she opened her eyes again and watched the waterskins passing so easily from hand to hand, it was clear that those lives had purchased something more.

"You disobeyed me," a voice hissed out of the darkness behind her.

Ely's head drooped. She had known he would come, but she had no desire to speak to the masked man, not now. This was a time for giving thanks, for helping those who could be helped and mourning those who could not. From his voice, however, Ely could tell that the masked man cared nothing for those things. She wondered how anyone could be so cold.

"That Masked is dead, like you wanted," Ely said, turning and stepping away from the tree that supported her.

"Yes," the voice said from the shadows, "but this was not the way. I told you what to do, and you disobeyed."

"But you were lying," Ely said bluntly. She was tired, too tired to act for him like she had before. It had come to her as soon as she had seen the now-dead Masked turn on his Aloise attackers.

"What did you say?"

"I said you were lying," Ely repeated, "just like you've been lying the whole time. You never cared about me, or this city, or justice." She wondered why she had not seen it before. "That Masked was no ally of the Aloise. You wanted us to fight him alone so that we wouldn't discover the truth. The Masked haven't sided with the Aloise at all, have they?"

The masked man made a disappointed sound. "The evidence is right in front of you. You've seen the Aloise wield our power. How did they get it if not through an alliance?"

A chill skittered down Ely's spine. "The same way we did. From you."

The masked man was silent for a moment. When he spoke, he sounded almost hurt. "All I've done is give you what you wanted, Elymia. Why turn against me now?"

Ely shivered, repulsed by his false emotion. Now that she could see his lies, she wondered why she had ever fallen for them in the first place.

"All you've given us is war," Ely said. "You've been pitting us against each other for your own benefit, not for ours."

"I'm not the one who made the Aloise torture and kill," the masked man said. "I'm not the one who gave your friend Tamalina her methods of fighting back."

Ely shook her head, wondering if he would ever stop lying. "You might not be the source of all our wickedness, but you nurture and use it. It's obvious that you want us to fight, and now you're trying to provoke the Masked as well. What I can't see is what you stand to gain."

The masked man fell into a menacing silence, but Ely could not bring herself to be afraid. He was ruthless, but there was some reason he needed her alive, or he would not have wasted his time with her at all.

"You saw something, didn't you?" the masked man said slowly. "When you looked through the keyhole. What was it?" It wasn't a question Ely had been expecting.

"Nothing," she said quickly. "I didn't see anything."

"No," the masked man said, stepping closer. "I think you did. You saw something there, and now you can see through this." He gestured to his furs and mask, but it was not the physical disguise he meant. "Tell me what it was." There was a dangerous edge in his voice.

But he was bluffing, Ely saw. Whatever his goals were, he would not risk them by hurting her.

"I think that is none of your business," Ely replied.

The masked man went rigid with anger, yet he did not lash out.

"The Masked will soon learn what you've done here," he said, his voice cool, as if the prior exchange had never happened. "I suggest you be long gone by then." Then he faded into the night and vanished.

Ely let out a breath and pressed her still-shaking hands to her forehead. She was so incredibly tired. Leading men to battle and defying a Masked all in one day . . . . She had no idea where she was finding the strength. She closed her eyes once more, and found herself drawn to memories of the white bridge, the steel door, and the keyhole.

Ely sensed that what she had seen on the other side was something deeply private, something no one should be allowed to threaten or force out of her. There had been the light, yes, light so thick it had seemed to crowd out everything else in her head as her eyes drew it in. But there had been something else. There had been a boy, perhaps a few years younger than her, gazing back through the keyhole with a face she had seen once before, though this time it was peaceful, unmarred by deceptions wriggling beneath its skin. His sad, dark eyes had met hers, and he had mouthed two silent words: "I'm sorry."

•••••

"Well I'll be snowstruck!" a familiar voice said from over Edwin's shoulder. "Ed, is that you?"

Edwin grunted as he dragged a dead man into the row of others on the grass. This one had been with the Aloise, he guessed, though his clothes were shredded beyond recognition. The right hand had calluses suggesting he had been an archer, and judging by his wounds, he had been one of the brave ones who kept firing even after the wall of spears had failed.

After folding the dead man's arms across his chest, Edwin turned to see who was calling him. To his surprise, he saw Ables using a spear as a crutch as he limped over. The last time he had seen the man was during Ely's attack on the Keep, and the intervening days did not look like they had been kind to him.

"Blow me off a mountainside, it is you!" Ables said, looking Edwin up and down. "You're supposed to be dead twice over now, but I guess death just can't keep hold of you." A grin cracked his face like a chisel across a granite block. "First you were supposed to be buried somewhere under all the rubble in the Keep, and then you were reported killed when we ambushed those rebel witches in the courtyard."

"An easy mistake to make," Edwin said, giving Ables a humorless smile. "But I'm not dead yet, though not for lack of trying."

Ables frowned. "You sure look like death, I'll give you that much. What in the peaks happened to your clothes?"

Edwin looked down at his bare chest, which was crisscrossed with claw wounds and dried blood. He had forgotten about losing his leathers. What did clothes matter when so many had died? "Battle. You know," he said numbly.

"'Course I know," Ables said, sticking out his injured leg. There was a thick wrapping tied around the thigh. "That wolf bastard didn't get me too deep, but damn does it hurt!"

Seeing Ables' injury, Edwin was reminded of the last time he had seen the man, covered with dust and blood and digging at a collapsed doorway as the Keep was falling to pieces around them. He felt a stab of guilt. "What happened to Gul and Van, back then?" he asked. "Did they make it?"

Ables rolled his eyes. "Those two," he said dryly. "They lived. Van screamed like a skirtless maid 'til Gul knocked him senseless, but we dug them out. Still wasn't easy." He held up one of his hands, and Edwin saw that half the fingernails were missing. "They aren't Knights any more though, not with Gul's broken leg and Van's shoulder. Both have been laid up with the rest of the wounded since then."

"And what about you?" Edwin said, realizing that Ables was not wearing any armor.

Ables turned his head and spat. "Lost my armor that night," he said bitterly. "Got crushed flat. Most of the others lost theirs too, one way or another. You too, I'm guessing." He looked at Edwin's bare chest pointedly.

"Something like that," Edwin said neutrally. Ables obviously cared more about the loss than he did.

Ables nodded understandingly. "Ten and Malbrand are the only ones whose suits survived intact. The rest of us got effectively demoted, even the captain. That's how I ended up in this nightmare." He sighed. "But how did you end up with another unit without us hearing about it?"

Edwin had been wondering when that would come up, but he still did not know how to answer.

"He didn't," a woman's voice cut in. "He's with me."

Edwin turned to see Ely emerging from the trees, Mae and Matrice at her side. Compared to Edwin and most of the other soldiers, those three looked practically spotless, and he felt suddenly self conscious. When they drew closer, Ely paused to give her two companions orders.

"Start spreading the word. We need to withdraw, and soon," she said. "But do it calmly. And remember to be courteous to our friends." Matrice nodded and Mae scowled, but both went without protest. Ely turned to Edwin and Ables.

"My name is Elymia," she said with a smile, holding out her hand to Ables. "Thank you for helping protect our city."

Ables stared blankly at her hand, then back at Edwin. "You're with the rebels?" he said, stunned.

"How do you know this man?" Ely asked Edwin, turning her back on Ables for a moment like he wasn't there.

Edwin looked uneasily between them. "He was a knight, like me," he said. "His name's Corris Ables."

"Can I trust him?" Ely asked bluntly. Ables, for his part, looked too bewildered to object to the rude treatment.

"He's as good a man as you'll find in the knights," Edwin said with a shrug. "If you can trust me, you can trust him."

Ely nodded. "Well then, Mr. Ables," she said, turning back. "Edwin is with us because Oridine tried to have him killed. I'm guessing the version you heard was anything but the truth."

Ables looked suspicious. "Why would Oridine want to kill one of her own blood?"

Ely glanced at Edwin. "That answer belongs to Edwin, not to me. But he will confirm that it's the truth." Edwin nodded solemnly.

Ables' eyes widened. "Shit," he said. "I knew something wasn't right when Oridine had her own daughter confined to quarters. We could hear her banging on that bloody door for most of the day and night. It made the men talk."

"Is she all right?" Edwin asked. "Do you know what's happened to her?"

Ables shrugged. "Couldn't say. It's been a few days, and I haven't seen or heard anything since. Malbrand's still posted to her door though, so I guess she's still in there."

Edwin opened his mouth, but Ely put a hand on his arm. "We'll see to Remiana in time," she said. "Right now, Mr. Ables needs to know how serious the situation we're facing is. What happened to Edwin isn't the only lie Oridine's been spreading, I'd wager. She also told you that the Masked were your allies, didn't she?"

"She said the ones who attacked us were imposters," Ables said slowly. "And that the real Masked wanted them dead."

"I don't know whether Oridine honestly believes that or not," Ely said, "but the fact is that the Masked aren't your allies. Nor are they ours. We're both being played by someone among the Masked, someone who's using their power to encourage us to fight."

"One of the Masked?" Ables said in disbelief. "They're peaceful, selfless."

"But I've met one who isn't," Ely said, "and that makes this situation all the more dangerous. With what happened here tonight, the rest of the Masked will be coming after both sides for killing one of their own, and I think that's exactly what this manipulator wants."

"But it was a trick!" Ables exclaimed. "We thought that Masked was an impostor!"

"We were tricked too," Ely said. "But we can't escape the fact that we took the life of a Masked. I doubt Oridine will calmly submit herself to whatever judgment the Masked deem fit, nor will I, knowing how we were deceived."

"What are you saying?" Ables said.

"I'm saying that in the eyes of the Masked, both our sides are guilty," Ely said. "If we're going to survive, we need to focus on that threat instead of on each other."

"You're suggesting we actually fight the Masked?"

"We've seen what they're capable of," Ely said, nodding to the long line of bodies, "and we've worked together against them once. I'm hoping that, if the need arises, we can again."

Ables scoffed. "Oridine won't like it."

Ely nodded. "That's why I'm not suggesting this to Oridine. All my people want are their homes, their lives, and their freedom. Oridine may claim that makes us your enemy, but when the time comes, it will be you and others like you who have to decide if that's reason enough to raise your spears against us."

"You speak of treason," Ables said, dropping his voice to a whisper.

"I speak of choosing our own paths rather than letting others choose for us," Ely said. "You came here because of Oridine's ambition and greed. Now you must decide if her anger is worth giving up the only aid you'll have against an enemy you can't hope to defeat alone."

Ables chewed on his lip. He was a soldier, Edwin knew, not a thinker or a politician, but he knew his tactics.

"You need not say anything now," Ely said. "But let me give you a token of good faith to prove my intentions, a piece of information to use as you wish. You know Tamalina Resposé?"

"The murderer?" Ables said. "Yeah, I know her. All the men do, after what she did."

"I'm going to stop her execution," Ely said.

Edwin raised an eyebrow, but remained silent. This was the first he had heard of it, though he had never really expected Ely to ignore her friend's death sentence.

"Why?" Ables asked. "Setting a murderer free won't do much to help your cause."

"I don't intend to set her free," Ely said. "She will still account for her crimes, but to our people, and in our way."

"Even though she's one of you, and she killed men of ours?" Ables said.

Ely nodded. "Here, a person's blood doesn't change the sort of justice she deserves."

"Strange people," Ables mumbled.

"Whether you understand it or not, a trial is her right as a citizen of Falls Gate," Ely said. "I will see she gets one. That goes for your people as well. Once the Masked are dealt with, I promise that none of your people will be executed. Those who have committed crimes will answer for them, but I won't tolerate mob justice."

"That's more generous than what you'll get from Oridine if things turn out the other way around," Ables said grimly.

"I know," Ely said. "But we have to start somewhere." She extended her hand again, and this time, after some hesitation, Ables took it.

"Whatever else there is between us, you saved us from that Masked today," he said. "None of us will soon be forgetting that."

"I only did what was right," Ely said. "I hope that example is what your men remember. Now if you'll excuse me."

When Ely was gone, Ables looked at Edwin bemusedly. "She's a live one. Wouldn't be surprised if she had a bit of the iron blood in her veins, the way she talks." He paused. "But I feel like I've seen her somewhere before."

Edwin smiled, thinking back to the great hall and the barefooted girl with the soiled dress and the determined eyes. She had been leading even then, Edwin realized. She just hadn't known it yet.

Chapter 36

Baiting a Shark

Donvin stomped along the white stones of the byssal bridge, the foul wind rubbing itself upon his furs. That wind was stronger every time he came here, as if its source were drawing closer with every passing day. Yet despite the unpleasant conditions of the trip, he did not rush. He needed time to think.

"She knows too much," Donvin growled.

"But she is too valuable to kill," Lith replied, her soundless footsteps matching his pace across the stones. The wind played havoc with her black hair, yet it never seemed to tangle. "She leads those people effectively. Without her, the resistance will crumble too soon to fight the Masked."

Donvin made a hissing sound. There were only a few days remaining, and everything was nearly in place. Why had Elymia chosen now, of all times, to develop such cursedly accurate insight?

It was the door, of course. Donvin seethed at his mistake of leaving her and the Aloise man alone on the bridge for so long. He had tried to rescue all four of them, Maewell and Matrice included, by dropping them into the same portal, but something had bent the byssi, jogging Elymia onto a parallel path. By the time he found her, she had looked beyond the door and seen something that had made her begin to doubt him.

Donvin looked up as he passed the center of the bridge. The door was there, as it always was, and it had retained its appearance of steel. No matter how much he yearned to know what it hid, it would open no keyhole for him, not since the time Lith had briefly taken over his body.

"Don't forget the other use that Elymia will be to us," Lith said. "She is better bait for the final part of the trap than any other." Lith was right, but that did not alleviate the itch Donvin felt to destroy Elymia for the way she had spoken to him. For seeing what he could not.

"I won't kill her," Donvin said halfheartedly.

"That's not good enough," Lith insisted. "You need to control yourself. You should know by now the consequences feelings like these can have."

Donvin smiled grimly. Oh yes, he knew. It would be the same thing that had happened to Keth, and to Evana, and almost to Bird. His little guardian angel would pay her a visit.

"If she dies," Lith warned, "it will put everything we've worked for at risk. I don't think you're that stupid. Selfish enough, maybe, but not stupid."

Donvin shrugged. "Fine," he said, burying his anger at Elymia deep in the pit of his stomach, where its coals could linger until it was time to feed them again. "But once her purpose is served, I trust you won't stand in my way."

"Once our work is complete, you will never hear from me again."

"Is that a promise?" Donvin said.

There was no reply. Donvin turned his head, but the bridge was empty. He snorted. For all Lith's promises about making him a free man, she never stopped telling him what to do. When this was over, he would be glad to see her gone for good, whether she went voluntarily, or otherwise.

• • • • •

The gray-haired man sat at his desk in the tent, untroubled by the flapping of its canvas walls as the wind assaulted them. The lantern on the tabletop was lit even though it was midday, for the heavy clouds and snow blotted out most of the natural light. In its flickering aura, the man's sturdy hands scrawled out a name again and again as papers moved from the desk to the drying rack: General Gelavar Celundine; General Gelavar Celundine; General Gelavar Celundine.

Suddenly, the hands stopped. The pen paused in the air, a bead of ink collecting at the nib and wobbling over the page waiting to be signed.

"Finally," he said to the air, his hands resuming their repetitive work. "I knew one of you would come, though I confess I thought it would take days, not months."

Donvin stirred, but remained in the shadows at the rear of the tent. The furnishings were spartan for the leader of an army, he noted. The overturned crate that served as nightstand did not even have a single book on it. All it bore was a yellowing, wrinkled envelope with the word "Father" penned across the front.

"Are you the one they call the Grayfin?" Donvin said.

"You would not be in my tent if I wasn't," the Grayfin said, scribbling his name once more with the pen. "Come, sit where I can see you."

Donvin obeyed. He needed to play nicely with this man, for in his own way he was even more important to the plan than his daughter.

Gelavar Celundine eyed Donvin's furs and mask as he emerged from the back of the tent.

"You aren't the one I was expecting," he said, finally setting down his pen. "One of your kind has visited me before, on more than one occasion. I assumed he would be the one to administer punishment for my men's transgression."

Donvin looked into the man's eyes, but he saw no fear there. Intelligence and calculation, but no fear. "I'm the one your men attacked," he said. "But much has happened since then, and I have not come to speak of punishment."

Gelavar's thick eyebrows lifted quizzically, but he did not speak. In the silence, Donvin scanned the papers on the desk. They were all copies of the same letter.

"No pigeon could survive this weather," Donvin said, nodding to indicate the howling wind. "It doesn't matter how many you send."

Gelavar looked down at the stack of signed letters on the drying rack. "Not all will go by bird," he said. "Some will go with men on foot, and they will have a copy sent from every village or manor with a rookery they pass."

"Even men might freeze before they get far," Donvin said.

"Yes," Gelavar acknowledged. "If I were a better leader, I might be able to stop those who wish to go, or deny them letters to carry." His eyes fell to his pen. "But if I were young again, I would have demanded the same duty, and gone with or without sanction. I've learned that even the best commander can't lead men away from the place their hearts desire to go."

There was a scratch at the tent flap, and both men turned their heads.

"Are you all right, sir?" a voice called over the wind. "I thought I heard voices."

"Quite all right, Torman," Gelavar called back. "I have a guest. See that we are not disturbed."

"A guest?" Torman repeated from outside. "I've been on watch right here for hours, sir. No one has entered your tent while-"

"Thank you, Torman," Gelavar said loudly. "That will be all."

"Yes sir!" the voice called back, and then was silent.

The General gave Donvin a thin-lipped smile. "My men are concerned for me," he said. "They have been since the news came. They fear an attempt on my life in order to slow our return to Falls Gate, now that we know of the Aloise treachery." He watched the wall of the tent ripple and snap. "My opinion is that anyone being paid for that task is making easy money. A good snow stops an army better than any assassin's blade."

"True," Donvin said, "and winter comes early and strong to these north-lands. It's already begun, and a full thaw won't come until spring."

Gelavar's eyes returned to him. "It seems you're well informed about the problems I face."

"They are why I came," Donvin replied.

Gelavar leaned back in his chair, frowning. "The Masked do not intervene in the affairs of men, either to assist or to impede. What interest are my problems to you?"

"They interest me because I share them," Donvin said. "All my people do. You've heard that the Aloise now control your city, but you don't know all that has transpired within, nor do I have time to tell you. What's important is that in two days time, without your aid, your daughter will be dead at the hands of the Masked."

The man was as still as stone, but Donvin could smell the maelstrom in-side him.

"What do you know of my daughter?" Gelavar said evenly.

"I know that she is alive," Donvin said. "I know that she has organized a resistance against the Aloise. I know that to aid that resistance, she stole from my people a power that is not for any but us to wield, a power she has used to great effect, but also one that my kind intend to see reclaimed." As he spoke, Donvin smelled something new emanating from the man across from him. Pride.

"And what happens in two days?" Gelavar said.

"That's when the Masked will go to war against your city and your daugh-ter." It was not true, of course. At least, not yet.

Gelavar slammed his fist on the desk. "Is this my punishment?" he de-manded. "For you to describe the death of my only child while I am weeks, if not months, away from reaching her? I did not think our protectors so cruel!"

Donvin let him fume for a moment before answering. "This is not punish-ment. This is a plea for aid." That caught the general's ear.

"I don't speak of this lightly to an outsider," Donvin said quietly, "but there is a division among the Masked. Some of us believe it is our duty to control the use of our power at any cost. Others believe it would be a terrible wrong to make war on those we are sworn to protect. I am one of the latter."

"You would stop the Masked from doing this, then?" Gelavar said, a piercing intensity in his eyes.

"If only I could," Donvin replied. "But I cannot. We have tried and failed to reconcile our differences, and there are more who favor war. I still think, however, that there is a chance to prevent it."

"A chance that involves my aid?" Gelavar said. "What can I do from such a distance? Even a bird could not reach Falls Gate in the next two days."

"Perhaps," Donvin said, "but I can get you there in one."

Gelavar did not so much as blink. "Men and equipment?" he asked. "Wagons and beasts?"

"Yes," Donvin said, "but those are less important than you yourself. You must convince your daughter to give the Masked what they want. Only that will prevent bloodshed now. If you need your men and arms and wagons and beasts to do it, then I will gladly transport them all."

Gelavar saw the opportunity that Donvin wanted him to see, of course: the chance to move his entire force to the doorstep of Falls Gate undetected. To a seasoned commander, it was hardly any different from offering him the city on a platter. It would also put him in a position to protect his daughter by force of arms. The offer had to be disguised as something an honest Masked would support, of course. It would not do to have the General suspect that there was more afoot than he was being told.

"I can't speak to your internal squabbles," Gelavar said, "but if you think it will avert war, I will of course try to make my daughter see reason. I won't abide any harm coming to her, however. If your fellow Masked demand blood payment, then I'll become your enemy as well as she."

"We would never ask such a thing," Donvin said, doing his best to sound offended. "Once the power she has taken is secured, no true Masked would still pursue blood. Any who did would be traitors to our code, deserving of anything that happened to them."

Gelavar was silent, but his smell said that he had heard the subtle authorization of violence.

"I owe you a debt," he said after a moment. "You are a good man for seeking peace even when the tides of the world favor war. It could not have been easy to go against the will of your people."

"Not easy," Donvin said, "but necessary."

Gelavar nodded. "You have my word that I will do everything in my power to prevent the Masked from making war on the people of Falls Gate. Now, how soon can you send me and my men?"

"Dawn tomorrow," Donvin said. "That will give you time to prepare. But before that, there is something I must do to make the way ready." That part was true. There was one final step to ensure that the Masked would willingly play their part before the path to war would be prepared.

Chapter 37
Reclamation

Edwin peeked around the corner of the alley, scanning for any sign of the man he was to meet, but leaned back against the wall in disappointment. A few stray raindrops spattered the cobbles, fallen from a sky trying to hold back its tears as it looked down on a beautiful city sliding into ruin. The alley was disgusting, filled with piles of human waste dumped from windows after the sewage channels had dried up, no doubt another of Oridine's punishments for the city's failure to render up Elymia. Mounds of other garbage added to the pungent aroma, making the place repulsive, and therefore the perfect spot for a secret meeting.

"Ugh," a voice said. "Could you have chosen a dirtier place?"

Ables appeared from around the corner, his face scrunched, though he did not cover his nose.

"Don't complain," Edwin said. "I know you've smelled worse."

"Smelled like worse, you mean," Ables said, coming to a stop in the middle of the alley. "And the same goes for you." He wore an ill-fitting doublet accented with an absurd amount of lace, clearly something pilfered from a captive nobleman's wardrobe.

"Can't argue with you there," Edwin said, remembering all the times he had been trapped inside his coffin of steel with nothing but his own stink for company. "Did you bring it?"

"Sure did," Ables replied, holding up a burlap sack. "Though I don't know why. We're mates and all, but this could get me killed." He looked down at himself and grimaced. "And having to wear this stupid thing might be even worse than that."

"It's a good disguise," Edwin said with a mocking smile. "No one would ever guess that you were a knight."

"Former knight," Ables corrected him. "Don't be giving me more rank than I have. I'm happier without it."

"Are things in the Keep that bad?" Edwin said. He could only guess at Oridine's fury after the slaughter her troops had walked into at Crossing Grove.

"You left us, remember?" Ables said. "It's not your problem any more."

"I didn't really have a choice," Edwin reminded him, "and I still have something to take care of there. That's why I needed this favor."

"Don't say any more. I don't want to know," Ables said, tossing the bag to Edwin. "Take it."

Edwin caught the heavy sack with both arms, and the object inside gave a muffled clang.

"All right," Edwin said. "It's safer if you don't know anyway. Any news on Elymia's proposal?"

Ables rolled his eyes. "Shit, Ed, I don't know. It's not like all us men get together and meet every night after Oridine goes to bed. I'm not in charge of them."

"But you must have some idea what they're thinking," Edwin pried.

"Yeah," Ables said bluntly. "They're scared. Nobody knows what the truth is any more, but they know that a lot of their mates got killed in some pretty awful ways by an enemy they don't understand. They've got no one they can trust, what with Oridine still insisting the Masked are on our side and the knights mostly dissolved. If Elymia's expecting them to suddenly grow a spine and a taste for treason, she'll be disappointed. They'll follow orders because they've got no idea what else to do, and no one they respect to tell them otherwise."

"I'm sure they respect you," Edwin said.

Ables snorted. "And what would I tell them? I'm in no better position than they are."

"You know what you've seen with your own eyes," Edwin said. "You know about Oridine's lies."

"So what if I do?" Ables said. "I trust you and all, Ed, but it's a lot to ask a man to hang his life on the word of a disgraced knight and a rebel. Not all of us can just run off with some local girl at the drop of a hat. You might not have family back home any more, but plenty of us still do."

"All right, I get it. But keep thinking on it. I don't want us to end up on opposite ends of a sword."

"Neither do I, but you don't have to want a thing for it to happen," Ables said.

•••••

Edwin nodded to the lookout as he slipped through the door of the modest home in the shadow of the city wall's northwest corner. Like most buildings within the walls, it was made of ancient stone, though no wooden additions topped its squat bulk. It was the sort where the common laborers lived, often two or more families to a building.

The grayness of the day made the house's interior dim, but it was not hard for Edwin to find his way. There were only a few rooms, all dark and square, and he followed the sound of voices. Ely was there, sharing a bench with a woman of middle years who was dabbing her eyes with a handkerchief. Matrice stood silently in the corner with her father, but otherwise the room was empty.

"Thank you," the teary-eyed woman said to Ely. "It was proper kind of you to come."

"I'm truly sorry," Ely said. "If there's anything you need, all you have to do is ask."

"You've already helped so much," the woman replied, her hand going to a pouch in her lap that clicked with the sound of coins. "My husband would be happy to know that he earned this for us."

"What about your children?" Ely asked. Edwin noticed that there were a few well-worn toys lying about the room: a blue glass beras with a missing leg; a stuffed doll with yarn for hair; a wooden sword.

"We're used to families without fathers around here," the woman said. "Sailing the ships keeps most of them away, and not all come back. It won't be easy, but some day they'll be proud to know their Pa died a hero."

"I won't let his death be in vain," Ely said soberly.

The woman smiled at her. "I know you won't, child. My father served under yours, you know, way back. He was just a footman, but when I'd tell him he was too old for it, he'd say, 'That Celundine is a wise man, and I'd follow him to the ends of the ocean and back again. Men like that need us as much as we need them.' My father was already gray then, mind you, and speaking about a man half his age! He served 'til he died, and I never understood why. Now, meeting you, I think I finally do." By the time she had finished, there were tears in Ely's eyes too.

Edwin waited in the doorway until Ely excused herself and her entourage, then joined them on their way out of the house.

"Did you get it?" Ely asked, her eyes on the bag under Edwin's arm. He nodded. "May I?"

Edwin opened the sack, and out of it Ely lifted a knight's helmet with a blue visor, slightly dented but otherwise intact. Matrice and her father looked suitably impressed, but Ely just shook her head.

"I wish he hadn't been able to find it for you," she said.

"Why?" Edwin asked.

Ely looked over the helmet at him. "Because what you want to do is foolish. This will all be decided, one way or another, at the execution tomorrow, and then Remiana will be safe. Why risk your life trying to save her an hour or two early?"

"You're concerned about me?" Edwin said. "I'm touched."

"Stop that," Ely said, her face coloring briefly. "I think we've been through enough to drop the sarcasm."

Now it was Edwin's turn to flush, and he looked down at the floor. "Sorry," he mumbled. "But still, I have to do it. What if there's fighting tomorrow? What if you have to storm the Keep again?"

"Then she'll have to make her own choice about where her loyalties lie," Ely said. "I promised you I would give her a chance, but she has to meet me half way. If she takes up arms against us, then I won't hesitate."

"And that's why I have to get her out," Edwin said. "Battlefields are no place for deciding anything, and you may well kill each other before you realize what you've done. I have to make sure that doesn't happen."

"You're too valuable," Ely insisted. "You have training and the best steel we've got. We'll need those against the Masked, if it comes to that."

"Then why not stop me?" Edwin said. "Why not deny me what I need? My plan won't work without them. Hells, I wouldn't even get as far as the gate."

Ely looked down at her reflection in the warped surface of the helmet. "Because I promised," she said, "and because you'd do something even more drastic if I did." You can't lead men away from the place their hearts desire to go. Her father's words, long ago, but now that everyone was looking to her for direction, she felt their truth all too clearly. Her job was not to herd them. It was merely to remind them where they wanted to go.

Ely held out the helmet, and Edwin accepted it with thanks in his eyes. Where he wanted to go now, where he needed to go, was to his sister.

Chapter 38
The Final Straw

Donvin had promised Gelavar Celundine a war, and now it was time to make good on that promise. The first blow had already been struck. All that remained was to make the Masked feel its pain.

Donvin entered the camp of the Masked without fanfare, cradling the cloth-wrapped body against his chest. Bird's corpse was not heavy for that of a man, but it was still an awkward load to bear. Yet even being forced to carry his adversary's cumbersome remains could not dampen Donvin's mood for long. Watching Bird die had been a pleasure worth savoring, but using his memory as the weapon to finally break the Masked would be even sweeter.

It was nearing the hour for their evening meal, with the sunlight slanting low and rich through the trees, and many of the Masked were in the camp laying out wood for fires or preparing food. Donvin's entrance quickly put an end to that. He came to a halt in front of one of the huts, and the other Masked began to gather around. After a few moments, the flap across the entrance drew aside and Limp emerged.

"What's this?" he said, looking over the multitude gathered before him.

"I return with dire news," Donvin said. "One of our own has fallen, and it is our fault." He dropped to one knee and lowered Bird's body to the ground.

Limp sniffed the air, and like the others quickly realized who Donvin was talking about.

"Ah, so the traitor is no more," he said. "There is no shame in that. Justice has been served."

Donvin bowed his head. "But he did not betray us."

The Masked around him made noises of confusion, looking to one another with uncertainty.

"It pains me to say it," Donvin said, "but it's true. He was no traitor. In the end, he proved it with his life."

"The evidence of his lies is strong," Limp said uneasily. "What is there to counter it?"

"Only what I've seen with my own eyes," Donvin said, "but the body itself will speak to the truth of my tale."

"Well, don't keep us waiting," Limp said. "Speak."

Donvin rose and faced the rest of the Masked. He could sense their anticipation. His efforts among them had turned their thoughts dark, taught them to expect the worst. He had sown within them the seeds of doubt, made them wonder if the way of the Mask was not so infallible as it had long seemed. Now they were ready.

"I have learned much as I sought the truth among the coastmen," Donvin said. "I have learned that, though he was flawed, our fallen comrade was true to our cause. We were the ones who were too blind to see it." He looked down at the folds of stained cloth that wrapped Bird's body. "When I sought him out and confronted him, he did not try to hide. Instead, he told me a story, one that I was too arrogant to believe until it was too late. He told me that he had not gone to the coastmen to betray us, but to protect us."

"A traitor's words are full of lies," Limp said dismissively. "Where's the proof?"

"He told me of a deceit greater than we dared suspect," Donvin said, "of a plot so devious that we were caught completely unaware." He put a hand to the scar on his side. "He told me that the first attack against us by the coastmen was no accident, and no fluke."

Donvin surveyed his audience. Of all the lies he could have told them, he had chosen this one for its intrigue, and they seemed to be eating it up.

"It was part of a plan," Donvin said, "a plan to steal our power. And we, unwittingly, played right into their hands. Him most of all." He nodded to the body on the ground. "The coastmen knew that once attacked, we would gather to decide our response, and while we were distracted, it was all too easy for them to approach our forest undetected and steal its sap."

"Humph," Limp said. "All this on the word of a traitor?"

"I've seen the trees they tapped," Donvin answered. "I can take you there myself." There were such trees, of course: the ones from which he had drawn the vials for Elymia and the Aloise.

"But what of his lies?" Limp said. "What of his poisoned wine? There was no poison, it is a fact!"

Donvin nodded. "True," he said. "He did lie, but I know why. He discovered the truth of the coastmen's plot while investigating the 'poisoning' in Falls Gate. When he did, he was overcome with shame for having so easily fallen for their scheme. In his anger he lashed out, striking down the woman who had orchestrated the plan and a boy who defended her."

"So he did violate the code!" Limp declared gleefully.

Donvin just shook his head. "I can't imagine the agony he felt when he realized what he'd done, nor, I suspect, can the rest of you. Fearing for his own life, he hid his misdeeds from us. Yet even in his disgrace, he had our welfare at heart, and he was compelled to warn us of what he had discovered. To do it without betraying his greater transgressions, he lied about the poisoning in the hopes it would lead us to discover the truth for ourselves."

Donvin let his words sink in. "We all know what happened next," he said. "We turned on him. Rather than trust our own sworn brother, we let our feelings and our suspicions rule us. And when his one little lie was discovered, we felt our betrayal vindicated, and we condemned him."

Donvin pointed at the body on the ground. "Yet even then, even when we turned our backs on him, he did not turn his on us. He took it upon himself to do what he could. He went south, alone, to put an end to the coastmen's plot and take back our stolen power. When he came to me to confess, he was making ready to confront them. You see the result before you."

Masked faces turned from Donvin to the still form on the ground.

"I let him walk to his death alone," Donvin said, "because I did not trust him. He fought to the last, but many coastmen wield our power now." With great effort, he squeezed a tear out of one eye. "In the end, I watched as they held him down and killed him. I watched as they stripped him of his mask and furs and desecrated them in celebration. Only then did I believe. Only then did I realize it was my doubt, our doubt, that truly killed him."

He had them, Donvin thought as he listened to the sniffs and moans from the onlooking Masked. They believed him because he told them the easy story, the one they longed to hear: that while they might have their flaws, the Masked were still whole, still fighting on the side of good. Unfortunately for them, it simply wasn't true.

"This isn't our fault," growled Limp.

Donvin smiled. As ever, Limp was right on cue. If his story stabbed at all the Masked with feelings of guilt, surely it cut straight to Limp's heart. Limp, after all, had been the first to accuse Bird, never mind that Donvin had put him up to it.

"None of this would have happened if not for those cursed coastmen!" Limp spat. "It's not our fault, it's theirs!" The sniffles among the Masked quieted as they looked to the man who had established himself as the closest thing they had to a leader.

"It's always been them!" Limp seethed. "They fear us, attack us, deceive us, steal from us, and now murder us! All these years we've protected them, but they've made it plain they don't deserve our protection!"

A murmur of agreement passed among the Masked.

"If we've failed each other, it's because they made us this way!" Limp raged. "We honor the pact while they flout it! How can we be expected to endure the hardships we face when the people we serve show us nothing but contempt? Is it any wonder we lack trust when we're surrounded by hate wherever we go?"

"All they care about is what we can give them," Furrow's voice added from the crowd. "All they do is ask, and ask, and ask, and never once do they wonder what our service costs us!"

"They treat the Dedication like a holiday!" another man's voice called out. "They don't understand us at all!"

"We've been too kind! It's time they gave us some respect!"

"They've gone too far!"

"Punish them!"

Donvin felt like laughing. His part was done. Only one more voice needed to be heard, and then the preparation of the Masked for the slaughter would be complete.

"Stop this!" Boulder's voice roared over the rising din. "Control yourselves!" The voices quieted, and the crowd of Masked parted as Boulder's large frame moved toward the front.

"Listen to what you're saying!" he called out to them. "Why not think before you judge?"

"Think?" Limp asked. "What is there to think about? We all know what they've done, and what we have to do about it."

Boulder crossed his arms. "Yes, our power is no longer ours alone. But before we do something rash, ask yourselves: is that such a terrible thing?"

Limp sputtered. "It's in the hands of our enemies! They'll use it to destroy us!"

"Think," Boulder rumbled. "Where is it written that our task is to keep the power to ourselves for all time? We are preservers, not tyrants who horde the wealth of the world. You all think this is a tragedy, but perhaps it's an opportunity. This could be the beginning of a new partnership, a chance to come together for the sake of the world as equals, not as masters and servants.”

“He thinks the murder of our brother isn’t a tragedy!” Limp cried, and several jeers rose from the rest.

“Our brother died because he tried to take from the coastmen what they believe is theirs by right,” Boulder said. “But who’s to say they’re wrong? This power hasn’t always belonged only to us. We were the ones who took it from them, in the beginning!”

“Yes, to protect the world from their mistakes!” Limp shouted. “They were cruel and wicked then, and they are cruel and wicked now! Humans have always been the same, and always will be!”

“You speak as if we aren’t human too,” Boulder said.

“We aren’t!” Limp fumed. “Anyone can see that! We’re better than they are! We spend our whole lives learning to be better, to resist temptation, to sacrifice ourselves to the cause, and for what? To be looked down on! The people we serve certainly don’t think we’re human, and they’re right! But we’re more, not less, and I say it’s time they recognized it!”

Boulder fell silent, his shoulders slumping as more of the Masked cheered at Limp’s words. If Donvin could have felt emotions like sympathy, he would have felt for Boulder then. Rationality would never conquer emotion, not once the Masked had given themselves license to feel.

“Nothing more to say?” Limp jeered over the noise. “Then let’s put it to a vote! Who’s for taking back our power and teaching those miserable humans a lesson they can’t ignore?”

Fists rose into the air on a chorus of shouts. Not all the Masked cheered for Limp, but it was enough.

“This is wrong,” Boulder said. “You talk of killing those we are sworn to protect.”

“Only if they resist.” Limp said. “Without punishment, children never learn.” He raised his voice. “And who’s for letting those who kill us and steal from us keep their ill-gotten gains?”

A round of boos greeted the invitation.

“That’s what I thought,” Limp said.

Boulder hung his head. “Agreeing on a thing does not make it right.”

Limp ignored him. “It’s settled!” he cried. “Tonight, we prepare! Tomorrow, we go to Falls Gate!”

Donvin remained quiet in the eruption of shouts and cheers, offering a silent, mocking thanks to the body that lay neglected on the ground. Yes, he thought to himself. *Tomorrow you go to Falls Gate, and to your end.*

Chapter 39

A Soldier Again

The preparations were finished by midnight, but no one in the warehouse harbored any thoughts of sleep. The rebels huddled in circles among the crates and boxes, some talking, others just staring silently into a candle's lonesome flame. No one knew whether tomorrow would bring peace or war, and the prospect of having to fight once more was heavy on their minds.

Edwin sat on an overturned box, his sword across his knees, polishing the blade with a cloth. It felt odd not to hear the rattle of the chain that had bound the weapon to his arm. The steel bracer was still locked about his wrist, but its chain, broken by the monster wolf's jaws, was gone, leaving the sword unteathered.

Not being chained to the weapon meant that he no longer had any obligation to fight, Edwin realized. He could easily pass the blade to some enterprising youngster and walk away a free man. His hands, however, continued to polish the metal, which shone yellow-gold in the candles' soft light. Gold, like his sister's hair. Yes, the sword could still shine a bit brighter. It was not time to leave it behind just yet.

Close by, he heard hushed voices.

"Do you really think we can win?" a young voice whispered.

"Of course," a second said. "This is our city, isn't it? Everyone will join with us, and it'll be over in an hour, just watch."

"But what if . . . what if we have to fight the knights?" the first said worriedly.

"There aren't even that many of them. Even if we do meet them, they can't be that tough. We'll kill them just like all the rest!" the second boasted.

Edwin stood and rounded the boxes that separated him from the speakers.

"No, you won't," he said, resting his sword on his shoulder.

Five youthful faces turned to look up at him, the candlelight softening their features even more than their tender ages. They were armed with a haphazard array of weapons, some real, some improvised, but not one looked trained in their use.

"You don't have anything between you that could hurt a knight," Edwin said. "If you see one, run. Their armor makes them too slow to chase."

"Oh yeah?" one of the boys said. "How would you know?"

"Because," Edwin said, stepping closer so they could see his blade, "not even this sword can do that. They aren't called the invincible knights for nothing." He lowered the blade so the would-be warriors could gawk at it more closely.

"That's Lady Elymia's knight!" one of the two girls said, pointing excitedly at his face.

"Yeah!" one of the boys said. "My pa saw him fight the monsters at Crossing Grove!"

Edwin shook his head. "I'm not a knight."

"But you have a sword!" one of the boys exclaimed.

"You can tell us how to kill them! You know how, right?" another added.

Edwin gave them a grim look. "No. If you see a knight, throw down your weapon and run, just like I told you."

"But-!"

"The man's right," a deep voice said. A shadow congealed on the edge of the candle's glow into a large man with a maul slung over his shoulder. "Run like the serpent o' the sea were behind you, and don't look back for nothing."

The Wharfmaster gave Edwin a respectful nod before addressing the youths again. "Enough tongue-flapping. I want all of you at the perimeter guarding the exits. No one leaves here to spoil our surprise. Understand?"

"Yes, sir!" the children said in staggered echo, scrambling to stand and collect their weapons as they marched off at double time.

"They shouldn't even be here. How old are they?" Edwin asked the Wharfmaster, who was tall enough that the light of the candle barely reached his beard. "Where are their parents?"

"I don't expect you have as many years on them as you think," the Wharfmaster replied, settling his bulk onto one of the vacated seats. The maul he carried thudded to the ground, revealing itself to be his massive sea drum minus the strings, the same one that had ended the battle of Crossing Grove.

"They still shouldn't be fighting. It's not right," Edwin said.

The Wharfmaster looked sideways at Edwin. "That's not the sort of sentiment I'd have expected from one of your kind. I thought you were about trial by fire, burning the chaff, melting the slag, and all that rubbish. You yourself probably held a blade at a younger age than those little ones."

Edwin sat, laying his sword on the crate beside him. "Just because that's the Aloise way doesn't mean it's the right way."

"Ah, from the mouth of one who knows," the Wharfmaster said, nodding. "Well, if you can keep those young 'uns off the field tomorrow, then you'll be a master of more than just the sword. I doubt any force between here and the great deep could hold them back after what your people have done."

"Maybe so, but you didn't have to arm them," Edwin said.

The Wharfmaster stared at the candle. "You're a cold one, if you'd have them out on the killing field with nothing but slingshots and wooden swords. Better an arrow than a stone. Better a spear than a stick."

"That still doesn't make it right."

The Wharfmaster snorted a half-laugh. "Did I say it did? None of this is right, Edwin, not one damn bit of this whole business." He clasped his hands under his bearded chin. "I just want those children to live 'till suppertime tomorrow. If that means I have to put a spear in the hands of every babe not yet a year grown, tides help me, I will."

"Now who's the one sending the weak into the fire?" Edwin said softly.

The Wharfmaster smiled wryly. "Don't die tomorrow, Edwin," he said. "I'm beginning to like you enough to miss you." He reached out and snuffed the candle with his fingers, plunging them both into darkness.

Chapter 40

Dawn of the Day

The light of dawn sparkled on the freshly fallen snow between the rows of tents. Donvin inhaled the cold air deeply, letting his mind rest for a moment as he relished the breaking day. The sun shone and the wind blew just as on any other, but Donvin knew something that those eternal forces did not. This was his day, the day he had been born for, the day he would make his mark upon the world. Today would be the final day of the Masked, and the first day of his freedom.

Within the camp, the army of Falls Gate was making ready for war. Crossbows were strung and bolts gathered; spears were sharpened and armor donned. Donvin's keen ears heard no wasted movement, no idle chatter among the men, just the hum of a body working as one, their hearts set on a common goal. This was an important day for them as well, the day they would liberate their city or die trying.

"They'll be ready within the hour," a gruff voice said from behind.

Donvin nodded to acknowledge Gelavar Celundine's presence, though he did not turn. "Good," he said. "The path I promised you is quick, but not instant. The sooner you depart, the better. Have you erected the archway I requested?"

"It's done," the General said.

"Then show me," Donvin said. "If it's satisfactory, I'll prepare the way and leave you to use it as you wish."

"Of course," Gelavar said.

"And what of the weapons?" Donvin inquired.

"We have precious little steel," Gelavar answered. "Crossbows, however, we have aplenty. The archers will march at our head."

"As it must be," Donvin said. "But that alone is not enough. If the Masked are already in the city, then it will be too late to avoid battle. If you want your men to live, they must fire at the first sighting of the enemy. Surprise and numbers are your only advantage."

"They've been instructed," Gelavar said. "But they fight for their homes and their families. That is more than enough to ensure their aim is true."

"You had best pray that's so," Donvin said. "Now, take me to the gate."

Donvin followed the old man down into the camp, where black-armored soldiers paused to salute as they passed. They looked ready, like a hammer poised above the anvil. This army, the rebels, and the Aloise would come together with terrible force, and in the center would be the Masked, enemy of all and friend of none. Donvin's hammer would shatter them like glass, and the heat of his forge would melt away their remains.

Of course, no plan could be perfect. Most of the Masked would surely die within this trap he had prepared for them, but no doubt a few would escape, and he would have the pleasure of hunting them down personally. His spine tingled with anticipation. Today was his day, and it was going to be the greatest day of his life.

•••••

Edwin moved to the window of the burned out storefront and peered out at the crowd gathering in the cathedral square. The morning was windy and cold, threatening rain from a dense cover of clouds, but nevertheless they came. Hundreds streamed in from every direction, swarming about the foot of the scaffold that had been erected beside the square's dry fountain. For many, this was the first time they had been able to gather like this in weeks, and there was an undercurrent of energy that seemed strange, given they were there to witness an execution.

Withdrawing into the shadows, Edwin checked over his gear one last time, squinting at himself in a cracked mirror to ensure that everything looked just right. It would have to if he was to have any chance of reaching Remiana without being discovered.

The getup Edwin had put together was not perfect, but it was as good as he could have hoped. The key was his old steel helmet: even with the dent, its shape and shine were unmistakable, and it would draw the eye away from the imperfections in the rest of the disguise. Getting his hands on any more true steel armor had been out of the question, so Edwin had resorted to the next best thing: boras chit-iron plates covered with silver-gray paint. Though they were far too light and clicked rather than clanged together, the color was close enough to dust-covered steel that a glance from a distance was not likely to catch the difference. A large green cloak draped over the armor would protect it from too much scrutiny, and the sword strapped to his side was certainly real enough. All together, it would make him appear as a passable knight to anyone who did not look too closely.

Satisfied with his appearance, Edwin paced the confined space, his boots crunching through the mixture of ashes and glass on the floor. His steps did not ring out as true metal would have, but there was nothing he could do about it. Hopefully the noise of the crowd in the square would cover that small defect for him.

Elymia was probably already out there somewhere, though he had not been able to see her in the throng. Mae and Matrice and the others would not be far off, ready to defend her while she did what she had come to do. The fighters he had passed the night with would soon be taking up their positions around the city, ready to strike the Aloise positions at the stables, waterworks, and docks if the signal was given. Ely had stressed to them that a true victory would be one without resort to weapons, but Edwin doubted that was possible now. Things had come too far. From what Ables had reported, the Aloise troops would break and yield if Oridine fell, but they were far too scared of her and the rest of her clan to do anything but follow orders while an Aloise continued to issue them.

Through the window, movement atop the gates of the Keep caught Edwin's eye: soldiers manning the battlements overlooking the square. He took a deep breath and went to the door. It was time.

●●●●●

The gates were open, and Ely strained to see over the dense crowd while keeping her cloak's hood firmly in place. First out of the Keep were five ranks of soldiers with their black lances at attention, the white and gold of their uniforms bright against the dinginess of the onlookers' apparel. Ely could see apprehension in their eyes as they took in the size of the crowd.

Next came a grim-looking figure who could only be the executioner, garbed in concealing black from head to toe. A short axe of steel glittered in one hand. Despite the dark coverings and veil, Ely noticed that the executioner's posture was that of a woman - one of Oridine's Impelars, no doubt.

The executioner did not walk alone. At her side, dressed in his finest robes, strode Councilman Tulloch. Weeks of captivity had clearly not been so hard on him: his eyes were pinched, but he walked erect, his raiment spotless and long hair neatly bound. In his hands he clutched a parchment wrapped with crimson ribbon. It was he, then, who would pronounce the sentence. And there, following him, were Gerard Orndas and Tallomi Shima.

It was not betrayal that Ely felt, watching three of her city's councilors march with the Aloise. That had come before. Now all she felt was sadness.

The procession moved on. Tamalina came next, held up by a soldier at each elbow and trailed by a yellow-visored knight. Her feet dragged behind her on the cobbles, and a bag hid her hanging head.

Ely wanted to look away, but she forced her gaze to remain steady. This struggle was not just about her and her feelings, nor was it only about her friends. It was about the duty she had accepted, a duty to something greater than herself, and that duty demanded that she not shy away from the truth, no matter how much it hurt.

After Tamalina and her escort came more Aloise troops, and then the gates of the Keep ground shut. Ely had not seen whether Edwin had managed to slip through in the other direction, but she hoped he had.

The crowd made way as the procession approached the scaffold, the last scatterings of conversation dying as the executioner and her victim passed. The soldiers fanned out around the base of the platform, pushing the crowd back to clear a small ring around it.

Ely's eyes immediately sought out Matrice in the pack of bodies. She was at the very front, as close to the platform as possible, but the Aloise were not stupid: the cleared area around the scaffold was large enough to put it outside the reach of her powers, which meant that Ely would be on her own once she mounted those steps. She tried not to let that frighten her. Fear was a private luxury she could no longer afford.

Chapter 41

The Joined Battle

By the time Donvin returned to the forest, flecks of snow still dotting his moccasins, he found the huts empty, the fire pits vacant and cold.

"Beautiful, isn't it?" Lith mused, stepping from behind a tree. "Soon, no trace of them will remain. They will never return, and the forest will absorb every hint that they were ever here."

"As if the Masked cared about a few huts," Donvin said sarcastically. "It's the trees that matter to them, and those will stand for a long time to come."

"I should think you'd have them cut down, after all this is over," Lith said. "I doubt you'd want their power sowing any seeds that might one day grow to threaten you."

"I'll do whatever I please," Donvin replied, looking up at the Scarwoods' majestic height. "They're going to be mine. Everything will be mine."

"Indeed," Lith said. "Even what lies beyond the door."

Donvin's head jerked around. "What?" he demanded.

Lith laughed. "The door will open, when the Masked have fallen. Consider it a reward for a job well done. When they are gone, you will have your answers along with your freedom. But not before."

"Why tell me this now?" Donvin said suspiciously. "What's inside?"

Lith shook her head coyly. "I wouldn't want to spoil the surprise. You'll just have to wait and see."

With a flick of his will, Donvin opened a portal between the tree trunks. "Even if you told me, it would only be a lie."

She had toyed with him for the last time, Donvin decided. Letting her depart when this was over would be far too kind after all she had put him through. Once the Masked were eliminated, she would be next.

•••••

Edwin strode through the corridors of the Keep, measuring his pace to avoid drawing attention. The soldiers and servants spared him no more than a quick glance, for they were as preoccupied with what was going on outside as the crowd in the square. They could feel the tinder of anger that Oridine had been stacking against these ancient walls, and they feared that now she was preparing to strike a spark.

The Keep was a far different place from what Edwin remembered. The wall hangings now had a musty smell, and once pristine chambers were stamped with dirty footprints and stripped of valuables. Much of the rubble had been cleared from the halls, but twice Edwin found passages blocked by collapsed ceilings or floors. Bloodstains darkened the stones at more than one intersection.

In the end, the particular door Edwin was looking for was not hard to find, for it was the only one guarded by a knight. Edwin swore to himself and slowed when he saw the armored figure seated on a stool, white-visored helm resting beside him. It was Malbrand. The man was scratching his beard with one hand while the other drummed a clanging rhythm on his knee. A sheathed sword was belted to his waist, and the chain connecting it to his bracer rattled faintly.

Edwin hesitated a moment, for he held no grudge against Malbrand. In fact, he hardly knew the man at all. Even as knights they had never shared more than idle conversation. He didn't know if he had a wife back home, or a family. He didn't know whether he would flee to save his own skin or fight to the end even when all seemed lost. The latter, at least, he was about to find out.

Edwin was the only other person in the long hallway, so Malbrand noticed his approach quickly, and he studied the oncoming figure with puzzlement. Then his face darkened.

"Do you think that's funny?" Malbrand growled, rising with an angry clatter. "You've got some nerve, wearing a dead man's helm like that. If that's you, Van, so help me I'm going to break your neck a second time."

"Open the door," Edwin said, pitching his voice low and letting the helmet distort it beyond recognition. "The Mistress sent me directly. I have a message for her daughter." He came to a halt and drew himself up, hoping the extra inch or two he had on Malbrand would aid him.

"I don't care if the king himself sent you from beyond the grave," Malbrand said. "Nobody goes in. I don't know what you're trying to pull, wearing that armor, but . . . ." His eyes slid down to Edwin's breastplate the first time, and he recognized the fake instantly. His eyes widened, and in a second his sword was bare. "Assassin!" he spat.

Edwin drew his blade too, and it flashed a bright greeting to its twin in Malbrand's hands. "Open the door," he demanded. "I'm not here to kill anyone, and I don't want to fight you."

Malbrand shook his head, a grim smile on his face. "I told you, nobody goes in. Nobody." He nodded to Edwin's sword. "If you think a stolen helmet and some fake armor will let you wield that thing like a real knight, I'd be happy to show you how wrong you are."

It was a waste of precious time to speak further, so Edwin let his blade answer for him. He lunged, hoping to finish the fight quickly with a jab at Malbrand's unarmored head. The other man's sword came up in time to parry, but only just, and a look of surprise crossed Malbrand's face.

Edwin struck again, this time swinging for the neck. His sword whistled as it parted the air, singing as it rushed to meet its brother. Malbrand countered with a rigid block, realizing now that he was facing a man who knew how to handle his weapon. There was a ringing clash that buzzed up Edwin's arms, the swords crying out as they met.

Edwin straightened and stepped back, wary of engaging too closely. Malbrand's metal armor would give him an advantage if it came to grappling, and if they went to the ground it would be all too easy for the knight to crush Edwin beneath him.

Seeming to sense Edwin's thoughts, Malbrand stepped forward to follow him, keeping the distance short but making no move to strike. He knew he had the advantage now that their blades had crossed, since it was only a matter of time before others arrived to investigate the noise. Edwin tensed with frustration; did he have any chance of finishing off Malbrand, so heavily armored and no slouch with a blade, before more soldiers came to his aid?

The seconds slogged past, the two men staring at each other, neither blinking. Killing Malbrand was not his goal, Edwin reminded himself. He just needed to open that door, grab Remiana, and flee. If he could do that, the true knight's armor would let them outrun Malbrand's pursuit. Stealing a glance at the wooden portal the knight was guarding, Edwin noticed that it, like many of the others in the keep, was in a state of only partial repair. Thick ropes held it to its frame in place of finely carved hinges, and a deep crack ran down its middle. That gave him an idea.

Edwin renewed his attack with a shout and a wild overhanded chop. Malbrand blocked the blade, but it had its desired effect: he stepped back, in front of the door. Edwin followed, making the same attack a second time, hoping Malbrand would read the move as it came at him again. He did. Instead of blocking, Malbrand made the proper duelist's counter and simply sidestepped. The sharpened steel whistled past his ear, burying itself in the door's rope hinges and sticking there, leaving Edwin momentarily unable to guard.

"Big mistake," Malbrand growled. He countered, swinging his blade straight at Edwin's unprotected flank. Edwin prayed that boras plate was as strong as he hoped.

The steel bit deeply into the chit-iron, and Edwin's ribs howled at the force of the blow . . . . But there was no chill of metal meeting flesh, no rush of lifeblood spilling from the crack in his armor. The boras plates had protected him.

Malbrand looked perplexed, unable to understand why Edwin was still standing after taking a direct blow in anything less than full steel plate. He struggled to free his blade from the painted armor, but Edwin did not give him the chance. He let go of his own sword, grabbed the collar of Malbrand's breastplate with both hands, and shoved him into the door with all his strength.

The steel of Malbrand's armor hit the weakened door with the weight of two bodies behind it. The partially severed hinges gave way, the wood cracked, and the door toppled inward with the two struggling men atop it. Edwin's helmet came off and rolled across the rich red carpet, coming to rest at the foot of an immaculately made bed.

"Remiana!" Edwin shouted, his eyes searching the room as he held his arm across the sputtering Malbrand's throat. The place had been made up to look like her room in the tower, with the same desk and curtains even though this chamber was windowless. Everything was perfectly in its place, from the pens to the pillows, just as Remiana had always liked it. Only one thing was wrong: there was no one there.

"Ed?" Malbrand choked out in surprise. Edwin looked down at him, a sudden fear spiking through his heart. Had he come too late? He leaned down on the fallen knight harder, making Malbrand's eyes bulge.

"What have you done with her?!" he shouted. "Where is she?!"

Malbrand gargled something unintelligible, flecks of spittle spotting his beard.

"What did you say?" Edwin said, leaning closer and letting up just a little.

Malbrand rasped out his answer. "She's saving us."

•••••

"Behold the face of the criminal," Councilman Tulloch read from the parchment he held, and one of the soldiers lifted the bag from Tamalina's head. Her face was heavily bruised, with great dark patches around both eyes, and her short hair was tangled and matted with blood.

"The criminal, Tamalina Resposé, daughter and firstborn of Nantala Resposé, has earned the punishment of death for the following crimes," Tulloch read out, the wintery wind adding a hint of mist to his breath. "Cowardly murder of a soldier in the line of duty – three counts; attempted cowardly murder of a soldier in the line of duty – six counts; despicable maiming of a soldier in the line of duty – one count. . . ." The list went on and on. By the time he had finished, Ely's ears were growing numb despite her hood.

Tulloch rolled up the parchment. "The prisoner being guilty of the foregoing crimes, her sentence shall be carried out before you all as witnesses. Let this stand as warning to those who would disturb our precious peace." He looked to Gerard Orndas awkwardly, having reached the end of his script. Orndas and Shima, however, were silent, their presence merely symbolic.

The Aloise contingent knew what came next without prompting. The knight put his gauntleted hands on Tamalina's shoulders, forcing her to her knees. The executioner took a step forward.

"How do you know she's guilty, Mr. Tulloch?" Ely demanded, lowering her hood and raising her voice. She had spoken, and now there could be no turning back. There would be no more hiding, no more scampering from house to house, no more planning for some future day when they would win back the lives that had been taken from them. This was that day.

The people surrounding her stepped away, as if afraid of being condemned by association. Ely kept her gaze focused on Tulloch, and one by one the rest of the crowd began turning to him as well, awaiting an answer.

Tulloch looked around the platform for someone he might defer to, and his gaze settled on Orndas, a pleading look in his eyes. Orndas gave a slight nod, and Tulloch stepped back in relief. The executioner watched the exchange through her dark veil, making no move, yet, to carry out the sentence.

"Our Mistress of house Aloise has declared this woman guilty," Orndas intoned.

"I wasn't speaking to you," Ely said curtly, moving forward. The people made way for her. "I'm asking you, Mr. Tulloch, whether you know this woman to be guilty. I thought it was the declarator's job to speak no verdict he doesn't believe to be true, and announce no punishment he doesn't believe to be just?"

"Now look here, Elymia," Orndas said, "I will not allow you to disrupt-"

"We will have his answer now, please," Ely insisted, and a ripple passed outward through the crowd, a surface disturbance as something large in the depths began to stir. Whatever it was, Orndas could sense it, and he fell silent.

Tulloch looked uncomfortable at being singled out again. "This is not a trial," he answered, attempting to end the exchange there.

"Oh," Ely called back. "She already had her trial, then?" She could see Matrice just a few paces ahead of her, and the ring of soldiers just a bit beyond that. She continued her slow advance, choosing a path that would take her right beside her friend.

It was clear that Tulloch did not want to answer, but even he could sense that everyone, including the Aloise soldiers, were waiting on him. "She was declared guilty," Tulloch repeated, evading the question. "That means she's guilty. That is the iron law, and that is our law."

"No," Ely said, coming abreast of Matrice and signaling to her as she passed. "I don't think it is."

She continued to walk toward the guards and their ring of spears, but almost immediately felt a small flutter in her stomach as Matrice's power lifted her feet off the paving stones. Slowly, gracefully, she rose into the air, floated over the soldiers' heads, and settled back to the ground behind them, where she continued her stately progression as if nothing had happened.

The moment of flight had been so smooth and natural that no one thought to react before it was over. The soldiers stared at Ely with lowered jaws, as did Councilman Tulloch, but there was no panic, no rush for arms.

"Where is your wife, Mr. Tulloch?" Ely asked as she ascended the steps of the platform, mindful now that she was outside the reach of Matrice's power. From this point on, she had nothing to depend on but her words for protection.

"My wife . . . . My wife has nothing to do with this!" Tulloch insisted, looking to the soldiers as if wondering why they were not stopping her.

"That's not true, is it?" Ely said sympathetically. "Right now your wife is a prisoner of Oridine Aloise, just as you have been these past weeks, and she'll be killed if you don't play your part, isn't that right?"

"That's ridiculous!" Tulloch said, looking suddenly afraid. His eyes flicked nervously toward the Keep.

"And you two," Ely said, turning to Orndas and Shima. "What has Oridine offered you to pretend you believe in this farce?" Orndas's jaw worked, but no sound came out.

Ely shook her head. "It doesn't matter. You might think you can sell this city to the Aloise, but you can't sell them what you don't own." She looked out over the intently watching crowd. "You know this is wrong," she said, addressing them as much as the councilors. She saw hunger in them, the same hunger that had led her to accept the shadow's gift that she now realized she had never needed. The power that would cast off the Aloise was stronger than any born from a glass vial.

"You know this is wrong, but you do nothing to stop it. Why?" She looked down at the ring of soldiers, many of whom were looking back up at her. "Is it because you're afraid of death? Is it because the Aloise can't be beaten?" She paused. "I don't think that's why. This city has never lacked defenders willing to die for what's right." Her hand went to the back of her head where her mother's comb would have been. "I think you cower because you're afraid that if you stand, you will stand alone."

The crowd was held in thrall by her words, as were the soldiers.

"You can't be blamed," Ely continued. "Oridine is skilled at sowing fear. She attacked us when we were weak, with many of our leaders away fighting for a cause that she herself championed. She placates our Council with deceptions and empty promises, and uses our own people to confuse us." Ely pointed at Tulloch's chest. "She does these things because she knows that there is only one way we can defeat her, and it's the very thing she claims to bring us: unity."

Ely smiled. "But we are a free people. We know that true unity isn't about sharing a king, or a city, or a name. It isn't about borders, or taxes, or trade. It's about making a family greater than the one you were born to. It's about choice and honor. It's about knowing that when you stand, you will not stand alone."

As she spoke, Ely felt her fear fading away. It was only the fear of one woman, after all.

"I choose to believe that we of Falls Gate are more than strangers who share a city. I believe that even though my mother is dead and my father gone, I still have family here who would die for my sake, and I for theirs. It's a family I've made, not one that I was given. That's why I stand before you now, even though I'm afraid. I stand to show you that you are not alone.

There is room in this family for all of you, and I pledge myself to the last breath to anyone who chooses to stand with me."

Ely turned to face the shrouded executioner. "Tamalina Resposé is my family," she said, tears in her eyes. "So was her sister. So was her mother." She held her chin high. "The laws that govern us are the ones we choose, and it's by those laws and her own family that she'll be judged, not by you. I will not stand by while any more of my family are taken from me."

The executioner stepped toward her, but Ely did not back away. No suffering could be greater than losing more people she loved without a fight. The power she had hungered for was not the power to kill or destroy, she understood now. It was the power to stand and challenge the wrongs of the world, regardless of what came after. It was the power to be like her father, and like her mother before her. Its name was courage.

Ely prepared for the blow of the axe, but instead the executioner's hands went to her veil, lifting it like a receding stormcloud to reveal the shining gold of the sun beyond. Blonde curls tumbled out as the hood fell back, and amidst them two emerald eyes sparkled like perfectly cut gemstones, fierce and hard and bright.

"I would not take them from you, Elymia," Remiana said, "for they are my family too."

Chapter 42

The Hungry Dark

Ely could not hide her shock as Remiana revealed herself. By the look on the three councilors' faces, they had not known it was her under the executioner's garb either.

"I confess, I did not expect to find myself so upstaged," Remiana murmured, leaning close so only Ely could hear. Even here, of all places, with an axe in her hand and the cold wind tugging on her hair, she smelled of sweetness and fresh linens, that odor of perfection that had so burned Ely's nose when she had been forced to kneel before her.

"Upstaged?" Ely said, conscious of the crowd around them who had taken in this turn of events with uncertain eyes.

"I had prepared a speech," Remiana said, "But yours was superior, I think."

"It wasn't a speech," Ely said. "I said those things because I meant them."

Remiana smiled. "I am aware. And that is why my rehearsed words would be poor by comparison. I suppose I will just have to speak plainly, as you do."

"And say what?" Ely asked, but Remiana had already stepped past her to the edge of the scaffold.

"Know me!" Remiana proclaimed to the hundreds who filled the square below. "I am Remiana Aloise of the Iron Blood, daughter of Oridine Aloise and first heir to the house of my name. With you as my witnesses, I wish to swear an oath!"

At her beckoning, the yellow-visored knight offered her his sword hilt-first. She took it, then turned and offered it to Ely.

"No," Ely whispered when she realized what was being asked of her.

"Please," Remiana said.

"No," Ely repeated. Her neck was tingling, and memories of pain and helplessness assailed her.

"You make me beg, then," Remiana said. "It is your right." She dropped to her knees, bowing her head to Ely, still holding out the sword. "Please," she said again over the whispers of astonishment from the crowd as they saw the gesture of subservience. "Please let me make my peace. I ask this favor, though I have lost all right to call you friend."

"This is your way, not ours," Ely said, still unwilling to accept the blade. But then she looked to the faces in the crowd, every one of them full of amazement at what they were witnessing. They saw an Aloise, whose pride was the stuff of legends, placing herself at the mercy of one of their own. They saw an offering of trust, a glimmer of something new through the fog of hate that had choked them at every turn. They were watching Ely too, watching to see whether she would embrace that tiny light, or snuff its new-born glow under the sole of her boot. Once she saw the longing in their eyes, her own reservations dissolved like so much salt in the tide.

Ely gave a stiff nod. Her fingers wrapped around the leather-bound hilt, and she lifted the sword from Remiana's offering hands. It was heavier than she expected. Remiana bowed down with her face to the boards, and Ely extended her arms so that the suspended blade gently touched the back of her exposed neck, just as Remiana had done to her.

"Hear my oath!" Remiana said, nearly shouting so that her words would reach the ears of the crowd. "I swear under threat of death that I speak the truth."

She hesitated, the plain words she had promised to Ely taking some effort to find. "People of Falls Gate, I am the reason for your suffering," she said. "Your city was taken so that I, a woman, could make a claim to the throne of our lands." There was utter silence. Even the wind fell off, as if holding its breath.

Ely's arms were quivering from the weight of the sword. It was a deceptively hard position to hold, she was quickly realizing, but she dared not adjust her grip for fear of letting it slip.

"What has happened . . . what I allowed to happen, was wrong," Remiana said. "I was to be queen, but a queen must serve her people as much as they serve her. One who takes her throne by spilling the blood of her subjects has no right to rule them. Most of all, a queen must never let herself be shamed or threatened into silence in the face of wickedness. In each of these ways I have failed you, but I swear to you now that I will make amends. I will accept no throne won through your suffering or purchased with your pain. I will put an end to this unjust occupation. I will not be queen."

Beads of sweat gathered on Ely's brow as her arms burned with the strain of keeping the sword aloft. The hilt shook between her palms, and a spot of blood appeared on the back of Remiana's neck where the tip scraped her skin. Ely clenched her teeth and struggled against the pain, fearing the weapon would slip from her grasp at any second.

That was it, she realized with sudden clarity. That was the purpose of this ritual, of the oath under the sword. The blade was not only a threat for the swearer: it was a bond for the bearer. For every second Remiana spoke, it was Ely who had to fight to allow it. If she did not, the sword would fall. By holding the blade, she was preserving both oath and life, proclaiming her belief in them. In that way, she became a part of the swearing as much as the woman at her feet.

The strain brought tears to Ely's eyes, but she gripped the sword as if her life depended on it. *I do believe,* she thought. *For what this promise means to my people, I will never let go.* And she did not.

"You have heard my oath," Remiana said as a small trail of blood worked its way from her neck to her chin. "By the iron in my blood and the honor of my name, I will keep it." She moved her head to the side, and Ely let gravity finish its work and plunge the sword into the wooden planks at her feet. Her fingers were wracked with aches as she pried them free, but the pain was bearable now that she understood.

Remiana rose, wiping the blood from her chin and giving Ely a look of gratitude, and of respect.

"You have heard my oath," she said to the crowd, "now hear my orders to make good on it." She turned her gaze down to the ring of soldiers looking up at her. "I order all who are loyal to my name to lay down their weapons! We have no conflict with the people of this city!"

The soldiers looked at one another, then at their lances, and then at the crowd that surrounded them. Without their weapons, they would be torn to pieces if the onlookers turned hostile.

"You heard her, lay 'em down!" the knight beside Ely barked. He made a show of yanking his sword from the wood of the scaffold and laying it at Remiana's feet, which earned him an approving nod. It was enough. Seeing one of the knights obey, the other soldiers quickly followed suit. One by one, lances were lowered to the ground.

"I declare myself speaker for the house of Aloise," Remiana said to the soldiers. "My mother has proven herself unfit. Her actions have caused great damage to our honor, turned our family against itself, and put all our lives at risk. She is to be apprehended and brought before the family for judgment."

She turned toward the Keep and its massive gates, pointing at the gate-houses where guards could be seen peering from their high windows. "I order the gates be opened and Cliffhome Keep returned to its people!" she shouted. "I order all soldiers inside to lay down their weapons and make ready to depart in peace! I declare the city of Falls Gate to be free!"

There was noise then, wave after wave of it as the emotion that had been rising inside the crowd boiled over, shouts and howls and sobs of jubilation and relief. Gerard Orndas, his face wracked with fury, took an angry step toward Ely and Remiana, but that was as far as he got. Tallomi Shima, who had been standing quietly at his side, laid him low with a sharp elbow to the gut, dropping him with a grunt to his knees. Then she gave Ely a slow, deliberate nod, standing as tall as her slight frame would allow, before hauling the sputtering Orndas off the platform with a bewildered Tulloch trailing behind.

The outpouring of the crowd was thunderous, like nothing Ely had imagined. Even at her most optimistic, she had never expected anything like this. She had never expected to be helped in her cause by a woman for whom she had felt such violent hatred. She felt dazed, almost ill, yet delirious with relief. The time of bloodshed was finally past.

Then she remembered Tamalina. The woman, who had until moments before been a prisoner, still knelt, head sagging to her chest, oblivious to the incredible change that was happening around her. As Ely watched, the knight in the yellow visor put an arm around her and helped her to her feet, taking her toward the stairs down from the platform.

"She is drugged," Remiana said over the noise of celebration, noticing Ely's concern. "It would have been cruel to make her endure a march to her death when I had no intention of letting it happen, yet I could not risk telling her my plan. When she recovers, she will remember little." She squinted at Tamalina and the knight as they descended. "I have given up my right to judge her, but that does not mean she is worthy of forgiveness. That determination falls to you, and I do not envy you that."

"Nor will I enjoy it," Ely said softly. Victory, just like defeat, came with its price.

"But first, we must make this official," Remiana said, picking up the executioner's axe and offering it to Ely. "Take it, as a symbol of peace. No more shall our weapons fall upon your people."

Ely nodded. There would no doubt be documents to sign later, explanations and assurances and agreements. For now, however, the axe would do. Its surrender meant more to an Aloise than any markings of ink ever could.

Ely accepted the weapon with as much dignity as she could muster. No truce could be complete with the promises of only one side, however. Ceremony demanded that Ely offer something in return. Thankfully, she had just the thing.

From the pouch at her waist she produced a small glass vial, the same one she had carried for weeks, its stopper still fixed in place. She felt a strange pride now, as she held it out to Remiana, in the fact that she had never used it. One look at those emerald eyes told her she knew exactly what was being offered.

"Take it in peace," Ely said, "and know that our weapons too shall be still."

Remiana looked taken aback. "You would trust me with such power?"

"The price of peace is trust," Ely said. "I pay it gladly."

Remiana blinked and looked away. "I still do not understand you and your kind," she said. "You are my enemy, yet you offer so easily a trust I was refused even by my own-" She stopped herself short. Ely saw the pain behind those eyes, though Remiana was doing her best to hide it.

"I think you might still learn, someday," Ely said. "Someone told me that the two of us are very much alike."

Remiana's gaze returned to Ely. "Ed survived?" she said, suddenly intent. "Is he with you?"

"No," Ely said. "He's in the Keep, trying to rescue you."

"Peak-blasted fool!" Remiana cursed. "He should have known I could manage my own affairs! There will likely be some men who stay loyal to my mother, and he's gone and put himself in the thick of them. Idiot!"

Ely gave a crooked smile. "We agree on one point, at least. Now take this damn vial already so we can see about getting him out. We're going to need him and every last soldier you have if a certain Masked decides our truce isn't to his liking."

"Very well," Remiana said, resuming her formal tone. "With this, our truce is made, Elymia Celundine. May it last a thousand years." She reached out to take the vial from Ely's hand.

Without warning there was a roar, sharper and harsher than the merry noises of the crowd. The boards trembled beneath Ely's feet, and a gale crashed into her with the force of a winter squall. On the edge of that devilish wind hovered a faint, twisted odor that Ely had smelled once before. She cried out as her hand ignited with pain, and the vial she held shattered in an explosion of acid and glass.

"You should have bloody told me in the first place!" Edwin shouted at Malbrand as he slammed the door behind him.

"And you shouldn't have hidden your damned face!" Malbrand answered, panting as he helped Edwin hold it shut against their pursuers' assaults.

"I was wearing my own blasted helmet, wasn't I?" Edwin retaliated, grunting as the door took another heavy hit. He glanced around the room, but saw nothing that would help to brace it. The chamber had the look of long disuse, containing nothing but a dusty, rolled up carpet under the west-facing window. What was worse, it had no other doors.

"We thought you were dead!" Malbrand protested, his metal boots searching for traction against the floor. "How was I to know it was you?"

"I met with Ables twice in the last week!" Edwin shouted, venting his frustration at the man beside him. "That topic never came up, did it?"

"Ables wasn't a part of this," Malbrand growled, wincing as the beatings from the other side of the door intensified. "He was at Crossing Grove, and half those men have lost their marbles since. We couldn't risk having him go off his rocker and spill the whole thing!"

"I was there too!" Edwin yelled indignantly.

Malbrand's laugh dripped with sarcasm. "And look how bloody sane you are!"

Edwin had no response for that.

Outside the room's lone window, the crowd in the square was still roaring with noise, the same sound that had interrupted Malbrand's explanation after Edwin had finally realized he was not an enemy. Not but a minute later, a full squad of soldiers had shown up at Remiana's room, and they were not in the mood to talk. A short, hectic melee later, Edwin and Malbrand had found themselves fleeing for their lives from the troops who were clearly still loyal to Oridine. Whatever had happened out there to stir up the crowd like that, Remiana's plan was obviously secret no more.

"You said you have allies among the troops," Edwin said over the pounding on the door. "Any chance they could help us out of here?"

"I said we have some, not a bleeding army," Malbrand said. "We'd have more if the rest could see that the knights are siding with your cousin, but I can't damned well show them while we're stuck in here. My job was to lead anyone who would follow and detain Oridine, but you've pretty well botched that plan, haven't you?"

"It wasn't supposed to be like this!" Edwin said. "I didnt-"

There was a hideous roar, and the glass from the window blew inward, spraying the two armored figures with razor shards. The whole Keep vibrated with a deep thud, and the noise of the crowd suddenly morphed from a triumphant cheer into a howl of fear. The pounding on the door halted.

Edwin turned slowly toward the destroyed window, the wind that had forced its way through rustling his cloak with its dying breath. What it left behind was a smell. A horribly familiar smell. He took a step toward the glassless opening.

"What are you doing?" hissed Malbrand, still bracing the door.

Edwin reached the window and looked out. "Oh gods," he whispered.

•••••

Donvin grinned as he gazed down from the highest of Cliffhome Keep's towers, the sea wind tousling his hair as he watched the beautiful chaos unfold below him. The people seemed so small, no larger than ants swarming about after he had kicked their nest. The Masked too looked tiny, fragile, and so very few. The ring they formed around the crowd, despite being nearly a hundred bodies strong, looked thin and weak, a leather noose trying to encircle the raging sea.

"It's almost over," Lith said, stepping up to the brink and peering over the edge.

"Yes," Donvin said, "thanks to me." Even from such a great height, his keen vision let him pick out individuals, and he watched Limp climbing the stairs to the platform that the Masked had cleaved with their power. The two women with the vial of Scarwood sap, which had been the object of the attack, still lived, and they were beginning to stir from where the blast had knocked them down.

Donvin lifted one hand and pointed, and a portal opened itself at the northern end of the square, just outside the ring of Masked. It was time to introduce the next player into his pageant of death.

"Will you miss them, when they're gone?" Lith asked as more tiny figures, these ones covered in dark armor, poured out of the fresh gateway.

Donvin just laughed. What an absurd question that was.

Chapter 43
The Pride of Ants

Ely's eyes fluttered open. The first thing that reached her was the noise: the screams she heard before blacking out were still fresh in her ears, and new ones hit her like continuously breaking waves. She must have been unconscious for only a few seconds.

Next came the pain, rushing in when she tried to move. So much pain! The right half of her body was on fire, dotted with tiny coals burning under her skin. Her right hand also felt somehow wrong, but she hurt too much to distinguish that sensation from all the rest.

Blurred colors condensed back into images, though the things she saw did not seem real. The scaffold was sheared in half not a few inches from where she lay, ruptured in a line of splinters like the wounded earth after a quake. Whatever did it it had sundered the paving stones of the square just as easily. Bodies lay along the trench's sides, though unconscious or dead she could not tell. Around them, others screamed as they tried to flee the packed square. Over everything hung that awful, rancid smell.

"Get up, Elymia!" said a voice beside her. Ely saw Remiana clambering to her feet, her black garments shredded by shards of glass. A red blotch stood out on her left cheek, a burn from the vial that had shattered between them. Far worse, Ely noted with shock, her left sleeve ended in emptiness. Blood dripped from the cuff in a quick, regular rhythm.

"Get up!" Remiana repeated, seizing Ely by the collar with her good hand. Ely cried out as Remiana hauled her to her feet, but her legs held despite the pain. She looked down at herself, terrified by what she might see.

The right half of her body was embedded with bits of glass, and much of her arm and leg burned by Scarwood sap. A hot pounding had begun behind her eyes, and she had a sudden flash of Matrice convulsing pitifully, rendered so helpless by the sap that she had been unable even to cry out in pain. Ely reached out to Remiana's shoulders to steady herself, but doing so brought another shock: the last two fingers of her right hand, the one that had held the vial, were missing.

"We must flee!" Remiana shouted at her. "Can you walk?" She had lost her hand, and still she was more concerned about Ely than about herself.

"You aren't going anywhere, you most wretched of mankind," a strange voice said.

Onto the broken platform mounted a bark-masked figure, the shadows in his eye slits full of menace. He moved with uneven steps, favoring one leg as he drew closer.

"You have broken the pact," he said. "You have touched the sap of the tree of ruin. Already it acts upon you, poisoning your minds against us. Already it spurs you to war and murder, toward a repetition of the suffering that we exist to prevent. That poison must be purged now, before it spreads. For your own good, you must be destroyed."

•••••

"Open the door? Are you crazy?" Malbrand said, refusing to budge.

"Look outside," Edwin said. "Oridine's troops have bigger things to worry about now than a couple of rogue knights."

Malbrand looked unconvinced, but the hammering on the door had indeed ceased. Reluctantly, he went over to the window and had a look for himself.

"Snowspit!" Malbrand swore, gazing out on the scene in the square. "Masked! And those black soldiers . . . ."

"Falls Gate men," Edwin said, tapping on his own armor with his knuckles. "Boras plate is what they're wearing, just like this stuff, before I painted it."

Malbrand swore again. "They were supposed to be hundreds of miles away!"

Edwin shrugged. "They're here now. And best be thankful too, else we'd be facing those Masked alone."

Malbrand's face was awash with disbelief. "The Masked . . . . Why in the blazes are they getting involved?"

"Crossing Grove, for starters," Edwin said as he cracked the door and peered out. The corridor was empty. "But that's not the real reason, though I'll be damned if I know what it is." He wondered if even Ely really knew why all this was happening.

"So what the hell are we supposed to do?" Malbrand said.

"We follow orders," Edwin said, opening the door wider. "We still have a mission to finish."

Malbrand raised his bushy eyebrows. "What's this 'we' you're talking? I thought you were here for your cousin?"

"My first attempt didn't do much to help her," Edwin said. He felt a pang of regret as he glanced toward the broken window. Remiana was out there somewhere, probably fighting just to stay alive between the Masked, the rebels, and now the Falls Gate army, but there was no way for him to find her. He was going to have to trust her to take care of herself.

Malbrand rubbed the bruise on his neck. "Damn right it didn't," he muttered.

"The best I can do now is make sure the orders she gave are carried out," Edwin said, "and that means we're in this together."

"Suit yourself," Malbrand said, "but it ain't going to be easy."

"No," Edwin said, drawing his sword, "but dealing with Oridine never was."

•••••

Remiana stepped in front of Ely, scooping up the steel-headed axe from the ground.

"Stay back!" she warned, pointing the weapon at the Masked who threatened them. "We have no quarrel with you!"

"Your greed and your pride are our quarrel," the masked man snarled. "Was it not enough that your ancestors doomed our world once? When faced with extinction, the way of the Mask saved us, and all mankind agreed that our power must belong to no man, but only to the Mask. Yet now you flaunt the wisdom of a hundred generations, and for what?" He pointed at the steel in Remiana's hand. "All you've done is use it to make war, just as it happened before. And just as before, it's up to us, the Masked, to save you from yourselves."

"No!" Ely exclaimed. "We didn't want this! We were deceived!"

"You were human," the masked man said coldly. "That was enough. This is not a matter of guilt or innocence, of right or wrong. It's a matter of survival. For this world to survive, our power must be contained, and you must die." The masked man lifted his hands toward them, and Remiana readied her axe.

"How can you say this isn't about right and wrong?" a rumbling voice challenged. A second, larger Masked ascended the platform, his steps vi-

387

brating the wood. "You can't escape responsibility that easily. We have a choice, even if you refuse to see it."

"This isn't the time for your damned philosophy!" the first Masked said, whirling. "The vote was had, and you lost. Now do your duty! Kill these humans before they kill us all!"

"No," the heavyset Masked answered in a growl. "We're just as flawed as they are. The only difference is that we're better at hiding it. If they should die for being touched by the tree, then so should we."

"You're mad!" the Masked with the limp spat. "They're nothing more than children playing with fire!"

"If we're so much better," the large Masked said, gesturing to the chaos around them, "then how has it come to this? Why couldn't we stop it?"

"We are stopping it!" the first Masked raged. "Right here, right now!"

"All we're doing is making ourselves murderers," the large Masked said, "and that I cannot do. We have no right, because our guardianship is a lie. We may treat the symptoms of the world's ill, but we are not its cure, and year after year our efforts only hasten its death. Is our monopoly on such paltry treatment worth the blood you're about to spill?"

"That's nonsense!" the other Masked cried. "Blasphemy!"

"I would rather speak the blasphemous truth than a pious lie," the large Masked said. "Such is my right. Did you not say that we must act as our duty compels us?"

Ely thought she could hear the first Masked's teeth grinding.

"My duty is to stop this massacre," the large Masked said. "I will not let you kill these people."

The limping Masked quivered with rage. "Then you will die with them, traitor!"

They lunged at one another, arms raised, the air between them boiling with warring energies. Then there was a noise, a hissing that Ely and Remiana recognized in unison.

"Down!" they yelled together, dropping to the ground as a flight of crossbow bolts zipped around them. Many shot harmlessly overhead, but some found their targets, punching through the heavy robes of both struggling Masked, who were too focused on one another to have sensed them. The grappling figures stumbled and fell from the platform to the stones below, dropping out of Ely's sight.

An explosion rocked the northern part of the square, from the same direction as the bolts, and the damaged platform shuddered under Ely's prone body. When the worst had passed, she lifted her head and looked north. Black-armored soldiers were pouring into the square and unleashing salvo after salvo at any Masked they could see, while the Masked were wasting no time in fighting back. As she watched, a second explosion tore the face off a three story building, spraying the soldiers with chunks of flying rock and enveloping them all in a swirling cloud of dust.

Ely lowered her head back to the rough boards, and she felt a wetness trickling down onto her cheeks. She had been wrong. She had prayed that when her father finally came home, he would be greeted by a city stronger than the one he had left, whole and proud despite its scars. But it was too late for that now. The army of Falls Gate had indeed come home, but all that waited to greet them was war.

•••••

Donvin strolled through the streets, soaking in the pandemonium. The road he walked was far removed from the epicenter of violence, but its symptoms were everywhere. Armed civilians dashed across his path, some equipped well enough to be with the rebels, but most carrying nothing more than broom handles or kitchen knives. Most fled at the sight of him, and the few who did not quickly became crimson stains upon the cobbles. There was little joy in killing such feeble creatures, however. It was the Masked who were his true targets. Should any try to escape the battle, he would be waiting for them. In the meantime, however, there was one last place he wanted to visit.

"The stables?" Lith said to him as she stepped around the remains of a bow-wielding rebel who had thought he was faster on the draw than Donvin. "For what purpose?"

"To add a dash more fuel to the fire," Donvin said, spotting the tall silos over the rooftops to the east.

Lith attempted to hide a smile. "That's my Donvin, always the clever one."

"Don't start sounding proud," Donvin said in disgust. "You're not my mother."

"Not of your flesh, certainly," Lith agreed, leaving the rest unspoken.

Donvin snorted. He only had to put up with her a little while longer.

They were roughly halfway to the stables when a familiar scent reached Donvin's nostrils, making him draw up short in the middle of the street. It was a smell that made his hands tingle with anticipation. It was the smell of his mentor.

A moment later, three haggard-looking Masked, rather than the one he had been expecting, stumbled out from a shadowed alleyway. Donvin's mentor was not among them.

"Which way did he go?" the first in the group said worriedly, looking up and down the street and spotting Donvin. "Hey!" he called out. "Did one of us pass this way?"

Donvin shook his head, approaching the three on a hunter's deliberate feet. How fortunate that they had gathered for him like this.

"He said he could lead us to safety! Are you sure you haven't seen him?" the second Masked, a woman, said.

Donvin grinned. Perhaps it was not fortune alone that had presented him with this gift. "You've reached your destination," he said, silvery threads uncoiling like razor whips from his body, "but I'm afraid you'll find no safety here."

•••••

When Donvin and Lith arrived at the stables after their short delay, they found they were not the only ones who had sought them out. The outer wall was breached in several places, and within the yard rebel fighters were locked in a deadly struggle against a contingent of Aloise troops defending the main building. Bowmen rained arrows from the roof while the soldiers below tried to hold their ground with spears, but the rebels outnumbered them at least five to one. The fences that had once divided the yard were smashed, and the soil had been churned to mud by the shifting lines of battle.

Donvin walked blithely into the center of the melee, going largely unnoticed in the fighting. One of the archers on the rooftop made a foolish attempt to fell him with an arrow, but Donvin caught the shaft with his threads and sent it shooting back to its source, knocking its owner clean off the roof. He marched right through the line of Aloise spearmen unchallenged, for those near enough to notice were either too surprised or too scared to stop him. The sliding doors of the stable building slammed open at his command, and he entered unopposed.

The last time he had been there, the place had been orderly and clean. What a difference a few short weeks could make. The smell of dung was so thick it was choking, and the floor was filthy with the stuff. The door to every stall in the whole building was rumbling as the creatures inside rammed against them, driven into a frenzy by confinement and hunger . . . or perhaps by something else.

"The beras aren't merely a gift of the pact, are they?" Donvin said to Lith.

"Perceptive," Lith said. "Though they are indeed a part of it, compensation for the pledge not to contest the Masked's stewardship. They gave the people a way to sustain themselves without turning to the power for their every need like they once did."

"But that's not all, is it?" Donvin said. "That doesn't explain why the Masked still inspect them at Dedication."

"It's tradition," Lith suggested coyly. "Isn't that reason enough?"

"No," Donvin replied. "The Masked have existed too long for that. All traditions that served no purpose must have died out long ago. Everything they do now, they do for a reason, even if they don't understand it."

Lith nodded slightly. "So what do you suppose the beras truly are?"

"Insurance," Donvin said.

Lith laughed with delight. "Please, go on," she said.

"I've seen the way they react to the power," Donvin said. "That's no coincidence. I think the Masked made the beras to be everything the people needed, but they also made them a weapon, one that could live undetected among the people in times of peace, yet should the pact be broken, one that would turn on its violators without warning."

Lith clapped her hands approvingly. "My, my, I had no idea you were so observant." She paused. "There is no record of such a plot, no rumor of it, not even among the Masked."

"Of course not," Donvin said. "Only a fool would have left a trace."

Lith smiled "We were many things, back then, but we were not fools." She turned her hands upward in a gesture of regret. "Alas, I'm sorry to say that the idea was not my own."

"I'm surprised," Donvin said. "It seems cowardly and manipulative enough to be yours. I suppose this was just one more thing you didn't deem important enough to tell me?"

"Now, now, a general never reveals all her strength at once," Lith said. "Had you needed an additional weapon, I would have offered it. Consider it a mark of praise that I did not."

"I'm flattered," Donvin said sarcastically. "But today is our final battle." In unison, the doors of the stalls burst open. "What good is a weapon that never sees use?"

Chapter 44

Call to the Forge

Ely knelt with Remiana against the inside of the fountain's wall, the trickle of water that remained at the bottom wetting her knees through her bloodied leggings.

"We can't stay here," she said breathlessly as arrows and rocks pinged off the fountain and whizzed overhead. "There won't be anything left of the whole square if the Masked keep at it like this."

"There is nowhere to go," Remiana said, leaning heavily against the fountain's side. "All the streets are cut off."

Ely risked a quick glimpse over the top of the wall, trying not to look at the mess of bodies that littered the ground. What she saw, however, gave her little hope.

The Masked seemed to be everywhere, their powers turning paving stones and streetlamps into missiles. The Falls Gate troops were firing and retreating, doing their best to stay out of range of the worst the Masked could do while still containing them within the square. The strategy had been largely successful, though judging by the occasional explosion that sounded in the distance, at least some of the Masked had taken the battle elsewhere. The constant exchange of fire riddled the open ground with a hail of deadly projectiles, and most of the civilians trapped between the two forces had already fallen.

"I know it doesn't look good," Ely said, "but we have to chance it. You're not in any shape to be waiting here for . . . ." She trailed off as she saw Remiana's face. It was even paler than usual, and she was slumping against the wall more than a moment before. A small pool of blood was forming beneath her handless left arm.

"Damn it," Ely said, reaching over to feel Remiana's pulse and finding it weak and racing. "We don't have time to argue! We need to get you help!"

"No," Remiana said, shaking her head weakly. "We must stay here, where it is safe."

"It's not safe!" Ely exclaimed. "If we wait any longer, you'll . . . you'll . . ."

"Die?" Remiana said, her green eyes catching Ely's. "Wounds like this bleed swiftly, Elymia. Even under good care, losing a hand can be fatal. On the battlefield, it's a rule." She lifted her eyes to the sky and the clouds that refused to release their rain. "It seems as though the gods have a sense of justice after all. Or perhaps a sense of humor."

"Stop it," Ely said tearfully. "Please, save your strength." How recently had it been that she had wished to see Remiana die in front of her? How had she not realized, even then, that having such a wish come true would be so painful?

"Will you do something for me?" Remiana asked calmly. "Please tell Edwin that I am sorry . . . for everything. Tell him that we are still family, no matter what my mother says."

Ely nodded, unable to stop her tears from overflowing and running down her cheeks.

"You need not cry for me, Elymia," Remiana said softly. "My people think battle is a noble end."

Ely hung her head. "But do you?" she asked in a whisper.

Remiana smiled. "You say such strange things, Elymia," she murmured, "stranger even than the rest of your people. I suppose that is why I always liked you." Her eyelids fluttered and drifted shut.

"Please, don't die!" Ely cried out, throwing her arms around Remiana's body. "I'm sorry! I should have trusted you! I shouldn't have let this happen! I . . . ! I . . . !" She choked on her sobs. Remiana couldn't die. She had always been so strong, far stronger than Ely would ever be. It was impossible that she could die while Ely still lived.

A flying hunk of stone knocked the head off the statue in the fountain's center, but Ely did not even wince. All she could feel was a crippling ache. This battle would be over soon enough, but there would be no victor. Not even the ghosts of the dead would be sated, knowing the awful price paid to avenge them. And worst of all, much of the blame was hers.

"You did what you thought was right," a woman's voice said from behind her, startling her with its closeness. "No human can know the future, Elymia. You should not blame yourself for that."

Ely turned her head. Through her tears, she saw a dark haired woman in a green dress standing upright in the fountain, paying no mind to the arrows that hissed through the air around her.

"You can feel it, can't you?" the stranger said. "That agony of losing and finding and losing again. That anguish of knowing that you have played a part in bringing about untold suffering."

"Who . . . who are you?" Ely said.

"A messenger," the dark-haired woman replied. "I am here to tell you that your part is not yet finished, Elymia. This world has need of your pain, and of your forgiveness. He has need of them."

There was no doubt who the woman meant. Ely remembered the boy beyond that strange steel door, the boy whose words refused to leave her mind.

"Soon it will be time for him to make a choice, a choice that will bring him pain worse than even you can imagine," the woman said. "And when he does, you must be there, Elymia. You must help him make his choice. Because just a little, you understand."

There was a sudden roar as one of the buildings at the edge of the square collapsed, and the cries of the soldiers within were silenced in an instant.

"Why should I?" Ely asked, feeling Remiana's head loll against her neck. "Why should I ever leave this place? I helped make this happen. I deserve to die here."

"Because not all the gods are cruel, Ely," the stranger said. "Some of them know mercy." She reached out and lightly placed a finger on Ely's forehead.

Ely gasped as she felt something shift inside her mind, a subtle reordering that made the world seem just a little clearer. The burns on her arm and leg pulsed with her heartbeat, but their pain receded, as did the ache behind her eyes.

"My child gave you the gift of destruction," the strange woman said. "Now let me teach you of restoration. The future will have need of both."

There was knowledge in Ely's mind that had not been there before, but it felt natural, right, as if it had always been a part of her. She realized suddenly that she could hear the beating of a heart other than her own. Remiana's. It was faint, but it was there.

What she had to do came as second nature. She saw beautiful silver threads blossom from her skin and grow into Remiana's body, feeding it with the warmth of their light. She felt them binding up Remiana's wounds like bandages of the softest silk, massaging her heart back to life and calling rivers of blood into the dry banks of her veins.

Remiana suddenly jerked upright, shoving Ely away as her eyes flew open and her hand grabbed at her chest in panic. The silver threads withdrew, their glow fading to nothing.

"What in all the deeps was that?" Remiana said. Ely flung herself shamelessly on her, weeping now for relief.

"Thank you," she whispered. "Thank you." She loosened her grip on Remiana and turned to the strange woman who could only be one of the divine, but she was gone.

It was then that Ely heard an odd clattering sound, distant but getting closer. Remiana must have sensed it too, for her look of bewilderment quickly turned to concern. Together, they slowly lifted their heads above the lip of the fountain, wondering what new terror this day could possibly bring. They did not have to wonder for long.

Into the square burst a living tide of insectoid bodies, their thrashing horns as fearsome as any sword. The clattering grew to a roar as they advanced, the sound of their armored legs striking the paving stones as they ran.

The fighting in the square halted, men and Masked alike struck dumb. The beras were ordinarily so placid that it was difficult for them to accept what they were seeing, and perhaps it was that confusion that stopped the first of the soldiers from getting out of the way.

That proved to be a fatal mistake. Even the smallest of the beras weighed hundreds of pounds, and they were moving with incredible momentum. Instead of halting, the animals merely rolled over anyone in their path, crushing men's bodies like living battering rams. Only then did the others begin to flee.

Ely looked down at the wall sheltering her and Remiana. It was nearly two feet thick, but against what was coming, it might as well have been made of paper.

"Run." Ely said as the beasts thundered across the square toward them. "Run!"

Remiana needed no convincing. There was color in her face again as she easily vaulted the wall and helped Ely to follow.

Behind them, the beras charged on, swarming toward the first of the many Masked who dotted the square. One of the beasts was cut to pieces by whips of silver force, but more crashed over their fallen comrade. Seeing he was outmatched, the Masked barely had time to turn to flee before one of the beasts speared him from behind on its giant horn, lifted the body and tossed it backwards into the swarm of shells and stamping legs.

"We have to get inside!" Remiana shouted, but Ely knew that would be futile. Somewhere in her new knowledge resided the fact that the beras were enraged by the use of the Masked's power, the same power she had just used to save Remiana's life. The residue would be on both of them, and the frenzied beras would sense it. They had to get far, far away, somewhere the beras could not reach. Once again, inexplicably, she knew what to do.

"Find a doorway!" she panted, "Any doorway!"

They had nearly reached the southern edge of the square, the rolling wave of beras close behind and gaining. Ahead lay the royal bank, its facade marked by marble columns that, so far, remained undamaged. Beyond them, tall doors stood slightly ajar.

"Too big!" Ely yelled as Remiana tried to guide her toward them. The lintel was well over ten feet up, much too high to reach.

"Are you mad?" Remiana replied. "We will be safe there!"

Ely, however, spied a smaller side entrance and dragged Remiana toward it, using the remaining fingers on her injured hand to open the bag at her hip. It felt empty now that the vial was gone, but she knew that it was not. She probed about inside and finally seized upon the broken tooth of her mother's comb.

Remiana gave up her protestations long enough to try the smaller door's latch, but the stout timber was barred from the other side and would not yield, not even to the vicious kick she gave it.

"Stand back," Ely said, placing the piece of bone against the bottom corner of the doorframe. She held the fragment firmly, knowing now how precious it was. It was a thing out of place, still bound to the remainder of the larger whole, which made it easy to find and manipulate those connections . . . . Ely tried not to let the racing of such foreign thoughts frighten her. As quickly as she could, she traced the frame of the door. She did not know precisely what she was doing, but whatever it was, it felt right, and her gut told her it meant escape. A faint silver glow remained in the wake of her tracing, like moonlight on a restless sea.

"What are you doing?" Remiana said, her voice nearing panic as the crush of beras came closer, smashing through the fountain where they had been hiding. Evidently she could not see what Ely could.

"I'm getting us out of here," Ely said. She touched the bone fragment to the lintel, and a thousand radiant filaments poured down from the tiny white tooth, hanging like a curtain over the closed door.

"It's done," she said, grabbing Remiana by the arm. "Let's go."

"But the door is closed!" Remiana said, resisting Ely's pull.

Over Remiana's shoulder, Ely could see that the beras were no more than a few seconds away.

"Do you trust me?" Ely said.

Remiana spoke without hesitation. "You have held the sword for me, and I for you. There is no greater trust."

"Then trust me now," Ely said. "Close your eyes, if it helps."

Remiana smirked, a strange expression with the deadly horns of the beras so close. "You know me better than that, Elymia." Eyes open, she walked purposefully into the closed door . . . and vanished.

Ely did not close her eyes either as she followed, for the filaments of light that wrapped themselves around her were far too wondrous. Time seemed to slow as the silver curtain gathered her up in its arms, and then, moments before the impact of the beras brought the bank's columns crashing down, she was gone.

•••••

Donvin paced in front of the steel door, leaning into the foul wind that was trying so hard to pick him up and hurl him down into the limitless depths. The door's surface was warped, small cracks appearing even as he watched.

"Soon now," Lith said, sitting cross-legged on the lumpy stones a few paces away.

"How long?" Donvin demanded.

"There is no rush. Take a moment to enjoy this, my Donvin," Lith said. "This is your triumph. I'm sure that must make you feel something?"

"How long?" Donvin repeated. His longing to know what lay beyond was a physical burning in his chest.

Lith sighed. "Of course you can't appreciate it," she said. "In you, there is only hunger. No matter what you achieve, you will never find contentment. That is how it had to be."

"Stop your blabbering and answer me. How long?" Donvin said.

"Until the last of the Masked are gone?" Lith said. "Minutes, perhaps, or hours. Not long, in any case." There was a pinging sound as another crack appeared in the metal.

Donvin continued his pacing. "You told me it would open. I should be out there hunting Masked, not waiting around here!"

"And it will," Lith said. "Have a bit of patience. I have waited far longer than you have."

Donvin kept his silence, but he also kept moving. He did not care to stand still in that place. When he did, the vile smell seemed to grow even more powerful, bearing down on him in a way that excited a primal urge to flee. There was no doubt it had grown stronger, many times stronger, since his first trip through that place-between-places. He could almost feel whatever was causing it hovering over his shoulder, drawing ever closer. Donvin shuddered, turned on his heel, and paced back the other way.

Chapter 45

Giants

"Forget it, Ed, she's not here!" Malbrand said as the Keep gave another weak rumble. "We have to get out while we can!"

Edwin spun around, eyes narrowed and searching, but Oridine's luxurious bedchamber was as empty as before. She was nowhere to be found.

"He's right, sir!" one of the soldiers who had joined them chimed in, saluting Edwin with his spear. "If the bracings on the core supports beneath the tower fail, the whole thing could come down." The stones shuddered again as he spoke, as if expressing their agreement.

Edwin turned reluctantly to leave, the taste of defeat sour in his mouth, but something made him hesitate. He looked back one more time at the large bed, the chests of drawers, the carved stones of the fireplace, and the thick rug, but none of it looked out of place. What was it about this room that was bothering him?

"Come on, Ed," Malbrand said with a touch more sympathy. "There's no more time. Your cousin wouldn't want you to throw your life away for nothing."

Edwin knew the danger. War of the worst kind was raging just outside the walls, ready at any moment to bury them under a mountain of rubble if they stayed a moment too long. Even inside his helmet, his face was covered with the mortar dust that was leaking ominously from the ceilings, and the smell of soot from the fires outside seared his nostrils with every breath . . . .

Edwin froze. This bedchamber had no windows. That smell couldn't be coming from outside.

Lifting his visor, Edwin stepped over to the fireplace and knelt down, sniffing the air. Something had recently disturbed the ashes within, enough to fill the entire room with their scent. At the edges, clear as day, he saw a set of handprints.

"There's a passage here," Edwin said with sudden conviction. He reached out and tested the stones of the fireplace's rear wall, but they were solid. The sides also felt immovable, and a glance up the darkened flue revealed it to be too narrow to climb. He could feel the seconds slipping away. If Oridine had escaped from this room, each moment he wasted put her farther ahead.

Malbrand shook his head as he watched Edwin crawl partway into the fireplace. Then he raised his voice so that the soldiers waiting outside in the hall could hear. "It's not safe to stay here. You men go and join up with Lady Remiana if you can. Tell her that her cousin still lives. Got that?"

Most of the Aloise troops were eager to obey, but one of the younger ones hesitated. "And you, sir?" the remaining soldier asked.

"Someone has to stick around to keep this fool alive," Malbrand said, jerking his thumb toward Edwin's backside sticking out of the fireplace. "Now go. You're needed out there more than in here."

The soldier nodded. "May the gods meet you with joy," he said. Then he turned and ran.

Malbrand spat a curse. "I'm not planning to die, you idiot!" he shouted after the departing soldier, but he was already gone.

"If that's true," Edwin said, coughing as he found the edges of the false bottom under the ashes and hauled it out of the fireplace, "then you had best not follow me. This passage looks darker than a mine, and narrow. We'll be helpless if there's an ambush at the bottom."

"You talk like I've got a choice," Malbrand grumbled, walking over and peering down at the darkened hole and the rope ladder that disappeared into it. "Remiana would skin me alive if she found out I let you out of my sight."

"Then let's get going," Edwin said, shedding his gauntlets to better grip the rungs.

It was indeed dark in the narrow hole, and the descent was not a short one. They were well below ground level, by Edwin's estimate, when his foot reached down for the next rung and hit a dirt floor instead.

"Hold up," Edwin called up to Malbrand. "I've found the bottom."

"Yell it a bit louder, will you?" Malbrand hissed back. "Are you trying to let her know we're following?" Edwin held his tongue, reaching out in the darkness to feel the way forward. They should count themselves lucky if Oridine was still close enough to hear.

Though Edwin could not see a thing at the bottom of the pit, that did not worry him. He had navigated mines far worse than this. Unlike the wandering layout of a mine's intersecting shafts and passages, bolt holes like this were designed for one purpose: leading straight to a safe exit.

As he suspected, Edwin felt solid walls on three sides and an empty space dead ahead. The opening faced due south, toward the water. The docks, he realized. It was the only logical place for an escape route to lead. If the city were under seige, the best chance of escape would be by water.

"Leave your armor," Edwin said as Malbrand dropped from the ladder. "She's far ahead of us. We'll have to run if we want to catch her."

"You must be joking," Malbrand said, but Edwin was already unbuckling his own battered breastplate.

"I don't know which one of us is madder," Malbrand muttered in the darkness, reaching for the clasps on his pauldrons.

The two men quickly stripped their outer layers of armor, dropping the pieces into a heap on the bare floor. It felt good to be able to move freely again, but Edwin took only a moment to savor it. Then, they ran.

The floor beneath their feet was well graded, and no ledges or bumps rose up to trip them in the dark. Edwin ran with arms out to his sides, letting his fingers scrape along the walls in search of tributary passages, but he felt none. The tunnel continued southward, straight as an arrow, and soon they were far from the Keep, somewhere between its walls and the high southern cliffs that faced onto the ocean.

A faint rumbling reached them through the thick rock, and Edwin called a brief halt.

"Thunder?" Malbrand panted from behind him.

The clouds had indeed looked ripe for rain before they had ventured below ground, but Edwin doubted it. In the absolute darkness, his mind was quick to conjure a hundred forms of destruction that that would make such a noise, and always he saw Remiana's face among the victims. Sometimes Ely's was there too.

"Come on," Edwin said, blinking the visions away. Whatever was going on outside, there was nothing they could do about it until they found an exit.

They ran for several minutes more, following the passage as it curved gently to the right. At first Edwin thought it was his imagination that it was growing slowly brighter, but soon the grayish light coming from ahead was impossible to ignore. A minute more, the end of the tunnel loomed before them. A vertical slit in the wall stood open, hardly larger than a man, and through it Edwin could see the ashen sky.

Though the dark passageway had brought them all the way to the seaside cliffs, it had hardly descended at all, and through the crack Edwin was able to look down upon the docks below from a dizzying height. Yet even from such a great distance, it was not hard to make out what was happening.

At least half the ships were aflame, sending up columns of oily smoke as their hulls burned. On the docks themselves, tiny figures were locked in battle, rebels struggling to breach the Aloises' defensive lines.

Edwin searched the melee below, trying to discern what the Aloise troops were defending, but a roll of thunder-that-was-not-thunder put the question to rest. The muzzles of six cannons on the largest ship in port, docked in the farthest berth, gushed mouthfuls of flame, and a moment later a section of the docks erupted with the force of a volcano, throwing splinters and rebel bodies into the air. Through the clouds of smoke that poured off the now silent muzzles, Edwin could make out a figure in red upon the deck of the massive ship.

"That's not one of ours," Malbrand said, looking down at the vessel. A blue and white Falls Gate flag fluttered from its highest spar.

"No," Edwin said, "but it's the one Oridine's taking." There was no mistaking the Falls Gatekeeper, whose cannons had been promised to Jonner Ceer in addition to Edwin's armor.

It was easy to see why Oridine had chosen as she had. The transport ships that had carried Edwin and the other Aloise soldiers were not built for battle, and in any case it looked as if most of them were either at the bottom of the harbor or well on their way. It only made sense that Oridine would commandeer the most battle ready ship she could for making her escape. Yet that choice was also probably why she was still in port. Her men were readying to sail an unfamiliar vessel, one that required a larger crew than they were used to.

"I don't envy those rebels down there," Malbrand said, "being blasted to pieces by their own ship."

Just then, as they were observing the battle from above, something dark whipped past the opening in the cliff face.

"The hell was that?" Malbrand exclaimed, drawing back.

Edwin leaned forward and eased his head out of the crack.

"It's our ride," he said.

The wind carried the dangling rope back toward him, and Edwin stretched out his arm to catch it, but it swung beyond his reach. Looking down, he could see that the rope, as well as several others, dangled all the way from the top of the cliff to the lifts at the bottom. The Aloise troops must have severed them at their base to keep the lifts from being pulled back up.

"You're not seriously thinking about what I think you are?" Malbrand said.

"We've got to get down there somehow," Edwin said, bracing himself and waiting for the wind to bring the rope back. "Complain to Oridine if you think she should have left the lifts working for us."

The rope swung back toward Edwin, and he leaned out as far as he could without falling and snatched it.

"Here," he said, dragging it partway inside the tunnel and handing it to Malbrand. "Hold it steady while I slide down, then I'll secure it at the bottom for you."

Malbrand's face looked decidedly green, but he just swallowed and nodded.

Edwin leaned out over the void and looked down again. The rope was swaying less now, but it was still a long way down.

"Be careful," Malbrand said gruffly. "I don't want to be fishing your body out of the bay."

"I'll be fine," Edwin said with more confidence than he felt. "Just don't let go."

Malbrand gave him a sarcastic salute, which Edwin returned in kind. Then, holding the rope in both hands, he steeled his nerves and stepped out into the air.

His grip slipped as soon as his full weight was on the rope, and he plummeted twenty feet before he managed to get his legs wrapped around it and stop himself. He dangled there for several seconds, waiting for his stomach to settle, but every instinct was telling him to hurry. There was no telling when Oridine would be ready to sail, and then she would be as good as gone.

Easing his grip, Edwin slid another ten feet, and then another, his gloves and leggings warming from the friction. He glanced down at the staggering distance beneath him, beginning to appreciate what he had gotten himself into.

The wind shifted direction, peppering Edwin with spray from Cliffdiver Falls and making him shiver. The waterfall gushed off the cliffs half a span beyond the end of the docks, but its great size and roar made it feel much closer. There was another set of docks on the far side, Edwin knew, but they were wholly obscured by the falls.

Below, Edwin saw a tendril of seawater rise and wrap itself around one of the remaining Aloise transports. It crushed the ship about the middle, crumpling timbers and beams like parchment before dragging it down into the depths, the few men still aboard leaping from the deck as it went down.

Then it was gone, leaving nothing but a froth of bubbles on the surface. There was no question it was the work of the Masked.

Edwin hastened his slide. Every second put Oridine closer to her escape, and if she managed that . . . . He did not want to dwell on the consequences. If Remiana did not emerge from this day the decisive victor, it would mean civil war, with his sister on one side and her mother on the other.

Another cannonade roared its battle cry. Five of the cannonballs crashed through the docks below him, sending up geysers through the holes they tore in the wood. The sixth, off target, impacted high on the cliff above, raining down shards of stone that whirred as they passed him.

Then the rope gave a nerve-wracking jolt, and Edwin's heart leapt into his throat. He did not need to look up to guess what damage those flying chunks of rock had done. He slid as fast as he dared, praying the rope would hold long enough for him to get down. The docks were so close!

Then the rope snapped. So much for Malbrand following, Edwin thought with black humor. Hell, he's probably relieved. Gravity took over, and he fell, flailing, the remainder of the way to the docks below.

Edwin crashed through the roof of one of the passenger lifts, splintering its support poles and collapsing the whole contraption around him. He hit something yielding beneath, cushioning the impact enough to keep him in one piece. When he groaned and rolled over, the pair of white-uniformed legs sticking out from under the collapsed roof told him what it had been.

The sounds of battle were all around him now, men shouting and bowstrings twanging, and Edwin stumbled to his feet, trying to clear his head. He was not dead yet, and he still had a job to do. He stepped around a stack of crabbing boxes only to come face-to-face with a bark mask.

For a second, Edwin's heart stopped beating. Then his muscles moved without thought, tearing his sword from its sheath at the same moment the Masked reached out for his chest. Time slowed. Edwin imagined he could see the terrible energies crackling among those calloused fingertips preparing to rip through his body. His sword moved as if through water, aiming for the thin patch of flesh connecting the mask to the hairy robes beneath. He could not guess whether he would live long enough to see it connect.

"Stop!" a woman's voice shrieked. Time snapped back into place.

The sword came to a halt against the Masked's exposed neck. Five powerful fingertips hesitated as they dug into Edwin's jerkin.

"Stop!" the voice cried out again, its agony so sharp that Edwin understood why he had been compelled to listen. He turned his head and saw a second Masked just a few feet away.

"Please, don't," the female Masked pleaded, hands outstretched pleadingly. "Please, let us go. We just want to go." Her voice rasped painfully in Edwin's ears. Blood streaked her furs, and she listed to one side, barely able to stand.

The Masked under Edwin's blade looked to her as well. "We have to destroy them," he growled. "They can't be spared after what they've done!" His mask was unusual, Edwin noticed, for a crack that ran between the eyes . . . .

"Even if you have to die to make it so?" the female Masked asked. "Even if I have to die?"

"We have to protect the pact. We have to protect the world!"

Edwin shook his head slightly. It couldn't be the same one from way back then. It couldn't possibly.

The masked woman lowered her pleading hands. "I would not see you die," she murmured. "Not even for the pact. Not even for the world."

Edwin remained still, watching.

"It's blasphemy, I know," the woman whispered. "But it's true. I don't care any more that it's wrong. I don't want to die without saying it." She lifted up her hands and pulled the mask from her face. Behind it, two gray eyes stared out over wan cheeks at the masked man before her. A line of crusted blood ran from the corner of her mouth to her chin.

"I love you," she said. "I don't even know your name, but I love you. Is that foolish?"

The man in the cracked mask was silent, frozen.

"I don't want this fight," the woman said, letting her mask slip from her hands. "I don't want this code, or even this world, if it means I'll lose you." Her eyes shimmered with sorrow, and with hope. "If we have to die, I don't want to leave this life without having seen your face."

"We can't," he said, his voice barely audible. "We mustn't."

"You have a choice," the woman said. "We all do, and it can't be taken away unless we let it." She stepped forward and cupped the masked man's bark face in her hands.

For a moment it seemed he might pull away, but he did not. Instead, he lowered his hand from Edwin's chest and used it to brush away the blood from the woman's mouth. She smiled and her eyes watered, the two of them seeming to forget that they stood in the midst of a battlefield.

"I knew," the masked man said gently. "I knew how you felt, how I felt . . . . But still, we must defend the code. If we don't, the others will know too, and then . . . ." He trailed off. "Even living as we have been is better than death."

"The others?" the woman said, looking around. "What others?" She gestured to the burning ships, the smoke, and the bodies. "This is the end of the Masked. But that doesn't mean we have to die with them. We can leave it all behind." She nodded to her mask, discarded on the ground.

The masked man sounded uncertain. "I don't know if I can."

"You already have," the woman said. She took his hands in hers and placed them on the edges of his mask. "This is nothing more than wood, and we are nothing more than people. We hurt, and we love, and we cry. Hiding it doesn't make us better. All it does is waste our lives, alone."

The masked man's grip tightened on the sides of his bark face. "Will you come with me?" he said.

She smiled. "Anywhere."

The masked man bowed his head. Then the cracked mask lifted away from his face, and Edwin let the tip of his sword slide to the ground. He was witnessing something incredible, something no other man in living memory had seen. He was seeing the true death of a Masked.

The mask hit the ground and split along the crack that had already divided it. The face it had hidden was also marked with a long scar, but its brown eyes glowed with hope.

The woman turned to Edwin. "Thank you," she said. "Thank you."

Edwin opened his mouth, but could find nothing to say. What could he, who was just a man, say to those who had been so much more and chosen to give it up? He watched as the scarred man put his arm around the woman's shoulders and they walked, supporting one another, away from the fighting. He found himself hoping they would be safe.

A flash of white caught Edwin's eye, and he turned in dismay to see an array of gleaming sails unfurl down the Falls Gatekeeper's mighty masts. He had lost too much time. The ship was about to leave, and the docks between them were still a killing field of flying arrows, swinging blades, and shattered decking. Even so, he was not yet ready to concede defeat.

With few options left, he eyed the sloshing water in the closest berth. Compared to the path over the docks, the path to the Gatekeeper through the water was positively clear.

He stripped off his gloves and his boots, the last two bits of clothing he could afford to leave behind, and made sure his belt was secure. Then, taking a deep breath and regretting ever having found that hidden passage in the fireplace, he plunged headfirst into the water.

The cold sank its bitter claws into him as soon as he broke the surface, but he forced his arms and legs to start moving. Stroke and kick. Stroke and kick. He had learned to swim in the high lakes, so his muscles remembered the cold as much as they did the motions. The water was ice on his eyeballs, but he kept them open anyway, wary of the debris that floated around him. Much of the remnants of the destroyed ships had gone to the bottom, but plenty of broken boards and scraps of sail lingered near the surface.

Edwin stayed underwater for as long as his lungs could endure to avoid being seen, but he need not have worried. When he did come up for air, he surfaced in the midst of a clump of floating bodies that had collected in a corner between two piers. The rebels and Aloise paid no heed to one more head bobbing in the tide, and they did not notice when it vanished again.

Each time he surfaced, Edwin checked the position of the Falls Gatekeeper. It had begun to move away from its mooring, but its great bulk made it slow. He struggled to swim faster, fighting the numbness that was settling into his limbs, knowing that they would not be able to tolerate those temperatures much longer.

Increasingly exhausted, Edwin had drawn to within a few strokes of the Gatekeeper's hull when he felt something tangle about his leg. He gave an extra hard kick, but whatever it was held fast, wrapping itself around his sword as well. Cursing, he floundered the remaining few feet to the side of the ship and grabbed on to a trailing rope. The crew was either very small or very inexperienced to have left the lines dragging, but Edwin was more than willing to take advantage. With great effort he hauled himself out of the water by his arms.

Dangling from the rope, his feet skimming the surface of the water as the ship churned along, Edwin saw what had snagged him. It was a sizable piece of cloth, mostly white with gold markings: an Aloise flag, probably from one of the sunken transports. Edwin felt the urge to laugh. It seemed fitting that even the flags of his former house would be trying to kill him.

He tried to kick the offending thing off, but it was wrapped too tightly. Unable to both hold on to the rope and untangle the flag, he had no choice but to ignore it for the moment, hauling its waterlogged weight up to the deck along with him.

The line he had caught was trailing from the prow, and it was toward the prow he now climbed, hand over agonizing hand. He was nearly to the top when a man's voice rose in alarm from above. They've seen me, he thought in panic.

Then a body flew over the rail, over Edwin's head and at least thirty feet through the air before splashing down into the water.

"Enemy aboard! Enemy aboard!" More voices took up the cry. "To arms! Protect the cabin!"

Edwin pulled himself over the gunwales and rolled onto the deck, arms burning and legs aching. Two more Aloise soldiers screamed as they were propelled overboard, and Edwin looked about for the other infiltrator who was causing the commotion. She was not hard to find.

"Come out, you cowards!" Mae shouted as she strode down the deck, leaving a trail of wet footprints that led back to the anchor line. Like Edwin, she was soaked through, her hair hanging in a slick mass between her shoulders and her leathers clinging to her body. A dagger was in her hand, but it was not her weapon of choice.

"Come out!" she shouted again, using her powers to launch another Aloise soldier into the sea. The deck was virtually empty save for her and Edwin, most of the troops having either been forcefully disembarked or fleeing belowdecks. Two soldiers atop the sterncastle took aim with crossbows, but Mae dodged behind a mast and their bolts thudded harmlessly into the wood.

"What're you doing?" Edwin shouted at her, finally freeing himself from the Aloise flag and getting to his feet.

Mae turned in surprise, but as ever, she recovered quickly. "Oridine's in there!" she shouted back, pointing to the captain's cabin. "But don't even think about it! She's mine!"

"Don't waste your time!" Edwin yelled. "Just blow up the damn masts!" He pointed at the four tree-trunk-sized pillars that were supporting the sails. Without them, the ship would be dead in the water, along with Oridine's hopes of escape.

Mae opened her mouth to argue, but the look on her face said she knew his was the better idea. Even if the two of them couldn't kill or capture her, stalling Oridine would let someone else catch up and finish the job.

"Fine," she said haughtily, "but this doesn't mean I'm taking orders from-"

Her words were drowned out by a loud crack. A section of decking erupted as something powerful thrust its way up from belowdecks, spraying splinters and dust that forced Edwin to cover his face. He lowered his arms just in time to see the curved blade of a scythe hissing toward his neck.

With no time to draw his sword, Edwin stepped back, but he slipped on the Aloise flag at his feet. He went down hard on his back as the scythe whipped through the air above him.

When his eyes refocused after the jarring fall, he found the red-clad Impelar standing over him, the point of her weapon hanging a hair above his face. Even through her veil, Edwin could see that she was smiling with glee. Mae, on the other hand, was nowhere to be seen.

"We meet again," the Impelar said, pressing his cheek with her scythe so that he had to turn his head to the side. "I always knew there was something off about you." She smirked. "It's a stain on the good name of the Impelars, the keepers of order in the house, when a bastard like you escapes the blade. At least now I can remedy that mistake."

Edwin groped for the hilt of his sword, but the Impelar's boot came down bruisingly on his knuckles.

"You're a skilled fighter," she said, "but scum like you don't deserve a fair fight. I'm going to cut your throat, just as it should have been when you were born."

Edwin tried to look up at her, but she forced his head back down with her blade. The boards pushed the impression of their grain into the side of his face, and his damp, salt-stiffened hair fell into his eyes.

"You should have died in the dark, never seeing the one who came to take your life," the Impelar sneered. "You have no right to look at me as I take it now." Her scythe pricked his cheek, sending a drop of hot blood running toward his ear.

Though Edwin tried to muster the energy to struggle, his limbs were leaden, cold, and worn to the point of uselessness. Unable to even lift his head, he stared at the rail of the ship. It was too high to see over the top, but through a drainage slot at the base he could see the rippling waters of the ocean reflecting the dense clouds overhead. A bit farther off, the spray from Cliffdiver Falls created a vertical column of mist, a hazy pillar that would have been sparkling with rainbows on a brighter day. It was certainly a more comforting view than the one his infant brother had when the Impelars had come for him all those years ago. Yet in the end, after twenty years of hiding, pretending, and lying, the only difference between them was that Edwin could look at the sea as he died.

The sea . . . and something else. Emerging from behind the curtain of falling water, Edwin saw something darker. A ship? A moment later a sail came into view, and then another, and another. It was not just any ship, but a large one – possibly as large as the one he was on. Atop its masts, the blue eagle of Falls Gate fluttered proudly over the six cannon bays that dotted its side.

Edwin looked out of the corner of his eye, but the Impelar standing over him, for whatever reason, had not moved. He could barely see her, but high above he could make out the flapping of the Falls Gate flag on their own ship's mast. He also saw a hint of another, more human kind of movement in the rigging.

The Impelar lifted her nose, sniffing at the air as if suddenly catching a whiff of something other than the brine of the sea.

"Lost your nerve?" Edwin taunted her from the corner of his mouth. "If you're going to do it, just get it over with. Do you bore everyone you kill like this?"

The distraction worked. "You'll get your wish soon enough, bastard," the Impelar said. "I only wish to give the Mistress a chance to witness your death for herself. And look, your wait is nearly over."

A door squeaked in the direction of the sterncastle, out of Edwin's line of sight, and he heard footsteps approaching.

"Good work," Oridine's voice said. "Show me his face."

The Impelar turned Edwin's head so that he was staring straight at his captors. Oridine's face was gaunt, but as imperious as ever, while the Impelar's was unabashedly smug. But more interesting than the two women staring down at him was the one above them: Mae, moving slowly through the rigging toward a position directly over their heads. He wanted to smile, but he dared not.

"After all these years, I am still cleaning up the filth my husband left behind," Oridine said with disgust. "It is a good thing he did not live to see what sort of disgrace his spawn would become. It would have been better if he had not lived to sire you at all, but it took his infidelity to show me how unfit he was to be the first among our clan. I suppose that makes it your fault, then, that he had to die." She tilted her head in amusement. "If not for you, Remiana might have known her father."

Edwin snarled and tried to rise, but the Impelar's scythe forced him back down.

"He should never have let you live, no matter his humiliation at having accidentally ordered the death of a trueborn," Oridine went on, "but he feared having his mistake revealed. And look at the result! You have corrupted his only trueborn child, and my only daughter!"

Pinned as he was, only seconds from death, the fear that had kept Edwin silent his whole life no longer had any hold over him. Even if he was trapped, his tongue was free. "It wasn't me who did that to her," he said. "I wasn't the one who taught her to seek power over compassion. I didn't force her to live in fear of disgracing her name, or show her the only way to honor it was with blood. You should be pleased with what she's done. You've finally made her into a true Aloise."

"Ill-bred dog!" Oridine cursed, kicking Edwin in the ribs. "I am the Aloise matriarch, and you are lower than an ant! How dare you speak to me that way?"

Edwin's back arched from the pain, but he smiled. "Why not?" he said. "You're not my mother, thank the gods."

Oridine, livid, reached for the Impelar's scythe, but it was at that moment Mae struck. She plunged from the rigging, dagger in hand, aiming for the other two women's backs.

The Impelar's heightened senses must have alerted her, but she could not move quickly enough. She spun, the haft of her scythe knocking the dagger from Mae's hand, but that did nothing to stop her from crashing down on her targets, sending all three of them to the ground.

Edwin's hand was suddenly free of the Impelar's boot, and he reached out again, but not for his sword. His fingers closed around the white cloth of the Aloise flag, and he pulled himself up and staggered toward the ship's central mast. The other vessel he had glimpsed was nearer now, near enough for him to catch flashes of iridescence off the helmets of the crew. She looked almost identical to the Gatekeeper, right down to her devastating armaments. This, then, could only be the Falls Guardian, and she was in the hands of her true owners.

When he reached the mast, Edwin spared a glance back for Mae. He was just in time to see her plant her fist into the downed Impelar's face. Then she turned her attention to Oridine, who was trying to crawl away on her hands and knees.

Edwin found what he was looking for on the mast easily. The ropes that controlled the flags formed a loop around two pulleys so that pulling on one side caused the other to rise. Edwin tied the flag he held to the right rope, seized the left, and drew his sword.

Mae was kneeling over Oridine, her hands wrapped around the fallen woman's throat, so intent that she did not hear Edwin the first time he called out to her.

"What?" she snapped as he called again. "I'm going to kill her! You can't stop me!"

"You need to jump," Edwin shouted. "If you want to live, you need to jump. Now!"

Mae looked up at him, rage twisting her face. For a moment, it seemed as if she was blind with hate, unwilling or unable to understand what he was trying to tell her. Then she saw the flag, the sword, and the other ship over his shoulder, and she understood. She released Oridine and threw herself toward the nearest railing.

Oridine coughed, spitting a mouthful of blood onto the deck.

"Cowards!" she shrieked. "You run because you know you can't win! The Aloise can't be defeated! We rule this world!"

Edwin shook his head. "You always said the Aloise were giants, but there's one thing a giant can never do."

"And what's that, you miserable ant?" Oridine spat at him.

"Hide." With one stroke of his sword Edwin severed the rope below where he held it, ran to the edge of the deck, and leapt overboard. As he plunged toward the water, the Aloise flag on the rope's other end shot up the mast.

Edwin hit the surface with a deafening splash, and for a moment he was blind. After the water had closed over his head and its churning subsided, he turned over, suspended and weightless, to face the sky. The white and gold flag was waving boldly over the ship, defiant to the end, as befitting an Aloise. For a moment, everything was calm. Then came the roar.

Six cannonballs from the Guardian tore through the Gatekeeper's upper decks. Splinters rained down over Edwin's head, each one creating a tiny ripple across the image of the ship above. The forward mast teetered and fell with a great crack, hanging over the side and dragging its sail awkwardly in the water. The rear mast soon followed, falling backward to crash into the sterncastle with a muffled boom.

Edwin's lungs burned, and he came up for air just as the Falls Guardian unleashed a second cannonade, this one ripping into the Gatekeeper's mid-section at the water line. The sea bled in through the gaping wounds, and within seconds the ship was splitting apart, its fore and aft divided by a growing vertical crack.

Edwin tread water, unable to turn away as the once proud vessel fractured and sank beneath the waves. It took only minutes. At the end, the gold iron-smith's hammer on white fabric was the only thing that protruded above the waves, and then it too was claimed by the sea.

Chapter 46
The Tree of Ruin

Remiana's eyes widened in wonder despite the harsh glare and the hideous wind.

"Incredible," she said, taking in the white bridge and the endless sky. "I would never have believed such a place could exist."

"It doesn't," Ely said, trying not to think about how she knew. "Not really." In the distance, several tiny shapes were moving against the horizon. She caught a flash of green and red, the colors of the goddess who had appeared to her. She was being called.

"Lith," Ely whispered, then touched a hand to her mouth in surprise.

"What did you say?" Remiana said.

"Lith," Ely repeated. "She's the reason we're here, and she's calling me." She lifted her uninjured hand and pointed. "Out there, by the door to-" The words cut off as pain lanced through her head. There was a memory there, nestled in with the other foreign thoughts, but it was shrouded by a haze of harsh emotions.

The sky was lit by a flash like lightning. With it traveled a mighty groaning, the strained vocalizations of a sleeper greeting the unwelcome day.

"Did you see that?" Remiana exclaimed.

"It's opening," Ely breathed with awe and terror she could not explain. "Gods help us, it's opening."

•••••

Golden light oozed like blood from the cracks in the door as Donvin slammed his fist into it a third time, finally feeling it give.

Lith watched him with crossed arms, then turned her dark gaze to the empty sky, a wistful look crossing her normally impassive face. "It was a pretty fantasy, while it lasted," she said.

Donvin struck the steel one last time, his fist punching through with a mighty rip. A wash of light gushed around his arm, forced out by a pressure no longer held at bay. Donvin was forced to shut his eyes against the brilliance, the force of it so strong that it brought him to his knees.

Then, as quickly as it had washed over him, the torrent of light rippled out and was gone over the horizon. When he opened his eyes, however, it was as if he were seeing a different world.

"Now there is something I have not seen in a long, long time," Lith said. "I had almost forgotten how it felt."

While the bridge remained the same, everything around it had changed. Gone was the clear, sunless sky. In its place, millions of white bridges crisscrossed the air from horizon to horizon, layers upon layers of them ascending into the heavens without end. The scale of it was incomprehensible. The tangle just went on, and on, and on, paths connecting places so distant the whole of time itself would not be long enough to reach them.

In that gargantuan sky, Donvin was able to read a message that required no learning to understand. It carried a meaning unmistakable to any creature possessed of the glittering spark of life. You are small.

After everything he had accomplished, after everything he could ever hope to accomplish, Donvin saw now that he was and always would be nothing but a speck upon the face of creation. He was an ant ruling from the spire of a fallen crumb.

"What does a man feel when he catches even the faintest glimpse of infinity?" Lith said softly. "He feels the agony of knowledge, the pain of his pride burning to ash in his breast." She looked down at Donvin, who was clutching his chest with both hands. "Now you know how we felt, all those eons ago."

Donvin couldn't breathe. He tore off his mask, sucking in as much air as he could hold, but it tasted of death and did nothing to sate him.

"But man is not such a fragile creature as that," Lith said. "Though it wounds him to gaze upon it, something compels him to try. And what does he see, when at last he can look into the heart of the universe without turning away in shame?" Her voice grew cold. "He sees only power. He sees only conquest."

•••••

Ely recovered more quickly than Remiana from the sudden tide of light, but when her gaze fell after surveying the altered sky, she found their way blocked.

"Hello, Elymia," the masked man said. Remiana reached for a weapon at her hip that was not there, but Ely was still. Something about the way he spoke told her that he was not an enemy.

"Lith wants you to remain here for a moment," the masked man said. "They are not quite ready to see you."

"You serve her?" Ely asked.

"I prefer to think of us as partners," he said.

"Who is she?" Ely probed. "What is she?"

"She is a woman," he said. "I should think that is obvious."

"That's all?" Ely said with a frown.

The masked man grunted a low laugh. "Is that not enough? Even though she is only echo of what she once was, I think that is plenty."

"An echo?" Ely said. "She was real enough when she touched me."

"When she touched your mind, you mean," the masked man said. "She has no true body, no feet to walk and no hands to touch. Not any longer. That died long ago, in a war not so different from the one you fight now. Since then, I have been her hands, whenever she has need of them."

"You mean . . . she's a ghost?" Ely said.

"An echo," the masked man corrected, "though in your words, 'ghost' might serve as well. Death did not come unexpectedly to her; none of us truly imagined we would survive that war. Her greatest wish was that her work not end with her life, so she left behind the seeds of its continuation: the Masked, and an echo animated by her strongest passion."

"You make it sound as if you've been with her all this time, but that can't be," Ely said. "Not even the Masked are immortal."

There was just a hint of sentimentality in his voice when he replied. "Many things were possible, in those days. It was a time of wonder and change, one whose like has not been seen since. When Lith was born, things were not so different from how they are now. Yet by her thirtieth year, cities were float-ing on the clouds as if by magic, and people traveled across the whole of the world in a single day. Can you imagine it?" He shook his head. "I was there, and still I sometimes wonder if it was nothing more than a dream."

He tilted his head back, looking up. "But by her thirty-fifth year, it had all ended in ashes. The flying cities had crashed beneath the sea, and a third of the planet was poisoned or blasted to dust. She passed her thirty-sixth in a dungeon, and her thirty-seventh making ready for war. She did not have a thirty-eighth." He looked hard at Ely. "I tell you this so you can understand something of her life, and why she has written your part in her script as she has."

It was a great deal for Ely to take in, but the vague, ghostly memories that Lith had given her made the tale seem familiar. "What does she want from me?" Ely asked. "I want to understand."

"Her life was full of sacrifice," the masked man said. "The lesson it taught her was that sacrifice makes a person strong. It was this principle that guided her when she first imagined the Masked, and it is this principle that guides her still. That is why, for the sake of the world, she needs you, and you alone, to do something you will revile. She needs you to save Donvin's life."

Donvin. Ely had never heard the name spoken, yet somehow she knew it, and it made the bile rise in her throat. It was the name of a killer and a fiend, a creature of wickedness and evil.

"Are you mad?" Remiana challenged. "I will not leave her alone with the likes of you!"

The masked man was unfazed by her posturing. "You will," he said, "because if you do, I will heal you."

Remiana was caught off guard, a flicker of hope passing over her face before she could control it. She drew her handless arm closer to her body. "Liar," she said. "Just like the rest of your kind."

"Your skepticism is understandable," the masked man said. "The Masked would not have made this offer, but it should be clear to you by now that the Masked are finished. I will do it, but it can only be done in the real world, not here."

"I will not leave her," Remiana said steadfastly. Ely appreciated the sentiment, but it was unnecessary.

"You should go," she said softly to Remiana. "I'll be fine."

"How do you know that?" she hissed back.

"It's all right," Ely said. Please, trust me and go." Just as she had been able to read Donvin, something made her able to read this Masked too, and she knew he was telling the truth. She felt an odd mixture of emotions when she looked at him, most of which were not her own; more residue from Lith touching her mind, perhaps.

Remiana bit her lip, but nodded. "I will see you again," she said stiffly, a command as much as a farewell. "I will have your name on our treaty, and no other."

"I wouldn't miss it," Ely said with a sarcastic smile. The offer of shared paperwork was downright affectionate coming from Remiana.

Remiana shook her head, clearly not seeing the humor, before beckoning to the masked man impatiently. "Come along, then," she said, turning on her heel and striding back toward the end of the bridge, the image of dignity despite her wounds.

The masked man let out a soft chuckle, then followed. Ely stepped aside to let him pass.

"It will be hard," the masked man said quietly as he passed her, "but more rides on Donvin's choice than you can imagine. I know you will do the right thing. Your father raised a fine daughter."

Ely blinked. "You know my father?" she said, but he was already past her, and did not slow to answer.

•••••

The pain that gripped him was fading in Donvin's breast. The realization of how small he was had staggered him, but he was still alive.

"What's up there," Lith said as she nodded to the sky, "grand as it is, is not the reason I've brought you here. That lies below."

Donvin, still on his knees, crawled to the edge of the bridge and looked down.

Like the sky above, the pit below was no longer empty. It too was full of a tangled mess of bridges, so many that the void beneath was utterly hidden from view. The bridges below, however, looked very different: they were rotting.

Donvin recoiled, choking. A blast of rancid air gusted up as one of the countless spans, its surface webbed with blackened cracks, shuddered and collapsed, breaking into a cloud of grayish dust as it fell. Another bridge caved a second later, and then another.

"What's happening down there?" Donvin asked, transfixed by the vastness of the destruction. The corruption was widespread, and while it affected the deepest bridges most strongly, it was creeping visibly upward.

"The past is happening," Lith answered. "Our past, reaching out to suck the life from your future. Our greed, demanding the payment that has been so long deferred."

"The past?" Donvin said skeptically, still looking over the edge. "You expect me to believe that was what's been hidden behind the door all this time?"

"Yes," Lith said. "That is the way of things among the branches of this tree that nearly ruined our race. Everything is connected, even the past and future. That is why we were forced to conceal the truth, including from the Masked. Not even they could have beheld it without temptation."

Donvin suddenly realized what she meant. "If that's the past, then by going down there, could I . . . ?"

Lith laughed. "That was always the first question they asked, even in my day. I will tell you what I told them. It is perhaps possible, if you knew how far to go and could find a way out again. But the paths are numerous beyond measure. More likely you would become lost, doomed to wander for eternity. If going back were so simple, I would not have needed to work so hard to prepare you and bring you here to fulfill your purpose."

Donvin snorted. "My purpose? I've already given you what you wanted. The Masked are dead, or near enough. Our business is finished."

Lith gave him a secretive smile, her dark eyes glimmering with hidden knowledge. "So you mean to say you still haven't figured out why it had to be you, and no other, to defeat the Masked and see the truth of the world?"

"Of course I have," Donvin said, knowing he was rising to her bait but hardly caring. He had won. What could she possibly do to him now? "The Listeners can't sense me. If they could, the Masked would have found me out in an instant. That's why you chose me."

"You're wrong," a shockingly familiar voice said from behind Donvin's back. "That isn't the reason she chose you. It's the reason she chose me."

Donvin spun around, but he already knew what he would see.

A young man stood there on the bridge, his face a mirror of Donvin's own, though he wore a tattered tunic and trousers rather than Masked furs. There was sorrow in his eyes.

"He speaks the truth," Lith said, looking back and forth between the twin Donvins. "I needed a body that could deceive the Listeners, and for it I was forced to wait a long, long time. Long enough for the passing of the ages to rearrange the scattered particles through which the Listeners listen. Long enough for a child to be born whose body contained not a single one."

Donvin scrutinized the young man who wore his face, picking over the shabby clothes and messy hair with keen eyes. They were damp, as if he had recently been in the water, and the scars of sap burns visible under his ratty garb were fresh, not faded like on Donvin's own body.

"What trick is this?" Donvin demanded.

"There is no trick," Lith answered. "I told you that the door concealed the past. Come now, do you not recognize yourself?" She flourished her hand, as if presenting a piece of art. "He is your past, hidden from you just as the greater past has been hidden from everyone. But now it is time for you to remember him. It is time for you to learn why I need not just one, but both of you."

Donvin turned to glare at Lith. "Even if this isn't just another of your lies, even if that thing really is what I once was, what makes you think I'd want it back?" His lips curled in disdain. "I've looked, and what I see is dirty and pathetic and weak. I'm better off without it, just like you once said." When he turned back, the disheveled doppelganger was gone.

"I'm sorry, Donvin," Lith said, "but I can't allow you the luxury of self deception any longer. I crafted you to kill the Masked so that we could finally end this creeping curse of the past, but we can't finish that work if you remain as you are, fragmented and incomplete. First, you must remember."

Donvin felt something strange inside him, a sensation like a dry sponge slowly filling with water. The inside of his head felt thick, and his limbs slow and stiff.

"Stop it!" he demanded, pointing angrily at Lith and putting a hand to his head. "Whatever the hell you're doing, stop it!"

"What I'm doing is killing you," Lith said calmly, "just as I did once before. The Donvin I made, the cruel, selfish Donvin without a past, has served his purpose. I'm sorry, but you were never meant to stay."

"You dare betray me?" Donvin yelled, staggering towards her on legs that felt more like unbending stilts. "I killed the Masked, and I can kill you too!" He called with all his might for the glowing strands, but, as always in this place-between-places, they would not come.

"I know you would, if you could," Lith said sadly, "but this is a place of the mind, of potentials rather than realities. The only kind of power you wield here is the power of understanding. You were born to rage, to hunger, and to kill, but not to understand."

Donvin reached inside his furs and withdrew the metal tree sculpture, the one from the cover of Lith's book that he had carried for months.

"I'll break this!" he snarled. "We'll see how long you live then!"

Lith gave him a pitying look. "In the physical world, perhaps" she said, "but not here. You would first have to understand what it is, and you have not the slightest clue."

Donvin took the sculpture in both hands and tried to snap it in half, but he could not so much as bend it.

"You know the meaning of brutality," Lith said, "so here you can be brutal. You know the meaning of terror, so here you can be terrifying. But you do not know the meaning of that one little tree, and so there is nothing you can do to it."

"Damn you!" Donvin cursed, hate lashing from his mouth like a forked tongue. He had been so close to his freedom, and now she thought she could rob him of everything he had worked for, everything he deserved! "Damn you to the eternal pit!"

Lith shook her head slowly. "Can't you see that we're already there?" She gestured to the endless white web that spread out in every direction. Its intricate weavings were reminiscent of a nest. Or a tree. Or a cage. "This is the Pit, and the Kingdom, and all the places man has ever sought or longed for or feared. But it is empty, Donvin. There are no gods or monsters here to do the damning, only us." She glanced down at the decaying threads of the past. "But that is all we ever needed to make a hell."

Donvin fell to his knees, the sculpture slipping from his hands and skittering away across the stones. He could no longer speak, for it felt as if his lungs were swollen with whole oceans of water. Every part of him was full, full, painfully full! He wanted to feel that beautiful emptiness again, that simple, wonderful freedom, that painless void . . . .

But the void was gone; the emptiness was gone; the freedom was gone. He was whole again, and it hurt like nothing ever had.

"No," he whispered, his forehead pressed against the warm stones as his memories returned. "Go away, please go away." Yet they would not leave him. He remembered his parents and their careful, almost obsessive care. He remembered their fear as his illness grew worse, as the blight on his chest threatened to consume him. He remembered his flight from home to spare them the pain of watching him die.

He remembered finding the Masked. He remembered his hope, brief and strong, that they might be able to save him. He remembered his despair, crushing and long, when he realized that they would not. He remembered trying to convince himself that he had never expected anything else.

Had he been alone in those days, he might never have found the strength to go on living. But, he remembered, he had not been alone.

Donvin blinked, discovering that there was wetness in his eyes. He remembered her. Her smiles, her chastisements, and her earnest, wholehearted desire to be one of the protectors of the world – he remembered as clearly as if he had seen her only yesterday. But he had not seen her yesterday. In fact, he had not seen the girl since . . . .

"Where is she?" Donvin said, rising slowly from the pale stones. His legs felt foreign beneath him, as did the tenor of his voice, but those oddities hardly mattered to him now. "Where is she?"

Lith's face grew solemn. It was clear that she knew who he meant. "She wanted to help you," she answered. "She chose to save you."

"Where is she?"

"She did not care what it meant for her, so long as she could be with you."

"Where is she!?" Donvin's voice thundered through eternity, and the bridge shuddered beneath their feet with echoes of his anger. Lith looked down at the quaking stones, and the corner of her mouth twitched upward.

"If you wish to see her, then she will come," she said.

Flicker.

Donvin saw the movement in the corner of his eye, and he caught a hint of her familiar smell. Gods, all those times, how had he not recognized that smell?

"Go on," Lith said. "You wanted to see, now look."

Donvin turned.

At first glance, it looked to him as if another Masked was standing there on the bridge with them. Yet where the mask should have been, there was no face, nothing but more hair. The figure was slouching, leaning forward so that the folds of its furs concealed something held close to its chest.

"Show me," Donvin commanded, his voice distant. Were it not for her unmistakable smell, he would not have believed his eyes.

The hairy figure shuffled reluctantly, but it straightened, its furs falling back. Two arms protruded from the hanging furs: the right was long and dark, armored and multi-jointed and ending in a curved blade like the horn of a boras. The left, however, was short, slender, and pale. It ended in a small girl's hand that clasped the other, monstrous appendage as if ashamed to show it.

"How?" Donvin asked, stepping toward the tall figure in a daze. "How can this be?" The thing stepped back.

"She can't answer," Lith said, her words reaching him as if though a fog. "Language is not a function Dolmon possess. Most of her natural tissues were used up repairing the damage that the corruption had done to your body. After that, this was the only way to keep what remained of her alive. All she can do now is listen, and obey."

A tingling ache washed across Donvin's skin, his nerves afire with sensations it seemed they had not felt in ages. He felt pain, but not the pain of indignity or shame or fury. It was the pain of sadness, of loneliness, and of loss.

"She wanted so dearly to help you," Lith said. "I imagine that's why she looks as she does now, with a form like your own."

Donvin's jaw tightened "How could you do this to her?" he said, reaching out to touch the creature that had once been his only friend, but the thing stepped away. He let his hands fall to his sides. "I didn't want this!"

"She wanted to save you, and she wanted to stay with you," Lith said. "All I did was grant her wish."

"But I didn't want to be saved!" Donvin cried out, turning on Lith. "Not like this!"

Lith's eyes were hard, the red cloth of her sleeves dancing in the wind like whips of flame. "I know. That is why I could not give you the choice. The world needs you, Donvin, yet you would have died rather than lived on at the expense of a single life. You would have made the noble choice rather than the one that would save our race. That is a weakness." She sighed. "Unfortunately, this final choice is not one I can force on you."

"Haven't you tormented me enough already?" Donvin said, wiping his eyes. "Is it too much for you to just leave me in peace?" His emotions were too confused to allow the tears to flow properly. "What choice could possibly be worth all of this? Everything I did while I was . . . . Oh gods . . . ." His dark deeds seemed to fill every corner of his mind, leaving him nowhere to hide.

"You know what choice. The choice whether to save the world from what is coming to consume it." Lith nodded over the edge of the bridge at the decay creeping upward. "And your suffering is a small price to pay. That is a good thing, for this will cost you even more than you have already paid."

"No," Donvin said. "No more. I won't. I can't."

"You have only two options," Lith said. "Now that you are here, you cannot avoid choosing, one way or another. If you, the one whom I have prepared for this final task, do nothing, then you will have chosen to let the world die. I do not believe you will find that option to be a painless one."

"And the other?" Donvin said, hardly daring to ask.

"The other option is to save it," Lith said with her predatory smile, "but that too carries a price. You will have to be unspeakably cruel. You will have to do to the whole of the world what I have done to you."

A knot of dread was rising in Donvin's gut. "I don't understand."

"I think you do," Lith said. "I took away your past, and in its absence you became an animal with no care for anything but yourself, unable to recognize the things you had once loved. This world, if it is to escape destruction, must also be set free from its past. The connections to its history must be severed, and only one who truly understands the meaning of such an act can do it." Lith looked him straight in the eyes. "The only one who can even begin to understand what that means is you."

Donvin was stunned, unable to speak.

"That is why I have made you suffer," Lith said. "You had to understand, so that on this day you would be able to choose. No one else can make this choice, because no one else truly understands what they would be choosing."

Lith raised her hand and pointed at Donvin. "Your work for me is finished. What comes next is up to you. Will you do as I have, and preserve the world by being its torturer? Or will you let it end, and save yourself from the responsibility for its suffering?"

She nodded to the tree sculpture on the ground. "I crafted that long ago, hoping it would never need to be used. It represents every thread connecting past to present, every path the people of my era used to steal from yours to fuel our empires and wars. We stole our powers from the future, not knowing or caring that we were draining it dry. But now you can stop us. All you have to do to is to cut down the tree and divide past from future forever." She knelt, using her finger to draw a line across the tiny metal trunk. "You will use the power of your own past to do it, the power you forced me to reveal to you. And you will need every ounce you can muster, reaching back to your very beginning."

"You're insane," Donvin breathed.

"It doesn't matter what I am," Lith said. "All I did was prepare you. In the end, you are the one who must choose."

•••••

As Ely drew closer to the bridge's center, she could see that neither of the two remaining figures was Lith, for both wore the hair mantle of the

Masked. One sat on the side of the bridge, his legs dangling over the edge, his face bare. Ely knew him instantly. Donvin.

She stopped, unsure what to do. The standing figure turned to regard her, and she noticed with surprise that it had no visible face. Even more alarming was the dark, scythe-like arm at its side, tipped by a blade so long that it scraped the lumpy stones at its feet.

"They're bodies, you know," Donvin said, speaking out into the void.

"Excuse me?" Ely said, having trouble taking her eyes off the creature with the bladed arm.

"At your feet," Donvin said. "Look down."

Ely did. At first, all she saw was the uneven surface of the white bridge. Then, after a moment, she noticed it. There was a pattern to the bumps: long, then short; long, then short. Like the curved backs and bowed heads of bodies encased in stone.

"That's what I think of people," Donvin said. "Nothing more than backs to tread upon." He kicked his dangling legs like a bored child at the edge of a lake. "Our minds manifest the paths to suit our expectations. And this is mine."

Ely did not know what to say. This was the same man she remembered threatening her, driving her to kill the people she had once called friends, yet something about him was different.

"I've been waiting for you," he said. "Lith told me you would come."

"Did she tell you why?" Ely said.

Donvin shrugged. "I can guess. I hope you brought a knife or something. I'd like it to be quick."

Ely crossed her arms. There was definitely something different about him. Unlike the wicked shadow who had promised her revenge, he was no longer menacing. There was no hidden power pulsing beneath his skin, no venom in his voice.

"I didn't come here to kill you," she said.

"Great," Donvin said, his voice thick with sarcasm. "I would have done it myself, but I figured the least I could do was give you the first chance."

"I'm here to help you," Ely said.

Donvin laughed, finally turning to look at her. "You must be joking."

"It's what Lith wants."

Donvin snorted. "Lith is a monster. I did what she wanted, and just look where it got me."

"She saved my life," Ely said, "and the life of someone I care for. She's not evil."

"She saved mine too," Donvin said, "but I wish she hadn't. If she helped you, it's because she needs you, and if she needs you, you're better off dead."

"But I'm not dead," Ely said. "I'm alive, and so are you." She felt, oddly, as if she were talking to a child, not a liar and a murderer who had nearly made Falls Gate tear itself to shreds.

"That can be fixed," Donvin said grimly, looking over the edge of the bridge.

"I won't let you," Ely declared, more confident now. This could not be the same Donvin who had used her as a tool of war. He was more pathetic now than hateful; she could almost feel sorry for him.

"You should," Donvin said coldly.

"Well, I won't," Ely said. "You can't control me any longer."

Donvin cocked his head, contemplating her like a challenge.

"I killed Evana," he said out of the blue. Ely felt her heart freeze in her chest.

"That was her name, wasn't it?" Donvin said. His face seemed younger than when he had masqueraded as Keth. All but the eyes, that is. They were lumps of volcanic stone, pitted and brittle from the fire that once filled them. "Now ask me why I did it."

Ely's mouth felt numb. She uttered something that might have been a word.

"Because she laughed at me. No other reason than that. She died because she made me mad."

Ely's hands clenched into fists. All this time she had thought it was Oridine's doing, but Jonner Ceer had been right all along. It had not been a sword that killed Evana. Ely's eyes crept over to where the Masked-beast stood with its long, bladed arm hanging at its side.

"That's right," Donvin said, noticing where her eyes had gone. "I killed Keth as well. Because his clothes fit me."

Ely found herself moving toward him.

"It makes you angry, doesn't it?" Donvin said, keeping his eyes locked with hers as she approached. "But I've done much, much worse." In those dark, wounded eyes, Ely could see that it was true.

She reached down and hooked her arm around Donvin's neck, hauling him to his feet. Beneath the layers of fur, his frame was thin and light, hardly more than bones.

"Do you still feel like helping me now?" he gasped with a leering smile, not even attempting to escape.

This was the Donvin Ely hated. She wanted nothing more than to choke that smug look off his face and hurl him from the bridge to his death.

"No," she whispered, pulling her arm tighter about his neck. "I don't feel like helping you. I feel like hurting you." The masked man's words to her and Remiana echoed in her head, but they seemed ridiculous. This boy was supposed to save the world? He was a creature of evil; he could never be a savior. She would be doing everyone he had hurt, everyone he had killed, a service by putting him out of his misery.

Donvin wheezed out a weak laugh. "Good."

How Ely hated him! After everything he had done, he could still laugh! She squeezed his neck harder.

There was a scratching sound behind her, and Ely spun, thinking immediately of the misshapen Masked-creature and using Donvin's body as a shield. Yet no blow fell.

The creature was there, but it was not focused on them. It was leaning over the ground, scratching the white stones repeatedly with its long claw.

"What's it doing?" Ely hissed. She felt Donvin's shoulders shrug against her in response.

The creature finished scratching and stepped back. At its feet was a crude mark, hastily made with lines that failed to meet at the corners, but the word they formed was unmistakable. Forgive.

Donvin began to laugh, a genuine laugh this time. Ely released him in surprise, and he dropped to his knees, shaking with barely controlled mirth.

The creature moved forward, kneeling beside him and placing its human hand on his head.

"But you can't forgive me," Donvin said, his cheeks stained with wetness. "I did this to you. I hurt you more than anyone else. Gods, all the things I made you do . . . . You just can't!"

The part of the creature that would have been its head bobbed, but its small, pale hand did not move. Then it turned to Ely.

She swallowed hard. The thing had no eyes, but she still felt as if she were being watched. Just as they had when she faced down Oridine, a cloud of invisible eyes seemed to settle around her, transfixing her from a thousand angles. Once again, they wanted something.

Go away! Ely tried to tell them. This isn't about you! But even as she thought it, she knew that was wrong. If she had defied Oridine for the people of Falls Gate, who had no voice but hers to speak for them, countless more depended on her now.

But what would they want her to do? This Donvin might be different from what he had been, but that would be no comfort to his victims. Why should he go unpunished while they forever bore the scars he had inflicted upon them?

But he will not go unpunished, said a voice in Ely's head, and suddenly she realized that the message the creature had scratched into the stone had not been for Donvin alone. She understood, finally, why Lith had wanted her there.

"I forgive you," Ely said.

Donvin looked up, agony in his eyes. "No. You can't, not after what I've done to you."

"But I can," Ely said. "Now ask me why."

"Why?"

"Because forgiveness is the best revenge against you," Ely said, remembering the words he had mouthed from beyond the keyhole. "I've seen the part of you that wants to accept responsibility for what you've done, the part that understands the magnitude of what you deserve. The worst tortures we could inflict would only give you the satisfaction of seeing justice done. But I'm not going to give you that. If you want suffering, you'll have to make it yourself: by choosing the painful path and enduring the consequences."

"But that won't make up for what I've done," Donvin said. "Nothing can."

"Maybe," Ely said, "but that's not for you to decide. Your punishment is to seek forgiveness." She stooped to gather up the tree sculpture that lay on the stones. "Starting with this. Cut off the past, right here at this moment, and we'll enter a new world where nothing you did ever happened."

Donvin shook his head. "It wouldn't change anything. We'd lose contact with our past, prevent Lith's ancient empire from stealing from us through the breaches, but that won't alter the present. It wouldn't bring back the dead. And the cost . . . ." He shuddered. "Even I don't really know what will happen. I understand enough, Lith claims, but how can anyone know for sure? That's why this was never tried before. Will we lose our memories? Our selves? Or will the whole world just unravel? You have no idea what you're asking."

He put a hand to his chest. "And then there's this. For the future to be free of breaches, to keep all of this from happening again, I can't reach forward for power like Lith's people and the Masked did. The power to do it must come from the past, from a place that will be forever cut off from us. But by doing that, by sucking the life out of my past self, I set all of this in motion." He nodded toward the creature that knelt beside him. "She saves me so that Lith can use me to kill the Masked, the only ones who could have stood in the way of her plan, and bring me to this choice. If I do it, it will be no better than saying I wanted it all to happen. Every bit of suffering and every bit of death."

"Then want it," Ely said. "Let it be one more reason you don't deserve our forgiveness."

Donvin looked up at her with those wounded eyes, but for the first time, there was an odd sort of peace in them. "Could it have been coincidence that you were the one to discover me that night in the Keep?" he said.

"It could have been anyone," Ely said.

"Perhaps," he said with a slow nod. "Perhaps." Then he rose and held out his hand. Ely pressed the metal tree into it.

"I think I understand now," he said. "Lith said that I was born to a great destiny, but it was never anything more than what I chose. I thought she was the one who forced me into this, but I was wrong. It was me. It will be me."

He turned to the creature with the girl's hand. "If I'm going to do this, then we have to make sure it will never be necessary again. Will you help me, one last time?"

The girl-creature nodded silently, and then she vanished. Only a second passed before she reappeared, and when she did, the blade of her arm was wet, but not with blood. For a moment, the smell of fresh sap overpowered the evil wind.

"Thank you," Donvin said as she moved to his side. "Now, let's do what we were meant to do. What we choose to do. Together."

Donvin lifted the tiny metal tree over his head, and a crackle of dark energy flickered to life in his chest. It coursing out and up along his arms like foul effluent from a stopped-up drain. "I accept my purpose!" he shouted. "I choose it!"

The shadowy radiance reached his hands, igniting them like dark stars beneath the byssi's pale glow. Between them, the metal trunk was a tenuous connection between two nodes of incredible power.

Then, in the air before him, a hazy image began to take shape. It was an infant child, resting atop a metal disk in the arms of a Masked. Donvin quivered, but did not look away. The image solidified, growing sharper by the second. Donvin let go of the tree with one hand.

"I'm sorry," he murmured as he reached toward the ghostly child. "I'm sorry, but this is going to hurt." His hand shot forward, plunging itself into the child's chest. The baby screamed. Ely gasped.

Donvin clenched his hand into a fist, and then he pulled. It emerged, drawing with it something long and black and viscous, like a blood serpent dragged from a vein. It glittered like the Masked's silver threads, but with shadow rather than light, a thing born from the dark finality of the past rather than the brilliant hope of the future. Its shape was fluid, but to Ely it was clear that the darkness was a weapon more deadly than any she knew.

No sooner had the thought crossed her mind than the shape of the blackness snapped into place. It was a sword, its hilt gripped firmly in Donvin's hand, its tip trailing off into a dark umbilicus attached to the screaming infant's chest. Donvin blinked, eyes flicking toward where Ely stood for just a moment before refocusing on the small metal tree.

"Goodbye, Lith," Donvin said.

Goodbye, my Donvin, Ely heard Lith's voice whisper.

Donvin gave a nod to the girl-creature at his side. Then he released the sculpture. Donvin and the girl struck together with blinding speed, his sword of shadow and her blade of chitin cleaving through the trunk as easily as a passing cloud cleaves the sunlight.

Well done, Lith's voice whispered. It sounded proud. Well done.

The two halves of the tree fell apart, each dropping off an opposite side of the bridge. And just like that, without so much as the faintest of whimpers, time itself was cut in two. The world, as it was, was ended.

The wind, a wind which had hissed and wheezed and gasped the sorrow of the past for millennia, finally died, and silence, perfect and pure, fell once more like shining snow upon the branches of the tree of ruin.

Chapter 47

Dawn from Below

In the skies high above Falls Gate, under the afternoon sun's cloud-dimmed gaze, something miraculous was happening. From the south, a cool wind began to blow in off the ocean. It swirled over white-capped waves and the dark, hidden deeps as it gathered strength, surging as if drawn to the fires that lit the city atop the cliffs like lighthouse beacons.

Over the broken streets and shattered buildings the chill wind blew, dissipating the stagnant smoke and working its fingers through the clouds that hung like a widow's veil overhead. In its wake, tiny motes of moisture, held apart by the hot, violent updrafts from the battle below, met once more. Together the particles became a mist, and within the mist formed a droplet, the first and bravest harbinger of things to come.

What sensations might this droplet have felt as gravity worked upon it, drawing it out like a teardrop from the dark haze of the clouds? Would it be saddened by this transformation of old into new? Or would it marvel as the mists parted and the land below revealed herself, reveling in the beauty that something so small as a breath of cool air could bring?

And if, at the terminus of that droplet's journey, it was scattered and divided upon the rocks, would its fragments remember the fear and wonder of their shared descent into the realm of man? When the time came for them to seek the sea, would they go with reluctance, afraid once more to lose themselves in change they could not comprehend, or would they go gladly, embracing with joy the countless others who were their kin? Perhaps such questions have no answers. Perhaps not all droplets are the same.

Edwin started awake as a raindrop struck his forehead with a faint plock, giving him a cold, wet reminder that he was still alive. He found himself staring up into the gray cloudscape overhead, its contours damping the afternoon light into a soft glow. A second drop struck his bare chest, and he looked down at himself in surprise to discover that he was lying unprotected on a narrow, rocky jetty that reached out like a finger into the sea.

He tried to recall how he had gotten there, but the last thing he remembered was Oridine's ship going down, and then winter waters dragging his already battered body into the arms of oblivion. By all rights he should have drowned, or frozen, or both, yet here he was.

A popping sound made him sit up sharply, and he twisted his stiff neck to see that a fire had been built just a few feet behind him. His clothes were haning on a drying pole beside it, but they were not alone. An assortment of black leathers hung there too, and beyond them he could see Mae's still unconscious body stretched out on the rocks opposite his own.

A few more raindrops fell, sizzling when they landed among the flames, but Mae did not stir other than the steady rise and fall of her chest. Clearly she had not been the one who made the fire.

Edwin scanned the the jetty's length, but it was bare save for the gulls that stood watch over their nests. He squinted toward the docks, but he could see no signs of fighting. Most of the fires were out, and no more ships seemed to be sinking.

The pitter-patter of the rain hastened, and Edwin scooted closer to the fire, grateful for its warmth. Yet as he basked in its glow, he could not help but wonder where the wood had come from. Not so much as a shrub grew along the bare rocks of the jetty.

Something within the blaze caught Edwin's eye, and he leaned forward. There, burning merrily alongside the dry branches, was one half of a bark mask.

Mae coughed and shifted as a raindrop fell onto her nose, drawing Edwin's attention from the flames. She sat up, looking dazed.

"I knew jumping was a bad idea," she muttered to herself, folding her arms across her breasts for what modesty she could manage. Then she turned her back on him and the fire, hunching her freckled shoulders against the rain.

Edwin smiled wryly. It was as close to a "thank you" as he was ever likely to get, no matter the fact that his warning before running up the Aloise flag had surely saved her life. He stood, wincing as the blood returned to his legs after a long absence, and realized immediately that his sword was not at his waist.

The blade stood upright, tip wedged between two rocks at the water's edge. When Edwin approached, he saw that two small, black bags on sinew cords hung from the hilt, one from each arm of the crossguard. Picking them up and loosening their drawstrings, he found an odd collection of tid-bits inside: a few pebbles, some dried grass, one or two twigs, and a tiny ball of clay. Most interesting, though, was a thin strip of pale bark into which a short message had been scratched with a fingernail. *We will not forget.*

Edwin smiled again, remembering the two Masked on the docks. He would not forget either. Returning their contents, he took the two black bags and placed them about his neck. They felt comfortable there, touching the same place on his chest the Aloise ring once had.

A whistle from over the water drew his attention, and he looked up. From the direction of the docks, a small rowboat was making its way toward him, a bulky man sending it surging through the calm waters with each haul on the oars. Behind him, a standing woman with brown hair lowered her fingers from her mouth and waved both hands over her head. It was Matrice. And next to her, seated, was a second, her blond curls bright even amidst the rain.

"Do us all a favor and put on some clothes before they get here," Mae said from behind him, tossing Edwin his vest and pants. "We wouldn't want to look a mess for your sister." There was mockery in her voice, but not malice.

A brief light drew their eyes upward to the great tower of Cliffhome Keep, which still stood tall despite all the ravages it had suffered. At its peak, a shimmering silver beacon appeared for a short moment, and then it winked out. Then, as if they had been waiting for just that signal, the clouds broke open and the rain became a downpour, one that traced clean, cool rivers from the top of Edwin's head all the way to his toes. He opened his mouth to the sky, and the droplets that fell into it tasted fresh, and pure, and new.

•••••

Ely stepped from the portal and Donvin followed, closing its silver curtain behind them. For a moment she thought they were flying until she realized that they were at the very top of Cliffhome Keep's highest tower, the city of Falls Gate stretching out around them in every direction.

No sooner had they set foot back in the real world than it began to rain, a heavy, pounding rain that spattered loudly on the small circle of the tower top, turning the stone a deeper shade of green. And there, lying out in the open on the rain-speckled stones, was Ely's mother's comb.

Ely knelt and picked it up, feeling its familiar contour in her hands, though the sensations were different now. Her hands were toughened from wielding blades and scaling walls and handling ropes, and she could no longer feel the delicately carved lines against her palm to mark where one animal shape ended and another began. All she could feel was the bone: solid, whole, and comforting.

Ely looked over the tower's battlements to the city. Smoke was rising once again from its streets, though the rain was quickly dousing the fires and the sounds of battle had fallen quiet. Between the buildings, she could make out darkly armored men tending to the injured and clearing debris from the roadways. To the east, north, and west, all of the city's gates were open, and people were flocking around them, dancing and jumping for joy in the rain. The city had suffered, there was no denying that. But it had survived.

Beyond the walls, the grass-covered headlands soaked up the rain, and the Cliffdiver River charged onward, just as it always had, leaping bravely from the heights to plunge into the sea below. Ely was not sure, in truth, what she had been expecting to see.

"It doesn't look any different," she said to the man who stood silently on the tower beside her. "Even after what you did, nothing's changed."

"I told you it wouldn't," Donvin said as he looked down, the rain dripping from his unkempt hair and matting down his heavy furs.

"But the breaches will stop?" Ely said. "There will be no more need for the Masked? We'll be safe?"

"There will be no more breaches," Donvin said. "The past can no longer touch us. But beyond that, I can't say."

Ely frowned. "I can remember everything," she said. "That means it must have worked out okay, right? We didn't all die, or disappear, or forget."

"Do you think those are the only possible consequences of wounding the universe in a way even the Creator never imagined?" Donvin said.

It was a question for which Ely had no answer.

"So what are we supposed to do now?" she said.

"That's up to you. Lith's plan is complete. This world is yours, free of everything that came before. Yours will be the first generation to truly choose its own destiny."

"And what of you?" Ely asked. "What's your part in this new world?"

"To be punished," Donvin said simply. "You've shown me a better way than I could have imagined. Thank you." He went to the spiral stairs leading into the tower, and a moment later he was gone.

Alone once more, Ely looked out on the city she called home. What she saw, more than the destruction the Masked had wrought, the suffering the Aloise had inflicted, or carnage in the wake of the rampaging beras, were a thousand promises waiting to be fulfilled. For the dead, there would be honors and burials. For the living, there would be consolation and aid. Homes would need rebuilding, families reuniting, trust reestablishing. When she came down from this tower, a thousand duties would be awaiting her, duties that would wear her to the bone and draw from her everything she had to give, and more. Yet those duties did not frighten her, did not make her want to bury her head in a pillow as she had so often done before. There were things now that only she could do, and to be needed in that way was a privilege, not a burden. She and the people of Falls Gate had bled together and fought together, and in the end they had stood together, united by choice, not by accident of birth. Their blood might be mingled in the dust of the battlefield rather than in their veins, but it bound them together them no less tightly.

Ely's heart swelled with pride, seeing how, despite its injuries, her city still rose from the headlands as prominently as ever, a story in full written out in the rise and fall of its buildings, the cursive swirl of its avenues, and the capital pronouncements of its towers. It was a story of loss, and bravery, and triumph. But more than that, it was a story that was not yet finished. And somewhere down there, among the ever-changing words of the tale that was both new and old at the same time, her father was waiting.

Ely turned, flinging raindrops from her loose hair, and took the stairs two at a time. She could not wait to show him how much their family had grown.

EPILOGUE

"Pa, come look at this!" Lendil called, hopping over the narrow stream and trudging up the bank on the opposite side. He eased the tension on his longbow, the rabbit he had seen utterly forgotten.

Lendil's father, Pordon, emerged from the trees behind him a moment later, the two rabbits slung over his shoulder bouncing against his fur-lined cloak. Winter had made game scarce, and even after venturing far beyond their usual range, their hunt had been poor.

"What's all the racket?" Pordon asked, his own bow nocked and pointed toward the ground. "You'll scare off our dinner like that."

Lendil, though only twelve, had hunted with his father countless times before. He knew well when something was worth shouting over. "Look up there," he said, pointing toward the top of the grassy hill and an odd gap in the tree line.

Pordon squinted, his graying eyebrows coming together. "Someone's been logging?" he said. They were two full days out of their village, deeper into the woodlands than most anyone ever ventured. There was supposedly nothing but wilderness all the way to the western foothills.

"But nobody lives out here," Lendil said, youthful excitement raising the pitch of his voice. "I'm going to take a look."

"Be mindful of others' land, son," Pordon said, following the boy's quick steps up the hillside on knees that did not bend quite like they used to. Raising four sons did a lot to slow a man down.

It was possible that someone had come this far out to establish a homestead, but Lendil and Pordon soon saw that was not the case. When they crested the hill, they discovered that not just a few trees had been cleared. A vast swath of forest, perhaps several hectares in size, was simply gone. As they moved warily into the open space, they came upon the stumps, massive things leveled perfectly to the ground.

Pordon knelt by one of the buried stumps and brushed a hand over its surface. The cut was smooth, like none made by axe or saw. He made a cursory attempt to count the rings, but they were so many that he quickly lost track.

Once again, Lendil was the first to spot the next oddity. "What is that?" he breathed.

At first glance Pordon mistook the grayish smudge over the deforested area for a cloud, but even his aging eyes were able to tell that it was much too close. Unable to deny their curiosity, the two moved toward it.

The thing turned out to be a tree, though a tree unlike any other the pair had ever seen. The gray color was because it was made of solid stone. The leaves, the twigs, the branches, the trunk – every part was an even, pale gray, without so much as a speckle or smudge.

"I don't think we should go any closer," Pordon said, catching Lendil's wrist while they were still a good twenty paces back, but his son pulled away.

"It's just a tree, Pa," Lendil said, coming to a halt before the trunk.

Pordon remained where he was, hands going to his bow. Lendil was not old enough to remember, but Pordon had witnessed other seemingly impossible things in his lifetime. In each case, the Masked had never been far off, and the only person who did not flee from the Masked was a fool.

"Come away from there, Len," Pordon warned. "This is no place for us."

Lendil shrugged, but did not move back toward his father. He had always had a good sense for danger, and he felt nothing threatening about this tree. He wondered why, out of all the others that had been cut down, this one had been spared and preserved.

He made a slow circuit of the trunk, pausing when his eyes fell on an irregularity in the stone. There, at about chest height, was a simple carving. Lendil put out a hand and traced the lines in the bark. They formed two figures, one short and one tall, their hands joined between them.

Lendil felt a sadness in the childish illustration, though he was not sure why. It seemed almost as if the figures were trying to speak, though in a language he did not understand.

"It's time to go," he heard his father's voice call from the other side of the tree. "We're wasting good daylight."

Lendil let his hand fall back to his side. Whatever this was, it would not help them in their search for game. The world was full of strange and wonderful things, but a fantastic story of an oddity in the wilderness would not fill a family's bellies.

Lendil and his father departed that empty forest, their eyes peeled for rabbit or bird, leaving behind them the great stone monument to something they did not understand. Yet the figures preserved in that petrified bark continued to smile as they held hands, alone once more among the ghosts of the Scarwood trees.

www.ingramcontent.com/pod-product-compliance
Lightning Source LLC
Chambersburg PA
CBHW060756210726

48292CB00013B/171